TRAINEE

SEEDS AMONG THE STARS
BOOK II

MARGARET McGAFFEY FISK

TTO
PUBLISHING

Cover Design by Deranged Doctor Design
www.derangeddoctordesign.com

TTO Publishing logo design by Blue Harvest Creative
www.blueharvestcreative.com

Custom scene break by ddb Design
i-ddb.com

Trainee

Published by
TTO Publishing

ISBN-10: 1631390147
ISBN-13: 978-1-63139-014-2

First Print Edition, Second Printing

Visit the author at:
Website: www.margaretmcgaffeyfisk.com
Twitter: @Marfisk
Google Plus: +MargaretMcGaffeyFiskAuthor
Facebook: MargaretMcGaffeyFisk

PRAISE FOR THE BOOKS OF MARGARET McGAFFEY FISK

SHAFTER

"Trina's life revolves around protecting her family and as a shafter, the lowest of Ceric society, her choices are limited to what she can steal. However, a chance at a new life aboard a colony-bound ship teaches her a new way of life and the price of unquestioned loyalty in this exciting tale, rich with cultural world building and science fiction adventure. This is a story you'll love, with a tale you won't want to see end!"

— Lazette Gifford, author of *Glory* —

"While the heroine yearns for another world, you'll crave any universe, any tale, created by this exciting new speculative fiction author. In Shafter, McGaffey Fisk delivers an inter-planetary colony system and populates it with complex and sympathetic characters. Travel from the tunnels of Ceric to the stars beyond with a master thief and her master storyteller."

— Valerie Comer, author of *Majai's Fury* —

SECRETS

"Through her young heroine and hero, the author breathes life into a curious, exciting and often dangerous world of steam, sail, sentient machines, loyal friendships and deeds of quiet bravery undertaken in the face of widespread fear and bigotry, to deliver a clever, entertaining and unique new take on Victorian Steampunk."

— David Bridger, author of *A Flight of Thieves (Sky Ships)* —

OTHER WORKS BY MARGARET McGAFFEY FISK

SEEDS AMONG THE STARS
(science fiction adventure)

Shafter

Apprentice

The Captain's Chair (Indie Traders short story)

THE STEAMSHIP CHRONICLES
(steampunk adventure)

Safe Haven

Secrets

Threats

Gifts

Box Set 1 (Books 1-3)

UNCOMMON LORDS AND LADIES
(sweet regency romances)

Beneath the Mask

A Country Masquerade

An Innocent Secret

SHORT STORIES (eBook only)

Forged

War Child

Curve of Her Claw (illustrated by Star Olsen)

Visit margaretmcgaffeyfisk.com for more information about these and other titles

The shuttle docked with a clang of metal against metal. Trina didn't jerk in surprise like some of the candidates. She'd chosen a seat toward the front and could just make out the pilot's screen through a gap in the panel separating the two compartments. Their shuttle had been approaching the station for a while now, weaving among many other shuttles.

She'd been watching the others connect for a short period then pull free and vanish out of view for some time. She knew exactly when their turn had come.

Trina had met the candidates with her in the orientation training on her colony ship, but she wouldn't call them friends. Everyone she had considered such would be continuing on to the colony or other spacer assignments. This shuttle was her last tie to that life.

The gate hissed open, offering a glimpse of a large room on the other side, bigger even than the cargo space where she'd spent so much of her time on the colony ship. The ceiling towered overhead, and she could not see the full width from their position. Opposite them stood an interior wall on which she could see the tops of many openings above the gathered crowd. Some of the doorways seemed sized for people while others were wider by four times or more. This must have been where they transferred all kinds of cargo, not just spacer candidates.

"Candidates, grab your things and get on out," an unfamiliar voice called from beyond, making Trina aware of how she lingered in the entrance. "The shuttle must return to its ship."

The others started talking at once, asking questions as though unwilling to step free, but Trina knew the shuttle had a short time before the next would need this spot. She twisted to pull her bundle free and strode through the open door only to stumble.

One second in the cavernous space, with what seemed like hundreds of voices echoing and pounding at her, cut Trina's confidence. She hadn't thought much about candidates from other ships. Their group of twenty seemed large enough for anyone's purpose.

Yet, who knew how many places had sent candidates? Judging from the sheer numbers, many. Without a high vantage point, she could not make a true estimate, but wherever she looked, layer upon layer of bodies stood between her and the internal doors she'd identified at first look.

"Keep together for now. It'll make things easier," said a woman in the purple suit designating an instructor as she waved them toward one side. "Another shuttle's coming in."

Trina joined the others, the woman's meaning clear without her saying they should move out of the way, but they had no further instructions. Her only relief came in seeing how none of the candidates from her colony ship seemed to know what they should be doing.

They kept walking along the outer wall, passing more shuttle hatches and stacks of cargo boxes. There never seemed to be a good place to stop.

Finally, they came to a disorganized halt when the room ended in a wall.

She moved through her group until she could brace against the metal curve. This wall stood too far from the engine to feel its beat, or so she thought until Trina remembered she lived on a station now. If it even had an engine, she doubted it would be of the same type or set off the same resonance.

Her shoulders hunched, but she forced them straight, unwilling to make her discomfort visible to any observer. Instead, she distracted herself by observing the others.

Not since coming onto the colony ship had she been in a space with so many strangers. She scanned those nearest, using an unfocused gaze so as not to draw attention.

The candidates came in many guises, skin tone ranging from pale white to a deep bluish tinge nothing like her spacer friend Nishan's dark color. Clothing resembled what she'd seen among the candidates from her ship except where it didn't, some standing out as much as her own Ceric clothes did. Hair had as many variants in colors, styles, and lengths.

The variety dizzied her at first. Trina wondered how she would figure out enough to blend in. How could this society work with so many differences?

The urge to run back to the shuttle, to the safety of a ship she knew, threatened to overwhelm her, but that shuttle had already undocked. She'd find no comfort in sneaking aboard any of those now connected to the station.

Trina sucked in a slow breath and narrowed her focus to just those gathered nearest to them.

Little variation existed in that group. All twenty-three wore uniformly tan-colored clothing that lay close to their bodies, and whether male or female, their hair hung down in dark, black sheets. Every one of them stood out in contrast to her, thanks as much to their clothes and hair as to having deep blue skin.

The next had fewer candidates than either hers or the blue-skinned ones, but these matched in both dress and overall look to those they stood beside.

She shifted to see another further into the room. This one had a greater variety than the first or second, but in comparison to the room as a whole, they still had more in common than not.

Her vision blurred then, calling up festival days on Ceric. There she'd seen the same mix of similar but not the same between laborers and polits. Even shafters wore colors and styles on par with the other classes, those shafters whose clothing wasn't stolen from polit rooftops in the first place.

With this realization, Trina could see how each collection must have held candidates from a specific ship. Every once in a while, there'd be someone like her who matched none of the others, but her group had clearly not been the only one told to stay together.

The room started to filter in her perception, becoming something like her sister's patchwork blankets. Each group made up a different fabric, but a fabric all the same. One composed of candidates.

Relief washed over her.

With so many candidates and so many differences, her own oddities would stand out less. She didn't have to understand everything about this society because no one would. No one would question her background. No one would even know she came from a colony planet and not a ship like the rest, though some of these others could be from planets as much as she was. Nishan had even come from something not so different from a shafter's life.

A disturbance rippled through the candidates, raised voices bouncing off the ceiling to travel to their corner as a jumbled mess.

Trina caught sight of purple-suited instructors moving through each section. They extracted one or two candidates at a time, who left to trail after the spacers.

"They're splitting us up."

Two others hushed the boy who spoke, but from the pinched look on the faces around her, Trina could see her shipmates all felt a twinge of what she had when the shuttle left.

They'd counted on having each other to lean on. She'd left everyone she could count on behind already.

DELUTH ADJUSTED THE UNCOMFORTABLE STRAPS on his pack. He'd never worn one before. The satchel had come from a random collection, each of The Headway's twenty-seven candidates using something different. Most were abandoned by colonists who'd hitched a ride, not that his ship did too much of that kind of commerce. They were traders.

He shook off the thought.

It didn't matter anymore. He'd chosen the Spacer Guild as they all had. Whatever they were destined to be, the Guild would assign them where they were needed, as they had the spacers who ran The Headway. Orientation hadn't covered methods of assignment, but somehow he doubted assigning candidates to their home ships was high on the list. Every spacer he'd met came from somewhere different.

"Just look at them. Scared little bots all huddled against the walls. You'd think they'd never seen a cargo bay before."

Deluth followed Redel's pointed finger to see some of the candidates had chosen a spot where the skin met the chill of space unlike his shipmates who'd marched to the very center of the room.

"At least they have something to lean on," he said, tugging on his straps. One of the group caught his eye. Smaller than the others, with dirty yellow hair and pale skin, she didn't seem all that impressive. But her very stillness drew him to her, a point of calm in the chaos all around him.

Redel slammed him on the shoulder. "Don't fool yourself. They're not in that place for comfort. Too close to the hatches. No, the instructors probably took one look at them, the tiny one especially, and arranged for them to be sent right back where they came from."

Now Deluth had a different reason to rub his shoulder thanks to his best friend and bunkmate since they left the separate dwellings of their parents at the age of six. "They don't seem all that different to me."

Redel turned to stare at Deluth with a familiar narrowed gaze, one that usually ended with a rough and tumble to wipe away whatever they'd disagreed about. He hoped Redel wouldn't try that here. He didn't want to be the one sent home, and he didn't think Redel would be foolish enough to chance it either.

Before that belief could be tested, one of the instructors came to a halt next to them, his head buried in a screen. He glanced from the screen to each of them before reaching out an arm and snagging Redel. "You're with me. A Pilot."

Deluth waited for the man to call him as well, but instead he faced a purple back as the instructor strode forth, Redel in tow.

"Wait. There must be a mistake. We're supposed to be together." Redel jerked free and moved to stand next to Deluth.

The instructor's expression had a lot in common with Redel's earlier narrowed stare. "Shipmates are divided into separate groups as much as possible. You're here to make new connections and learn how to deal with strangers. Not to hang out with those you've known your whole life. You could be assigned anywhere, with anyone."

Something oddly like relief washed over Deluth. He'd miss his friend, but they'd come here to change who they'd been. If they stayed with the same folks, it would be much more difficult to become something new.

The man waited for Redel to move, his scowl deepening. Then a whistle sounded loud enough to cut through the background murmur, and he shrugged. "We're behind schedule. Your group is too big to split up completely anyway. I suppose you two together is no different than any others of this lot." He poked the screen then waved both of them to follow.

Redel linked arms with Deluth and pulled him along with a big grin. "I knew we should be together. Isn't that right, bunkmate?"

"Right." If his response lacked enthusiasm, it was only because it had been a long trip. He was tired and cranky.

His annoyance faded as he realized the same most likely caused Redel's cutting remarks about the other candidates.

They'd taken the test together, planning all the adventures they'd have once free of the strict rules that made up their ship culture. They'd been excited about meeting new people from other places.

Pointing out those who were different in a sarcastic way didn't match with anything they'd shared before catching the shuttle.

Deluth held onto that thought as the instructor picked seven more candidates, but when they circled the edge, his focus changed to the girl. Would she be part of his group?

No sooner had he considered the possibility than they turned toward one of the station doors.

"Keep up now, and don't get mixed into the others. You're red, after all. Pilots don't get lost."

Redel pushed forward until he walked next to the man. "Does this mean we've been chosen for that section?"

Their instructor laughed. "Don't get any grand ideas, candidates," he said to the lot of them. "The designations are so you can mix and mingle, but will always know where to find your room. You have to complete all your training before you'll be assigned to a division based on your primary aptitude. And you may serve in more than one over the life of your career. This is just the first step. No one would tolerate an untrained rookie pilot. They'd rebel and throw every guild member off the ship first. Too much at stake. And they'd be right about it too."

He hadn't stopped to deliver this speech. With the last word, he stepped into a moving air stream and whisked away, leaving the rest of them to leap on after.

Deluth tilted into the current to speed his movement, as did the rest. A feat of safety engineering kept them from slamming into each other as they adjusted to riding a pressure wave.

He reached their instructor first. "Our room? We're all in the same bunk?"

The man raised an eyebrow as he shook his head. "No, you'll be in the same section, and you'll share eating and gathering areas, but each candidate has a separate room. I don't know what it's like on your ship, but things are designed to maximize your focus here. No staying up too late chatting after the lights go out."

"Our own rooms," Redel said, coming up on his side. "Just like the single adults. But don't worry. I'll take the one right next door so you don't have to be scared all by yourself."

Their instructor shoved them out of the air stream before Deluth had to answer. He fought to stay upright even as the others were pushed out almost on top of him. The man relaxed his grip on a handhold Deluth hadn't noticed and joined them.

"You're Pilots, remember. Red's your color. You get lost, find a red strip and follow it to the end. It'll be your rooms…or you'll have to turn around and go the other way."

Deluth scanned the colored strips marking various corridors, but one of the others found their color first. He joined the scramble to reach the section and see what would become their home for the next year at least.

TRINA TRIED NOT TO SHOW how nervous she felt as candidate after candidate was chosen and led away.

The bells chimed two more times, but she had no idea what they signified. She did notice how the instructors increased their pace as they plucked a girl here and a boy there.

A space that had seemed large when filled with students grew even greater with each group departing. She'd seen seven leave already, each numbering between ten and fifteen candidates, and she might have missed some in the crowds. There were many still waiting, but the choices had become slim.

Something caught her attention, and she turned to see a tall, dark-haired instructor staring at her.

He looked her up and down, then nodded as though he now understood something more than as a greeting.

She tensed when he strode toward her, no longer sure she wanted to be chosen, at least not by him.

"You are Trina of Family Menthak. From Ceric, correct?"

She hadn't heard any of the other instructors who'd collected from their group use names.

"Come with me."

He hadn't waited for her response when she'd hesitated, perhaps taking her lack of a protest as consent.

The name, the absence of other students, and something about his manner sent a spike of panic through her. For one horrifying second, Trina knew it had all been a mistake. She didn't belong; she hadn't passed the test; they'd realized she wouldn't be a good fit after all.

The instructor had set off, assuming she'd follow in his wake. What else could she do? Her steps dragged, but she had no other place to go, and no good would come of finding a tunnel to hide in here.

Trina stopped dead, her indrawn breath loud enough to attract an irritated look from the instructor.

He stopped as well, one eyebrow raised in inquiry.

Nishan had told her what the test did. It wasn't her answers but how she'd answered the questions. The political officer said the Guild needed spacers like her, like Nishan, as well. People who'd grown up in the depths of a colony, who'd experienced the dark underside. There had been no reason to lie. No purpose for it when they had the option of imprisoning her for what she'd done.

"Are you coming?"

She'd used up the instructor's patience, but it didn't matter. Trina squared her shoulders and sped to his side. She wouldn't be here if they didn't think she'd be an asset. They wouldn't have waited until the station.

"Yes, I'm coming."

Instead of collecting other candidates and leaving the area as the rest of the instructors had done, he led her toward a group against the front wall. Other purple suits brought in one candidate at a time as well only to abandon them.

Her instincts twinged, but she forced the worry aside. Whatever the plan, she could survive it. She'd proved often enough she had what it took to come out on the right side in the end, and she'd never been one to shy from hard work.

"That's the last of them," her instructor said as she joined the others. "Good luck to you."

It took only a heartbeat to realize he'd been speaking to someone else. He wasn't to be her teacher after all.

She watched him stride away, a little lost despite her instinctive caution around him.

"Can I have your attention please?"

The man speaking had dark brown skin and stood a head shorter than the one who'd walked away, but he wore the same purple uniform.

She might have been cast aside, but at least it was into the care of another instructor.

"Thank you," he said as the last of their group turned to face him.

Though she appeared to be focused on their latest instructor, Trina scanned the other candidates' expressions in her peripheral vision. They seemed equally wary of this separation.

He coughed, clearly uncomfortable with the role he'd been given.

"It's not often there are so many of you, but we've shuffled some of the instructors to ensure you get the training you need."

Another candidate raised his hand when Trina would have bided her time until the information revealed itself.

"Yes?"

"Why are we here?"

"Ah." He coughed again. "All of you are from places where technological access was not universal."

She kept still, but many of the others nodded their agreement.

"Your orientation scores show you may need remedial training in technology." He held up a hand to stay the many questions brewing among the students. "Your candidacy is not at risk. It's just that you would struggle with some of the training exercises and might not get the full benefit because of your weakness in this area. To ensure there will be no problems, you'll complete a full technology assessment. Many of you will be sent into the standard rotation without any further delay once your skills are confirmed. For the rest, we have special training sessions to bring you up to the level of a standard candidate. We'll be covering the same material, just not in the same way. You'll be released once you've attained the necessary mastery."

Trina's face stayed blank thanks to the practice of keeping her emotions from Fence when trading the polit goods she'd stolen for coin, but inside, she boiled over.

Why had they not performed this assessment, and provided any extra training needed, in the orientation sessions back on the ship? Why not tell her this might happen? Why wait until now?

Once again, she'd been set apart as if they could see her shafter background written across her face. She'd worried about blending in earlier. Now she knew she wouldn't even get the chance.

Whatever questions the others had asked, she heard none of it.

Instincts had warned her, but she'd ignored them in favor of believing the spacer test infallible. No one thought to tell her because they'd never had a shafter among them. That the instructors identified her limitations, weakness as he'd called it, should have been a blessing. But Trina knew all too well how societies worked and how they treated those on the outer edges. She'd have preferred to struggle with the others than come in late but fully prepared.

CHAPTER 2

Deluth had expected the stripe of red to lead directly to their quarters. Instead, it laced through classrooms, common gathering areas, and other sections their instructor didn't bother to call out. By the time the man came to a halt, Deluth had started to wonder if the red stripe had any meaning at all or if this was part of the ritual for new candidates much like the tricks played on those just moved into the bunks on his home ship.

"And this, candidates, will be your home until you either pass your training or are dumped from the program."

The instructor stepped aside to reveal another gathering area, this one much smaller than the common areas and with a door as an entry rather than an open wall.

Deluth went to step through at the same time as a tall, brown-haired girl did. She gave him a tense look, but he shrugged it off, stepping to one side to let her go.

Redel pushed between both of them. "Stop blocking the doorway. We all want to see."

Redel's broad shoulders obscured Deluth's first sight of their quarters as his friend stopped directly in the path to look around.

Before any of them could decide to say something, their instructor shoved Redel to one side, ignoring a surprised, "Hey!"

"Everyone come inside. Don't block the corridors. That should have been part of your orientation. This station has more going on than just teaching, and emergencies happen."

Deluth shot Redel a glance, annoyed at the scolding when he'd had little choice. At least the man didn't seem to be holding it against any of them as far as he could see, though in the area's dim lighting, it would be easy to miss something.

"Sit anywhere. The table's good for shared projects and discussions. There are six terminals should you need one. The vid gets standard programming and can access any of the educational programs produced by the Spacer Guild. You might find some useful. After all, few candidates arrive at training with the same set of knowledge. The vids are one of the ways to even things out."

The instructor waited for them to settle before continuing. "I'm Kenner Plank. You can call me Kenner or Plank. I don't answer to 'instructor' so learn my name."

One of the girls laughed, and he gave her a raised eyebrow that only made her laugh again.

"Right. I'm your main instructor. I'll tell you where to head in the morning, where you'll need to be in the afternoon, and whether I've arranged a gathering with one or more of the other teams for socializing. You'll have many teachers, but when you have questions or problems, come to me. Got it?"

They answered as a chorus, but Deluth noticed he wasn't the only one to glance toward the opening in the back wall. It stood far enough from any of the seating to prevent a clear look, even from one of the lounge chairs where Redel had taken the name as a direction and stretched across three seats.

"Thank you for your attention," Plank said with a sardonic twist to his tone. "I hope you'll do better when I'm passing out your assignments. Focus is critical for success in the Guild."

Deluth's cheeks heated, but he hoped his skin was dark enough to cover it in this light.

"Despite what you might have heard, the instructors are not cruel. I know you've traveled far and are eager to settle into your rooms. Only one more thing. You might have noticed the light level. Our lights cycle on a standard daylight scheme based on our synchronous orbit with the planet below. It's evening now. There's enough light to watch a program, and the terminals have their own light enclosures if you need to work, but generally this is your time to think on the lessons of the day. Use the cycle to gauge when you should be resting."

"We don't control our lights?"

The question came from a boy seated at the table, but Deluth had wondered the same. It was one thing to share the lighting controls with seven others as they had in the bunks, but they'd known each other. With the exception of Redel, every one of these were strangers.

Plank nodded. "In the main areas, you do not. In your rooms, you will, though you're advised to keep to the same schedule as the rest. Too much deviation will affect your performance."

"Can we see our bunks now?" Redel drawled the question as he shoved to his feet, earning another raised eyebrow from Plank.

"The next room is your meal section. There's a standard replicator and seating. You can load your own meal requirements within reason. A palm-scanner activates your allotments just like on most ships."

"And our rooms?"

Plank smiled at the girl where he'd not greeted Redel's demand as well. "They're past the meal area to provide separation should you need to study in your rooms while others are gathering. Official gathers are in the larger section, but you'll have a good bit of free time to study or use as you think best."

He rose, and everyone else did as well, except for Redel who'd already been on his feet.

Deluth fell into step behind Plank, unsurprised when Redel slipped in between as they approached the opening.

He mulled over what their instructor had said, or more specifically what he hadn't. They would have a lot of freedom, freedom he'd never had before, and he suspected the same would prove true for many of the others.

"Are you coming or not?" Redel demanded from across the meal area.

It took a second for Deluth to realize he was the target and that several others had made their way into the bunk section already. He picked up his pace, as eager to see the rooms as Redel, half expecting them to be curtained bunks despite what Plank had said.

They entered a tight corridor with doors opening on either side. Dim light streamed from along the walking path, most likely adjusted to the time of day.

Redel raced to the very end, shoving two candidates out of the way in his eagerness. "I'm taking this one."

The girl who'd laughed before gave a shrug and stepped toward the one next to it.

"That's Deluth's room."

Deluth glanced up from the room he'd been looking into to meet her startled frown.

"I'm fine with this one."

"No," Redel said, glaring at the other candidate. "You're next to me. I promised to hold your hand if you get frightened at night, remember?"

Deluth was about to object, annoyed at the repeated tease, but something in Redel's stance made him wonder if his friend was the one needing hand holding. After all, they'd never had rooms of their own. As babies, they lived in their parents' room, and then they moved into the shared dorms. They'd never been alone.

He turned to the girl. "Would you mind?"

She opened her mouth as if to reject his request, but ended with a shrug. "It's not like it matters. The rooms look much the same. I thought it might be quieter here."

"I think that one's still unclaimed." Deluth pointed to the room opposite Redel.

She laughed once. "I think I'll take this one instead." Her hand touched the door to the one Deluth had been considering.

He nodded his thanks and switched positions with her, sending his friend a questioning look.

"You're my right-hand man. My buddy. Who else would I want sharing a wall? You're my second in command."

A laugh burst out at the statement, Deluth shaking his head at Redel. "We're not in command of anything. We're the lowest rank on the whole station."

"That's what you think," Redel's voice lacked a teasing tone as he implied a command structure already coming into being.

Deluth turned to his door, embarrassed for his friend. "Be careful, Redel. We're all a team, and we need to work together."

"Every team needs a leader."

He chose to ignore the response in favor of keying his room to his palm. Maybe by morning Redel would have regained his equilibrium. If he'd tried such games on their ship, he'd be locked in the thinking room. Here, he could be expelled from training.

Deluth glanced at the panel, only then noticing what he'd done while lost in thought. He'd set his lights to shift red if anyone entered without him, or even right behind him, a warning system they'd come up with in his bunk to stop the older boys from playing tricks on them in the night. It shouldn't be necessary here, though with the way Redel was acting, he didn't bother changing the setting.

THE LAST IN A LONG line of purple-suits pushed Trina and the others out of another bewildering air stream.

"You were told your team section and color. Find it and follow the stripe to your new quarters."

Trina was not the only one to gape when the woman stepped into the stream again and disappeared.

"What are we supposed to do now?" a boy asked. He looked too young to be a candidate.

Trina thrust her shoulders straight and scanned the area. "We're to find our colors and follow them. If you think today's been hard, perhaps you're not ready for the training."

A couple of the others turned to stare at her for that, and she felt a flash of guilt, but her statement stood not just for him but for herself as well. Half of her wanted to find an instructor and ask to be sent back. To the ship, to Ceric, to anywhere but here.

The testing had been nothing like the spacer test. She'd been locked into a room all by herself with only a terminal, not even an instructor. This hadn't been a simple matter of colored buttons either.

Half of what the terminal asked of her she couldn't understand much less do. And the other half she could read the words, but many seemed to have different meanings. She wanted nothing more in that moment than to be on Ceric Colony still with her knives safely stowed in her sheaths.

Both hands twitched, but no solid blades slid forward.

Nishan had explained how she wouldn't be allowed weapons in training. How that would mean being removed from the program. Trina hadn't wanted to chance being dismissed, and right now, she appreciated their reasoning. She could do much worse than snap at a young boy.

Her gaze scraped over a stripe of the right shade, and she marched toward it, ignoring the others.

"You shouldn't take your frustrations out on the others."

The words gave too little warning as a hand landed on her shoulder. Trina dropped to a crouch—ready to run, to attack, to disappear— before she could control herself.

The candidate stood quite a bit taller than she was. Most of them did. He had dark brown skin to match Nishan's tone, but where the political officer's hair hung in straight black lines, this boy's auburn ringlets surrounded a gentle face before twisting down almost to his waist. He showed a keen intelligence as he raised both hands in surrender and stepped away, recognizing the danger in her stance.

Trina shook herself and rose. "Sorry. You're right." The short, staccato phrases came out in clipped shafter speak.

He relaxed at her apology. "I guess we're all a bit thrown. Were you told to expect extra testing?"

"No. I guess they forgot."

He gave a lopsided grin. "Too used to their own understanding to remember there are those not afforded the same privileges." He thrust out a hand with palm facing up. "Azizi. From Shekal."

She stared at his hand before laying her palm on top of his. "Trina of Ceric. So you're planet-bound?"

He didn't object to her gesture, only dropped his hand down to his side. "And clearly not of the ruling class."

"Me neither." She didn't bother to explain how none on her planet used technology beyond the few technology workers, nor the complexity of her heritage.

"None of us are. But once we finish our training, it won't matter."

Whatever class he came from, he seemed to have been free of the power dynamics she'd navigated from the moment she stepped foot outside of the space her father had found for them. He didn't understand how the training would set them apart, but he'd learn.

"So, I'm an Engineer, not that it matters beyond sleeping. Black stripe."

He paused, waiting for her answer. She almost wished they had the same team.

Azizi might not have come from a colony as resistant to technology as hers, but he had been neither ship-raised nor polit, whatever they were called on his planet. As they'd been talking, some of her anger had eased, though the concerns remained.

"Red. Pilots." Again, her tongue took on a shafter tone, so much so Azizi frowned at the short words.

"Well, then I guess this is your path." With a wave to the stripe she'd been heading for, he turned away.

Trina caught his arm. "Maybe we'll see each other in training? At least if it's not in the single rooms again."

He spun back, that grin showing off bright white teeth once again. "They're sure to train us together. I'll look for you."

With a relaxed wave and none of the tension of his first leave-taking, he strolled off.

A slight smile curved Trina's lips as she started down her stripe.

She'd made a friend of sorts. Only time would show if they'd continue as friends, but Trina felt less isolated already.

At least until she reached the end of the stripe and stepped into a dimly lit room full of lounging candidates.

A quick glance showed terminals against the wall, only known to her because of the testing she'd just suffered. A girl sat at one, but her body shielded the screen. A vid much like the ones shown in orientation played on another wall with eight more candidates present, at the table, on the lounges, or standing.

All but the one on the terminal turned to stare at her.

"Who are you?" a tall young man demanded.

"A Pilot." Though she'd promised herself not to act the shafter, this time not just her words but her stance went into alert. Her hands twitched, but still no knives slipped down.

One of the female candidates tipped her head to assess Trina. "You're awfully young for this, aren't you?"

Trina winced, remembering her own assessment of one of those who'd needed extra testing. "I'm old enough."

"She's probably exhausted," another young man said from the table. "You came in on a late shuttle, didn't you?"

The first young man shrugged and waved her through, acting the host…or big man.

She didn't stop to explain. They'd figure it out soon enough, and she'd caught sight of an entrance across the room.

A few quick strides and she was in another space, one blessedly clear of people now, even if they'd been in here recently from the layered smells.

Her stomach rumbled, but she wanted to secure her belongings first. At least she knew they'd all have individual rooms. No one would be messing with her things for all this felt like a shafter warren already, one with a big man shoving his weight around.

The next opening revealed what had to be their rooms.

Trina paced the length, but every door except the first one before the meal area glowed a faint green around the palm screen. She'd have preferred the last room rather than the first, but in this like the rest, she'd had no choice. She got what the others discarded.

As she keyed the room to her palm and stowed her belongings, Trina tried not to grit her teeth. She'd thought that part of her life was over when she joined the Spacer Guild. Both her past and her present seemed determined to keep her on the outside.

IT DIDN'T TAKE TRINA long to set up her things. She found a shelf to display her father's pen, spread one of Katie's quilts across the bed, and tucked her clothes into a drawer.

She sat down on the quilt and scanned the room. It was much smaller than the cabin she'd shared with her sister, and had no separate place for eating or even a cleanser.

One wall had shelves and drawers above a bed. The other held a screen indicating a terminal near the head of the sleeping surface, and when she looked below the screen, she could see a stool that folded out when needed. She saw no sign of a replicator.

These quarters were clearly designed for sleep and maybe some studying. Not much else. No wonder the others had gathered in the rooms beyond.

The thought of those rooms, especially the nearest, made her stomach rumble. She had no reason to stay here, and even if she saw little need in meeting the others, she had to eat.

The door slid open at her command. She confirmed it had accepted her palm print by closing it with an elbow, or rather trying, before using her hand. Satisfied, she went into the meal area, expecting to find it empty.

A chair scraped the floor as she entered, and she turned to see the same candidate who had attempted to bar her way.

"All settled in, then?" he asked, as if he were in charge.

For all Trina knew, he had been elected by the others in her absence. She kept her response to a noncommittal nod as she crossed to the replicator.

He leapt up and strode beyond her to reach the replicator first. "This is the replicator," he said in a voice pitched to carry over into the next room. "It will give you your meals. You only need to—"

Trina brushed off the hand he'd laid on her shoulder. "I know exactly how to get my meal. I don't need any help."

He raised both hands into the air and stepped toward the main gathering area. "I apologize for intruding. I just thought you might need assistance since you missed the introduction to our space, coming in as late as you did. Wouldn't want you too hungry for our first exercises. We can't afford a weak link."

Any thought Trina had of offering an apology of her own ended with his words.

He spoke not to her but to those listening from the other room. With every phrase, he emphasized what she already knew would happen. She was the outsider, the one who scrambled behind the team without proper training.

It would only get worse once they realized she had not been a late arrival, and that she wouldn't be participating in any of the team activities for a while. She didn't even have to try and she'd been labeled a liability. How could she contribute less than not being there at all?

Trina called up one of the basic meals she'd grown used to on the ship, relieved to see something had stayed the same.

The machine spit out her food, and she took it to the nearest table, not coincidentally the one out of direct line of sight from anyone in the gathering area. She refused to be a source of entertainment any more than she'd already been as she choked down her meal.

A wave of homesickness crashed over her, not for Ceric and the shafts, but for Katie. Her sister had accepted Trina no matter what. Here, she would be constantly required to prove herself, and by the very nature of her background would come up wanting.

Even Azizi came first to scold her.

The difference between him and the Pilot big man lay in the intent behind his action. He'd quickly offered friendship when she revealed herself not to be as cruel as her comment had seemed.

CHAPTER 3

The last bite came no easier than the first, but the would-be big man had spoken the truth. She would need the energy food offered.

Trina glanced at the dull knife that came with her meal. If she could find a way to sharpen it, at least she wouldn't be unarmed. She froze, remembering Nishan's warning again. A weapon would harm her the most of all.

She stowed the knife with the rest of her dishes, half-tempted to return to the room she'd claimed rather than going to the gathering area that held all those curious strangers, ones who might be just as quick to reject her.

A burst of laughter came through the opening, taunting her.

Was this how she planned to begin her new life? Would she hide out in the shadows, too timid to chance an encounter when she most likely could handle herself better than any here? She'd walked that path on the colony ship, and it had lost her the chance of becoming a part of the colony group just as her sister had warned.

She stilled the twitch of her hands. Even had she tucked away some knives, or made them, using a blade would cost her more than she was willing to pay.

Her life on Ceric had been worth little once her mother died. Katie would have found a way to survive. Here, she had the chance to leave her years of thieving behind. If she managed to complete her training, she'd walk off this station as a spacer, one destined to roam the stars and welcome on every planet out there, even Ceric.

No arrogant candidate could take that from her. Only she could throw away this chance.

Trina straightened to her full height and strode toward the gathering area. She half expected the same young man to jump out at her as soon as she passed the entrance, but everyone seemed occupied.

In front of her, one candidate sat upright on a lounger, apparently lost in thought as a vid about the history of the Guild played on the screen. The large table held five more, absorbed in some sort of card game. She wondered whether it had anything in common with the games she'd learned from her sister and the others on the colony ship, but couldn't tell from this distance.

She could not see any more from where she stood and didn't want to be seen as hesitant. Trina wished she knew where the one who had accosted her ended up, but she had to take this chance.

With the table full, and the terminals on the far side so she'd have to pass by everyone, Trina chose to perch on one of the loungers and watch the vid. She knew less about the Guild than anyone here, she'd guess. All her time spent at the fence separating First City from the spaceport taught her little, and orientation focused more on doing the ship proud and not getting in trouble.

The other candidate didn't look up when she joined him, confirming her assessment of his mental state. She looked at him long enough to take in his reddish brown skin and the straight, black hair hanging past his shoulders, but he didn't even shift under her gaze.

That very fact reassured her.

It seemed others were having difficulty with the change to this new life as well, if in their own ways.

She felt less of an outsider as a result, the first step in becoming a member of the Guild in truth. The Guild offered a family much bigger even than the one her father had sprung from.

"You can't want to watch that," came a voice from behind her.

Trina didn't bother to turn and see, already suspecting the one candidate who had decided to make himself her very own annoyance.

Sure enough, he strode up to the screen, contemplated the settings, and switched the program.

From the way he'd pondered, she suspected the whole thing an act, something he'd planned when he left her in the meal area. Trina didn't intend to show how he'd rattled her no matter what he chose.

It took a moment for her vision to adjust from the bright picture of the previous vid to this dimly lit scene with occasional flashes of light, but when she did, Trina had to suppress a grim smile.

He had turned it to images of a brutal war, an active one from the way the picture formed. Dark came from the sun having already set on this world, but also from the blood pooling around some of the bodies.

Perhaps those raised on ship had less exposure to the more deadly side of life what with security patrols and monitoring in all known areas, but the shafts had no such luxuries. This had been what Nishan had tried to explain. Where he thought to scare or shock her, she'd lived a life so much more deadly than his, and at least with a war, eventually it would come to an end.

She kept both her humor and her boredom masked, watching stoically. While she could probably figure out how to switch it despite her technical limitations, she had no intention of giving him the satisfaction nor of fighting him for the privilege.

After a long pause full of expectant tension, the candidate laughed once. "You are a tough one, I'll give you that. Good. You'll need to be."

A LOUD EXPLOSION DREW DELUTH out of his thoughts where the murmur of voices didn't draw him. He glanced at the vid, wondering just what it would be showing.

A brutal war met his gaze, a planet war of the type that didn't happen in space with the exception of pirates.

"You ready to deal with this?"

At first, he thought Redel spoke to him and began to answer, but his friend looked toward the other lounger.

He turned to see the same candidate he'd noticed in the cargo bay. She was part of his team, after all.

The jolt of happiness surprised him, though he suspected curiosity lay at its root. Even in that short time of observation, she'd seemed different from the rest. Intriguing.

She offered no response to Redel, staring at the vid as if engrossed, but from the way her jaw muscle moved, he thought her attention fake.

Deluth sighed inwardly as he pushed himself up. They were here to become spacers, not bullies. The changes in his bunkmate were unwelcome, and unfortunate. He hoped Redel would soon find his place and stop pushing.

"What are you doing?"

This time Redel did direct the question to him.

"I was watching the other program, Redel, and have no interest in planet wars."

"You know all there is to know about Guild history. Nor were you paying attention. I think our newest team member likes this one."

Deluth swallowed his true reaction. He'd try to find time to speak with Redel alone, but he would not start the argument here. Humiliating his bunkmate would serve little purpose, and Redel would never forgive him.

"We start lessons tomorrow. Until we have our schedules, we don't know what they'll entail. A refresher seems wise, and why else would they have put this in the queue?"

He looked to the young woman, but she ignored him, perhaps unwilling to admit she had a problem even to one trying to help her. She did not, however, protest when he restored the history vid. She did not react at all.

Deluth settled onto his lounger, expecting his mind to return to the puzzle of their new circumstances and what they could expect come morning. He'd had such high hopes for a different world, and different it was, but some of the differences, especially in Redel, proved more troubling than not.

He shifted so the newcomer appeared in his peripheral vision. Redel might have to be reminded of their purpose, but the young woman seemed to focus on the right things to the exclusion of all else. Again, she'd settled into stillness, a pool of calm amid the activity around them.

The group playing cards erupted in crows of laughter and groans of loss, as though to emphasize the contrast.

Had he not been watching her, he would have missed how she tensed for a second, her relaxed appearance as much an illusion now as in the confrontation with Redel.

TRINA KNEW SHE SHOULD BE focusing on the Guild vid. After all, unlike the other candidate who'd said he wanted a refresher, she had little knowledge beyond what they'd crammed into her in orientation. Still, as fascinating as the history should have been, her mind wouldn't settle.

She listened to identify where the first candidate, Redel this one had called him, had gone. When he settled with the card-playing group, she focused on their comments in the hopes of learning more about them.

They spoke of little beyond the cards.

The young man opposite said nothing and appeared to be absorbed in the vid again. From how long it had taken him to react to Redel's actions, she suspected his thoughts had wandered much as hers had.

She forced her mind to the display, but her gaze fell on a busy terminal screen in the vid behind the person speaking and lost focus.

All those days in orientation, and no one had thought to give her a system rundown so she wouldn't have been quite so ignorant from the start. Perhaps they didn't think her capable of learning without formal teachers. Perhaps they didn't think about it at all.

A flash of anger rushed through her at the memory of standing there waiting when no one chose her, of being singled out from the start. Would this Redel have picked her for the target of his power games if she'd been collected at the same time, just another candidate? And how quickly would she be able to regain her standing when she would have a schedule very different from the rest?

The vid switched to starscapes as it talked about the different roles the Spacer Guild enabled, from colony ships like the one she'd been on to trading vessels, and even militia support. Her eyes narrowed at that, wondering how often spacers engaged in warfare like the other program.

As though it heard her, the vid focused on this aspect, explaining it was space support only to help colonies suffering from ship pirates. With so many settlements spread out across the galaxy thanks to folded space, few had the resources to mount their own orbital protection, and official governments were often too far for help. Most received all their contact through the Spacer Guild or independent traders.

Ceric had been one of those colonies, and contact had been limited even more by the rules and shunning of any who used the crutch of technology. At least the pirates found little to draw them there.

The very incongruity of her position threatened to overwhelm Trina.

She might not have been a leading member of Ceric society, but her ignorance of technology made her one of the devoted by nature. She'd followed the doctrines about the work of her hands as much by lack of choice as intent.

Now, she sat in a space station maintained by any number of mechanical contraptions. The very air she breathed came not from a planet's atmosphere but out of more machines she didn't understand.

This ignorance made her vulnerable, and the ways she knew to hold her own would cost her more than suffering the attention of would-be big men. This Redel had failed in his attempt to shock her, but that he tried showed no matter what those on the colony ship might believe, not everyone was focused on becoming a good Guild member and learning what they needed. For some, like Fence on Ceric, the need to dominate, to find your place by crushing those around you, came naturally.

Her teeth pressed together in the tight-lipped grin of a shafter in battle. She had no intention of being his outlet. He'd soon learn he'd chosen the wrong target.

Trina crushed that thought as soon as it crossed her mind.

He might be willing to chance expulsion for posturing. She was not.

She would keep her head down, do as she was told, and learn everything she needed to so she could become a spacer in truth. Only then would she be able to get as far from people like Fence and Redel as possible.

That he'd made it into the spacer candidacy program made no sense, but perhaps he had virtues she could not see.

Her thoughts turned then to the other young man, the one who had intervened though she hadn't asked for help.

He'd shifted to a more upright posture, his face turned toward the screen and his body still except for the occasional sip he took from a glass in his hand.

Perhaps he had just wanted to watch the program after all.

She should take a lesson from his dedication instead of evaluating the situation the way a shafter would.

The spacers on the colony ship had shown her that those in authority didn't have to be conniving and power-hungry. They'd had the chance to punish her for helping her grandfather. Instead, they'd assessed her value and brought her to this point. Nishan had sponsored her, but so had Lenat and Patty. She had the support of a political and medical officer, but even better, one from security.

The idea of a security force working for her instead of against still amazed Trina. If she could find a ship like that one, where spacers worked together instead of cutting each other down, maybe then she could put the past far enough behind her to give up her shafter ways.

She'd hoped to do so in training, but it would take more effort than she'd expected. She had no tunnels here.

She refused to seek them out though they must be present behind the walls. This training offered a turning point to remake her life. She would not let old habits destroy it for her.

Trina pulled her gaze from the other candidate, unaware until then that her focus had shifted. She could afford no distractions, not from enemies nor from young men who seemed to draw her attention no matter what she tried.

She pushed to her feet and headed for the room she'd chosen, not waiting for the program to end or saying anything to the others. She had a long day ahead of her tomorrow and couldn't have repeated a single bit of information from the vid anyway, not even if her life depended on it.

Her rescuer she could have described well enough for someone with talent to take down his likeness. She suspected he wouldn't slip free of her memory as easily as the spacer history.

CHAPTER 4

Noise outside her room woke Trina. Only then did she become aware of the insistent beeping of her alarm. She'd been up late into the night despite her best intentions, her mind tearing apart the technology assessment one minute and dwelling on the motivations of the young man who'd helped her the next.

It seemed wrong for her to know the name of her enemy, but not the one who just might turn out to be a friend.

She rolled off the bed, banged her arm on the terminal, and snatched up the first clothes she could get her hands on.

It wasn't until she caught sight of herself in the reflective surface of the terminal that she realized she'd chosen a tunic emblazoned with the sign of Menthak.

Longing for her sister hit her so hard she bent double, her body mirroring her mind. She'd never been alone before despite all the time she'd spent on her own. She'd always had Katie waiting for her. She'd had her mother and Piper on Ceric as well, while Marcus had become a close friend on the ship. Here, she had a dubious rescuer and a quick conversation that started with a scolding.

Her frowning face stared at her from the terminal, but she didn't linger as voices outside reminded her she'd be late if she didn't hurry.

She might be alone now, but she had made positive contact with two different people, Azizi and her rescuer. She hadn't known Marcus until he ran Samuel's errand, and though her grandfather made the connection to cement his position in her life, that did nothing to change her friendship. Trina had only to make an effort rather than hiding in her room.

The last was enough to motivate her, and she ran her fingers through the straight blond hair that never seemed to tangle as she triggered the door and stepped into a busy hallway.

Except it wasn't busy.

She moved through the empty kitchen and reached the gathering area in time to see the others on their way out the door.

Though she started after them, Trina froze when she saw the last two to leave: Redel and her rescuer.

Redel had a hand slung over the other candidate's shoulder, and they were laughing about something, clearly both familiar and friends.

Maybe he had just been watching the program after all. Maybe his coming to her rescue had less to do with her and more to do with his own wishes.

She gritted her teeth against a disappointment much too strong for such a short connection.

Her grandfather had betrayed her. This young man had not even noticed she existed while she'd spent the better part of the night considering what she'd say to him this morning.

It had to be homesickness for her sister. Trina never had been one to put much stake in ties with others, but she'd never had to since she seemed to find those connections without much effort.

Remembering Azizi, she shrugged off the last bitterness. While she'd have liked a friend on her team, she would find others. And perhaps in the evening, she'd make a point of introducing herself to the rest of the Pilot team. Redel did not stand for the whole group. He couldn't with them being strangers until yesterday.

"There you are," came a voice from the opening. "I'm to take you to your technology training. Hurry along now."

She glanced from the woman in an instructor's purple suit to the meal room entrance and back. "I'm coming." She'd go hungry, her punishment for failing to wake with the rest.

A smile slipped out when she realized she had Redel to thank for what little energy she had, though she'd swear it had not been his intention. She might just have gone to meet the others had he not intervened, or at least she wouldn't have lingered and gotten such a full meal the night before.

"I'm glad to see you're looking forward to the training," the woman said, misinterpreting Trina's smile. "So many see it as a failure, but the Guild wouldn't have sent you here if they didn't see value in your abilities and your background. The lack of technological understanding is a part of that. I've been on Ceric once myself a bit ago. Never could understand your doctrine, but then, in space, there isn't much of a choice. If we turn off the technology, we'd be adrift without air or gravity. Instant death."

The last came in such a cheerful tone Trina laughed along with the woman. Perhaps the training wouldn't be so bad after all.

CHAPTER 5

Redel had monopolized Deluth from the minute they left their rooms, leaving no time to check on their newest group member.

As the female instructor swept them out of their quarters and into the air stream, Deluth thought he'd have a chance to speak to the girl before class. Maybe he could even choose a seat near her.

He didn't understand what about the candidate drew him, but he planned to enjoy finding out.

"What do you suppose our first lessons will be?"

Redel's shout cut through Deluth's thoughts with the force of a blow, worse when he realized any attempt to get to know the new girl would be hindered by his friend's unwarranted dislike.

His shrug came just as the air pressure lowered, indicating one of the disembarking spots.

Sure enough, their instructor had already left the stream with the others.

Deluth scanned those gathered, but neither her height nor her hair stood out in the crowd. He moved to the side and sped up to catch the instructor. "I think we're missing someone," he said.

She glanced at him, her eyebrows raised. "I have everyone I'm supposed to collect."

When she would have kept going, he caught her arm and pulled her to a halt.

"There was another candidate. She came in late last night. After the rest of us. She's not here."

The woman frowned and glanced at her screen. "I don't have anyone else listed."

Redel shoved another candidate out of the way to reach them. "Why are you asking about her? Maybe she stowed away on a shuttle and isn't even a student."

This time Redel received the raised eyebrows. "Candidates do not stow away, and neither do non-candidates." She bent over the screen and tapped a few times. "Ah, yes. Trina of Menthak. She was part of a colony group. They don't all have the access ship-bred do and sometimes require extra sessions to catch up. She'll be joining us once she tests out."

Deluth tested her name on his tongue even as Redel lashed back with, "Once she gains competency? And how long will that take? She'll come in knowing nothing and expect us to carry her."

The instructor looked to her screen again. "Redel from The Headway, right? Let me explain a few things to you, Redel. Spacers come from all sorts of places, and with all sorts of skills. Because of that, we help each other. It's not a burden, and often you learn more by helping than by learning on your own. Besides, her lessons run parallel to yours just with a different emphasis."

She didn't give him the chance to respond, only turned and strode down the corridor to their first class, leaving Deluth to suffer Redel's glare.

Deluth said nothing, knowing any response would only provoke his bunkmate. He couldn't imagine growing up without basic skills, but then he'd only been planetside once. She most likely had abilities he wouldn't.

TRINA ARRIVED AT THE STUDY hall when most of the chairs were already filled. The woman who'd guided her gave a quick wave and stepped into the air stream again, leaving Trina no choice but to go forward.

She scanned the area, seeking a secure spot against the wall.

"Trina," a voice called out. "Over here."

She turned toward the voice, startled, only to recognize Azizi from his riot of long curls.

He sat toward the front and well away from any of the walls. He'd chosen a position vulnerable from all sides.

Trina drew in a slow breath and crossed to the chair beside him. If she wanted to become a spacer, she had to put her shafter instincts aside. None of those in this room would attack her with knives or whatever weapon they'd claimed. The worst she'd suffer would be words like from Redel, and those she could ignore.

"Quickly. The instructor's coming."

At Azizi's urging, Trina slid into her seat and rested both hands on the desk, mimicking those around her.

The simple surface came to life with a series of sharp notes.

She jerked, half rising out of her chair. The seat only stayed upright because she had one leg wrapped around its support.

"Ah, a perfect introduction," said the woman in an instructor's purple as Trina took her place again with hands carefully folded in her lap. "I am going to be your main teacher, though you'll have sessions with others as necessary. I am Fredrika Florence Remintralia. You will call me Fred."

That brought forth a few chuckles, the noise a reminder of just how many candidates sat in this room. Trina guessed more than fifty crowded this space. She'd never thought other worlds would have any strictures on technology.

"This is the initial meeting room. You are to come here every morning until you are released into the general program. For some of you, that may happen by the end of this day. For others, it will come when it is time."

Fred did not glance in Trina's direction, but she felt the words directed at her all the same, an instinct proved true with the woman's next statement.

"Your desks are specialized terminals. They will help guide you through the program and will be where you do the majority of your work. Each of you has been assigned an ID tied to your palm print, so you can access study materials from any terminal. Your ID also provides access to the on-point machines such as the replicators should you wish to add something to the meals in your rooms."

Fred continued explaining what she called the basics, but Trina found her head spinning with things she didn't understand.

She'd felt isolated by the choice to pull her aside, thinking it would make her stand out, but how much worse would it have been to suffer the humiliation of not knowing what even those here clearly knew. They might not have had access to the same level of technology, but it seemed from a quick look around that everyone else could follow what the instructor said without difficulty. Most looked eager to set their hands on what had been denied them.

"Though few of you will have had this ability before, when we're finished with your first section, you'll be able to customize your living quarters to respond to your needs. Only your individual rooms will be unlocked for you, so you can't change the settings for everyone in your group, but you can establish your lighting preferences per time of day."

"How can you lock out a switch?"

Trina hadn't meant to say the words aloud, but within a heartbeat she realized she had from the rustling of the other students as they turned to give her odd looks. She stared resolutely at Fred, unable to change her outburst but neither could she change the need for an answer.

Their instructor stared back, a baffled look on her face that cleared after a moment.

Fred gave a breathy laugh. "That's right. I'd heard there was a Ceric candidate. We've never had one before. We've suspected politics prevented applicants, but you came off a colony ship, didn't you?"

She shrugged, unwilling to give a verbal answer. At least the woman hadn't called her out for the shafter she'd been. Still, having her colony set aside as unique made her as much of an outsider in this group as she was with the Pilots.

"For those of you who don't know, Ceric is a colony that chose, because of early tech failures, to limit technology to critical aspects only, and all knowledge is kept restricted to a particular class. For Trina to have made it this far is nothing short of amazing. If you thought your flight hindered, hers was a thousand fold more difficult, and yet here she sits among you."

Trina slumped in her seat, wishing she could disappear into a shaft right then. Now, as well as being the most ignorant, she would be seen as one to be pitied.

"What about the switches?"

She turned to glare at the voice only to realize Azizi had been the one to speak and he tried to redirect Fred to the knowledge she needed. Trina gave him a slight smile as she straightened to watch their instructor once again.

"Right. Switches. She wouldn't have had access to light conditioning at home because such would be considered wasteful, even blasphemous. On a colony ship, the tech exists as much as any ship. However, the colony sections are isolated from the ship sections in case of troublemakers. There have been cases of pirates using a colony contract to take over a ship, or rather there were before the precautions. We will be covering light conditioning shortly."

Though the explanation had been more for the other candidates than her, Trina felt some of her tension ease as they moved onto the next topic, at least until she considered just what Fred had mentioned.

She'd been the troublemaker in their colony, and their precautions had meant little when some of the crew could be bribed.

How much more damage could she have done in her grandfather's name if she'd known how to change things on her own beyond figuring out the colored buttons on the device he'd given her? How many places had she passed where understanding this technology would have given her access to everything?

Without her, Samuel would not have known remote listening devices were possible.

He hadn't believed her when she first suggested them.

If she hadn't, perhaps he wouldn't have known how far he'd slipped from the power he sought. Perhaps he wouldn't have released the deadly virus that brought his activities to the attention of the crew and cost some of the colonists their lives.

But then he'd have waited to release it on the colony itself where they would not have had the technology or skilled medical staff available on the ship to stop the spread so quickly. The thought made her gut churn.

She had not known his intentions, but even so, she'd known she had passed beyond the expectations of the colonists. It should have been enough to make her question his motives. Had he been a shafter, she would not have been so willing to consider his wish to help everyone, but now she knew big men came in every class. She had only to look at Redel to see the spacers were not free of them either.

She caught the tail end of something Fred mentioned and realized the class had moved on while her thoughts spun down dark tunnels. The panel in front of her flashed key definitions, but she lacked the context either from listening or in her background to understand what they meant.

Trina split her focus between the screen and the instructor's words, concentrating as hard as she ever had when learning the routine of a new polit house she'd planned to rob. Bit by bit, her efforts paid off now as then. She began to see how the definitions built on one another, connecting much like the shafts under First City did, to form a system of knowledge. As much as she could see their relationships, the overall concepts teased but did not settle.

She glanced around only to see concentration but no confusion.

Trina was less capable than anyone else in this class of those least able to perform the tasks of a spacer. The gap between her and the worst student here stretched longer than the longest shafter tunnel. Trina fought down a sense of despair as she realized even if she were willing to present herself as a fool for a second time in the same day, she didn't know what questions to ask. She lacked a base context they all seemed to share, and she had no idea how she would be able to change that.

CHAPTER 6

Instead of a classroom, they arrived in a large open space that Deluth knew very well. He and Redel had spent all their spare time working on ship drills for the past two years, determined nothing would keep them out of the Guild.

"I'm turning you over to Kenner, your group instructor now. He'll run you through a ship drill at some point of each class day," the woman who'd led them so far said at the doorway they'd just entered. "He'll tell you the full schedule." Without waiting for a response, she spun and walked away.

A snap echoed through the chamber as an open panel he hadn't noticed closed and Kenner strode toward them. "The drills are about knowing how to survive malfunctions, knowing the right steps to take, and what the options are, but more than that it's about learning how to work together as a team. You might not know the spacers you're assigned with at first, but you have to become a cohesive group from the minute you step onto your new ship, from the minute you start your new assignment. There's no time for feeling your way and learning your position. Problems happen at all times in a flight. You must be able to integrate into an existing team or bring in a new member without hesitation."

As though timed to the end of his speech, the empty room transformed into a facsimile of a bridge with all the necessary equipment, a warning chime telling them the scenario had begun. The fault would happen at any point in the simulation, so they had to move fast.

Deluth crossed to the nearest station, expecting all the others to do the same, but then he heard Redel.

"I'll take the pilot station. You go to navigation, you're on communications…"

Redel sorted everyone out and made sure they understood the console before them, taking more than the pilot's position but that of the captain. There was not a single person he didn't check out and school beyond Deluth, who he left alone after jerking to a halt when he tried to assign one of the other candidates to the post Deluth had already claimed.

The others seemed to accept his leadership without question, much like the confrontation over rooms. Whether the battle did not seem worth fighting or they truly didn't care, he couldn't tell.

For all he knew, they could welcome someone with an obvious understanding of the ship drills. Perhaps they hadn't had the access or ability to do them before now.

He scowled down at his panel, labeled ship's systems in glowing letters at the top. This station controlled the on-ship gravity, air, humidity, and half a dozen other aspects making a metal shell in space habitable.

Because of its very complexity, there were also endless ways things could go wrong. He needed to concentrate.

Instead, he kept turning to watch Redel move among the others.

His friend was everywhere. He told the candidates how to work their stations, often without asking first what they already knew.

Deluth's fingers gripped the sides of his console hard enough for his knuckles to whiten, but he forced them to relax.

He didn't know what had gotten into him. Ever since they'd left the ship, he'd been finding reasons to question, rebuke, or frown on his friend. No one else seemed to resent Redel's behavior. Kenner had told them to act like a team. The others were falling in line.

A sigh surprised Deluth as he wondered if that could be the problem.

He'd grown up with Redel. They knew each other better than most married couples. Could he be jealous of how easily Redel had found his place even as Deluth hung back, assessing the possibilities?

While he pondered the question of a lack in his own rather than Redel's actions, the simulation moved from station to system to slipping into folded space. His console remained steady, everything within marked parameters. It could change at any time, so he kept scanning the readouts.

The alarm sounded just when they'd settled into the rush of folded space where time compressed a million moments into one.

His heart jumped and one of the other candidates let out a squeak.

The simulations were designed to feel real, and they succeeded. Everyone knew the dangers of folded space. A problem here could mean a ship lost forever, or a ghost ship appearing a hundred years later with crew that hadn't aged a day.

He glanced over to see which console showed an error. A navigation issue. The worst possible while in folded space, but then none would be good.

Before he could offer a suggestion, Redel stepped in to guide them through the possibilities. Where the two of them had always debated the choices together, now Redel ran through the options aloud, but the choice would clearly be his alone.

It made sense. There were nine of them. If each got an equal say, the ship would be lost before a decision could be made, at least for a navigation issue. They had a limited amount of time until the ship lost its bearings and floated at random. Even if they could find an anchor point to cut through to normal space, they had no way of knowing where they would end up, or if they'd be close enough to civilization to enact the repairs they'd be sure to need.

"Return to your station," Redel barked at one of the other candidates who'd drifted over to see. "Just because we have found an issue doesn't mean there won't be more."

Deluth couldn't disagree, one of the reasons he'd stayed at his station once Redel moved over. But at the same time, how would the others learn if they couldn't see. They'd only know what Redel chose to describe.

He considered stepping in, suggesting a rotation through the stations so everyone had a chance, but that would take too long and the simulation would complete with them adrift. If they were truly running a simulation every day, chances were that each would get to experience all stations, and more likely than not, a problem at that station.

The options ran through his mind as well, this a common drill on their ship. As a supplier, they often went below, as folded space was called.

"Systems, shift the internal gravity balance."

Redel's barked command took a second to filter through Deluth's evaluation. Not the choice he would have made, but sometimes navigation problems could be caused by a conflict between gravity waves as the fold passed too close to a black hole capable of stretching into even the below.

He went through the calculations, sent a quick warning pulse to the areas affected, and shifted the gravity to oppose the pull even as Redel had the thrusters reversing them away.

The risky move would throw them off their expected course, but if they tracked their shift, they could restore the course once past the black hole. Below didn't function exactly like normal space, but some things were comparable.

The alarm bell quieted as they successfully passed the gravity intrusion and restored their course. The consoles faded away, and Kenner moved from where he'd hidden during the simulation.

"Not bad for a first run. I see you have some experienced crew onboard. Very few complete the first scenario with the ship intact."

Deluth was surprised when the instructor nodded to him as well as Redel, though he had completed the gravity maneuver without issue.

"However, you forgot a crucial step. You cannot assume everyone will have either the skills or the capability to escape that pull. A cargo ship with only crew quarters under gravity, for example, would not have the systems in place to throw a counter weight in to assist the engines. Your job as spacers is to mark and report potential dangers for those coming after. Drop a signal beacon and mark the coordinates in your logs."

Kenner moved to the candidate who had been at the communications panel as he spoke, explaining even without the console how such would be achieved.

Deluth thought they'd done pretty well on their first run out. He glanced to Redel, thinking to congratulate his friend for organizing, but Redel didn't notice. Instead, he glared at the candidate who had failed to drop the beacon.

Moving up to Redel's side, Deluth said in a low voice, "They did fine for their first time. Remember how many times we failed before our first success? Even a partial one?"

Redel's mouth tightened into a thin line, then relaxed. "You're right. It's easy to forget they're just beginners. They should have practiced like we did."

Deluth swallowed the reminder that not all ships bothered with, or could afford, a simulator system. He'd managed to distract Redel. For all his friend's assumption of command annoyed him, had he not driven the team, perhaps they wouldn't have performed as well.

"Deluth, right?" Kenner dropped back to walk at his side as they headed for the next session. "If you want to do some extra drills, there are simulators open to candidates during your free time. I suspect our drill banks are a bit larger than those on your home ship."

Before Deluth could thank the man, he'd taken off again, regaining the head of their group with ease thanks to a long-limbed stride.

"THAT'S ENOUGH FOR TODAY. Don't be worried if not everything sunk in." Fred gave them a quick smile. "We laid the foundation. As we build on it, you'll come to understand more."

Trina stared at the terminal in front of her, the terms from the last session scrolling past still, but though she could read almost every one of the words there, the meanings escaped her. She'd spent their lunch break trying to grasp the morning's session with little success, and now it looked like she'd spend her evening doing the same. So much for meeting her team.

She thrust a hand through her hair, trying to ease the pressure on her skull.

Brown fingers cut between her vision and the terminal, blocking her view.

She jerked upright, mouth open to demand no interference, only to meet Azizi's concerned gaze. Her lips snapped together in time not to offend the one person who'd shown any interest in being kind, but her teeth gritted with annoyance anyway.

"You'll give yourself a headache if you haven't already. You heard our instructor. You're not expected to understand it all from the start." He shrugged.

Trina pushed away from the terminal. "Too late for that. My head already aches. And every single one of the candidates in this room understood more than I did."

He grinned for a heartbeat before controlling the expression. "You know this how? Telepathy is rare, and not something that would put you in the basic spacer training."

His deep brown eyes twinkled with suppressed mirth.

Trina let herself relax. "If I had telepathy, I wouldn't need this class. I could pick up how to do things from your mind."

He tugged one of his ringlets. "Not this mind. I caught a few training classes before a ship passed that could take me here, but you notice I'm still not up to the basic standards. Otherwise, I'd have missed the opportunity to meet you."

"Some opportunity. I'm the only one who thinks turning on a light with my hand is normal, and that's just the start of my backwards upbringing." She used the word she'd heard whispered earlier, but where the candidate meant an insult, she saw value. "Everything is so automatic. You have no responsibilities at all."

He pulled his chair over and sat down again, seemingly oblivious to the now empty room. Even their instructor had left to go wherever it was the instructors gathered after hours. They had no idea how much trouble Trina could get into, or maybe they did considering she couldn't figure out the simplest aspect of what they'd learned today.

"I can help you if you want," Azizi said, breaking into her morose thoughts. "I don't know much more, but in showing you, I'd guess what I've learned will stick better. And you wouldn't be here if they didn't think you had the ability to figure it out. Together, we might understand more than anyone else, the ship-bred included."

She stared at him for a long moment. While she'd thought spacers helped each other, she'd learned that not to be true for all, at least among the candidates. Some of the shafters had pretty faces and welcoming smiles, tools they'd used to get close so they could learn secrets to use to their advantage.

"Why would you help me?"

His eyes widened at her response. "Because it's what people do. I might not have been from the richest among my people, but I never lacked for anything important. When I wanted to attempt the Spacer Guild, every effort was made to give me the chance. Once I passed the test, training and access to things I never needed in my normal life became available. When one is weak, all are weak. When one is strong, all become strong."

A laugh escaped her lips before she could stop it, stunned at such a different world, a different life.

He pushed his chair back and rose. "I'm sorry I misunderstood our connection. I will not bother you again."

Trina caught his arm, but Azizi looked as if he would shake her off so she spoke all in a rush. "No, I'm sorry. I didn't mean to mock you. It's just your life is so different from mine. I can't imagine it. Where I was looking for how you would gain from it, you were looking to my needs."

He stared at her, his eyes narrowed as he judged her just as she had him.

She held her breath, waiting for his decision. She'd felt alone before, but she now realized that feeling a lie. They had just met, but a connection had formed much as she'd found with Marcus, and Piper on Ceric. Nurtured, it could grow into a strong friendship.

If he forgave her reaction.

The wide smile she'd found welcoming before came again, and the tension swept out of her.

"They told me the world beyond my planet would be different. My parents, my teachers, even the city leaders warned me not to expect anything. They'd thought to dissuade me. Instead, it made my longing only stronger. I wanted to see the differences, to come to understand how people chose to be the way they were. And now, facing it the first time, I'd thought to reject you."

"But you won't?"

His auburn ringlets flung out around his face as he gave a vehement head shake. "No. I won't reject you for being different from me, though I can hope to change how you see me and those around you."

She laughed again, but this time he took no offense. "You can try, but some lessons are strong ones. I gave my trust before, breaking all the rules of my upbringing, only to risk myself, my sister, and everyone."

Trina hadn't thought to tell the tale to anyone, but the words seemed fitting. She didn't know if she'd feel the same when he asked for details.

"Have you never had someone you can count on? Was your life so rough?"

Her eyes slipped closed as she considered his question. "Rough, yes. And there were many who could not be trusted no matter how much I wished it weren't so. But I had my sister, my mother, and a few others who rewarded my trust with faithfulness. It's hard to remember that when my world grew out of striving only for yourself. Everyone around you would be as likely as not to put a knife in between your ribs."

He nodded. "See. I start to open your eyes already."

When she would have objected, he sat once again and pointed to the screen. "Now I open your eyes to this technology so tomorrow you might have more understood and less puzzled over."

His cheerful statement made even the thought of going over such strangeness more appealing. Rather than contest whether she could change her upbringing, she let him go over each and every term they'd learned throughout the day. She would understand what this meant if it took all night. After all, the replicator was one bit of tech she'd mastered already.

She could get a late meal and avoid the strain of sharing the time with those assigned to her group. At the very least, she would not have to hear everything they did without her, and it reduced the chance of crossing paths with Redel once again.

Her thoughts drifted to his friend for a heartbeat, but she resolutely turned them back.

She had made a friend already, and one who was willing to help her navigate this transition into a completely new world. Azizi had set his goal at getting her to put her shafter past behind her. Hadn't that been her wish as well?

Then she should not waste time wondering about someone who saw no harm in Redel's behavior, or at least not enough to shun him for it.

KENNER PICKED THEM UP FROM their last class of the day, a session on colony practices with specific focus on how the Spacer Guild interacted with those planet bound.

Deluth half-expected their missing member to appear for this one. Several of the lessons over the course of the day had been taught to a combination of teams rather than just theirs.

He saw no sign of Trina.

Redel paced at his side as they made their way to their rooms, preventing Deluth from asking Kenner as he'd queried the other instructor. When they finally reached their quarters, Redel pulled him aside, letting all the others go inside first.

"What's your interest in the colony girl anyway?" Redel demanded when they had a moment of relative privacy. "Don't think I haven't noticed you looking for her."

Deluth shrugged and tried to step through the entrance, but Redel moved to block him.

"She's part of our team," Deluth said when it was clear he wouldn't be able to avoid the confrontation. "Aren't you curious about her? It's going to be awkward if none of us know her when she's included in the drills."

Redel gave him a tight look, but Deluth did his best to offer a disinterested expression. Somehow, he didn't think he could tolerate more teasing when he hadn't quite managed to shake his annoyance from this morning. It wouldn't take much for him to lose his temper. If these two days were a measure of their training, he wondered whether they had a chance of remaining friends through the whole.

A short laugh came from Redel as he threw his arm around Deluth's shoulder. "It'll be awkward no matter how well we know her even assuming she isn't cut from the program. She'll be unskilled and untrained while we'll be a team with no rough edges. We'll all suffer for her stumbles. We managed an almost perfect success this morning. How is everyone going to feel when she turns that around and our drills become a series of failures?"

"I'd hope we would be able to bring her up to speed."

"As do I, but she's much more likely to bring us all down. Which is why, my friend, you should turn your attention to the good spacer girls here who would be happy to spend time with you."

They'd crossed the threshold at that point so Deluth swallowed his comment, not wanting to argue in front of the others. Somehow, he didn't imagine anyone who passed the spacer test, especially without a basic understanding of tech, would bring the team down.

"Sharna, there you are," Redel said, striding toward the same young woman he'd ousted from first his then Deluth's room.

Deluth headed for the meal area, relieved his friend had finished with him, yet another inappropriate feeling when he should treasure the time they spent together. If only things hadn't grown so complicated.

He couldn't tell which of them had changed, or if they both remained the same but the place made other parts of them more prominent.

Something to drink and maybe eat would go a long way toward restoring his balance. Their lunch break seemed so long ago. If luck rode with him, he would find all this confusion washed away with a little nutrition.

"Deluth, where are you going? You watched that history program all last night, and this morning was such a rush. I don't think you had the chance to meet Sharna properly."

Redel's voice brought him up short. For a heartbeat, he thought to pretend he hadn't heard. So much for a meal. Apparently his turn had not ended with the change in focus but had tightened.

Schooling his expression to pleasant interest, he turned to face a young woman he'd only shared a pained look with before.

She seemed unaware of the undertones and met his gaze with a smile.

"Sharna is from a ship," Redel said, as if that wasn't obvious from the absence of their one colony-bred team member.

She rolled her eyes. "As are we all, right?"

"One of our team is colony-bred. She's in separate classes," Deluth said.

Redel sent a scowl in his direction, but he focused on Sharna instead.

"Really?" she said. "How interesting. I wondered that they'd chosen a number lower than the stations on the drill. What do you think she's studying?"

"Most likely how to use a palm reader."

Redel's sour tone removed any chance of it being a joke.

Sharna's eyes widened. She frowned toward Redel, earning Deluth's attention as little else would have.

"Why do you say that? Surely she can figure out something so simple if she made it this far. I don't know about the spacer test you took, but ours was quite detailed."

"Aptitude is different from experience," Deluth interjected, not wanting to hear another long rant from Redel. "She may not have had access to the same technology as we had, but clearly they thought she had the ability to pick it up."

"Yes, they must have. Unless she has some extraordinary ability or something." A mischievous twist of her mouth transformed Sharna into clearly the best looking of all of them male or female, not that she hadn't been beautiful before. "Maybe she's a mutant. We heard of those. Like she can walk in heavy gravity, or breathe methane?"

Deluth laughed, feeling the tension drain out of him. "Those are just stories, I'm sure. I'm less sure of the ones about telepathy."

"Imagine being able to read minds."

"I think it would be tedious. As for me, the only thoughts in my head are of food."

He didn't think of the double meaning there, just wanting to escape from Redel before his friend said something else to irritate him, but that sentence wiped away the frown gathering on Redel's face.

"That's a great idea. Why don't you and Sharna go eat something? Talk about ship life. Get to know each other."

There was no good way to bow out of it, especially when Sharna added, "That sounds like a plan. I'm certainly hungry, and good company is always welcome."

Before he knew what had happened, she'd looped her arm through his and he was escorting her to the meal room.

Not that he regretted the chance to talk further. She seemed an inquisitive sort, and more interested in exploring than condemning. It was a relief after Redel's behavior even if he'd orchestrated this connection.

They talked through the meal about their different ship lives, hers driven by the pursuit of perfection while his focused on forming bonds between community members that held stronger than blood ties.

"No wonder you and Redel ended up on the same team. They split everyone from my ship up, probably a good thing. No one here meets our standards—no offense—and so I don't have to worry about competing for my place on top of learning."

Deluth let her comment pass, unsure what standards of perfection her ship held to, and answered her other statement instead. "We were supposed to be split up. Redel changed that."

"He does that a lot, doesn't he? Charismatic is what my people call ones like him. If he weren't so ordinary looking, I'd be measured against him."

It didn't seem the right time to remind her everything had changed when they'd left their shuttles, that here the measures were very different than on either of their ships. Redel seemed to have forgotten that fact as well.

He wondered if he stood alone in hoping things would be different on the station, and everyone else thought to have their normal ship life. If so, he imagined there would be more than a few clashes in the coming days just judging from how different his ship had been to hers.

"You want to spend the next break day together? I hear they're planning a multi-team gathering, and I'd appreciate having a familiar face at my side."

"I'd thought to do some extra training," he said, focused on what the instructor had said rather than her question.

She slumped in her chair and stared at him as though stunned by his answer.

Deluth dragged his mind to their conversation and realized she'd asked him a favor he hadn't bothered to acknowledge. To make up for it, he could see no other way but to agree. "But I can practice later. After all, it's important to meet the other teams."

Her frown lightened into a smile. "Yes, and important to make a good show of it."

As much as he wondered what she meant by that, his thoughts had already turned to the one person who seemed to draw him in. Would they let those in separate training come to such a gathering? Surely they had to give all candidates a break day.

CHAPTER 7

For the first week, Azizi and Trina had stayed after every session to study, but even with the extra effort and Azizi's help, she still struggled with concepts others found easy.

She brushed the hair out of her eyes and stared down at her terminal. "It's more energy efficient?" Trina asked, once again puzzling over the use of elaborate programs instead of manual switches. "It doesn't take that much effort to turn on the lights."

"No, it doesn't. And in those terms, I can understand why this is hard for you. But what happens when you forget to turn them off?"

A sharp memory of her shafter home rose before Trina's eyes, the power coming from the city above and not within their control. Somehow, she didn't think he wanted the solution they'd come up with. Their lights had been always on, but a few blankets tucked over the sources dimmed it enough to sleep. Her thoughts veered away from the blankets they'd hung over the front window only once they'd been discovered. He needn't know just how different her upbringing had been.

She shook her head to cast the memories aside and thought on his question. "Nothing."

He grinned. "Exactly."

At first, she didn't understand, but then First City drew its power from the sun. A ship didn't always have access to transformable energy sources. "That's the problem, isn't it? If you forget, the ship continues to provide light where it isn't needed. Light is energy." She triggered a flip of screens to where she'd learned about transformable energy. She'd never thought much about the source of their lights on Ceric beyond knowing her father had arranged a power drop for them to tie into. All that happened before she was born.

She'd been much more focused on finding items to sell to Fence so she could help her mother and feed all of them. How the power came to be mattered less than that they'd had power. And that her father had loved Mother enough to arrange it even when he wouldn't be there.

Her grin matched the one on Azizi's face as she confirmed she'd remembered correctly. Ships had limited power, and even when they did not, wasteful use could mean a lack later when an emergency occurred.

"So making the system manage your lighting means it's never wasted. It's not laziness at all."

"Only in so far as it recognizes the likelihood of our forgetfulness." Azizi laughed.

"But what about the energy the ship uses to watch for us?"

As though to remind them of how easy it could be to forget, the lights in the classroom dimmed as the ship went into its night cycle.

Trina's stomach growled in confirmation they'd once again stayed on much too late, making her question fade in importance.

"Time to head to our quarters," Azizi said with none of the enthusiasm that should have come after a breakthrough from his only student.

She caught his arm, holding him back. "I know why I have to stay so late, and why I'm not eager to return to my quarters, but surely you should want more time among your team. I appreciate what you're doing, but I won't have you harmed by it."

He gave a short laugh. "If you think it's all for your benefit then you're missing half the value. Like your last question. I was taught it's more efficient, so I have to assume the energy loss is less than that lost to lights left on, but I don't know. Even more, I wouldn't have thought to ask the question. You have a way of thinking not just about a problem but under, above, and around it as well."

"It comes from studying polit houses," she murmured, shaking off his questioning look. She'd planned to leave the past behind her, but it haunted her every decision and thought. Not as easy a burden to discard as she'd hoped.

"So you get something from it," she said after an awkward pause, "but not enough to make up for failing to integrate with your team. I have to do this. You don't. All this stuff we're going over you know already...or well enough to understand what the instructors teach us. You have the choice not to be a stranger when we're returned to our groups."

"Some choice." His mutter came out with a bitter twist, as bitter as the thought of his reaction to learning she'd been a thief when his people had everything they needed.

He started toward the corridor, and she followed on his heels, unwilling to let it go. "What do you mean by that?"

Azizi stopped so suddenly Trina almost ran him down. He turned to face her with a scowl marring his normally gentle expression. "I stay with you because you look at me and see a person, a friend. My assigned team is not so clear sighted."

"They don't know you."

"And they never will." He tugged on a strand of hair. "They see my smooth skin and ringlets as assets. They say I used my looks to get into the Spacer Guild because I don't have the skills to make it here."

Trina stared at him, surprised though she shouldn't have been considering her own experience. "The ship-bred will use any excuse."

He started walking again with an abrupt, angry movement. "You think it's that easy? The worst of the teasing, for that's what they claim it is, comes from a candidate who rode the same ship I did. She's not from my colony, but she's colony-bred as much as any of us. She says I give the colonies a bad name because I need all this special training. Better only candidates like her, who were raised with the same tech as any on a ship, are chosen."

"Do you believe that?" Her voice came out breathless as she matched her shorter stride to his, a sign she needed less studying and more physical activity.

Azizi paused when they reached the air stream, turning to face her once again. "Sometimes it's hard not to believe, but when I'm with you, when I can remember how hard I worked to be here, then no, I don't believe it one bit."

Trina gave him a smile. "Good."

She stepped into the stream, leaving him to ponder both her questions and her answer.

She'd seen herself as the only one punished, but why would the other groups be any less demanding and critical of those who were separated from the normal path?

They would just have to work harder. When they rejoined their teams, they had to be as good if not better than the other candidates were, ship- or colony-bred.

From what they'd been told, the classes covered the same material. Theirs just went into greater depth. And with the extra studies she and Azizi had begun, whether big men or bullies, the others would regret their choice to scorn the colony-bred candidates.

Trina came here to become a spacer, nothing more and nothing less. If that meant suffering those who thought it better to fight for dominance as a candidate than to prepare for a future among the stars, it seemed little enough to endure compared to what she'd survived to get here.

Knowing why Azizi stayed as she did now, Trina would make sure he came to see this treatment as nothing more than an inconvenience as she had. After all, he'd wanted to open her eyes. Why shouldn't she share the value of her experiences with him?

Right then and there, she decided they wouldn't stay as late the next day. They wouldn't stay late at all.

She'd invite Azizi back to her team quarters to share a meal. They'd face her tormentors first, then his, and show how little of an impact the ship-bred, and those like them, really had.

CHAPTER 8

The consoles are designed so that if any of the crucial functions are compromised, a less critical console will switch to support the missing one. That's what happened in the drill today." Deluth couldn't remember when he'd first seen the safety in action, but he didn't imagine he and Redel had been any quicker to respond. Still, their first complete failure grated on all of them.

Sharna gave a sour laugh. "They told us that in class. Knowing didn't help at all."

The other four at the table nodded their agreement.

"Which is why we have drills as well as lessons." Deluth leaned his weight on both hands, standing where the others had taken seats. "And why it's important to work at every station. Spacers don't encourage specialization beyond your team for this very reason. If navigation goes down while in the fold, the dangers of below don't sit still and wait for the navigation officer to search around the bridge for the new navigation controls. Whoever is at that station is now the navigation officer."

The young man who'd been at the new station scowled. "Easy to say, but not so much to do. I was reaching for the adjustment dial before the switch and there wasn't time to stop."

Deluth gave him a hard look. "The controls lock out for long enough to notice the transfer. If it had been as immediate as that, nothing would have happened, Peter."

"It all happened so quickly," Sharna broke in. "And it was confusing."

Deluth just kept his gaze on Peter until the other candidate looked to the table.

"I wasn't watching my console. I was distracted by the navigation panel going out like everyone else."

Deluth gripped Peter's shoulder and gave a tight squeeze. "That's why they do this in the drills. It is distracting, and scary, especially while disconnected from normal space. The drills expose us to circumstances we hope never to experience in truth, but if they do happen, we'll be ready."

Peter pushed to his feet. "And excuses won't save us. I get it."

"Any of us would have made the same mistake, and will. The important part," Deluth glanced around at the others, "is to understand what went wrong and prevent it in the future. That's the strength of the drills, and much more important than getting them right each time."

He could see the tension they'd held since leaving the drill chamber easing, proved out when the five of them laughed.

"I wouldn't count on Redel holding the same position," a soft-spoken young woman said.

Deluth gave a twisted smile in response to that. "He'll just have to remember our early tests. Everything you're struggling with now, Redel faced already. It's easy to forget once you're past that, but the drills could always throw something new at you. Never believe you've grasped every possible scenario, not now and certainly not when it's a real console under your fingers."

"I'd like to have seen his face when his assigned station went blank," Lorise muttered, having received a heavy tongue-lashing for her panic.

"I seem to remember him using curse words picked up from some of the spacers," Deluth told her, as much to lighten the mood as because he remembered the specific event.

His mind wandered to the lessons earlier in the day before the disastrous drill.

They'd had another session on colony relations that focused on how different the cultures could be on the ground. Not that any two ships shared the same traditions, or so he'd learned from the rest of the Pilot team, but colonies could be so strange. And the planet mentioned as having the strongest difference caught his attention fully when Kenner, who had taught this session, commented that the Pilots had one from that very colony.

Members from the other teams glanced around as if expecting some kind of reaction from the Ceric-bred candidate, but Deluth knew exactly whom Kenner must have been referring to. No wonder she'd needed some additional training. He didn't look forward to Redel's comments once his friend returned.

Motion at the main entrance to their quarters drew his gaze, expecting Redel to march back right then. His bunkmate had stayed to discuss their failure with the instructor, leaving Deluth to help restore the team's spirit.

Instead, the Ceric candidate stood in the doorframe.

He'd looked for Trina every day, but she tended to come very late, eat, and go to her room.

Deluth's gaze expanded to take in her companion, a striking young man with dark skin and an abundance of curly hair.

Before he could think through his actions, Deluth had left the table and marched over to meet them.

"We were given to understand you were studying hard while the rest of us drilled. I can see we were misled. Training just not important enough for you to participate?"

Though he regretted the snap as soon as it came from his mouth, he could not see a way to pretend he hadn't said it, especially with every person in the room now focused on him. Deluth pivoted and stomped over to one of the terminals, pretending it had been his goal from the start and the pause in the doorway unplanned.

He stared at the blank screen as conversation resumed, but his focus stayed on the faint reflection of the two of them as they crossed the gathering area on the way to the meal section.

She owed him nothing. He had no right to be angry, but that didn't change the fact that he was.

While she'd been making new friends, he'd wasted his time looking for Trina, wondering about her, and even learning about her colony. He'd wondered so much about the change in Redel, but now his actions showed him no better. He'd defended her to Redel only to attack her himself for no good cause.

The chair scraped against the floor as he rose to follow them into the meal section. He had wanted to talk to her for so long, and yet the one time he could do so without Redel around, she brought a stranger, or rather clearly not a stranger to her.

While his interest had grown almost to the level of obsession, apparently he'd made little impression on her at all.

Well, he'd made an impression now, and not a good one.

That last thought changed his path, and he walked away from the table they'd chosen instead of offering an apology, no longer able to trust what would come from his mouth.

"I can see what you meant," the stranger said, the humor clear in his tone. "Though not much like my quarters at all."

Deluth strained for her answer as his fingers poked the drink selections to lend some truth to his behavior.

Trina spoke too softly to be heard, but the shared laughter was enough proof they came together out of choice rather than an assignment.

The first sip of the liquid in the glass his hand automatically closed around when delivered almost made Deluth spit. He'd chosen some overly sweet stim.

Deluth took the bright yellow drink with him as he retreated to the gathering area.

Listening to the two of them would do little to improve his grumpy mood, and with the drink he'd chosen, he'd be unable to escape into sleep for some time. Still, he knew better than to be wasteful, and even so, he refused to let them know how distracting their presence had proved to be.

"I THOUGHT YOU SAID YOU didn't know any of your team?" Azizi didn't look up as he took small bites of the meal he'd chosen, something with a rich, sweet scent.

Trina glanced over to watch Redel's friend disappear into the gathering area. "I don't know him. I don't even know his name."

Azizi laughed. "He sure seems to know you."

"He doesn't." She'd wasted too much time pondering their earlier interaction as it was.

"On my colony, such behavior would be followed with a visit to your parents. Are you sure he doesn't think you're a couple?"

She glanced up at Azizi, worried despite his laughter. Her meal became less appealing all of a sudden, and she shoved it away.

He shook his fork at her and pushed the plate back. "I was only teasing. Don't let the thought put you off your food. We have another big day ahead of us tomorrow."

"You don't think the same, do you?" Trina needed to know, needed him to know, if they were to continue being friends.

Azizi shot her a puzzled look then a grin spread wide across his face. "About you and me?" He waved the fork between them. "Of course not. We're just friends. I'm only curious, not jealous. The way he singled us out when we arrived seems interesting."

She relaxed, pushing aside the fear of losing her friend to consider his words. "We were lucky he saw us instead of Redel seeing. His friend has no interest in when I'll be joining them. He'd prefer I get cast out of the program before that happens."

A grunt was the only response she received, reminding Trina why she'd suggested he take his meal in the Pilot team quarters.

"What do you think the drills he mentioned are? I thought they were in classes just like we are."

Azizi finished his bite and took a sip from the milky liquid in his glass before answering. "From what I've heard in my section, they're running scenarios as well as taking classes."

She waited for him to say more before realizing his simple "from what I've heard in my section" covered any number of events, most likely ones resembling the confrontation they'd just suffered, or worse, rather than sharing information. Again, she wondered at the choice to isolate them. It must serve some purpose greater than she could see for the instructors to overlook all the ways it tore the teams into two groups, or one group with them on the outside.

"Drills would be interesting, don't you think? My head is aching from all the information, and my body feels soft."

He gave her a curious look, the strain falling away from his features. "I thought you were on a colony ship. And for quite some time. I'd think you would grow used to the lack of physical activity. Or did you have access to the drills too?"

Trina laughed, her gaze pinned to her meal. "No, not spacer drills," she said so the pause wouldn't grow to an awkward length, "But I kept active."

He settled in to watch her finish her serving, his plate empty. "They must have different accommodations for colonists than just transporting passengers. After all, you're on the ship for a lot longer as you head out to the newer territories. It was just luck you passed the exam when you were close to this station instead of one of the others, like the one near your home planet."

Grateful for a topic that didn't veer all too close to revealing just what kind of colonist she'd been, Trina described the colony sections. She borrowed some of Katie's tales to fill in the activities she had not participated in, but she hadn't realized how much she'd connected with the Menthak family in her time before Samuel tore her away once again.

"You must miss her very much."

Trina gave a stiff nod. "But she had a different future planned, one that would not have suited me at all. It's better this way."

Azizi brushed her hand. "It doesn't make this any easier. I, too, have siblings at home, and a girl I plan to ask to marry. Coming here…well, I don't know if she'll wait for me."

She looked at him with new eyes.

Just as she'd failed to consider why he lingered rather than going to his quarters, she'd never really thought about the other candidates and the people they'd left behind. Shafters kept their lives private. "You planned to become a spacer. Didn't she know that?"

The smile he offered had little of the warmth she'd grown used to. "Yes, she knew. They all knew. It did not make the leaving any easier on them or on me. You make it easier. Having a friend makes it easier."

This time the stiffness left her nod as she smiled at him. "It is better with a friend. And some day, you'll go to see your girl. I'll go find Katie in her new life, too. We'll go there as spacers like we'd always wanted."

CHAPTER 9

The drink had kept Deluth up later than he'd planned, but he hadn't noticed until just now as the last few Pilots headed for their rooms. While Trina and her friend kept poking into his consciousness, the others stayed focused on the drill failure, though not with the despair of earlier. The whole team, or at least all those present, spent most of the evening figuring out how to avoid another failure. Only Redel, who hadn't returned, and Trina were not involved.

Smiling, he triggered his door. He refused to let his annoyance with Trina strip away the satisfaction of the team coming together. They'd worked hard and effectively, but now he needed rest if he wanted to be alert in the morning.

The lights came up to a low orange, just enough to see by. He didn't need much when his plans now focused on crashing into a deep sleep.

Deluth blinked to clear his eyes when the light turned darker at the same time as a hand landed hard on his shoulder.

He spun, recognizing the warning in the color shift too late.

Redel scowled at him.

"You're here. I wondered if you'd get any sleep at all."

Redel didn't respond except to step further into the room and let the door close behind him.

Deluth shot his friend a questioning look. "It's late. Can't you tell me what you were up to over breakfast tomorrow?" He smothered a well-timed yawn.

"I'm more concerned with what you've been up to."

"Me? I've been here all night. You're the one off on adventures."

Redel slammed his hands into Deluth's chest, pushing him hard enough to hurt. "You've been undermining my authority while I was gone. One minute out of my view, and you're stabbing me in the back. That's not what friends do."

Deluth shook his head. "What are you talking about?"

"You've been having secret meetings with my team. Telling them anything that will get them on your side instead of mine. Deny it. I dare you."

"I don't know what you think you know, but I have no interest in leading the team. I'm here to learn, like we all should be. My studies are my first priority."

Redel gave a sour laugh. "Studies. Right. And that's what you've been doing here all night, I suppose."

A glimmer of comprehension teased Deluth. "Yes. We've been analyzing what went wrong with the drill. Some good ideas came out of it."

"You told them failing didn't matter. Jessine told me all about it just now. He said you thought I needed to remember my own failures."

Deluth sank onto his bed. "Yes, I did say you and I went through our share of failures when we first started drilling. You know we did, and we will again. It wouldn't make sense if they were all so easy they could be passed on the first go. There wouldn't be any reports of lost ships or disasters if every crisis could be solved by a bunch of untrained candidates."

Redel clenched and unclenched his fists, a clear sign he wasn't ready to let this go.

"Look, it wasn't planned or organized. We just got talking over the meal, and kept going afterward. If you hadn't gone off to talk to one of the instructors, you would have been in the thick of it." He swallowed the "as always" though he felt it more strongly than ever with Redel jumping down his throat. Deluth also kept his tongue in his mouth when he wanted to point out the failure came from assigning everyone a role, including the leader. They all needed to learn how to balance and manage the team as much as any other station.

His friend stood there for what seemed like forever, clearly trying to control his temper. Deluth appreciated the effort, not just because Redel was an even match in a fight. If it came to one, they could both be thrown from the program.

Redel released his breath slowly, the air hissing between his teeth. His laugh this time sounded a little more normal. "I would have been, wouldn't I?"

Deluth gave a cautious nod, unsure whether the danger had passed. He'd thought Redel sought out the instructor, but now he wondered if Redel had been pulled aside because of his reaction. This anger seemed out of proportion with the circumstances, but Deluth couldn't ask without questioning the very authority he'd been accused of undermining.

"Why don't you tell me what everyone came up with then? So I can consider their ideas."

Again, Deluth smothered a yawn, this one a grand bit of acting. "Sure, Redel. I can tell you everything we considered, and you can add your thoughts into the mix before we test it out tomorrow. But how about we do that over breakfast. We're planning to ask our instructor to run the same scenario, or at least with the same parameters, so we can test it out. If we want to do better than today, we all need our sleep."

Redel looked like he was going to argue then slapped Deluth's shoulder instead. "That's good thinking. We wouldn't want you at less than your best when you try to correct the errors you made today. And I forgive you for running the examination without me. After all, you couldn't have known the instructors wanted to consult with me, or how long I'd be. It's good to have some groundwork when I make the plans tomorrow morning. I don't know why I thought you were trying to take the command from me. A moment of foolishness. We both know you don't have the charisma to carry off the task."

Deluth just stared at him, knowing any response would be an argument. He didn't want the team, but he didn't think Redel should claim it either. They should each have had a turn at that role along with the rest.

He remember Sharna's comment about charisma and realized only she shared his immunity. Deluth had grown up alongside Redel while Sharna set her standards higher than even Redel could achieve.

An awkward pause filled the space between them, then Redel gave a haphazard salute. "You really do need your beauty rest. You're too tired to chat. I'll see you first thing tomorrow. You'd better be alert and ready."

The door opened when Redel waved a hand over the trigger panel then closed after him, leaving Deluth in a now orange-tinged room. Exhaustion took the place of tension, and he rolled to lie flat, too tired even to strip off his clothes.

When they'd dreamed of the spacer training together, he'd never imagined it turning out like this, or that Redel would decide he was some sort of a commander with Deluth the willing lackey.

CHAPTER 10

Trina had a rough night's sleep, haunted by her discussion with Azizi. Homesickness, or rather missing her sister, had been only a part of the disruption. The question of why the other candidate singled her out offered the greater distraction.

"…and that's the optimum temperature for evening hours."

She blinked, startled out of her thoughts not for the first time. Trina glanced at the terminal, words scrolling past that made as little sense as the light automation had, though this time she understood the terms well enough.

Environmental controls. Sure, she knew the ship had to keep the temperature somehow, but she'd never given it much thought. The chill of space existed only in concept while weather, real weather, affected everyone. Even polits and leading laborers suffered the weather. Shafters might not feel the rain on their heads or the burning sun, but what produce reached their market changed depending on the surface conditions.

This seemed another way in which Ceric had been different. Again, the others seemed aware of methods to control the environment. She wondered if any of their people accepted what nature wrought or if even the poorest on their worlds had the ability to change their environments.

The word "vents" appeared on her terminal as their instructor spoke of redirecting the flow of air to shift the temperature.

She stared down at it, heat warming her cheeks.

The doctrine called for acceptance, but she'd be more than a fool to believe polits did nothing but accept. She'd used ventilation shafts to slip into some houses while even the tunnels had such to bring in breathable air. The vents here would connect every part of the station.

Trina brushed away the thought. She would not hide between the walls here. To do so would risk the person she wanted to become.

She focused back on the topic at hand. If simple vents counted as environmental controls, she had no cause to look down on the other worlds for using technology to ease their way. Every person in First City, from highest polit to lowest shafter, used ventilation to survive the hot desert. No matter how simple, they all used technology.

Chastened, Trina pushed the screen to view the other terms again. Her head ached as she struggled not just with alien concepts but with the realization they weren't as alien as she'd first believed.

She concentrated not on what she'd thought was true but what she had observed on her own.

Ventilation shafts released hot air so it wouldn't collect in the finer houses. Underground rooms helped preserve foodstuff so it lasted longer in every house she'd searched, but she'd been after something more valuable when all of the shafts stayed cooler than anything on the surface.

Instead of seeking the cold, her mother had quilted endless blankets to keep them warm before she got too sick and Katie took over the task.

Thoughts of Katie distracted her as she remembered how her sister figured out the colored buttons in the colony area because of her practice making patterns out of fabric scraps until her blankets held as much beauty as the pictures in the books their father left them.

They'd thought themselves so clever to figure out how the ship worked without any training, and as far as their knowledge went, they had been. Now Trina knew just how little access they'd had as colonists, and how much more complicated everything had been.

She rubbed her temples, the headache growing, but she refused to give up. If she could only map this new information to what she already knew as Azizi had been showing her, she'd understand everything she could about environmental controls and exactly why they were important.

"Think of a ship as a lidded meal plate. If you leave off the lid, the meal soon chills. If not for the sealed environment, the chill of space would freeze every last one of us," the instructor said as if reading Trina's thoughts. "It might seem simple to some of you—a matter of adding heat when you're cold and sending it away when you're warm—but this is about more than just you. Environmental controls ensure there is enough liquid in the air so your lungs don't dry out from within, but not so much that mold or rot occur."

That drew a groan from many of the candidates, and their instructor laughed.

"I see you've had some experience with those. Now imagine the same thing here without a sun to expose them to. And mold in the ventilation means mold everywhere, on everyone, in everything."

Where Trina had been looking for connections, she'd found one, though not to Ceric. The solution her grandfather sent her to spread went through the main rooms of that section rapidly thanks to the ventilation. A boon when she thought she spread a cure. A curse when she learned his true intentions.

She raised her hand, finally able to ask a question she'd pondered since that horrible day.

The instructor nodded.

"How can you stop the spread? Confine it?"

The question earned her an approving smile, but she hadn't asked for that reason.

"It's not part of this section, but since it's a good question, I'll give a quick answer. On any good-sized ship, there's the ability to isolate sections for this exact reason. If something gets into the ventilation system, if a fire breaks out, or a section loses pressure, there are ways to lock down that part of a ship or station so everything isn't lost. While mold might not be as critical, other types of spores cause disease or debilitation that certainly would require such dramatic actions. There are also partial containments where access is through a decontamination chamber so medical personnel can get in. What you want to avoid is something so virulent the whole section is sealed with everyone within it until the contamination fades on its own. The loss of a whole section—especially when carrying passengers or colonists—is painful, but your first priority is always the ship. Better to lose some than everyone, no matter what the contract says."

Trina shuddered, remembering how Samuel had wagered on exactly that priority. If not for her unique immune system, he might just have succeeded.

Now she understood the importance of the environmental controls in ways she wished she did not. Someday it might be her hand on the controls to lock out a section, sentencing everyone within to death so that the rest could survive.

"But as with most things, those types of circumstances are the extreme, and rare. Most of the time, the worst you have to deal with is foot rot. As risky as the spores, though, is an environment growing so warm as to harm the plants that provide the basis for the replicators and all the nutrition you consume."

The subject no longer seemed confusing as the instructor moved on to specific cases.

Trina swore to study this section harder than any of the others even if Azizi wanted to stop. The others might think cold or heat the greatest risk, but she'd seen with her own eyes how critical the ability to spread—and control the spread—of substances was. And weather had restricted the food available in the shafts often enough for her to know the pinch of starvation. For that to happen on a ship without the chance of a better season to follow did not bear imagining.

CHAPTER II

Azizi continued to work with her at the end of every day, but an instructor had pulled him away to explore an aspect of one of his questions this afternoon, leaving Trina alone in the classroom for the first time in two weeks of studying.

Where once the quiet space would have drawn her, now it held too many echoes of what she hadn't known and still needed to learn.

She headed to her room, preferring the terminal there if she were to study by herself even though she couldn't work on her assignments. She'd tried one night when still puzzling over what she had studied with Azizi only to discover the materials were there but all her notes and work existed only in the classroom.

The air stream swept her along, requiring nothing beyond her destination and leaving her time to consider all the ways she had not been prepared for spacer training.

She'd been arrogant from the start, thinking what she'd learned on the colony ship, both in sections open to colonists and ones where she'd done her grandfather's bidding, would put her ahead of all the others. Even after the decision to put her in extra training, she remained ignorant of just how little she knew until she couldn't recognize the terminal they'd used as a desk surface. She'd worried they would drop her from the program as it became clear how little she had to contribute.

Now, she wondered why they hadn't.

She'd started to see the logic behind the lighting systems and how spacers controlled every aspect of their environment. The artificial nature meant there was no reason to accommodate herself to circumstances beyond those places she shared with others. On Ceric, nature controlled everything. Here, the spacers did.

The idea disturbed her a bit when set out in those terms.

Trina might not have been devout, but even she had some concerns when setting the doctrine of living through the work of your hands aside on the colony ship. On Ceric, she'd accepted both the gifts and burdens given her as the doctrine stated. Trina might have taken the extravagances of others, but she'd done so personally. She'd never become one like Fence who lived off others.

Here, spacers controlled every aspect of life. No natural phenomena, driven by God or fate, set their circumstances. Here, spacers were like gods as they provided both nourishment and punishment for the candidates.

Trina blinked when a flashing light appeared in front and jerked her out of tangled thoughts.

It was too close. She had no time to react.

She twisted hard in an attempt to catch the safety hold before her stream crossed where someone was about to enter, but her hands closed on empty air. An opening appeared on her left, and she slammed into the person coming from it.

He grabbed her and shoved Trina toward the hold even though the safety system had cut both flows the moment of their collision.

She stumbled, her feet landing off-balance because of the shove combined with a return to normal, undirected airflow.

"I should have known. You're that ignorant colony girl. Of course you don't know to look for the signals. You probably leaned too far trying to go fast. You're a danger to everyone here."

Trina turned to face him, an apology forming on her tongue. She'd been so lost in thought, she hadn't noticed the light until too late. His accusation rang all too close to the doubts burning her.

The words evaporated.

It was Redel, the same candidate who'd made trouble for her from the start. More than that, something in his expression reminded her of Fence's enforcers when she'd found them beating a shafter almost to death for some unknown offense. She'd learned the truth behind the trader's polit manners and sweet talk that day, the same truth radiating from this candidate.

He wanted to show her up, wanted the least excuse to take her down.

Redel might have had some special knowledge allowing him to manipulate the air currents using spacer environment controls so she had too little warning. Perhaps she'd just been unlucky. But Trina had no intention of letting him have the satisfaction of seeing her beg for forgiveness.

She had as much right to be in the transport as he did.

Trina stared at him in a silence rich with tension, unwilling to speak first in case he took her words as the regret she refused to offer.

Redel scowled at her then took a quick step forward. "Stupid colonist," he muttered under his breath.

She twitched her wrists, but no knives sprang free to slide into her hands as he slammed her out of the way with his shoulder.

The attack she'd expected never came beyond that one contact.

He opened a panel in the wall beside her and air rose to cushion them once again.

Further proof he'd engineered the problem.

A faint call drifted back up the tunnel as he swept away. It took a second for her to work out the words, but she shook her head once she heard them.

He'd told her to keep with her own kind. As if she'd had any choice.

She'd been assigned to the Pilot team, and it wouldn't be Trina asking for a transfer no matter how much trouble Redel caused. He had no idea what her life had been like on Ceric if he thought simple bullying tactics would have an impact.

She waited long enough for him to have reached their corridor and their quarters, grateful no one requested the airflow she hovered in, one hand secured to the safety hold. He might take her delay as a further sign of her incompetence, but she had no wish to meet him in the hallways.

She'd made an enemy for sure if he hadn't been one from the start. There had been a choice in this encounter, a time when she could have bowed to his superiority and perhaps secured the lowest spot in his esteem.

Trina didn't believe for one second anything less than total surrender would have won him over, and that she would not give.

A shafter recognized the value of strength, not weakness, and she was enough a product of her upbringing to find his need to devalue those he collected a weakness.

"**Y**OUR COLONY GIRL WILL BE later than she expected," Redel said as he swung through the main door and crossed to Deluth. "She ran into a little trouble with the air transport."

Deluth rose from the terminal where he'd been researching and stood to block the screen from Redel in what he hoped would not be an obvious move.

"Why do you say that?" he asked as a further distraction. The last thing he wanted his friend to discover was that he'd been researching

Ceric. He ran a palm over the sensor by touch, saving his work and disconnecting his program stick as he ended the session.

Redel thrust his arm through Deluth's and tugged him toward the meal section. "Because I bumped into her during transit. He laughed. "She missed the warning light and the whole system had to shut down, inconveniencing who knows how many, instructors among them. When word gets out just who messed things up, we won't have to worry about her doing the same to our standing."

Deluth dropped into the nearest chair, watching Redel collect a drink from the replicator with narrowed eyes.

Visible bubbles danced in the glass he returned with, something Redel reserved for celebrations.

"You should have seen her, caught all speechless by her own failures. Probably the first time she'd been out on her own. Either an instructor or that pretty boy guided her before."

Though Redel must know his statement held little truth when Trina had been returning well after the end of classes for weeks now, Deluth had no chance to correct him.

Sharna slid into another chair at the same table. "What about a pretty boy?"

Redel stared at her, but she was looking at Deluth so must not have noticed.

"You mean the one with the gorgeous hair who visited us?"

"Yes. The one who helps our colony brat. I have high hopes he'll slip up and someone will recognize the mistake they made accepting her. I'd prefer to run the team one short than have her on it."

Deluth rose with a shake of his head. "You two don't seem to need me for this."

Both protested, but he didn't slow down until he'd reached his room, the one place he could find privacy. Deluth tried not to use it too often because it wouldn't do for his teammates to think him unsocial, but he needed it tonight.

The door slid closed and he sank on his bunk, hands folded behind his head.

Redel had become a master of the air transport on their ship, not just using it but manipulating the system so it tripped up all on its own with no record. Even if Deluth called attention to the prank, there'd be no evidence, and no one to stand with him. Siding with Trina openly would put an end to any friendship he still had with Redel, and it was unlikely to do her any good either.

Deluth stared at the unadorned ceiling, but the paneling offered no answers, only more guilt to lay on his shoulders.

She would have been a target regardless because of needing the extra classes, but everything in him screamed that his interest lay behind Redel's special attention toward the colony girl. And the worst of it came when he realized he couldn't even say a word of comfort.

Not only was Trina barely aware of his existence, but his petty attack the other night had done little to label him a savior, much less a friend.

He'd be lucky if she saw him as just another faceless team member. Deluth feared the more likely chance that she lumped him in with Redel as a bully.

He sprang up off the bunk with a sharp twist and turned to his desk terminal instead. A quick command brought up the information he'd been studying when Redel proclaimed his triumph over the very person driving Deluth to waste his free time in extra studies. He couldn't get her out of his mind, and nothing he discovered offered any answers.

She'd come from a strictly segregated world, with castes controlling who you were and what you could be regardless of interest or abilities. He'd learned almost everything there was to know about her planet, but it told him little about her. To understand her life before she'd passed the test she had to let slip which caste she'd been born into, something he doubted would ever happen at this rate.

He turned off the terminal and considered venturing back into the main area again. Nothing in the information would tell him what he wanted to know. Only she could do that, and Redel had said she'd been on her way to their quarters. She might have returned by now.

The thought of her returning to be accosted by Redel, or worse discovering she'd changed her plans and gone to spend the evening free time with that other candidate again made him drop the hand he'd raised to trigger the door.

He was not good company right now anyway between his inability to chase her from his mind and his suspicions about Redel. At this rate, he'd be likely to say something to offend both of them. Better he get a good night's sleep and leave figuring out a way to get Redel to leave her alone and getting himself a proper introduction to another day.

CHAPTER 12

Trina shot a distracted glance at the terminal screen, relieved to see it showed they would be discussing food. They'd spent a little more time on each section as they went, but still, as they approached the end of their first month in training, she felt as though she struggled to keep up. While she might not have had much experience with farming directly, she'd heard enough talk in both the shafter marketplace and among the colonists to find it familiar.

Or perhaps she should have wanted something difficult, something that could take her mind off the odd encounter she'd had this morning.

Her thoughts drifted to how Redel's friend had come up to her as she'd left their quarters. His group had already started off toward the training she couldn't attend, but he'd lingered, something like an apology on his face.

She shook her head to banish the image. No matter how much her thoughts clung to him, surely his behavior the other night proved where his interests lay. Only wishful thinking—wanting to have a friend in her group—put an apology on his features.

At least she knew his name.

Redel had yelled for him loud enough to wake the dead should any have been nearby.

Deluth.

A name as odd as that of his friend, but somehow the name suited him. It came on strong and tapered into a softer sound.

He'd said nothing at all this morning. Just stood and looked at her as though he wanted to speak but could not.

The only clear emotion came from the frustration and annoyance painted there when Redel called again. He'd made a sound between a sigh and a grunt, then turned abruptly and jogged after his departing group.

That more than anything had to be the explanation for why he seemed embedded in her mind. Curiosity had always been strong in her, and she still had no idea what his purpose had been in coming up to her in the first place.

Her cheeks heated as she remembered Azizi's interpretation of their previous encounter. She'd denied it at the time, but part of her wondered if he did seek her out for the same reason she found herself searching for him whenever she entered a room. Even here, where the chances of an encounter measured lower than the vegetable piles in the shafter market after a long stretch without rain, she looked for him.

She glanced at the terminal screen as it prompted her to save or discard her work. Class was about to begin, and this time she planned to let the information come into focus.

The terms scrolling down to fill her screen held no fraction of familiarity despite the comfortable-sounding topic. She couldn't hope to correlate them with what she'd already known as she had the environment controls because these definitions, what little she understood of them, spoke of the invisible elements that made up all materials.

Trina remembered how the tunnels did not connect to every cabin on the ship. She'd known then the replicators could not be supplied by armies of crewmembers or robots carrying food from the kitchens. From what the definitions implied, though, there weren't even mechanisms taking the unprepared food from the growing areas to the kitchens.

She sounded out the first term of "molecule" in her head, not daring to let the word come out even in a whisper for fear she'd mangled it. A desperate look to Azizi showed him with a furrowed brow. They'd reached material neither had a foundation in and so must work through it together.

The task overwhelmed her at first, no hint of something she could translate and any connection to her past one proving her ignorance. She couldn't even count on Azizi, who had always seemed one step ahead of her despite what he'd said.

The instructor, this one a young man who looked no older than the candidates he taught, clapped his hands.

"Most of the terms on your screen will be unfamiliar as words, but they're easy enough if you work in analogies. Since you all come from planets, you've probably seen a plant before. Even those raised on shipboard usually have a stint in the hydroponics areas to understand where our food comes from."

Whether because of his easy tone or the knowledge that, beneath these terms, there was some form of plant farm, Trina felt her growing panic ease just a fraction. No longer dangling from the eaves, the rest of his explanation reached her rather than bouncing off the shell of fear she'd been building. She'd seen plants in the gardens behind wealthier houses, or cut flowers used for decoration.

"Plants have leaves, a stem, a flower…components that make up the whole. This is true at every level of existence. They follow a pattern built by nature to achieve the form you've seen, but the closer you look, the more you'll see pieces of the pattern continue down far beyond what the unaided eye can see."

He pointed at the screen behind him as it showed a plant. Then it moved closer and closer until everything became simple shapes like the stones making up the walls in First City.

"You're looking at the microscopic view of a plant stem. This is what makes up all the food you've experienced through the replicators. Just as nature applies a pattern, so too can we take the base materials and put them together into a pleasing structure, pleasing both to the taste and to the needs of your body."

The instructor kept going, but Trina no longer trembled at the task in front of her. Like the walls, or even her sister's quilts, she could see the concepts behind the alien terms. A molecule would be a stone. The stones made different patterns depending on how they were laid just as the scraps of fabric could draw pictures.

The terminal screen blinked a warning then reformed to display a problem for them to solve. Had it come before the instructor gave the pattern, she would not have even tried, but where the problem showed a finished pattern, she plucked the pieces, molecules or representations of the same, and placed them to match. Her screen glowed green to indicate success, and she pushed the button for another, a surge of delight rushing through her at mastering something that seemed impossible only moments before.

An alarm sounded and red flashed out of the corner of her eye.

Most of the candidates abandoned their labors to watch the instructor move through the desks to stop at the one toned red.

"Only a slight difference lies between a pattern that provides necessary nutrition and its deadly counterpart. All the replicators and programming terminals are set to flag incorrect patterns that could cause harm long before they're entered into the catalog of selections."

While he'd spoken the first to the whole class, now he bent his head and focused on the specific terminal, speaking softly to the candidate as he showed the young man how to correct the error.

Trina wished she could both see and hear the correction, but soon enough she had the instructor over her shoulder as the fourth exercise flashed red.

"Look at the edges here and here," he said, pointed to where she'd placed a rectangular piece. "You've chosen the right shape, but not the right size. It doesn't line up correctly, which means there are some open receptacles that can bond to the wrong elements. Tap here to rotate through the available sizes and use this function to measure them."

She picked up his instructions quickly, earning a smile and a light squeeze on her shoulder as he moved to the next person. Overhearing another's would not have helped her. She needed to see where he pointed to learn, something that made her grateful for the error, especially as the problems grew more complex.

Trina wondered what had provoked the guard against incorrect measures only for a heartbeat before she realized either accident or one like Samuel must have been the cause. Still, while the food being a construct rather than natural made her squirm, she found the safeguards comforting. At least poison could not be transmitted through an appetizing item in the catalog.

FOR ONCE, AZIZI WAS THE one to struggle while Trina guided his studying. This food construction had no true match to her life on Ceric and so no conflict.

Still, she could pair the elements together on the screen much like she'd sifted through information she gathered when staking out a new polit house.

Katie would have seen quilting, but Trina's patterns had been neither as tangible, nor as consistent, as blanket making. She'd learned each member of the household, studied their behaviors, then matched that to the layout of the houses and when something worth lifting would be available.

She chuckled at the thought, putting faces on the shapes she sought to match up now, faces of servants, the polit masters, and the household children.

"I'm glad you find this all so amusing," Azizi bit out with none of his usual patience, "But I can't construct something more complex than a three layer. My head is aching. I can see the shapes behind my eyes." He pressed a hand to the offending body part. "And they don't fit even there."

Trina pushed away from her desk and came to lean over him, finding the three adjustments necessary after a quick scan of the screen.

"You need to make this one larger, and swap that square for a parallelogram."

Azizi lowered his head to the screen. "How do you do that?"

His words came out muffled, but the strain in his tone was clear.

Trina knelt so her face was level to his. "It's the first part of our training I can match to what I've always done. Well, not with shapes, but with pieces more complicated even than that spiky one. Everything else has been as though they tried to teach a tunnel crawler to sit at a table for dinner."

Azizi straightened, now much taller than her kneeling form. "I have no idea what a crawler is, but I have seen you struggle. You bore the weight of your confusion much more gracefully."

She patted his arm. "Don't worry. You'll get it. You're quick to understand most things, and it makes you expect that. But I've seen you work as well, and this will come in time."

He rose, swiping his terminal closed at the same time. "But not tonight. It's late, much later than we usually stay, and my brain is full. It'll be another long day tomorrow, especially if we're still focused on this."

Trina glanced at her own terminal to see it had indeed grown quite late. She'd been having so much fun with the first part of the training to click she hadn't noticed the time passing when usually it would have dragged as she struggled with alien concepts.

She saved her work and swiped her terminal closed as well. "You're right. We should get a good night's rest."

Energy hummed through her even as she sent Azizi a sympathetic look. Trina wondered if she appeared as worn after studying on most days.

He shook his head, not denying her statement but the way she said it. "I can tell you're pandering to me. If I could connect you to a ship, you'd cut the transit time by half with the crackle of power leaking from you."

She laughed and linked arms with him, pulling him toward the air stream transports and their quarters.

They'd talked about transit time as an element to consider when coming up with the standard meal for a journey. Ships were getting faster every day and controlled jumps through folded space longer. Soon they'd be reaching star systems considered beyond the realm of possibility, but though discovering untouched space appealed, Trina found more hope in the chance she'd be able to visit her sister before Katie's hair went white and her memory faded.

TRINA HALF EXPECTED TO CRASH when she separated with Azizi where the different corridors branched. Instead, she felt wide awake as she slipped into the gathering area.

No matter how late she'd arrived before, whether from studying or an awkward meal in Azizi's team quarters, there'd always been at least a few candidates about. They'd be working at the terminals, or hanging out at the tables here or in the meal area. She'd learned most of their names from overhearing, but had spoken to few of them. Trina didn't know how much was her own reluctance and how much Redel's influence.

This time, it seemed everyone had gone to bed.

Azizi and Trina had stopped for a meal break in the classroom hours ago, so she had no need to eat, but she didn't feel like entering the sleeping corridor, either.

Her mind swirled with squares, pentagons, ovals, and other shapes, testing them, turning them, and fitting them together in all different ways. She understood how they represented actual molecular structures. Or understood as well as she might having only seen such things in pictures that could have easily been from a fertile imagination.

The confidence filling her felt familiar, though.

When she'd studied a polit house enough to take action, or when she knew she could accomplish one of the tasks her grandfather had set for her, the same bright energy swept over her.

She'd never be able to sleep.

The replicator stood silent in its corner, no one having woken it in some time.

She moved to stand in front of the machine. Now she knew how it worked and felt a kinship within that understanding.

Still, nothing on the menu appealed when the machine hummed to life. She didn't need food, and it was too late in the night for hot tea.

Her gaze drifted from the list, dissatisfied but unwilling to give up.

For the first time, she noticed the major difference between this replicator and the one on the ship. Just like the terminals, the colony area replicators had limited functionality. No such attempt had been made to restrict access here.

She reached for the small button off to the side that said only "Custom."

The menu that sprang up in response to her touch resembled what she'd spent all day practicing, but instead of exercises pushing her to figure out a specific configuration, it had options to choose from.

Trina stared at the screen, struck dumb by the choices.

She could make anything, at least anything they didn't deem dangerous. While she could think of one of her group she'd be happy to see clutching his stomach, she had no real wish to cause harm.

She wasn't her grandfather.

Thought of Samuel brought with it homesickness not for him but for her sister and their time together. Katie would have delighted in discovering this ability, though they'd enjoyed the offerings listed on their replicator well enough.

She closed her eyes as the memory of exploring their first replicator rose. She compared the ship's options to what had displayed both on the replicator here and in the classroom. The selections focused around similar components, but now she could see how choices had been made to reflect the different expectations of the candidates.

The meals marked with heat would not have been included in the Ceric offerings because they would be too different from what the colonists were used to. Here, those responsible for the selection had to balance out the needs of candidates from all sorts of places.

This time her mind drifted not to the ship but all the way to Ceric where the heat and dust added a tang to the air even down in the shafts. Memories surfaced of the meals, simple but tasting just right, they'd made in their apartment.

A sharp taste grew out of her memory, not something from home but one she'd wanted nothing more than to share with her sister.

The apothecary's berry juice.

A memory so strong she could taste its nuances filled her mouth with saliva. Trina rapidly scanned the library of biological molecules, searching not for shapes as she had in the class but for the flavor profiles and source, options she'd ignored before.

A wide variety of berries, many she had never heard of, existed in the library. Trina considered each description, rolling the words around in her mind as though she swished the juice across her tongue.

She sought not just one berry, but a combination that would blend together and mimic the flavor she remembered. If she could succeed at this, then maybe she could memorize the combination well enough to bring it with her when she finally visited Katie and let her sister share in the delight even if many years had passed.

The thought gave her pause, wondering if Katie would reject such an offering once she knew it came not from the ground but from a program designed to rearrange base organic material. Would the new colony follow the doctrine at least as well as those on Ceric had? Or would they have their own set of rules to govern what they could do?

Remembering how the Menthak family had chosen a governing body from all levels over the tradition of a grand polit, Trina realized what she'd find might not resemble Ceric at all. But it wouldn't matter. She'd be with her sister.

A gift offered motivation to perfect this juice as if it tied her to the sister she'd left behind. Trina bent all the knowledge she'd gained to perfecting the flavor, testing her work with the small samples the replicator allowed without weighing against her allocation. Soon, she had one that fit with her memory.

Trina requested a full glass and exited the custom section. At the reminder to save, she laughed. Now she could have the juice whenever she wanted it, at least while she was at the station. She decided to study the pattern whenever she could so when she got a ship assignment, she'd be able to recreate it there.

A yawn broke through her victory, reminding Trina of the fast approaching morning. She drank the rest with more haste than she'd ever treated the original, but then, she could choose it at will. What had once been a twisted pleasure tied as it had been to the medicines keeping her mother alive—until they didn't—had become part of her daily life.

She controlled its presence, and she could share with whomever she wished, unlike the original. The difference mirrored all the changes she'd experienced since agreeing to leave Ceric on her grandfather's terms.

CHAPTER 13

The first true break day came at the end of a long month. Endless scenario drills were eased only by classes where they studied everything from the Spacer Guild rules to cultures on the oldest of settled planets.

Deluth remembered his plan to spend this day in extra training, as he did much of his unscheduled hours already, and laughed aloud. He needed the rest as much as anyone. Part of him wanted to stay stretched out on his bunk and do absolutely nothing.

Noise from the corridor reminded him that while they had no classes, this marked the first opportunity to meet candidates on other teams and reconnect with those from their own ships. He considered how eager he would have been to find Redel had they not shared a team. The others were known to him, but Redel had been his true friend.

His good mood soured at how well that connection had turned out.

It might have been different if they'd been assigned to separate groups, but different could as easily have been worse. At least the gathering held no surprises.

A sharp bang sounded on his door only a heartbeat before Redel called, "Wake up and get out here. There's not much time if you want a full breakfast and a chance in the cleanser before we go. I think Sharna's already waiting on you."

Deluth swung his legs out of bed and grabbed a set of clothing. From the amount of noise, he suspected most if not all his team had already moved on to breakfast, leaving the cleanser free. He didn't need more than a quick wash.

One of the treats with break day was the promise of a real, water-based shower, a luxury reserved for the highest classes on shipboard. He'd never earned that right, but he'd heard enough from others rewarded in this way to want his own turn. They only had to show up at the gather and use a replicator to record their presence. The shower allotment order would be revealed the next morning.

With that thought uppermost in his mind, he triggered the door and stepped through...right into Trina.

She jerked away, raising her hands in a defensive stance as if waiting for him to attack her.

Deluth raised his hands as well, but to his shoulders as he took a step back into his room. "I'm sorry. I forgot to look. I thought everyone had left already."

She tipped her head to see his face, making him even more aware of how small she stood. After a silence that oddly held no awkwardness, she nodded. "I should have noticed when your door opened."

He started to claim full responsibility once again, but stopped. Something in her attitude seemed to expect argument, though of what type, he couldn't tell. He'd never wanted to know someone's thoughts as much before.

"Are you going to the break day gathering?" he asked instead, hoping they'd have the chance to get to know each other outside of the tension Redel had fostered the few times she appeared in the Pilot areas.

Again she nodded, this time saying nothing.

He swallowed a request that they walk together, memory of his promise to Sharna rising just in time. Instead, he gave her a smile. "I hope to see you there."

What might have been confusion swept over her features so quickly he couldn't be sure of what he'd seen.

"Perhaps."

Before the word faded from his ears, she'd passed through the door to the meal area, their moment of harmony gone.

Deluth stared after her, dredging his memory for something to explain her reactions in his research of her world, but he could think of nothing. By the time he'd finished washing up, she'd been and gone, whether eating quickly or having made plans to eat elsewhere. Anger spiked through him at the thought of her eating with her friend, but he brushed it away.

He had no claim on her.

Sharna waved from one of the tables, but Deluth pointed to the replicator. He went to get his meal before taking the indicated seat. At least Redel had finished already, but even as he had the disloyal thought, he realized his friend would have chosen to eat elsewhere in a misguided attempt at matchmaking.

"Are you looking forward to the gathering?" Sharna asked him, her eyes bright with almost fierce anticipation.

He remembered his encounter in the corridor, and though he knew he shouldn't be thinking of Trina right then, he smiled. "Yes. Yes, I am. For the promise of a true shower as much as the gathering."

He'd meant the last as a joke, but from Sharna's frown, she hadn't taken it that way.

"I mean, I've never had one in all my life. It's a new experience, one only known from others. How about you?"

She shrugged, but the tension between them eased. "I've had a few. It's a strange feeling, but you get used to it quickly. And it's both not as effective as the cleanser and makes you feel cleaner."

He gave her a strange look at the puzzling description, but Sharna seemed unable to explain better.

She shrugged. "We should ask our colony girl," she said, peering around. "Water is available on all colonies from what we've learned so far, and Jessine said colony ships plan water use to include showers because it's easier than retraining all the colonists or dealing with the stink. They must devote a lot of space to water treatment."

"She's already gone," Deluth said as he processed the rest. "Our ship didn't carry colonists often, so I have no idea whether Jessine's information is true for the others. It seems wasteful to me, but then much of colony life is alien."

He remembered reading about Trina's world and how the colonists refused all but the most critical machinery. Water had been one of those if he recalled correctly, and yet they still chose to waste it.

This only made the gulf between them wider, but at the same time increased his interest. He'd come here to find something different. How more different could she be? He'd never touched soil except for one short visit as a child, and never thought of water as an almost unlimited resource.

Trina had done all of these things.

"There was talk of going to the observation dome before the gathering begins," Sharna said, jerking him from his wandering thoughts. "Would you like to go?"

Pushing aside the question of whether that's where Trina had gone off to, Deluth nodded even as he lifted the last of his protein blocks. The subtle flavor designed to encourage conscious eating failed to provide enough of an incentive to linger. He downed the juice he'd requested and shoved to his feet all before Sharna had moved.

"That eager to catch sight of the planet curve? Or is it the company."

From her smile, Deluth could tell she thought his eagerness had to do with her. He reminded himself though forced into the invitation by his inattention, he had agreed to spend the day with Sharna. She deserved better than that he let his mind wander.

Trina took another sip of her juice even though she'd failed to reproduce the same mixture in the classroom replicator. This one had a sweeter flavor and lacked the complexity of the first. Still, it offered something to swirl around in her mouth as she studied the environmental control problem before her.

Three elements, most likely simplified from a real scenario, all worked against her efforts to balance the temperature in the hydroponics area. A nearby sun, an asteroid belt shedding meteors, and a system malfunction.

No matter how she set one against the other or drew resources from different areas, the terminal flashed red. In addition, today, she had no instructor or friend to help.

A laugh from the doorway made her think the terminal had called for assistance before she turned to see Azizi.

"I should have known where you'd be," he said, striding over to drop into his own seat. "Trying to race ahead of me now?"

"As if I could." She pointed to the red-wash on her screen, a warning that would persist until she canceled it to try again. "I may have figured out the food system, but you understand the rest better than I do."

"What's that?"

Her motion must have revealed the glass of deep purple liquid.

"Maybe I don't have the food figured out as well as you might think." She explained about the juice and how she'd recreated it here from memory. "But I must have remembered some of the elements incorrectly, or put them in the wrong places. This version is much too sweet and simple."

He reached past her to swipe the glass, taking a sip before she could protest.

Trina stared at him, wondering if he did think their lives tied before remembering how he'd described his own people. Sharing food must have had little significance.

Azizi caught the edge of her stare even so and a ruddy color rose beneath his dark skin. "I'm sorry. I thought you wanted a comparison."

She shrugged and waved him to keep the glass. "If you like it, go ahead and have the rest. No matter what I tell myself, every sip is as much a reminder of my failure as this flash of red."

The terminal ignored her glare entirely, but it reset when she slapped the button, perhaps a little too hard. "If you want the truth, I came here to avoid a morning spent surrounded by the rest of my team. They know each other. I'm an outsider there, and some enjoy making that clear."

He shook his head. "You're not speaking of the one who confronted us the other night, are you? I swear his was more interest in you than a will to provoke."

Trina shoved the hair out of her face, hearing again the apology he gave just this morning. "No. Not him, but his friend. They came from the same ship, as far as I can tell."

"That doesn't make them friends."

"In this case it does. He jumps when Redel calls and does not protest the demand."

"Ah," Azizi said, drawing the sound out. "And Redel is the one with the air stream."

Trina tapped the terminal, setting another group of commands into action with little hope of success. "Yes. Redel of the air stream. I still don't know whether he did that on purpose or the system malfunctioned, but he surely made the most of the encounter. At the rate I'm going, I'll never learn to control even the largest systems, yet one like him can twist a basic one to dance at his tune."

"There are protections against meddling," Azizi reminded.

The red flashed twice before she hit reset this time, unwilling to let it go. "Protections only exist where someone has proved a vulnerability. He wasn't caught, so no one would prevent another attempt."

"If he did anything." Azizi shifted so he could peer over her shoulder.

"If he did anything." She repeated his words in a murmur as he reached past her to trigger a vent of the extra heat from the malfunction into space.

The resulting jet of steam acted like a drive and thrust her ship out of the incoming meteor shower. The steam cloud particles also absorbed or dispersed some of the radiation that was overloading the shields.

Her screen blinked green.

"Sometimes it's just a matter of turning a disadvantage to your advantage. Not all problems are problems solely, though you'll now need to collect more water."

She flashed him a grin. "Water is abundant according to these readings. I don't know why I couldn't see that."

"You were trying too hard, and you still are. Look at the time." Azizi pointed to the corner of her terminal. "Like you, I came here to avoid my team, but the gather is a chance to see how those you journeyed with have been."

Trina pushed her chair away from the desk but did not rise. She'd planned to spend all of break day here. She had no one to rediscover, and only trouble to find, or so she'd thought before the encounter with Deluth this very morning.

She didn't know what had prompted her to nod when he'd asked if she planned to come. Until that moment, she'd been sure she would not go.

Then he'd apologized.

Such a little thing, but so different from how Redel had behaved either in their quarters or when she'd missed the air stream's warning lights.

Part of her wanted to see more of him, to discover an ally among her team. They'd progressed far enough in the lessons she figured she'd soon be put back with her team as several of the candidates from her classes had already been. It would be a relief to discover Redel the exception rather than that all of her teammates were more interested in her failure than their own success.

If she did find it so.

"Surely there's someone you want to see," Azizi said as if aware of her weakening. "I would have noticed a shuttle disgorging one single person on arrival day."

Trina laughed and shook her head. "In the huge docking bay with ten or more shuttles at the same time and enough candidates wandering the floor to start a colony of our own?"

He waved a hand to dismiss her teasing. "Are you saying you did?"

She pushed to her feet and walked toward the door, unwilling to let hope of Deluth's nature slip away after all. "I barely knew any of the candidates I arrived with. We had a few weeks of preparation classes, but I spent every minute outside of them with my sister. I didn't board the ship to come here like you did, remember? I was a colonist right up until the testing."

A stunned silence echoed from behind her for long enough that she slowed until running steps pounded up to her side.

"You are coming to spend time with me, then," Azizi said, making no other comment about her isolation as he looped an arm through hers.

DELUTH AND SHARNA SPENT THE morning observing the planet they orbited, and talking about all the ways the Guild training proved different from their expectations. If not for how she seemed to want more from him, he thought they could become fast friends.

"I can see why it makes no sense now," Sharna said with a laugh, "but I truly thought I'd be piloting a ship already. Not a full one, but a shuttle at least."

"I'd expected to be thrown into battle against space pirates, myself. Not that my ship ever encountered any directly, but the stories some of the indie traders told were enough to expect a pirate around every corner and our safety a matter of pure dumb luck."

She struck his chest with an outstretched finger. "Pirates. I suppose you saw yourself as some sort of hero, then?"

He rubbed the spot though it hadn't really hurt. "And I suppose you were shuttling dignitaries."

Deluth caught a glimpse of reddened cheeks before she twisted to stare at the planet again.

"I thought the station was using its home planet to determine the light cycles, but I can see the dark of night coming already."

He followed her gaze and sure enough, a darkening curve seemed to swallow the planet below.

"We are matched," came a voice from behind them. "If you were on the surface, that dark wouldn't reach you for half a day. The anchor point for our stationary orbit is directly below us and we experience its light cycle. If we went based on vision, we'd have a shortened day because we can see that much farther."

They turned to see who had offered this information and met the smile of an unfamiliar instructor.

"The gather allows you to meet more of the staff as well even if it's mostly for the candidates," he said as if able to read Deluth's mind.

"You'll be part of a large crew for all first assignments and often for your whole career. You need to know how to relate to people from different ships, from planets, and even those outside Guild borders like the indie traders you mentioned."

Deluth felt a flush of his own rise at the realization this instructor had overheard their dreams.

"This gather is a small part of getting you ready for that reality. Attendance is by choice, but I suggest you come."

Sharna linked her arm through Deluth's. "Oh, we're coming. We just hadn't noticed the time passing."

She gave him a significant look at that, but Deluth stared straight ahead, pretending not to see. He could tell between her interest and Redel's matchmaking he'd have a hard time winding his way through this asteroid field without someone getting hurt. It would be so much easier if Redel didn't suspect his attention had fixed on Trina, but then, Trina didn't seem to share that interest any more than he did Sharna's.

Perhaps.

What had she meant by such a comment?

He got no answer when they arrived.

Sharna pulled him around the room, introducing him here or there, but mainly she seemed to be taking everything in before engaging.

It wasn't until the fourth introduction proved a careful assessment by the member of her ship, and he noticed her doing the same to both the person and those they stood with, that he started to become uncomfortable.

Soon he could identify her shipmates before she said a word, both from the stiff nod she offered them where he'd been expecting joyful greetings and the sheer beauty the candidates possessed whether male or female.

If these proved a true representation of her ship, it must have been a striking crew. A glance at Sharna made him wonder though.

With everyone so close to perfection, he supposed the definition would be redefined rather than enjoyed. He remembered her odd comment about Redel and how if he'd possessed a less ordinary appearance, she might have had to do something.

On their ship, both Redel and Deluth were considered handsome, but neither would stand up to a comparison with any of Sharna's people.

Deluth's realization quickly followed with another.

The assessment they gave him had little to do with his value and everything to do with his appearance. Worse, it seemed he was assessed as part of her aura rather than on his own.

He couldn't imagine growing up on a ship where your genetic predisposition to physical attractiveness held sway over all other factors. With so many of her shipmates here, they clearly didn't lack for intelligence either. Still, they assessed on the visible features alone from his short time in the presence of more than one.

Sharna swept passed a replicator, but Deluth slowed, pulling against her hold. "Let's get something to drink and find a group to talk with. Remember what the instructor said. You're supposed to expand your community, not stick with those you already know."

She looked as if she would protest for a heartbeat then targeted a nod just as stiff in his direction.

He half wanted to tell her to continue on her own if it was that important to her, but he'd seen enough to realize if he didn't stay with her for this event, she would be damaged in the eyes of her shipmates. As much as he wanted to make his wish for friendship, and nothing more, clear, he did not plan to hurt her in front of a crowd of all too interested onlookers.

Sharna had keyed in her drink when he turned to place his own request, but before he could do more than put his palm on the reader, he finally saw Trina.

She stood framed in the doorway with the same candidate as before, an escort easily as attractive as his own.

Deluth tensed at the sight, fighting down the urge to charge over there as he had the first time he'd seen them. He had no agreement with Trina. She'd shown hardly any interest in him at all. He had no right to debate her choice of companions.

The replicator beeped, confused by his palm on the scanner for so long with no request made.

Sharna turned to see what had distracted him, and remembering his thought about the assessment, he tried to come up with a reason other than his interest in Trina.

Before he could say a word, she tensed more than he had, drawing herself into a straight line and glaring across the room. A series of curses in her shipboard language came from her lips, or so he assumed from the venomous tone.

"She means nothing," he blurted, afraid what she would do next.

The confusion in her eyes when she glanced at him could not be faked. "Her? Can you not tell he's male? It's the pretty boy." Her glare returned to the dark-skinned candidate.

Deluth stifled a surprised laugh, knowing Sharna would not appreciate the sound

Of course.

He'd seen how her people assessed each other, and though he did not have that preference, even he realized the extent of the candidate's beauty. Trina's friend hadn't caused an issue when Sharna saw him in their quarters, but where everything weighed for or against her based solely on appearance, her reaction had changed.

If he'd been about to condemn Trina, Sharna looked as if she wanted to do Trina's companion bodily harm.

"Sharna, it's been long enough. Let's go to the observation dome and see if we can catch the sun rising on the other side."

She resisted his pull until he feared she would reject his efforts. Then, just when he thought he'd have to tell her outright that she couldn't risk being caught in a confrontation, she forced her gaze from Trina and her companion to smile at him.

If her teeth were clenched, at least she no longer seemed interested in gutting the other candidate.

"Fine," she said after a pause. "I have done what I needed to here."

They passed Redel on their way out, and he gave Deluth a wink.

Swallowing a groan in response, Deluth realized he'd trapped himself again in a situation sure to raise the very expectations he wanted to avoid. But they were already one member down with Trina in her separate training. He'd be a poor friend if he let Sharna be thrown out of the Spacer Guild because she couldn't work well with others who matched her beauty, and their team would suffer the loss of two members, weakening the training for all of them.

CHAPTER 14

Thought of a water shower didn't offer the same amazement Trina found reflected in the faces and comments around her. The station's pure sonic showers had taken some time to get used to when she'd arrived. It had been one of many changes, and she'd been much more concerned by whether she could learn enough to stay.

"I can't wait to properly wash my hair," Azizi said, brushing his fingers through the tight curls. "I know the sonic is supposed to be better and all, but it doesn't feel right."

Trina laughed before she could catch herself. Most of her life, she'd splashed copper-infused water over her body and called it good, scrubbing only to remove any scent that might mark her. Hair didn't smell, or not much.

Her hair had never been cleaner or better tended.

"Easy for you."

Azizi tugged a strand of her hair, and she didn't flinch. Her instincts were fading. She didn't know whether to be happy about that or not.

"Your hair doesn't need more than a quick sonic run, but mine—"

"Yours is a precious treasure that needs careful tending?"

He laughed so hard at her statement, the others waiting for their scheduled turn twisted to see what was so funny.

Trina scanned their faces, some instincts harder to break.

She noticed Deluth with Sharna in a line to their right.

She shouldn't be surprised at the pairing considering how she'd seen them leave together the previous day. Besides, the order of the schedule came from when they'd used the palm reader at the gathering. Otherwise, Azizi would be surrounded by his team and she hers.

Deluth turned her direction, Sharna following his lead. Trina ducked her head to avoid meeting his gaze only to track him with her peripheral vision.

"You have no idea how wild my hair can get when left alone."

She realized Azizi had been speaking to her while her thoughts wandered, but could only shrug in answer as Sharna stepped into the shower chamber.

Azizi followed her look. "It seems he's not the only one interested."

"He has a pairing already. She went in first."

"Just because they spend time together is no measure as you should know from the two of us. I tell you he's interested. The ship born are not that much different."

This time Trina laughed, though she swallowed the rest of the sound as soon as it broke free. He had no idea the extent of differences between his planet and hers, his life and hers. If the ship born had a fraction of that variance, his instincts could be just as worthless as what she would expect on his planet.

He stared at her, a question in his eyes, but she shook her head, unable to explain without costing the very friendship she'd come to depend on.

Some candidates near Deluth began an argument from what Trina could tell, but she couldn't hear what they were saying, or even the target of their ire.

Sharna stepped free of the shower, her appearance stunning the others to silence. Deluth entered the chamber, and she stepped to one side to wait for him, a further sign of their pairing no matter what Azizi might think.

The line moved forward, and Trina shifted so she'd present a shoulder to Sharna. She had no interest in speaking with the other candidate as much as she refused to accept Deluth as the cause. Trina had no connection to any of her team.

A tiny voice in the back of her head denied the statement, offering up visions of her encounters with Deluth, of his intent expression when he said he hoped to see her at the gather.

He'd left the room almost as soon as she'd arrived, showing his words to be nothing more than that. If she thought to find a greater meaning because of Azizi's suppositions, she'd only be disappointed.

The question had no importance anyway.

She'd come to the training to become a spacer, not to find love for all she envied Katie. If she'd been ready to settle down, she could have stayed with the colony and Marcus.

Her turn came next. Trina placed her palm against the scanner. A familiar, mechanical voice stated:

Candidate 15f. Confirmed. Preferences recorded. Water allocation: ten minutes.

She'd selected the basic shampoo and soap from the list they'd been offered, having experience with nothing else and amazed at the variety possible. Perhaps she should have stolen soaps instead of jewels from polit houses. Fence could have created a whole new culture among the shafters, though few had access to large water sources.

Trained by showers on the colony ship, she slapped the water off before it had finished, triggered the drying cycle. Trina stepped free in half the time to meet Azizi's puzzled look.

She shrugged. The showers offered neither a wonderful adventure nor a reminder of home as it did for others. She saw no need to linger.

DELUTH EXITED THE CHAMBER WITH a smile on his face. He wasn't quite sure whether he preferred a water shower to the sonic, but it had been all he'd been looking for in a brand new experience.

A quick glance around showed only those waiting their turn.

He suppressed his relief upon discovering Sharna hadn't stayed to walk with him. She didn't deserve his disgruntled thoughts.

He'd given her every indication he wasn't opposed to her interest thanks to the circumstances he'd found himself in. He would find the time and place, or create it if it could not be found, to make his hopes clear. With any luck, they'd continue as friends and put these misunderstandings behind them.

Just then, a gap opened in the line he'd been weaving through, giving him a clear view of Sharna where she leaned against the wall.

She straightened and waved, showing she'd caught sight of him as well.

Deluth increased his pace, determined to pull her aside right then, but slowed at the last moment. Not only would his quick step raise more expectations to quash, but he couldn't pull her out so publicly without increasing speculation that would turn against her once the truth came out.

"So what did you think?" she asked when he reached her side. "Wonderful, isn't it?"

The neutral topic offered some safety at least.

"It was interesting for sure." He ran a finger across the crease above his collarbone. "I swear I still feel damp despite the sonic dryer at the end."

She laughed, tipping her head back to give the best view of her beauty, or so he guessed from the admiring looks he could see directed her way. "The liquid absorbs into your skin. It's the same when you visit the hydroponics section. Ship—or station—air is kept much dryer than the skin craves, even on my ship."

"I was thinking to get in another training session before classes re-start this afternoon," Deluth said when their conversation fell off. If he could get her to agree, he could talk to her about how he saw their connection on the walk to their quarters.

Sharna shook her head. "I don't want to discourage your ambition, but they give us this break time for a reason. Study too hard and you'll wear yourself out before you ever make spacer. You think they want someone in a key role who has no stamina?"

Her argument made sense, and he'd thought the same a time or two, but his options for getting her alone were limited. "You can't mean to stay here all day?"

She glanced toward the showers as one of the lines shuffled for-ward, then shrugged. "I suppose I don't have to be here."

Relieved at her agreement, Deluth started toward the nearest air stream, expecting Sharna to follow.

"Look," she said instead. "Redel and some of the others are here as well. They must have been in a different line."

Wiping all signs of annoyance from his expression, Deluth turned to follow her pointed finger, knowing as he did so they had no choice but to join the others. One more chance to clear things with Sharna lost.

He couldn't lay the blame at Redel's feet this time as much as he wanted to. His friend had no way of knowing they'd caught sight of him as Redel stood with a group of candidates from their ship. Even there, he seemed the leader.

Sharna might dismiss his charisma, but from what Deluth could see, his friend had stepped into a leadership role as soon as they began training, and everyone, even those who had grown up at his side were affected—everyone but Deluth.

"Just look at the expression on that one? Afraid of a little water?"

They arrived to hear the others laughing at a young man next to en-ter the showers.

"As if you looked any better," Deluth said before he could swallow the words. "After all, you'd never experienced it before today either."

Redel turned slowly, and he made no effort to school his expression either. "There you are. Late to the showers as you were to the gather."

His gaze widened to take in just who Deluth arrived with and the scowl melted away. "I see you've been using the extra time wisely."

Sharna tossed her hair in answer, and the others, both male and female, shifted to watch her instead of those they'd been mocking. "We've already been."

Deluth shouldn't have been surprised. He'd grown used to her stunning looks, but even he stayed aware of how she affected everyone. If only she didn't consider Redel beneath her standards, they'd make a dynamic team. She'd catch everyone's attention, Redel would command them, and they'd both work the strategies.

As long as those strategies didn't involve him.

A loud string of curses cut through the air behind them.

Everyone, Sharna included, spun to stare at the showers where the commotion originated.

A door slid open and out poured some kind of beast, or so Deluth thought at first sight.

A second later, he choked on an unfortunate laugh as he recognized Trina's pretty boy. That definition, however, no longer applied.

Something had malfunctioned in the shower treatment so his long, auburn ringlets had become a brassy yellow, tangled mess of sharp strands sticking out in every direction. When he jerked free of the entrance, the mane swayed back and forth as though composed of living creatures.

Everyone nearby recoiled. Everyone except for Trina.

WHEN AZIZI CURSED FROM INSIDE the shower, Trina tensed and dropped into a fight-ready stance before she could stop herself. He burst free as she relaxed, but the sight of him only sent her tension higher.

The hair he'd complained about requiring careful tending had proved his point for him, and from the furious look on his face, he didn't think it an accident.

She grabbed his arm and dragged him through the group to the nearest instructor, curses still spewing from his lips in a low mutter.

"Tell him," Trina said, pushing Azizi forward.

Her friend stared before noticing the purple suit. "Someone tampered with the settings. Look what they've done." He jerked a piece of hair forward to demonstrate.

The instructor struggled to control his expression, the battle shown in a twitch at one corner of the man's mouth. After an awkward pause, he said, "Are you sure you read the instructions correctly when stating your preferences? Water and cleansing compounds are very different from sonic showers."

"You think I don't know how to request soap?"

Trina put a hand on Azizi's arm to calm him. They would figure out what had happened, but not if he antagonized the instructor and got himself into serious trouble for it.

Azizi shook her off, but he did temper his approach. "I selected the same hair treatments I used back home on the colony. I am not new to water showers nor to selecting the compounds."

Something changed in the man's face that Trina found all too easy to read. She'd seen similar recently enough in Redel's expression.

"I'm afraid our systems are much more sophisticated than those on the colonies as we have to keep them functioning smoothly. It's easy enough for those unfamiliar with the process to make an error."

"I did not make a mistake," Azizi bit out in a tight voice. "My settings were changed deliberately to harm me."

The man laughed once before forcing a serious expression. "That is very unlikely. The preferences were set in advance, and the showers go by order rather than person. Besides, your hair—though impressive—is not truly damaged. A harmless mistake."

If any water had remained on Azizi's person, Trina suspected it would have steamed as a deep red undercut his brown skin.

She stared around for anything to distract him before he was thrown from the program for assaulting an instructor no matter how much this man deserved the treatment.

"Look," she said, her voice a little too loud but enough to jerk Azizi's attention to her. "It's Fred. She'll help."

Sure enough, their main instructor strode across the room toward them. Unlike the first, she had no sign of humor on her face as she took in Azizi's appearance. "Michael, make sure no other incidents occur here. I'll deal with this and send another to take my place."

For a moment, Trina worried Fred would be harder on Azizi even than this Michael.

As soon as he'd gone, Fred waved a hand and started toward the entrance. "We'll get this fixed in the instructor section, Azizi."

Not quite sure what she meant by "fixed," Trina decided the wave had included her as well. She had no plans to abandon her friend. Even worse, she finally understood what the first man had said. The program ran on order. She'd cut her shower short, throwing off the timing. If this had not been a simple malfunction, she'd been more likely the intended target and she knew exactly where to look for the culprit.

Just before they passed through the opening, Trina glanced around to find her target not far from where they went.

Redel stood in a collection of Pilots and other candidates. From the grin on his face, he felt the results acceptable even if he'd failed his aim.

She had time for one quick glare that swept the group, her gut twisting to see Deluth among them, though he no longer laughed if he ever had.

Then they moved through and off to an air stream that would take them to the instructor's section, normally off limits for students.

DELUTH CAUGHT THE EDGE OF Trina's glare before she, her friend, and one of the instructors swept through the entrance and out of sight. It made him regret the startled laugh even more, especially since the others were still chuckling as they mimicked the young man's hair with their hands.

He turned to Sharna, but she'd stepped away without him noticing, destroying both the chance to catch her alone and the hope of one person not punishing the victim of an unfortunate system failure.

"That was amazing," Redel said, slapping Deluth's shoulder. "I've never seen such growth on a human head."

Deluth frowned at his friend. "You should be nicer to him. After all, the same could have as easily happened to you."

Redel ran fingers through his hair, a feature he'd always been proud of, and stretched it to its full length, almost the measure of his arm. "I don't think it could have. My hair doesn't have the wild nature of his."

The others joined in with renewed laughter, but Deluth had had enough. His mind kept fixating on the glare Trina had sent before leaving, and he started to wonder if her anger came from more than just their reaction. Could his friend have played another trick and just missed the intended target?

He reviewed Redel's expression in his mind. Though his friend had been as quick to laugh as any of them, surprise not satisfaction filled his features. Perhaps the result had been much greater than he'd hoped, but no, Deluth knew Redel's features well enough to recognize the delight a successful, or even spectacular, prank would have brought. Redel didn't do this.

"I'm going to our quarters," he called over his shoulder, waiting neither for a response nor company.

He didn't like the suspicions he'd started to have about Redel.

Sure they'd done many pranks on the home ship, and had the same done to them, but never ones so cruel. Why would his friend risk so much for so little cause? The air stream had been dangerous, but this one had too many potential witnesses.

Deluth wished he could be sure, wished he could be confident that Redel would never be so foolish or downright mean, but his friend's behavior since they came to the station had been just shy of vicious. That he held a grudge against Trina could not be doubted. Had his ill feeling spread to those she associated with as well? Or had the same charisma Sharna marked made some other candidates bold enough to strike out at a person few seemed to know.

He hadn't realized before, but Sharna had spent almost as much time asking after Trina's friend as checking her own shipmates.

Her curiosity, however, received little information of worth as many knew of the young man by description, but few had any more contact with him than being present in the same room.

Which brought Deluth to Redel, the only one he'd heard speak out against the two colony-bred, and all of those from a colony if he were being honest.

The uncomfortable feeling spread as he connected another anomaly to his friend. They'd done drills in conjunction with other teams the previous day. Both times, the other team failed to complete their portion of the tasks.

He wouldn't have marked the fact, especially since most teams failed more often than they succeeded from what people had been saying at the gather, but each time, Redel had been out of position and standing near the team member responsible for the failure.

Deluth stepped into the air stream, wishing he could punch something harder than the airflow itself.

He had no proof of his suspicions, and his friend deserved better than that he let jealousy twist what he observed.

Redel had found a role, a place in the team that everyone else accepted. They looked up to him. He'd made friends, or at least followers, of both the Pilots and now even of those who'd come from The Headway. Why would he risk all that on a prank?

In comparison, Deluth felt trapped by a relationship he didn't want and hadn't agreed to. He was ignored or scorned by the one person he wanted to know better. His teammates tolerated him as one among them, but he had no illusions. If they had to choose, they'd side with Redel over him every time, no matter what the circumstance.

He stuck out a hand to grab one of the support bars intended for emergencies and pulled out his program stick. It might be more sophisticated than they expected a candidate to own, but he'd won the stick, and its preset controls, from a member of his ship's crew. Not one of the spacers stationed there.

With the ease of habit, he manipulated the stick in his one free hand, never once chancing it floating free on the stream.

The pressure dropped suddenly before picking up to send him in a different direction—to the training area.

He might have accepted Sharna's advice then, but if he went to their quarters now, especially if Redel had already returned, he couldn't be sure he'd manage to control his temper.

Their friendship had weakened since coming here. He had no intention of alienating Redel any further, especially when all his concerns might have their roots not in fact but in other, less noble, emotions. They were supposed to be working toward a common success, not fighting over scraps like a pair of pirates.

Hard, physical stimulation could burn out this energy before he had something more to regret than an ill-timed laugh. One of the external repair scenarios would be perfect.

And if he let out his frustrations against the simulated hull of a spaceship, no one else had to know.

CHAPTER 15

Fred took them to a room with the instructors' cleansers, which were capable of both sonic and water showers.

"You deserve the reward you earned, and to enjoy it." She swiped her own palm across the panel, drawing from whatever allowance the instructors had for water usage.

She let Azizi configure his preferences, then added a dye remover and oil for an extra finish.

"Trust me. I have a spacer friend from your world. His hair isn't as nice as yours normally, so he uses the oil to refresh it."

Azizi gave her a long look before he nodded and stepped into the chamber with a measure of trust Trina wasn't sure she would have been able to offer.

"You're going to find who did this, aren't you?" she asked Fred while Azizi repaired his hair.

The instructor shrugged. "It's much more likely a system error."

"Azizi did not set his preferences wrong, and you know it. He's been helping me after class, and he's quick to understand most of the work you've given us. Besides, they had water showers on his colony."

Fred nodded, this information nothing new to her despite the attitude of the other instructor. "It's easy for people to assume because you came from a different background that it, and you, is therefore lesser. Michael should not have treated any candidate as he did."

Before Trina could celebrate, Fred continued, "But the fact remains that it is very unlikely any of the candidates have either the skill or the tools to change something like this, and even if they had, candidates were identified by place, rather than person."

"It could have been time."

That drew a faint smile from the instructor. "True. The duration of the showers was set in advance, and the pressure from those behind would have been enough to keep to that timing. A couple of candidates lingered within, but never so long we had to intervene. As I said, those who assume the candidates who require my classes are slow will soon learn better. Few would have identified a pattern where we try to have none. You've shown an aptitude for configurations when the terms are defined. This is a skill that should serve you well."

Trina felt her skin heat as she absorbed the compliment. Her instructors would never need to know just how she'd developed that knack, but it seemed her shafter life had not been a complete waste. Then the color drained along with her good humor.

"I broke the pattern. This malfunction should have affected me, not Azizi. And it's not the first."

"How so?"

Fred's question came out a command, her easy nature sharpening into a pointed stare.

This time it was Trina's turn to shrug. "We had water showers on the colony ship. The allocation was five minutes, and I'd grown used to that."

Again Fred nodded. "I'd forgotten you'd been more than a colony-bred candidate but part of a founding group as well. Your pattern skills will aid you, but be careful not to rely on them too heavily. Malfunctions do happen, especially on a station as large and as active as this one. Taking responsibility where warranted is an important quality, but claiming guilt where none is to be had will only weaken you. It's easy to see a pattern where there is none."

"But the pattern is there." As much as she wanted to accept the freedom of not bringing this down on her friend's head, neither could she ignore the facts.

With a laugh, Fred drew her over to a view panel. "Do you see the patterns in the stars? Our ancestors named them. They drew lines between to form pictures of their gods and heroes. They too saw patterns where none existed. They built their lives around those even so."

Trina vowed to look up star pictures to understand what her instructor meant better. Earth history was not something a shafter could access, nor were star charts among the books her father had left them. At the same time, though she understood the meaning, her stubborn nature made her point out, "You agree I've found the method. Why pretend I couldn't have broken it?"

The woman shook her head, resting one hand on the panel as if she could touch the stars beyond. "See this star? It might be surrounded with viable planets, or it might have no satellites at all. From where we stand, with only our bare eyesight, we have no idea what it holds, nor whether a colony ship has gone there or is on route. Yet, we assume it will have at least one place to plant the seeds of humanity until we prove it cannot."

Fred gave Trina a sharp look. "It's in our nature to see patterns and expect the universe to conform. Because most stars have satellites, we expect this one to. Because most stars have at least one viable satellite, whether it needs terraforming or is already suitable to support human life, we assume this one will. Whether it has or not, we cannot know. It would make more sense to withhold judgment, but we do not. This is humanity's blessing and curse."

"But what if it does?"

"What if it doesn't?"

Azizi stepped free then, his hair restored just as promised in both color and nature.

Trina thought his arrival would put an end to the odd lesson, but instead Fred waved him over.

"I will state this simply for both of you to understand. You, Trina, could not have been the target if this were a deliberate act. The timing might have aided the choice, but the malfunction came in preferences, and yours were much different than Azizi's I'd assume."

Trina had to nod then, and Azizi turned to stare at her.

"You think you're at fault?"

She looked away, unwilling to see the accusation in his gaze.

"If this was deliberate," Fred said again, using the same commanding tone, "the only possible target would be the one who suffered it, and so Azizi. However, I state once again the likelihood of such an act is slim at best. Evidence of same would be even harder to find. Anyone capable of making such an adjustment would be just as capable of changing all logs for it. A bumbling change I'd suspect. Something this elegant? Why use it for so simple a prank? The only cost came to your dignity, and soon the candidates will be busy with their studies once again, too busy to remember that trick. Anyone sophisticated enough to make such a change would know we could correct the consequences."

She glanced at both of them, but her gaze came to rest on Trina as she added, "I'd suggest you put this happening from your mind. You have a lot of work ahead of you, and soon you'll be rejoining your teams. Every moment you dwell on this unprovable question is time you've lost from learning what will help you excel as a candidate and as a spacer."

Because Fred seemed to expect a response, Trina ducked her head in a quick nod. Her words made sense if all Trina had known was the spacer life, but as a shafter, she knew well enough an attack ignored only encouraged another, stronger assault. She needed to figure this out whether Azizi had been the true target or not.

Chapter 16

As Fred had warned, Trina had a hard time concentrating the next day, though with a different teacher, at least she didn't have to worry about Fred calling her out.

Azizi seemed to have put the troubles behind him, and apart from a couple of sympathetic looks and a teasing comment or two, those in their class accepted the event as a system failure soon to be forgotten.

Trina examined what she'd observed a number of times, but could find nothing that would lead her to an answer. As far as she knew, Redel had been nowhere near the shower they'd used. She hadn't even seen him until they were leaving.

If Azizi had an enemy of his own, he hadn't shared that information with her, an unlikely event considering how many tales he had told her about his team and those who shared the transport taking them to the spacer training station.

Which brought Trina back to her own guilt.

Fred pointed out how the prank could not have been intended for her even if the instructor accepted it as deliberate. She'd failed to rule out an attack on Azizi, though. One not intended for Trina, but intended to hurt those who allied with her.

Trina had thought all this behind her, but it seemed she'd stumbled into a culture just as tangled and dangerous, if in very different ways.

She could not pretend she hadn't noticed.

Such a choice would make her weak and vulnerable in the eyes of their attackers. But she had to be careful and clever in how she went about it, both to keep them ignorant of her progress and to avoid any reprimands from her instructors.

Fred would be the first to condemn her this time when she'd been so quick to stand up for Azizi at first. She'd told Trina to let this go. Trina doubted the instructor would feel kindly toward her now that she ignored the advice.

"You're not even listening," Azizi said, startling Trina out of yet another attempt to find a pattern to follow. "Class is over. We might as well go to our quarters if this is all the attention you have. You're listening no more now than you were when the instructor spoke. What has you so distracted anyway?"

Trina shrugged, knowing the truth would only provoke him into a lecture as firm as any Fred gave her. "I'm just tired."

His eyes narrowed as he stared at her, but when she did not provide anything more, he slapped his terminal off and rose.

"All the more reason to head back early and get some rest. Perhaps tomorrow you'll be interested in completing your studies. I suppose you missed his comment about how soon all of us will join the normal classes?"

At least Trina didn't have to hide her surprise, Fred having indicated as much the previous day. "I'll be ready."

Whether she promised herself or him, Trina didn't know for sure, but he answered with his own shrug and left the room clearly disgruntled.

For once, she didn't want his company any more than he seemed to want hers. If she couldn't tell him the truth, best she kept her distance. She'd tell him everything as soon as she had something concrete to tell.

TRINA DOVE INTO THE AIR stream, tipping forward until she lay almost along the current, her frustration driving her to greater speeds than ever before. The world around her became a blur of movement.

She stared straight ahead, unsure what she could do next.

A shadow appeared in the stream ahead of her, someone else using the transport at the same time.

She put out a hand to change her profile and slow down. If she ran over the person this time, it would be all her own fault. Still, she'd been going fast enough that when the current slowed to let her off, the candidate had yet to cross the chamber and enter one of the many corridors leading to the different quarters.

He turned, clearly startled, and Trina recognized Deluth.

She almost laughed aloud as her mind, still caught up in puzzling out a pattern, threw images of him into the mix. Then she remembered how he'd confronted the two of them coming into the Pilot quarters. Another flash and she saw again the glare he'd directed not at her but at Azizi when they'd come to the gather, shortly before he left with Sharna.

He didn't move a step as she marched across to confront him.

All this time she'd been thinking his association with Redel an unfortunate accident, but what if he, not the other candidate, had been behind all the conflicts. This could be how he attacked—secretly—using others to do the work.

"Trina—"

"You did it. I know you did."

He retreated a step, shock in his widened eyes.

"You didn't think we'd figure it out. Thought us dumb colony candidates would never discover you were behind such a cruel trick."

His back hit the wall before she realized she'd been advancing steadily. If Trina had her knives, they would have been out and ready.

No one hurt her friends and got away with it.

Deluth struck so quickly had she been from any other background, he would have touched her.

Trina just knocked his hands aside.

He scowled at her. "I don't know what you think I've done, but I have defended you at every turn. I might lose a friendship for standing up for you colony-bred. Figures you'd attack me for it." He rubbed the side of his hand where she'd hit him and glared.

Trina glared back, his words and play at innocence only enraging her more. He wanted sympathy to distract from her purpose, but the pieces had fallen into place. His attempt to undermine what she'd seen only strengthened her resolve. If he'd been such an advocate, why had she caught him staring at Azizi?

She took one more step forward, not intimidated by his words or his size.

He dropped into a stance much different from hers, but enough of a reminder that though he'd never been a shafter, it didn't mean he'd never fought.

Trina mirrored him by instinct even as her mind started screaming a warning, not about a fight she could most likely win, but about consequences. Nishan made it clear she had to follow the rules as a candidate or be tossed from the program. If she wanted to succeed, she could not win the battle this way.

One backward step and then another, she ended the confrontation if not on her own terms.

A look of satisfaction crossed his face, and she fought against the need to wipe it away. "I'll get the evidence to prove you did this," she said, her voice low and intense. "Then we'll see how the instructors respond to your lies."

Far enough for safety, she pivoted and strode for her corridor, the same one he would follow. She'd hear him coming if he tried to run after her. In turning away, she showed the full of her contempt.

Fred had said it would have taken someone of extreme skill.

Trina might have started late, but she planned to reach that level and higher until she could prove he'd done this. When she informed the instructors, he'd be served far worse than if she won a physical battle, and she'd come out of it much better.

DELUTH STARED AFTER HER, FUMING. Everything he'd done for her, even setting himself against Redel, and she thought he'd been the one to change the shower? He didn't have half the skill necessary to do that. He doubted any of them did. But she hadn't accused just anyone. She'd come after him.

He clenched his fists, half wishing she had launched at him as he'd thought she was going to. He needed to punch something, violent urges he'd felt all too often of late.

She'd poured out of the air stream so soon after him, already on the warpath. If he didn't know better, he'd think she manipulated the stream to catch him where there was less chance of witnesses. She probably didn't realize the whole area could be scanned.

Deluth shook off that thought.

He wasn't going to fall into Redel's trap no matter how angry she made him. Just because her planet chose to ignore the advantages technology offered didn't mean she was ignorant of them, especially not after weeks of training.

She'd shown more control than he would have expected from what he'd read of her planet. Beyond the general information, he'd had to rely on spacer reports that often left him bewildered.

Sure, they'd had a rough beginning, but from what his research had told him, she'd chosen to live in filth long after the colony grew enough wealth to restore the machinery lost on landing. Her cities were patrolled with thugs carrying sticks to beat any wrongdoer into submission.

The thought stilled his angry pacing.

Coming from a background like that, maybe he should be grateful she'd found the strength to walk away. He'd been in his share of tussles, but he'd never had to fight for his life. Somehow, he doubted the same could be said of Trina, and instinct told him she'd be unlikely to drop her accusation either.

A flash of admiration surprised him.

She stood by Azizi when no one else would. The instructors announced it had been a malfunction, but clearly Trina found that answer too simple. His own instinct had been the same until he considered the level of skill to pull it off. And what if she was right with only her target off in choosing him?

The instructors seemed blind to the conflict growing between those held aside from the full training and the rest of the candidates, but he wasn't. How could he be with his friend a leading architect? It wouldn't take much for someone to go too far.

He had equipment that should have been out of his reach. Why should he assume others wouldn't have advantages as well? After all, not everyone passed the spacer test. It made sense for those with exceptional talents to have used those skills in their life before coming here.

Confusion mixed in with frustrated anger until he knew going to their quarters would be a mistake. She'd accused him, but Redel had encouraged the antagonism between her and the rest of the team. Even Sharna pressed him for something he didn't want to give.

He could understand what led Trina to suspect him, but it still burned. When he spent all too much time tracking her movements, she saw him as nothing more than an enemy. He didn't need another reason to admire her. She clearly hated him.

He needed a reason to walk away.

Deluth marched to the transport device and keyed up the training area. If nothing else, he could put all this frantic energy to use.

At this rate, he'd have more outside experience than a hull maintenance specialist by the time he graduated to full spacer.

CHAPTER 17

Trina went straight to her room, not even bothering with food as she raged at Deluth and at herself. The bunk groaned when she tossed herself onto it to stare blindly at the ceiling.

She'd seen his true nature from the start only she hadn't wanted to believe it. She'd pasted apologies onto his features instead of remembering what his sharp words taught her. She'd wanted him to be something else just because he'd caught her attention from the start.

She'd made kindness out of convenience when he overruled Redel's prank but she'd focused on the wrong aspect.

When she'd considered his motivations, she should have been looking at how Redel, clearly styling himself as a big man, bent to Deluth's will.

How many big men throughout First City had reported to Samuel? Her grandfather once said she, as a shafter, was the embodiment of the doctrine to live by the work of your own hands. He used others to do his work, a practice that made Samuel start to think of himself as a god.

For the first time in a long while, Trina let herself remember the times with her grandfather before he'd become a monster. He'd been a good man once, well respected by his people, kind to his staff, and even willing to discipline his unruly son rather than protecting him from the consequences of his actions.

That had been the Samuel she'd come to respect, come to admire. And he'd been the one to take her to the stars.

On Ceric, the machines would be blamed for twisting his mind, but she knew better.

Love of power, not the tools he'd used, was responsible for his choices. Blaming technology allowed those on Ceric to look away from the actions of the people, to excuse them rather than recognize the corruption that festered within.

An uncomfortable similarity between herself and her grandfather rose to tease her. He'd been obsessed with ensuring the Menthak legacy. So obsessed he'd been willing to do, or sacrifice, anything to make it happen even if it meant killing every single colonist not locked away in the freezers. He would have thrown away lives, knowledge, and preparation, releasing unprepared colonists onto a strange land with only Paul's feeble grasp of command to lead them.

Could she stand in judgment when she did the same thing here and now, if on a smaller scale?

She'd come to live her dream of being a spacer, but she threw that away to search for the cause of something even the instructors believed impossible. She'd searched her mind for any clue, wasting the time she should have been devoting to her studies, and for what? Because she suspected another, worse, attack would come if she did not?

There were punishments in place for those who acted against the rules in any significant way. Surely even if it had been a prank, the one behind it wouldn't try again and chance being sent home any more than she was willing to fight Deluth with that consequence.

Her mind stilled at thought of her teammate. She saw again the surprise in his expression, the anger when faced with her charge.

Had she done exactly what Fred warned against?

He had glared at Azizi. He had accused them of playing while all others worked. But did that mean he would have struck out against them?

Azizi assigned a much different meaning to those acts, one that offered as good an explanation, and perhaps a better one.

Her breathing slowed as she changed the framework of her vision and turned each encounter into that of interest. If he felt for her as Aaron had for Katie, or even if he hoped to reach that point, Azizi could seem a rival. He'd never spent enough time with them to learn they were only friends.

That would explain his anger at her accusation better. She could see Redel accepting responsibility whether or not he did it. Or laughing and delighted she thought him so skilled.

She let out a long sigh.

Redel bowing to his wishes on the first day suddenly seemed less a big man commanding another than the friendship of shipmates who were unwilling to fight over so simple a conflict.

The attack, if that was what it was, had brought all her shafter instincts to the fore. She saw both danger and power games in every motion, and even if there were those establishing a power base like Redel, the aim lay in recognition not control.

No one could harm another candidate without inflicting greater harm on themselves and their hope of a career in the Guild.

Fred had warned her, had shown how the instinct to find patterns could lead a person astray, but she hadn't listened. Instead, she'd attacked the one person on her team who had shown any sign of trying to help her.

She'd been so sure she would succeed as a spacer, but the hardest aspect turned out to be the same one she'd struggled with as a colonist, and this time she didn't have her sister to guide her.

As though responding to her need for guidance, her stomach rumbled its disgust with the decision not to eat.

She hesitated, wondering if she'd have to face Deluth as soon as she stepped from her room, or worse, face the whole team with him having shared her unfounded accusations.

Trina sat up and swung her legs off the bunk in one fluid motion. She'd done many things in her life, but being unwilling to acknowledge her mistakes did not sit well. She might have wished for more time, but she would not cower in her room to gain it.

TRINA FOUND THE CORRIDOR SURPRISINGLY quiet. The meal area stood silent as well as the gathering room beyond. She must have mulled over all the ways Deluth had been Samuel for longer than she'd thought, determined to convince herself if only to have a target for her rage.

She'd built up courage to face Deluth and all the others. To find they'd already gone to their rooms came as a welcome surprise.

She crossed the empty room to the replicator, but when she went to select a meal, her finger turned instead to request the juice she'd designed. The silence pressed in on her, and she needed something to remind her of home, of her sister, and of not being so alone.

As she lifted the drink free, the replicator's light making the contents glow, Trina tensed. Instincts honed in the shafts on Ceric made her aware she shared the space, though she'd seen no one.

Deluth stepped free of the opening to the gathering area, the stench of sweat rising from him to fill the room. He seemed cautious, and she could well understand why he might be.

She held her ground as he approached, the juice occupying one hand and the other along her side to show she meant him no harm.

"So you've discovered the addition too," he said, the words so unexpected that she jerked.

He snatched her glass up before it could spill, raising it to the light as if that had always been his intention.

"It's weird how the drink wasn't signed. That only happens if it's configured at the replicator, and no one would bother doing it that way with a terminal interface so much stronger, don't you think?"

He seemed to have chosen to ignore her accusations, making her apology even more difficult to produce without returning them to the earlier conflict.

Everything about him made her life more difficult.

She swiped the drink from his hand, annoyed with no good cause when he selected her juice as well.

"I didn't discover it. I put it there."

Trina saw him tense as though rejecting the possibility.

He stared at the replicator, seemingly fascinated with how the liquid poured out to fill his glass. When the chime announced it was done, he lifted his up to the light as he had hers and offered a smile. "It's a well-chosen molecular composition."

She'd been ready for him to deny her claim, to act surprised, or call her a liar. His compliment, especially considering their confrontation earlier today, threw her off.

"I didn't make it for you." The sharp words came from her mouth before she could stop them. "Besides, it's a shadow of the real thing."

He frowned, not at her but at the juice itself. "Compared to other juices I've tasted, it has a wonderful blend of tart and sweet. The real drink must be amazing."

Trina sighed in response, more at her own behavior than his obvious attempt to ease the strain between them. She didn't deserve the effort.

Her experience on a real planet, as limited as it had been, seemed her one advantage here. Nishan told her the Guild needed those who understood planet-based people as much as those born on ships, but there was so much she didn't know.

He hadn't been trying to hold his knowledge over her in mentioning the puzzle of the juice. She shouldn't have held her planet experience over him.

"I'm sorry for earlier." The apology she'd found so overwhelming before came from her as smoothly as her sharp words.

Deluth froze, even his smile becoming stiff just as she'd worried would happen. "So you don't think I tried to harm your friend?"

Trina stared into her drink as if it held all the answers. "Fred warned me about false patterns found if you look too hard, but I didn't listen. No, I don't think you did."

"You're a good friend to care enough to try to find an answer. Who is Fred?" His question, and the light tone he used with the statement, offered an escape from their awkward moment along with what could only be acceptance of the apology.

Trina almost sighed again, this time in relief. "She's one of our instructors. A good one."

He waved to a table and put action to gesture as he sank into a seat as though exhausted. "I haven't had a class with her."

"You wouldn't. She teaches those of us who have had less exposure to technology. You seem to know all about it."

A startled laugh came from him, but he shook his head. "Hardly. It might seem that way to someone raised with tech as a taboo, but you'd be surprised how much of the specifics are being taught in our classes as well. We're working on fine-tuning the environment and disaster response. Not exactly what the average ship-bred kid learns from the start."

"Most colony-bred have technology."

Had the light been brighter, she would have been sure about the flush she thought she saw coloring his neck.

"I was curious. I read up on your planet when I learned where you were from." He paused. "After all, you're part of the team, and we haven't had much chance to talk."

Though Azizi would have dismissed the last as an excuse, Trina could see how it made sense. Hadn't she considered his ignorance a failing only a short while before? Why not use the resources at hand to learn about her?

"I've been studying with my friend, Azizi. There are some things I struggle with." Why she felt the need to emphasize her friendship with Azizi, she couldn't have said.

She still felt drawn to Deluth, more so than before considering how well he understood what had made her accuse him.

"Don't let the other candidates' posturing intimidate you. I would guess there is something each of them finds hard as well. Most of us have faced a flashing red screen a time or two."

A laugh startled Trina when they'd been adversaries not so long ago. "I've fought the red myself. We're also studying crisis steps. Fred told us we would soon be rejoining our groups, so it makes sense our studies align."

"Too bad you'll have less time with Azizi." Deluth put a hand over hers on the table in sympathy, but withdrew it before she could react.

Trina shrugged, not having considered that when compared to their worries about finding a place in teams already settled into habits.

"How could you use a terminal?"

Her question came out of nowhere, a desperate attempt to turn the conversation, but he seemed to follow her train of thought with ease.

"Most port their code and work on it at any terminal. When we're assigned, we'll have designated storage, but here, the systems are isolated so a candidate error won't harm more than a small area."

She made a noncommittal sound and let the silence fall as she finished her drink rather than admitting his answer had failed to reveal anything. Memorizing his wording, she decided to ask Fred about it at their next class.

When no more liquid fell on her tongue, she rose to put her glass away, ignoring the need for a more substantial meal a second time. "It's late and there's much to learn tomorrow," she said by way of a goodbye.

He plucked at his shirt and laughed. "I think a visit to the cleanser first for me, but you're right. Time to head to our rooms."

She didn't wait for him, her mind spinning both with a deeper understanding of his character and the teasing bit of information he'd shared, one that hinted at how a change could have been made to the shower preferences after all.

CHAPTER 18

Deluth stared after her as he downed the last of his juice. He'd have given anything to prolong the conversation despite the importance of sleep.

The lingering tartness on his tongue returned him to the moment she'd claimed the juice as her own creation. Here he'd been challenging Redel for his assumptions, but he'd been just as quick to think she benefited from the work of others as he did. He hadn't considered whether she'd created the juice herself.

It never crossed his mind that she could have been part of the remedial group and yet progress to programming a foodstuff, and not a simple one at that. She, more than any other because of what he'd learned about Ceric, seemed least likely to have attained any level of tech mastery. Yet the drink she created had complex, layered flavors he could easily imagine came from something real.

His lips curled upward as he rose to deposit the glass.

She'd made assumptions too from her tone as she stated the failure in her juice. Unlike many ship-bred, he had been planet-side once when he was still young enough to bunk with his parents.

He could remember the feeling of standing under a wide-open sky with nothing between him and the stars. His teeth winced at the memory of dust gritting between them, and the berries he'd tasted there put all manufactured food to shame.

His mother had offered words with the berries that had stuck in his head all these years though he doubted he'd understood them fully then.

She'd said how everyone had been planet-bound in the beginning. Humanity had not sprung to life in the space between stars. He should never become so tied to a ship as to forget the true roots of their kind.

The gritty feeling rose again as it always did, the wind blowing dirt in his face and over the berries clutched in one hand as she stood up.

He'd demanded they return to the ship, his delight destroyed by the reality of uncontrolled climate, but now he wondered what it would be like to walk on a planet again when he was mature enough to understand the whole of what he saw.

The cleanser door closed him in, and he stripped to stand beneath the sonic waves. He barely felt their pressure, unlike the pounding of the water-based shower the previous day.

He'd flinched when the falling water hit his skin then, but he'd adjusted quickly.

Would he be as quick to accept the sky now as he had as a child?

In one of the lessons on colonies, Plank mentioned how not all spacers could survive a planet-based assignment. In many, the sky he'd loved as a child triggered uncontrolled terror and the fear of drifting off into space or burning up in the radiation.

He hoped he wouldn't be one of that group, and his younger self surely hadn't had any difficulty, but the specter hung over him.

A vision of Trina showing him her own homeland so he could better understand where she sprang from crossed his mind. He laughed aloud, stepping into the empty corridor on his way to his room.

They might have managed one civil conversation, but they were a far distance from planning a trip to her home world or his home ship for that matter. He'd be lucky to convince her to join him for a break day gathering, and then only after he'd made it clear to Sharna he desired a friendship but nothing more.

Still, the way she'd confirmed Azizi's status as a friend, and only that, seemed to indicate some hope. Enough of one to build pleasant dreams on at least.

CHAPTER 19

Trina found the next day's lessons much easier to understand, especially with her focus on them rather than being distracted by trying to uncover who had attempted to humiliate Azizi. Unable to trust her judgment or patterns, she'd decided to follow Fred's counsel at last and leave the attack unexplained.

"Finish off your exercises before tomorrow. We're moving on to a new section, and you'll need to understand what we've covered," Fred announced, bringing the final class of the day to a close.

Trina glanced at the terminal in front of her. She'd struggled a bit at first because of her inattention yesterday, but unlike the crisis management they'd been working on before, once again the class had turned to programs. Just as Fred had mentioned in a previous class, each of them had a strength. That was where they'd find the work turned easy.

She expected most of the class to stay after, but everyone filed out the door except her and Azizi. When Fred went to pass her, Trina caught her sleeve.

A wary look crossed the instructor's face, making Trina suspect her obsession had not been as well hidden as she'd supposed.

"Yes?"

"The others. They'll work on their exercises in their rooms?"

Fred shrugged, clearly relieved at what she must see as a simple question. "Of course. Those who haven't finished already. Didn't I see a success on the last one from you?"

Trina waved off the question, determined to get what information she could without revealing just how poorly prepared she'd been. Other candidates spoke of their sponsors who had provided the resources to get them to the training. She'd had sponsors too, but all they'd managed was to get her into the test.

Here, she felt much like a shafter once again, outside of the state everyone else saw as normal. If not for her father's efforts, she wouldn't even have grown up with water.

Her lips curved at the thought, realizing it would have made her more like the spacers than to live as a polit, though in her case she would have had no substitute, especially not the sonic cleansers used here.

"Is that all you wanted to know? If you want to redo any of the exercises, just put them on your program stick. Every one of the terminals available to candidates supports the training program. You don't have to stay here to study. I'd assumed you did so by choice."

She sent a significant look to Azizi before glancing toward Trina.

Trina flushed, catching the implication that she and Azizi were tied, but did nothing to dismiss it. "Yes, that's all I needed."

"Good. I have some plans this evening, so I'll leave you to it."

Clearly eager to be gone, Fred gave a quick wave and headed out the door, leaving Trina to chew on the implication that she was expected to have one of these devices. She'd learned about porting just today in an earlier class. The discussion covered when a program had been built on one ship and transferred, or ported, to another. Now she had a name for the device enabling the action.

A program stick.

"What was that about?" Azizi asked as Trina settled into her seat.

The screen showed she'd reached the end of the day's exercises, but it would do her good to review those from yesterday. She hadn't realized she had that ability.

Still staring at her terminal, she asked, "Do you have a program stick?"

He laughed. "I'm stuck on one if that's what you're hinting. I could use your perspective."

She rose to lean over his shoulder, grateful to return the assistance he'd given her with the crisis management as she pointed out where he'd chosen a command with secondary results that hindered him.

"I mean the porting device," she said once his screen flashed a welcome green light. "To carry your work from isolated systems."

Confusion swept his features then cleared. "You mean like sending to another ship? Is that what it's called? And why would I have one? We'll have access once we're spacers, I'd think."

"Some of the other candidates have them. Fred thought I did as well, so it's not just the ship-bred."

Azizi tapped one finger on the desk, sending random pulses across his screen as the terminal tried to interpret his intentions. "I've never heard of such a thing, but I suppose it could be available to some. My people recognized my strengths as organizational. Had I been focused on programming like you are, they'd most likely have made sure I had one. As it is, I don't think we'll be needing to transfer information to another ship any time soon. Why are you worried about it?"

Trina laughed and waved at the empty room. "All this time I've thought I was the weakest of even the colony-bred. You stayed out of kindness, but everyone else must have finished their work with the end of class."

A flush deepened his dark skin. "I've thought the same—about me, not you. I stayed to help those first few days, but you've helped me often enough once you found your bearings. At home, I was exceptional. Here, I'm just one of many, and not even close to the best."

She put a hand on his shoulder and squeezed once. "Is it so important to be the best?"

"Not here, maybe, but on my home world, if you want more than what you're born to, yes." He waved his fingers in the air to dismiss her sympathy. "You're given everything you need. No one goes hungry or shivers in the cold. But if you want more, you have to show you have something to offer in return, something worth what others must give up so you can have it."

"But you're here. You'll be in the Spacer Guild. How does that help them?"

Azizi shook his head. "Sometimes I forget how different we are. You must have been isolated from the politics of your world to think so."

She stilled, knowing just how isolated she had not been, but at the same time, she hadn't known enough to understand what Samuel would do.

"The simplest answer is they benefit from having one of their own in the Guild to speak for them and explain should there be a conflict. The more complicated one is the hope I'll be able to negotiate better terms and ensure their access once I'm a full spacer."

Trina didn't know what to say. She'd never been responsible for more than her sister and mother, not even when Samuel used her to further his political agenda. She couldn't grasp being responsible for a whole planet.

Azizi laughed as he rose to stand next to her. "Don't look so shocked. It's not that bad. They don't expect more from me than a portion of my earnings. The rest is only hopes. And speaking of hopes, I wouldn't mind answering those of my stomach right about now."

Trina walked with him to the replicator, but her mind had returned to the original point. She'd never guessed Azizi shared her concerns. "They don't leave because they're done," she said as they waited for their meals to disgorge.

"How would you know?"

She shrugged. "I wouldn't, not for all of them, but Fred as much as stated most would be working on their terminals. I tried, but all my notes were here. That's why they have a program stick. Not to port between ships but between the different terminals available to all of us."

As she queued up the juice that still didn't match what she'd managed in her quarters, Trina explained everything to Azizi, from her confrontation with Deluth to him revealing the existence of the sticks.

"And so I learned there's an important tool missing, for both me and you from the sound of it."

He gave her a sharp look. "And would you prefer it that way? Being able to take your exercises to your room instead of staying here?"

At first she didn't pick up on the cause for the tension that sprang between them, but then she reviewed his words in her mind.

"No, Azizi, no. I wouldn't give up our time together, the friendship that has grown out of it, for the most sophisticated tool in the world."

He relaxed then, giving her a lopsided smile.

"I just want the ability to work anywhere." She paused to take a sip and grimaced. "To move my juice program since my memory isn't strong enough to do it justice."

Azizi caught her hand. "Your company is worth the sacrifice, as I would hope is mine."

"**D**ELUTH."

He turned at the sound of his name. He'd been in a good mood since talking to Trina for the first time last night. Coupled with a quick training scenario at lunch break that had surprised him, nothing could bother him today, not even Redel.

"I'm disappointed in you," his friend said, continuing now that he had Deluth's attention.

He shrugged. "Not sure how you know about the loss, but don't worry, it won't go on the team's record. I'm not tracking them." He did the extra training to push himself, not to puff up his ego.

Redel caught his arm and pulled him through to the meal area. He chose a table off to one side, away from the three other candidates currently finishing their dinners.

Deluth didn't protest. His stomach had told him to seek food already. It had been a long day of classes on top of a morning training, the reason he'd set up only a quick scenario when they'd been released for lunch.

"I'll be right back. I need something to eat while we catch up. I'm nutrition poor."

Redel looked like he wanted to protest for a moment before waving him away.

Deluth took his time choosing a meal, adding Trina's juice to the selection with a smile that soon faded.

He did the extra training as much to avoid any more clashes with Redel than because he felt it necessary. Ever since his friend had chewed him out for meeting with the team without Redel present, Deluth had been careful only to offer encouragement on an individual basis. Though Redel didn't seem to care, Deluth saw no reason to destroy their friendship, and with it any chance he had of restoring the Redel he'd grown up with.

He missed that boy, but he refused to become a mindless follower like the others seemed to have done. Any one of them would do whatever Redel asked, no matter the consequences, and suffer his disapproval silently when the task went sour.

Every minute they spent together lately involved either Redel pushing him to support some decision that might or might not be good, or Deluth choosing to hold his ground on a principle Redel despised.

Whatever Redel had noticed this time, with such an opening, Deluth doubted it would be a friendly chat.

He'd have preferred to spend his meal reliving the previous night than this.

"I thought you liked Sharna," Redel started as soon as Deluth returned.

Deluth stared at Redel in silence. He still hadn't managed time alone with Sharna to clarify things. Until he did, he had no intention of discussing the muddle with anyone else.

Redel didn't look away, waiting Deluth out in a mockery of staring challenges they'd played when much younger.

Deluth didn't have the patience for it any longer. "What's between me and Sharna is our business, not yours or anyone else's."

Redel leaned across the table and said in a low voice, "Is that why you were having a cozy chat with the colony-bred failure after everyone else had gone to bed? Peter mentioned seeing you two last night."

Deluth could have groaned. He hoped Sharna didn't hear Peter and jump to the same conclusion, the right conclusion maybe someday, but not until he'd been straight with her.

Aloud, he said only, "I came in late to find her eating, well drinking. We talked for a bit. Is that a crime? She's a member of our team as much as Sharna, Peter, or any of the others. It'll do no good for her to be uncomfortable and a total stranger when the classes rejoin. That's coming soon enough."

"I suppose she told you that." Redel scowled at him. "Of course she would. The longer it takes her to gain basic competency, the more obvious it is how little she belongs on our team or any other." His hands came down on the table with a loud thwack, startling the other candidates from the rattle of their dishes.

Deluth didn't move. He'd seen this tactic too many times to be stirred by it.

"She didn't have to. They're studying much of the same information we are, just with some differences. If they weren't trying to converge the two classes, why bother?"

Redel slumped in his chair. "You think I don't know what's really going on here? You think I'm blind? She caught your attention the very first day, and you're not the type to let something go. Sharna is beautiful, smart, and talented. She's an asset to the team. Can't you see how much stronger we'd be with her fully connected? Can you say the same for your broken ship limping into port on antique engines? Rads, bunkmate. You are not that stupid. We need to present a united front here if we're to have first choice of the assignments. We have to be better than any other."

Deluth leaned back as well, though his posture had everything to do with relaxation, not strain. "Now I understand what you're up to. The Guild isn't like that. It's not some hierarchy where only the top rung get a spot like on our ship. It's an escape from that. There are positions enough for all of us and more generated every time a new colony comes up. You don't have to be the best. You just have to demonstrate your own talents, not crush everyone else."

Hope rose that they could end this constant bickering and return to the way things were.

"Are you that stupid?"

Redel's flat question crushed what little optimism Deluth had scraped together.

"There are new stations and new colonies founded practically every day as humanity casts its seeds among the stars, sure, but you think they are created equal? You think a position at a station in the middle of nowhere supporting one tiny colony on a barren rock is the same opportunity as one at a central hub? Do you think doing shuttle runs between planets of a single solar system is the same as folding space itself? It's a hierarchy all right. One just like our ship only bigger. I intend to end up on the top of our piece of the triangle. I'd hoped to have you with me."

Deluth pushed to his feet, grabbing his half-eaten meal as he went. "You seemed so different when we talked about getting out of there, of leaving the bunkhouse for the Spacer Guild, and now all you want is to carry that life with you. You want the top of our little piece? You're welcome to it." He didn't feel like making excuses for Redel any longer. If his friend couldn't see how his ambitions created the very dissension that would undermine any team, any crew, and any ship he was on, Deluth had no way of opening his eyes.

They'd grown up in that environment, one that tore children from their parents to avoid familial power bases and did nothing to halt the sometimes brutal pranks between bunkhouses. Deluth wanted to escape it. Redel seemed set on recreating the same wherever he went.

A lifetime of training in efficiency made Deluth drop to sit at another table, his plate hitting the surface a second later. Any interest in food had vanished, but he would not let it go to waste.

He turned away but could still feel Redel's pointed stare long after his friend—though they were hardly that any longer—had scraped back the chair and marched from the room. Even gulping down the complicated mix of berries Trina had created failed to settle his stomach or ease the twist of sadness at losing Redel's friendship once and for all.

CHAPTER 20

Trina went to the observation dome after they'd eaten and stared down at the planet. It looked so different from how she imagined Ceric to be, but she'd never seen it this way.

Still, what circled below felt more familiar to her than any station.

Down there, it wouldn't matter where she came from, or whether she had special tech tools. She'd survive where most ship-bred wouldn't know how to start.

It felt as if everything weighed against her here. And now against Azizi as well.

Fred had assumed she had one of these program sticks. That meant she wasn't denied one. It came down to resources.

Whether she traded stolen goods to Fence to pay for her mother's medicine or traded her skills for a pass to the stars, she'd always lived in that bargain. Only a fool would think things so different in the Spacer Guild. It might not be the same struggle, but still there were those who rode in the wagon, and those who pushed and pulled it.

She was tired of bending her back to someone else's labor.

Trina returned to her quarters frustrated and angry, but resigned for all of that. She could not change what she now knew any more than she could change what she had available to her.

Maybe Azizi had been right and once they succeeded, the Guild would offer every opportunity and provide what they required. Or maybe he saw the whole galaxy through the filter of his home much as she saw it through Ceric.

It didn't matter which proved right in the end.

If Nishan knew what she'd been talking about, the Guild had some purpose for Trina. Samuel, even Fence, had found a purpose in her. Why should the Guild be any different?

She'd been a space rat before. She'd hoped to move beyond that life, but at least she knew she could survive it. She didn't need any fancy tools or sponsors who made sure she wouldn't be left behind. Even when she'd had Katie and Mother, she'd been the one to ensure they had coin.

Again the gather space stood dark and empty when she arrived.

Trina didn't know how long she'd spent watching the line of light move across the planet's surface, but it seemed all others had gone to sleep.

"Good," she growled too low for any to hear even if there had been someone there. Her shafter instincts were driving her now, and she didn't want to chance what she'd do to anyone who tried to stand in her way.

She strode through the room and into the meal area, her steps silent despite her anger.

A bright light from one corner drew her attention before she saw the shadow standing next to it.

She dropped into her thief stance, aware though the other person was not.

Her eyes slowly adjusted and she made out Sharna, the candidate Deluth spent time with, but that mattered less than what the girl was doing with her hands.

Trina crept closer, fingers spread out to brush anything in her way before it could make a noise and reveal her presence.

It came too easily, just as it had when Samuel called on her the second time. She kept pretending she could be something else, but everyone around her knew better.

Sharna laughed as she pushed a button on the replicator. "That'll do it," she whispered.

The room filled with a bitter scent.

Trina thoughts ran first to poison, but both Sharna's presence and the safeguards protected against that, a belief strengthened when the other candidate lifted the glass and drained its bitter contents in one, deep gulp, after which she bent double in a coughing fit.

Before Trina could figure out how to make it look as if she'd just arrived, Sharna straightened with a grin. She poked some more on the screen, then jerked a small metal stick from the wall of the replicator. Stopping only to toss the drink container into the dish keeper, she wandered toward the rooms.

Trina waited for any sign of Sharna's return, waited until her calves ached from the tension, but the other candidate had finished her purpose and gone to bed, leaving Trina to learn from what she left behind.

A close investigation of where Sharna had placed the object showed a tiny slot in the front of the machine that Trina had never noticed. She'd never seen one before, but she suspected exactly what the object had been, a suspicion confirmed when she called up the menu and saw a new drink nestled next to the juice she had made.

There was a big difference between the two drinks, though. Where a blank space showed after Trina's juice, the other had Sharna written next to it, the tag Deluth had been expecting.

This candidate had everything handed to her while Trina still fought to survive without even knowing the rules. Sharna had access Trina never would, she had beauty to draw every eye, and she probably never questioned why Deluth would want to spend time with her.

Sharna was everything Trina was not.

Once again, frustration welled up in her, but this time it had a focus, and a target. If Sharna had everything, she could serve to lose some of it just as the polits had on Ceric.

The sound of a door opening made Trina creep to the final hallway in time to see Sharna open the cleanser. This late, she doubted the other candidate would stay for long. If Trina wanted to act, it had to be now.

The maintenance panel lay next to the keyed one, allowing repair crews special access. Trina would have liked to have the tool she'd used on the colony ship, but she'd spent the past two days, at least when she was paying attention, learning maintenance routines. The programming Azizi had bemoaned would serve her well.

She tried one of the override scripts she remembered, and changed an aspect each time because they would be unlikely to teach the current keys. But Trina had noticed a pattern between the scripts they'd studied. One aspect changed by an increment.

Her patience had grown thin by the time a quiet hiss of the lock releasing proved her instincts correct.

With a wary glance at the cleanser, she nudged the door open manually and stepped into the dark chamber.

She cursed, remembering too late that lights were tuned to the resident. She'd been lucky they hadn't been set to warn of intruders by shining too bright as she'd overheard some of the team discussing one morning. Instead, the room did not acknowledge her presence at all.

Seconds ticked by as she waited for her eyes to adjust to this new lighting, scanning from one side to the next for any clue as to where Sharna might have hid the program stick. Her muscles felt the strain of anticipation as she listened for warning of the cleanser door release.

A glimpse of light against the dark of the study area caught her attention.

She'd have to walk to the far end of the room. Though small, she would not be able to leave fast enough to mask her intrusion should Sharna return soon.

The gleam called to her, promising everything she needed to make her an equal to those bred on a ship.

She took one step then another, half hoping the shine would be a mirror or something simple. But once she reached the spot, what lay there could only have been a program stick.

Before she could think twice, her fingers reached out and plucked it off the surface, touching nothing but the object. She dropped it into a pocket.

The tool had been lying there out in the open, just like when she'd found real Earth emeralds in a polit house. Then as now, the fools did not deserve their treasures. If they'd taken proper care, she would have never succeeded.

Where her steps before had been slow and cautious, now she needed nothing more than to escape.

Halfway across the room, Trina heard the sound of the cleanser door. Her foot landed at an awkward angle but she swallowed her curse, pushing forward at a desperate pace. No matter what, she needed to get out of Sharna's room. If they met in the corridor, Sharna would have no reason to suspect.

In here, Trina would be caught.

A jolt of conscience and anger at her own stupidity raced through Trina as she reached the door. She'd let frustration and spite risk everything she'd fought for.

Only Sharna's door stood between her and discovery. She had no way of knowing if the other candidate had left the cleanser, or if she looked this way. Trina only knew delaying too long would make failure certain.

She slid the door open and stepped through, pulling it closed before turning. She half expected to see Sharna glaring at her, but the corridor stood empty.

Just then, the candidate stepped free of the cleanser chamber and wound her way down the hallway apparently oblivious to anything beyond her own unsteady progress.

Trina sucked in a quiet breath and backed up first one step and then another. When her shoe met the base of the doorframe leading to the meal area, she stopped. She could pretend to have arrived from this point.

She watched Sharna continue her odd path all the way to her door. The other candidate slapped a palm on the sensor with more force than necessary and seemed to throw herself within when the door opened.

Trina held still, waiting for the cry when the other candidate found her program stick missing, but none came.

A silence as deep as the darkness filled the hallway as if the whole team, the whole station, had gone to sleep while she stood frozen. After a long moment, Trina crossed to her room and entered it, dropping to the bed as she waited for the fierce pounding of her heart to settle.

Her head rang with chastising as though Katie were here railing at her as her sister had on Ceric. Katie always said they could figure out another way. Katie had thought thieving was in Trina's blood, that she lived for the excitement of it. She'd protested the charge then.

Trina pulled out the device, staring at it in the dim lighting she'd programmed into her room preferences to test her learning. The program stick seemed a little thing to carry such weight, and yet it did.

It held the burden of her sister's worries about thieving, the risk of being cast off the station, and more, the trouble she could have caused for Sharna no matter how foolish Trina had thought her on seeing the tool lying there unprotected. It had been behind a door that should have stayed locked against any harmful intent.

CHAPTER 21

Redel met Deluth at the door to the meal area a second time and pulled him over to a table with a broad grin. He acted as if their argument just last night hadn't happened. Or it hadn't meant as much to Redel.

Deluth started to argue when he figured out where Redel was headed.

Sharna already sat at the table, and she wasn't looking herself.

"She needs some cheering up," Redel said in an overly loud whisper. "And you're just the person to offer it."

Deluth swallowed his protest at having Redel command him and focused on the other candidate. He'd been worried she'd heard the same whisper about Trina and came to the same conclusion. This offered no better a time than any of the previous ones to have the conversation he'd been planning between the many interested listeners and Sharna's mood, but he couldn't let her suffer either.

He slid into the seat next to hers without stopping to get something to eat. "Morning."

She raised her head slowly to stare at him, her usually bright eyes shadowed.

Deluth drew in a deep breath. He told himself not to be a coward and harm her in the process.

Sharna twisted as though she'd been about to leave only to slump into the chair.

"Look," he said, delaying no longer. "I don't know what you've heard from Peter, but it wasn't arranged. We just happened to be eating at the same time."

That caught Sharna's attention. She swiveled to look directly at him, her brow pinched in confusion.

"About talking with Trina," Deluth clarified when she showed no sign of comprehension.

Sharna's frown deepened. "Why should I care who you talk to?"

"You shouldn't," he said at once. "I mean, it's not important. I wouldn't do anything about it with our situation unclear."

She stared at him in silence for what felt like forever.

He had no experience with this beyond watching some of the couples form and collapse in the bunkhouse on his home ship. He couldn't guess at her reaction when he didn't know whether she'd cry, attack him, or plan vengeance in the night hours. Nervous, he looked back for a bit, then dropped his gaze to the table.

Out of the corner of one eye, he saw her blink. Then she let out a quiet chuckle that grew into a full laugh.

"You think we're bound together?" she asked between gasping breaths. "You and I?"

She sobered, but the way her mouth kept twitching made her sympathetic frown less honest. "I'm sorry, Deluth. I never thought you would consider yourself qualified."

He straightened to glare at her.

Here he'd spent all this time worrying about hurting her, rejecting her when he'd never tried to make a connection in the first place, and she'd been looking down on him.

Sharna met his gaze and blushed. "I mean, you've got a lot to show for yourself, and I doubt you'll have any trouble finding... It's just...well...I thought you'd know you're not up to my standards. I thought we were just friends."

Any damaged pride he'd felt vanished at her last words.

They wanted the same thing. She'd never had any expectation of more, but she'd enjoyed his company all the same.

"That's what I wanted as well," Deluth said after a pause. "But I worried you'd think there was more. I didn't want to chance hurting you, and after you showed me off to your shipmates..."

Sharna nodded. "You've got a good heart, Deluth. It's one of the reasons I enjoy spending time with you. But it can never be more than that. I didn't think how little you understood or I would have been clearer. My people measure not just by each person's quality but by that of those they gather round. Your friendship reflects well on me just as mine should on you. But it's not any more than that."

Deluth offered a relieved smile even as he wondered at a ship culture so rigid that every companion had to be measured against an almost impossible standard before a relationship could develop. "I'm glad to hear that. I had hoped we could find our way to a friendship, but with Redel's matchmaking and all, it seemed risky."

She laughed and patted him on the hand. "I chose you to be in my presence. The choice was mine, not any other. I told you from the start what Redel has and where his weakness lies. He is not capable of driving me any place I did not already want to go."

They shared a significant look, one he felt sure Redel observed and misunderstood, never guessing the connection came not of interest in each other but from disinterest in his schemes.

"Besides," Sharna said, her eyes gleaming as if her earlier slumped posture had been a mirage, "everyone knows your interest is set on the colony girl."

Deluth jerked upright at that. "I never said—"

"You didn't have to. It was obvious from the start when you found her missing. Just remember our discussion about the colony sort, especially those without the basic skills required. They were let into training for some reason."

Deluth raised his shoulders in a shrug. "I've talked to her only a few times, most just an exchanged greeting. Whether there will ever be any reason to worry about what strangeness allowed her in is still unclear."

"If you think so."

As though the morning switched to night, the animation drained from her face. It reminded Deluth of how he'd come upon her in the first place. "If it wasn't what Peter saw, what is wrong?"

She waved a hand vaguely, not bothering to look up. "There's nothing wrong."

"I thought we were friends," he said, rather than pressing directly.

Sharna twisted her head to stare at him.

"Friends help each other. If you can't tell me, then you should find a friend you can."

He went as if to rise, not really planning to abandon her in this state, but if she didn't agree to speak, he could do nothing.

She mumbled something, but he couldn't hear her.

"What did you say?" he asked as he sank into his chair once again.

"I lost my program stick. I had it last night when I went to bed. Now I can't find it anywhere. I'm sure where I put it, but when I went to look, it just wasn't there. If I report it lost, they'll get me a new one, but my rank will drop, and my whole family's with it. They'll lose everything they've fought for their whole lives, and it'll be generations before we build up again even if I end up with a perfect career."

Deluth couldn't imagine a world where a simple mistake could have so much impact, but then he never lived in a place where how a person looked determined their value either. "I can help you search. It has to be around here somewhere. Where'd you see it last?"

Sharna dropped her head into both hands. "I think it was in my room, but I did something foolish to celebrate our win against the Mechanics. One of my shipmates led the team."

"I noticed," Deluth murmured, the visual perfection hard to miss and unlikely to have another source even without the stiff nod he saw them exchange.

"And this is the result," she continued as though he'd said nothing. "I could have sent it down the dish recycler, and I wouldn't know."

Deluth stroked her hand until she looked up at him. "I'd guess the system is programmed to recognize when something inappropriate is added. After all, it can't be the first time such a thing happened. You probably just dropped it. Someone will bring it back soon enough. You'll see. It's not like anyone would take it."

She managed a weak smile. "You're right. No one else would need one, and they have to know any work would be marked with my name."

With her worries relieved, they went to get something to eat.

Sharna now had an appetite, but her last sentence stuck in Deluth's head, distracting him. He knew of one person who didn't have a program stick, and he doubted she'd know about the signing either despite him mentioning it.

He pushed the suspicion aside. She wouldn't be so foolish. She only needed to ask for one, so why steal?

TRINA WOKE LATE WITH A sick feeling in the pit of her stomach. She listened to the noises outside her room but neither rose nor ventured out where anyone could see her.

Only when she could hear nothing more did she slip from her room and into the cleanser. Her body stank with the pungent burn of sweat—fear sweat, not that earned by honest labor.

She laughed at the thought as she stripped and set the sonic settings to as deep a cleaning as they would allow.

When had she ever had the chance to do honest labor? Her whole life had pushed her on a path to taking what she needed—wanted—from others with no thought to their loss. Why should now be any different?

Denying her even the peace of habit, her mind thrust forward discussions with Nishan about how every step marked a choice. They'd begun the same way, but the spacer took the lucky chance that brought her to the Guild's attention and used it to become a valuable member.

Trina remembered working with Katie in those few short months when she'd thought herself a colonist. That work had been honest as she labored side by side with others to make the new world they would colonize into a wonderful place.

The cleanser ended its cycle with a soft chime. Her skin no longer wore the results of her nighttime thievery, but that fact neither settled her stomach nor made the truth of it undone.

And she had needed the tool. Still needed it.

Sharna would most likely go to her sponsor and request another. She had that luxury just as the polits had theirs. No polit had to steal to pay for critical medication. Did it then stand to reason those who couldn't afford it deserved to die?

The rationalization got Trina through dressing. She skipped the meal, knowing she chanced being late to class already, but though her body was present, her mind stayed focused on the small piece of metal she'd thrust into another pocket this morning. She needed to keep it with her, a foolish behavior in a thief, but one she hadn't had the time to fight.

Even now, guilt kept all her thoughts focused on the tool. She had no idea of what had been taught this day.

"Are you planning to stay after?" Azizi's voice broke through her obsession.

She glanced up to see the classroom empty and the teacher gone.

"I could use your help on a couple of things she covered. Your strength, not mine."

She stared at him while her mind raced through everything she'd heard in the hopes of finding the lessons buried there. She remembered nothing well enough to help herself, much less Azizi.

"I have to go."

He stared at her, eyes wide at first then narrowing. "I thought you gave up trying to find out who played games with the showers."

"I did." Trina could have cursed as the best excuse vanished with her quick answer. "I just need to go."

She had no better explanation, not with all she'd hidden from him.

She couldn't be this person, not again. She was not a space rat. She planned to be a spacer. If she wanted to walk that path, she had no choice but to return the program stick unused, unharmed, and without being caught.

Azizi still didn't look satisfied—and why should he?—but he did not control her any more than Redel could.

"I'll be here studying if you change your mind," he said, suiting action to words as he bent to his terminal.

Guilt of a different sort kept her there for a second longer, but even if she stayed, she had nothing to offer him. At least from Azizi's comment, she had a chance of figuring it all out on her own. She'd be back to focus on the exercises, but she had to finish this first.

CHAPTER 22

Trina spent the trip to the Pilot quarters planning just how she'd manage to get into Sharna's room a second time with no one the wiser. She'd place the program stick half under the bunk as though it had fallen and bounced.

She'd accomplished more difficult tasks of a similar nature for Samuel, but never before had she been working to repair a wrong, as much as she'd believed she had been.

The thought froze her. Progress in the air stream slowed to a crawl before she noticed her posture resisted the flow.

Her mother, in the days before disease stripped her of speech, had told Trina often enough a wrong could not be repaired by another wrong. She'd meant it to stop Trina from attempting to harm those who'd poisoned her mother, but it lingered in Trina's thoughts now.

She'd violated Sharna's room and taken her property. How much different would it be to commit the same act a second time to return the program stick?

Somehow, she didn't think Sharna would see the distinction if she caught Trina where she shouldn't have been.

The air stream slowed for her to step off at the same time as someone came from one of the other corridors.

Trina checked, the reaction left over from when knowing exactly who was near could save her life.

She stopped so quickly she tripped and had to stumble so she wouldn't fall flat on her face.

Somewhere, fate was laughing at her.

Sharna glanced up at the noise, and Trina almost stumbled a second time.

The other candidate always looked beautiful, a goddess among mortals. But not today.

"Are you all right?"

The question burst from her without thinking.

She'd been wrong to ask. She knew exactly what had happened between the previous day and this one.

Sharna stopped dead and straightened out of her slump. She tried for a smile, but Trina could see it went no further than those lips.

Suddenly she understood what her mother had meant. Sneaking in and putting the program stick where it could be found would return Sharna's tool, but it wouldn't change the time in between. It wouldn't change the strain on her face or the weight on her shoulders.

Trina had created that pain, and making the other candidate appear clumsy would not heal it.

Standing as tall as she could, she marched right up to Sharna. "We need to talk. Will you come with me to the dome?"

The other candidate looked down at her, a good head taller, and one eyebrow rose.

Then a flash of animation showed in her features, and she managed a real smile. "Sure. We can talk. Deluth would like that."

Trina didn't understand what Deluth had to do with anything, but she didn't want to have their conversation here where they could be interrupted at any time, and the Pilot quarters would be worse.

They stepped into the air stream together, zipping past all the trainee areas in silence.

When they pulled free, Trina let out a quick sigh as she took in the dome.

Everyone else had gone to eat or study. They had the space to themselves, and she had the chance to convince Sharna to forgive her this one time.

"There's nothing between us," Sharna said. "You have no worry there."

Trina stared at the other candidate. "Why do you think I brought you here?"

"Why else? It's obvious he's interested in you, and he had the same concern that I believed us joined."

A strangled laugh came from Trina's lips before she could stop it as she realized whom Sharna meant. "I have no interest in Deluth," she said with a confidence she didn't feel. "I need to talk to you about something else."

Her words dried up at the curious look from Sharna, and with her silence, the other candidate's face hardened.

"What could we possibly have to talk about other than Deluth? You haven't said a word to me before this. You aren't one of those people who are out to fix everyone are you? You see me at less than my best and you think it's your purpose to make everything and everyone all right?"

Trina turned away, bracing both arms against the window. Her face reflected back at her. She wished, no matter how angry it made Sharna, that she had been interfering.

"It's not that. It's worse."

Sharna stepped closer. "What could be worse? You don't even know me."

Pivoting so she could slide down the wall, Trina made sure she could not run no matter how much she might want to.

Sharna sank to her side, looking as if she'd forgotten her own troubles.

Trina wished she could keep it that way, but what she said next would ensure those troubles rose to the surface and stayed there.

"I have something for you." She pulled the program stick from her pocket and held it out, palm up.

"You found it. Thank you so much." Sharna laughed, snatching the tool from Trina's hand to cup it between hers. "I've been so worried."

Letting her believe such a simple answer fought with the words of Trina's mother, and wisdom won. Whatever the consequences, she had to face them or she had no business trying to become more than the thief she had always been.

Trina turned so she could look the other candidate in the face. "I didn't find it. I took it. I thought— Well, what I thought doesn't matter. I didn't have one, and you did."

Sharna stared at her, a stunned look widening her eyes. Her lips formed a circle, and she didn't move.

Trina laid a hand on Sharna's knee. "You are within your rights to report me. I broke into your room and took it. I ask only that you consider I came to you first."

Her hands tightened around the tool, but Sharna didn't pull away. "You have no idea the loss of face if I'd had to request a new one. The first is given to all candidates, but if we damage or lose it, our sponsors pay the price. My ship doesn't look favorably on the family of those who incur unnecessary costs."

Trina sighed. "So I was the cause of your state as I thought."

The other candidate glanced up from where she'd been staring at the program stick. "I just don't understand. Why take it? Did you hate me so much? You couldn't have used it anyway. It's keyed to my name. The minute you tried to access anything, they'd have known."

Trina sprang up, not to run but to pace, unable to contain her energy. "I didn't hate you. I hated what you are. You didn't require extra training. You have sponsors who provide things like the program stick. I'm nothing but a thief who somehow made her way here where I don't belong."

Her progress jerked to a halt when Sharna caught her leg and tugged her down.

"You think I have everything? You think any of us do? Every day we struggle in our classes, but we can't admit it. I can't admit it in case word gets back to my ship and my family suffers. I have to be perfect, act perfect, look perfect. More than just my career weighs on each action, but no one here understands, not really."

They stared at each other across the gulf that separated their two lives, and Trina realized it wasn't so different after all.

"So you won't report me?"

The question came out more as a surprised whisper than a confident statement, but Sharna heard well enough to shake her head.

"If I did that, I'd be hypocritical. I know what the pressure can drive us to. I know how hard it is to leave the past behind, especially when it presses against us. Me in the form of the others from my ship who will report any failures. You because of your lack of training in things most of us think of as automatic. I've done things I regret, driven by that pressure when I should have been able to control myself."

Relieved she'd survived this failure, Trina laughed. "I can't imagine you doing anything close to what I did."

Sharna looked away, her fingers opening and closing against the rough fiber of the floor. "I destroyed that boy's hair. Your friend. I destroyed it because it made him prettier than I was, and because if he's drawn into the circle of some other from my ship, they'll be measured greater than I am."

Trina stared once again, shocked and starting to get angry. "You did that to Azizi?"

The other candidate gave a stiff nod. "So you see, I can't report you without you revealing what I did."

That froze Trina for a heartbeat, her anger fizzling. "I wouldn't have known if you hadn't told me."

Sharna stood this time. "I would have known. I would have stood judgment over you, a judgment I wouldn't have survived."

"And you have to be perfect." Suddenly both the reason Sharna would have acted and why she now confessed seemed clear. "More than just the stick was eating at you."

A grin spread across the other candidate's face. "Yes. And I had no one to confess to. I'm not as brave as you are or I would have confessed to the pretty boy."

"His name is Azizi, as you must know, and he has already forgotten. One of the instructors fixed his hair the same day, and he thought that was the end of it. Ask him yourself."

She left out how she had continued to search for a culprit. She'd never considered a driving purpose beyond malice, but Sharna had been right. She'd seen all those in the normal classes as privileged and without constraints.

She knew differently now.

"I can't." Sharna shook her head hard enough for her hair to keep swaying even once she stopped. "I can't chance it."

Remembering what Sharna had said, Trina dropped in front of the other candidate, catching one of her hands. "You can. When you're ready. I tell him first, to prepare him, so when you're ready to confess, he's ready to listen." Before Sharna could protest, she added, "After all, then you can claim him as part of your circle."

Sharna gave her a stunned look for only a second before she laughed. "You should have been born on my ship, Trina. You have the mind for it. Some days I'm not sure I do. It'll be interesting once you are added in with the rest of us. Very interesting if all those who needed extra training are as astute as you are."

"Don't forget how we came to be here at the dome in the first place. I doubt any would want to follow my path."

Sharna stood and tugged Trina after her. "We read something in class the other day when studying one of the colonies. It stuck in my head because I didn't quite understand it, but now I think I do at least a little. 'Though the path be varied, we all end up in the same place.'"

She laughed. "Your path might be very different than the one I took, but we're both candidates and soon to win our way into the Spacer Guild. It's about time we starting living that reality."

Trina suspected the phrase had a very different meaning. In the shafts, it would have stood in for a thousand sayings that all meant the same thing. *In the end, we all die.*

She liked Sharna's take better.

Trina would have thought it impossible when she'd stepped out of the air stream to see Sharna, but now they walked together with smiles on their faces.

Just before they crossed into the flow of air, Sharna caught her arm.

"There's one thing you had wrong, Trina, and I don't think you heard me when I said it. My ship didn't give me the program stick. The Guild did. Every candidate can request one. You or your sponsors bear the cost only if you lose or damage the first. They covered that in orientation."

The idea that she could have one of her very own without resorting to theft and deceit stunned Trina, but not for long. They'd been separated before the orientation Sharna referred to, and her instructors had not shared this right.

"Thank you. I didn't know that before, but now I will ask for one."

Sharna nodded and stepped into the transport without another word, unaware of how she'd exposed one more way Trina and her classmates had been kept separate from the rest.

DELUTH HAD BEEN KEEPING AN eye out for Sharna ever since he passed her heading back out after class ended. He didn't know what she'd gone to do, but he had a good suspicion.

They'd spent more of the midday break searching than relaxing and getting something to eat, but her program stick had vanished. He would have been with her after class, but he'd stayed to ask the instructor if things like the dish recycler would swallow up a program stick or reject it. He'd half hoped for a positive answer because then he'd have one real possibility that didn't involve Trina.

As he suspected, the device would have refused a program stick.

He took a bite of the meal he'd chosen at random, but stopped to stare at his plate. He'd grown up on flavored paste or cubes. Neither the spices nor the consistency matched anything he'd experienced before.

Poking with his fork revealed chunks of something, or rather many things, each a different color and texture. Some squashed under the pressure of his utensil while others skated across the brightly colored fluid to the other side of his plate. He wished he'd been paying more attention, though he couldn't decide whether he wanted to avoid this meal or try it again when he wasn't so distracted.

Voices pulled his gaze to the opening between the main room and the meal area in time for his vigilance to be rewarded.

Sharna stepped through, scanned the room, and strode right for him.

Where he'd been expecting dejection, her lips curved into a smile and her whole body looked more relaxed than she'd been this morning.

He frowned. He'd thought she'd gone to report the loss and expected her to return devastated, not like this.

"You have chosen well in your colony girl, Deluth."

She broadened her smile but did not stop on her way to the replicator when he'd expected her to sit down.

He watched Sharna carefully, waiting for her to return and explain herself.

Instead, she collected her meal and went to a different table. She joined none other than Trina, a candidate he would have sworn Sharna had no direct contact with before now.

Feeling the intruder, Deluth tried to concentrate on his odd meal, but though he could not hear what they discussed, the frequent laughter proved more of a distraction than his food could counter.

He raised the plate so he could continue putting the strange combination of flavors onto his tongue while watching them and trying to figure out how this all came together.

He'd suspected Trina of the theft, had spent a portion of his wait deciding how to confront her, but the only way Sharna could be this relaxed would be if she'd recovered the stick without drawing down penalties on her own head and those of any relatives.

As proof of his thought, she shoved to her feet and waved what could only be her program stick at Trina. She strode for the replicator, inserted the stick, and concentrated on the screen for much longer than it would take to transfer a new meal combination. When she disengaged the stick and stepped away, Sharna waved Trina over.

The two of them talked and smiled even more as they called up two of Trina's special juice from the color in their glasses. Only then did they stride from the room toward the gathering area.

Deluth sat there, unsure what to do or what to think.

At last, he rose and crossed to the replicator.

He reviewed the custom menu, but he could see nothing new she'd added, her change so slight he would never be able to find it without knowing every option that had been there before.

Disgruntled though he knew he had no right, he went to key up his own glass of the juice. It offered a welcome flavor to tone down the spices of his meal, and one he'd grown accustomed to having at the end of every day. They'd had little chance to get to know one another, but sharing the juice made him feel closer to Trina.

With that thought, he understood his unsettled feeling. Sharna stole from him the chance to spent time with Trina, filling one of the few opportunities when the colony girl had joined them at a reasonable hour. The realization didn't make him any happier as he stared at the menu.

He should be delighted by the sight. Far better Sharna befriend her than have him as Trina's only connection to the team, especially with Redel's disapproval.

Deluth found that answer far more satisfactory and decided he would focus on it rather than his own sense of missed chances. If expanding her circle was the goal, no one would question him joining them as well.

He reached to select the juice and paused, his finger hovering over the option.

The juice now bore the tag of Trina as if she'd added it from a labeled program stick like anyone else.

He could have sworn it had been unlabeled this very morning, though an instructor could have come by and fixed it. He glanced toward the other room and remembered how Sharna had called Trina over. Deluth suspected he'd been wrong about the programming abilities of some of the team, and about what tools might be loaded onto their sticks.

With this in mind, the friendship he'd observed seemed even less likely. Sharna had the tools to override a system, tools that would have made the attack on Azizi possible. Trina was the only candidate without a program stick, presumably because she'd lost her own and could not afford to get it replaced, though she'd acted more as if she didn't know they existed.

Suddenly the idea of sitting between the two of them lost its appeal. He turned away from the replicator without putting in his request and headed to his room instead. He could always do with a little more study time.

CHAPTER 23

Trina rose bright and early, for once not trying to avoid the other candidates but because she needed to get to class. She'd spent the evening with Sharna instead of returning to the classroom and still had to figure out what she should have been learning the previous day.

Fred arrived soon after and strode to her side. "I'm glad to see you here, Trina. When I checked the logs, you hadn't finished any of yesterday's work, not even those done in class time. If you can't be bothered with the training, you should speak up now. We don't like to see anyone get this far and fail, but it only gets harder. We certainly won't put someone out in the Guild who will endanger others. That includes those who put their obsessions over their work."

Any thought of confronting Fred about the tools vanished as Trina stared down at her screen to avoid the instructor's intense gaze. "I'm not quitting. I promise you that. And I have stopped looking for an answer to the attack on Azizi."

As soon as she spoke, Trina wished her wording better chosen, but now she knew it to be the truth no matter how much she accepted Sharna's reasons.

Fred sank into the chair in front of Trina's desk facing backwards. "I'm glad to hear it. You came with recommendations from some very qualified officers, but sometimes whether you'll fit in can't be seen until you try. It's hard being a spacer. You are moved around from assignment to assignment, forced to work with people from all over the galaxy—each with different rules and traditions—and that's not even looking at the job itself. You've shown a lot of promise, both in your work and how you made a connection early to help learn. Still, the life is not for everyone."

Trina kept her gaze steady. "It is the life for me. I promise. I've finished half of yesterday's assignments already, and I'll get the rest tonight."

She sucked in a breath to confront Fred about the program stick, but the others filed in, and the instructor rose.

"I guess I'd better make sure you learn something today then," she said before making her way to the front of the class. "I'll come check on you at the end of the day."

Somehow, Trina knew the promise had been to ensure she would pay attention rather than if she had any questions. How good her work had been before would not matter if the instructors lost faith in her determination.

Fred had been clear. If she didn't think Trina could succeed in the training, she'd make sure Trina never got the chance to.

After shuttling the exercise she'd been working on into the terminal memory, Trina concentrated on the lecture more than she ever had before. She didn't want there to be any question that she belonged. Not now when everything seemed to be coming together.

She examined the thought for a heartbeat, realizing what she meant had less to do with discovering the program stick, or even her facility with the programming itself. The very people Fred saw as a potential problem made Trina feel as though she could fit in, could find her place here.

Nishan had been the first to encourage her, in part because of how different her life had been compared to the others. Yet, she'd given up her weapons and her life on the streets to become, as Fred had mentioned, a highly qualified officer.

Add in both Azizi and Sharna—neither of whom fit Trina's image of a spacer candidate, especially now that she knew more of Sharna's culture—and Trina felt she could belong here as she had nowhere else before.

But she had to prove she did.

For the rest of the class, Trina concentrated on the lesson and mastering the exercises. Her inattention the previous day made that much more difficult. She accepted the punishment without complaint as she fought her way through them.

THE DAY'S CLASSES CAME to an end much faster than Trina had expected, especially with Fred's threat hanging over her.

She glanced at the terminal to confirm that she'd completed most of the exercises from today, proof of her commitment.

Fred didn't approach Trina's desk when she arrived. She went straight up to talk to the other instructor, most likely to ask for a report on Trina's behavior.

Trina sprang to her feet only to stop when Azizi caught her hand.

"You're running off again? Even if you don't want to help me any longer, you need to help yourself. This isn't a program where you can ignore half and still make it through."

She grimaced, hearing the echo of Fred's words in Azizi's, but she didn't sink into her seat.

"I'm not running off, and this time you're coming with me." She added the last in a lightning decision. He had as much at stake as she did, and both would find it easier if they could review their work at the other terminals rather than just using them for general research.

Confusion swept his features, and he didn't stand up. "I'm not getting into trouble. I respect my position here too much, and I won't be the excuse you use to throw away your career. Fred fixed the damage to my hair and it's done with."

She stared at him for a moment, never having considered in her crusade to defend him that she might have harmed his status as well. The thought sobered her. It had always been easy to take risks before because she kept all the sides of her life isolated.

That thought curdled in her stomach as she realized the delusion it had been. As much as the belief she could defend Azizi without getting him into trouble. She decided right then not to tell him what she'd learned until they were secure as spacers. Sharna could wait.

"I promise. It's no trouble this time. It's for your benefit as well as mine."

He gave her a wary look but trusted enough to rise and follow her to where the two instructors were still talking.

Fred turned to see them first and took in Azizi with a raised eyebrow, probably believing Trina brought him to vouch for her.

She'd deserved the scolding this morning, but the logs should show already how she'd dedicated herself to catching up, working through the lunch break and using the exercise sessions during class. This time, she would let nothing distract her from gaining access to the program sticks. She did this not just for her but for all of them. They'd been pulled out before the orientation. Even if every other candidate had a program stick, there could be other tools and resources owed them.

"I want to request a program stick. And so does Azizi."

Now both of Fred's eyebrows rose. "I hadn't imagined you were the careless type, Trina, but I'm more stunned that you have lost yours, Azizi."

Azizi had been staring at Trina like she'd lost her mind, but now he pivoted to look at the instructors.

Before he could say a word, Trina continued, "You'd be right about both of us. We wouldn't have lost them had we been given them from the start."

The other instructor straightened at that. He'd been the first to notice her programming skills, but never had he suggested she get a stick.

"We don't just hand them out. You have to ask for them." Fred kept her voice calm, but Trina could hear the impatience under it and decided not to draw this out any longer.

In a tone as even as Fred's had been, she said only, "Which we would have had we known that we could."

"If you'd paid attention to the orien—" Fred caught on first, cutting her words short, but then the other instructor groaned.

"The orientation you didn't go to," he said. "We never expected any of those needing help would ever have a reason to port their code. That's for advanced students who can work all on their own. It's never been a problem before, most likely because the candidate asks first."

They looked very uncomfortable.

Trina had expected to enjoy their guilt. Instead, his last statement bit deep.

She had known about the program stick before she stole Sharna's. Had she come to Fred or any of the instructors the next day with a straight request, they would have made sure she had the necessary tools.

Not wanting to reveal her own ignorance, she'd approached the topic sideways, gathering knowledge, yes, but not the one crucial piece she needed. The instructors had forgotten her lack of information, and she'd done everything possible to make sure they didn't become aware of it.

"It's our fault for not remembering when you and a few others showed remarkable talents. You're more advanced than many who grew up with the basic programs. Ignorance, not a lack of aptitude, brought your scores down." Fred grimaced. "And I knew you wouldn't have had a full preparation, either. Most know they want to be in the Guild at a young age and start preparing for it. I've been interested in your progress when the information included in your profile stated how you came to take the test and when."

About to ease her instructor's guilt, Trina froze. "How I came to take the test?" She'd thought the past her own to reveal or hide, but not if the official record laid out her misjudgments.

Fred shrugged. "Yes. It's rare for a colonist to take the test while on route to founding a new base. It doesn't happen often, and when it does, the candidate's potential is identified long before testing. They're pulled into the same classes as the local ship students. From your record, the only way you got into the testing room was because of your recommendations, and you had just a few weeks before being dropped off here where every other candidate studied for at least a year."

Trina relaxed for the first time since charging up here. "You mean there was other preparation?" She remembered thinking how the ship had failed her, but if she'd seen only the final days of the training, no wonder there had been holes.

A sigh came from Fred, and she stared down at the desk before meeting Trina's gaze. "And we, I, failed you there as well. It's one thing to drop a prepared candidate into a new program and monitor their progress, but we should have remembered how little preparation you'd been given. We should have acted instead of waiting for you to ask. How were you supposed to know there was even a question? It's amazing how well you've done."

Trina shot Azizi a smile. "I wouldn't have without Azizi's offer to help. I struggled with what are basic concepts for you because the framework had no place in my mind. It's like you said yesterday about my exercises. Part of my job as a spacer will be to work with others who have a different understanding."

"You do that so well," Fred said. "You and Azizi both have demonstrated a remarkable ability to learn from and teach others. I've recognized your hand in Azizi's progress just as his is clear in yours on different topics of study."

"What I find most amazing," the other instructor interjected, "is how you've done all this without some of the basic tools. The program stick, for example, does more than just carry your work around. It also contains templates you can apply to speed a task. That you've completed your assignments every day but the last here in the classroom without any templates to guide you is nothing short of amazing."

Azizi laughed then. "You need to check the logs. We didn't do it in class time. We stayed after, never understanding why the others didn't need to."

Fred looked from Trina to Azizi and back. "I made my own assumptions there as well. I can only apologize again." She paused. "You went through the full preparation, Azizi. Why didn't you know about the program sticks at least enough to ask after them?"

He shrugged and gave the same answer he'd told Trina before, "On my world you have everything you need, nothing less but nothing more.

As you have seen, I lack a talent for programming. Without Trina's help, I'd be at risk of failing the training. Why would they tell me about something they never thought I'd use?"

She frowned at that, unsatisfied no matter how much Azizi had come to terms with his culture. "We'll have to see about providing stricter guidelines for the preparation. Trina's ship had an excuse with her late addition. Your world does not. Spacers might have certain strengths, but we are all trained in every task to some degree. When an emergency happens in space, there's no option to wait for the arrival of an expert. Lives and ships could be lost too easily if the on-board specialist falls ill, is injured, or dies."

Azizi gave no reply to that, but Trina could see the sense of it. They'd studied closing off whole sections of the ship with the clear understanding that those behind the barriers most likely would not survive. If the specialist in a critical function was on the wrong side, everyone could be lost.

Fred shook her head and gave them a bright smile. "We'll worry about how this happened later. Right now, I'm taking you two down to supply and getting you program sticks. Tomorrow, we'll cover the parts of orientation you and your classmates missed in case there's something else you need."

Trina couldn't believe it had been so simple as she and Azizi followed Fred from the classroom. They were off to get a program stick free of any guilt or tarnish. She'd never been in a place where asking changed anything, but now it seemed she'd have to learn the habit.

DELUTH SPEARED A PROTEIN CUBE as he tried to figure out how to slip a question about Sharna's programming into the conversation. They'd discussed the fuel requirements of various ships, talked about a colony they'd touched on in class that had much in common with Trina's home, and reviewed their performance in the latest drill all without him finding a way to ask her about the label on Trina's juice.

He lifted a glass of the liquid in question, wondering if he should just blurt it out or keep silent. They had agreed to be friends, but tampering with systems would have major consequences if discovered. Maybe he didn't want to know.

"Oh, there she is," Sharna said, breaking into his thoughts.

Deluth twisted round to see Trina entering the meal area with a grin on her face.

Sharna nodded at the drink in his hand and raised her own. "You might as well join us. After all, we're enjoying your creation."

Trina glanced at him as if unsure of her welcome, so he mirrored Sharna's smile and waved her over.

She gave a quick smile in return. "I'll get a meal first."

He turned to Sharna. "You two seem to have become fast friends. I hadn't realized you'd spoken to her before."

Sharna glanced toward the replicator then shrugged. "Sometimes it doesn't take long to find understanding. She's certainly different, and I think it's more than just coming from a colony. When I look into her eyes, she feels like someone who has seen much and not let it destroy her."

The description seemed odd, especially when applied to someone so young. At the same time, he'd had a similar feeling himself though he'd never put it into words. "She's different for sure, and she knows how to stand up to Redel. A rarity around here."

Sharna laughed at that. "Sometimes it's easier to be the planet spinning round the sun than the ship trying to bounce off its atmosphere, Deluth. There are bigger issues to focus on."

Again her words connected, this time in relation to his ongoing battle with Redel. There were no prizes to be won by the victor, and many chances for both to lose everything.

Trina dropped into an empty seat, ending the conversation.

He glanced over at her plate to find it filled with objects of many different shapes and colors, so different from his tan nutrition cubes. He drew in a deep breath but could not smell the sharp scent marking whatever he'd chosen the other night.

She didn't start eating.

Trina glanced between him and Sharna, her shoulders tense. Then she shrugged and pulled something out.

"They gave me a program stick today," she announced, exchanging a look with Sharna though he'd been the one to tell her about them. "I was hoping you could show me how to port my juice to the classroom replicator."

"You can't port it. It's unsigned." Even as he spoke, Deluth remembered his discovery the previous night and fell silent.

"It's fixed now," Sharna said without taking responsibility or assigning it to an instructor.

Deluth told himself to stop. First he'd been suspicious of Trina when clearly she'd requested a program stick and had been waiting the assignment. Now he suspected Sharna of twisting the station programs. Next he'd think Redel capable of doing the same.

He sighed, remembering his suspicions about the air stream accident and the program he held on his own stick. His instructors would most likely be unhappy to learn it existed among the candidates. They'd all brought more than strange food and customs when they came on board.

Her meal forgotten, Trina followed Sharna over to the replicator where she studied every step Sharna took from the intent expression on her face.

They only returned when successful, according to the triumphant grin Trina now held.

"And you follow the same process in reverse to load one. Only this time, it'll be signed from the start," Sharna said as they took their seats once again.

Trina scooped up a forkful of her meal and put it in her mouth. The steam still rising from her plate revealed her choice was better able to hold its temperature than Deluth's cubes.

"Why do you want to move it there anyway?" he asked, more out of something to say than true curiosity. After all, she'd made a wonderful combination. Why wouldn't she want to show it to her instructors and have them commend her?

Trina finished the bite and waved her fork in the air. "Tomorrow, everyone in the class will have the chance to get tools they didn't know were available to them. I got my program stick early, as did Azizi. I want to show them why it's valuable and to celebrate our getting access to the same tools you've had since orientation. You like my drink as does Sharna. It seems a good reward for everyone's hard work."

Deluth stared at her, and through the corner of his eye, he saw Sharna do the same.

Sharna turned to him and mouthed, "See, she's different," an exchange Trina missed as she started scraping together another forkful.

Redel would never think to share something of his making without the reward coming down on his head along with the ability to hold it over everyone else. Even Sharna would think of how it could elevate her status, and his first thought had been to prove something to the instructors.

Trina seemed oblivious to just how unique her perspective was. She chose to reward everyone when many others would not have shared the opportunity in the first place even though sharing would cost them nothing.

He glanced from her to Sharna who had returned to her normal self-confidence so easily she seemed happier even than she'd been before losing her program stick.

Whatever she'd done, he suspected Trina had a hand in this improvement. She seemed to treat everyone as a treasured bunkmate, no matter how they were connected. He suspected her willingness to help everyone in her classes succeed would overwhelm even the delight of her juice.

He wondered what it would feel like to be on the receiving end of her attention, or rather of her wish to help others. He'd already faced her accusations.

CHAPTER 24

Trina arrived early again the next morning, but this time it wasn't because she still had exercises to do. Sharna had shown her how to access the exercises Fred had loaded on her stick when the instructor gave it to Trina. For the first time, she'd actually worked from the terminal in her room.

Though she'd enjoyed the freedom, she planned to stay after class. Azizi needed her help. She'd been a poor friend over the last two days when he'd done so much to make her current success possible.

The juice composition passed easily between her stick and the classroom replicator just as Sharna had promised.

Trina smiled at the sight of her name on the menu from the start, and now she understood why Deluth found the unlabeled one so unnerving. Her previous attempt sat there blank. No one knew where it had come from or why. This time they could ask her if they were curious but unwilling to sip.

The system allowed for three test measures outside of normal allocations. As students began to file in, Trina queued her samples up, one for Azizi, one for Fred, and one for herself. The others would have to decide if they wanted to use their allocations to sample the treat she'd provided or not.

Azizi arrived late enough to go right to his desk, and Fred appeared a minute later.

Trina chose a path that would lead her past both Azizi and her own seat, but stopped only long enough to hand him his drink and put hers at her place. She held the final glass in both hands as she approached the desk at the front.

Fred glanced up, already frowning, but her lips eased into a smile when she saw who stood before her. "We've been up for hours figuring out just what you candidates might have missed. We didn't want to waste time on the simple stuff, but even more importantly, we didn't want to forget anything important."

"I should have known you wouldn't be one to withhold something from us," Trina said, her voice soft. "I've made good use of my program stick already so you have a way to demonstrate it if you need one."

The caution in Fred's eyes gave way to delight as she took in what Trina held up. "You added something to the replicator? I wouldn't have thought you'd learned enough to make that leap." She paused to jot a note on her screen. "And yet another thing to make sure everyone understands."

Trina waited for the instructor to take the glass before clarifying, "I didn't just add it here. I used the stick to port something I'd added to the one in my quarters. I tried to do it manually, but it didn't taste right."

Fred sent a narrowed gaze at her. "The unlabeled drink. I should have guessed it was a student, but we thought the system had just malfunctioned as it does sometimes. You figured out how to add to your meals some time ago then."

Trina shrugged. "About when we first learned the meal programming, but I didn't have to figure it out. There were some specially programmed meals on the colony ship. The spacers did them, but it didn't take too much thought to shift what I'd done in class to the machine."

After taking a sip from the glass, Fred's expression changed from intent to eyes wide in surprise. She took another sip without speaking, then said only, "This is the best juice I've ever tasted. Your technique is nothing short of amazing for any candidate. For any spacer in my experience."

A blush heated Trina's face, but she refused to look away. She'd studied hard to make this happen. "It's as close as I can get to a juice I drank on Ceric."

Fred held up the glass to see how the liquid shone in the light. "If this is what things are like on a colony, I can see why some never come to appreciate spacer food. It's rarely this complex. A drink like this is meant to be savored."

Shuffling of chairs and a cough came from behind Trina.

Fred's expression hardened. "But now's not the time for it. We have a lot to cover today. Go take your seat. I will indeed use your juice as an example of what one can accomplish. I'm thinking there's going to be a lot of folks wandering into the classroom to try this."

Suppressing a grin, Trina did as she'd been told. She never had the chance to share this with her sister, and maybe never would, but the reactions she'd gotten so far had been well worth the decision to build it in the first place and to bring it here.

Trina sank into her seat just as a sobering thought crossed her mind.

She'd have to be careful.

Fred had shown such amazement at what she could do, but how long before the instructor started to wonder what else she'd been able to master.

At least Sharna would keep her secret, if not for their growing friendship then because she'd told Trina about the trick on Azizi.

The instructors might not take kindly to learning a mere candidate could override the programming on a door. They might get curious and look deeper into whom she was and what she'd done before coming here. As much as she wished to put an end to the secrets and that life, the risk to her spacer career had to carry more weight.

Besides, if she did nothing with those extra skills, that she had them should neither raise questions nor cause a problem. Maybe someday they'd come in handy as well. Fred had mentioned the risk when a specialist was not available. Trina could step in though they'd never suspect her capable.

CLASS ENDED EARLY AFTER A discussion of the tools available to candidates. Trina had considered each, but none offered her more than the program stick the other candidates already possessed.

"Everyone who needs to request any of the items discussed, please follow me." Fred strode through the classroom to the door, her energy high after she'd led each student through the steps of adding a favorite concoction and had them request Trina's juice.

Only after they'd tasted the treat, Fred mentioned that Trina created the juice in her quarters and used a program stick to bring it in for everyone to enjoy.

That had afforded Trina more attention than she found comfortable, but at the same time, she felt a happy glow at how much they appreciated her gesture. She'd always seen herself as isolated and alone beyond her family. If she'd reached out here, many hands would have been willing to grasp her stretching fingers.

"It's like we're a household back home," Azizi murmured, having decided like her that none of the other tools would be worth the trouble of keeping track of. "Fred's the head mother, and all the children flock after her."

"I wouldn't be quick to call them children unless you consider the same label applies to you and me. I'm small, but I'm fully grown. Besides, yesterday, that was us."

He shared a grin with her. "Thank you. I didn't get the chance to say it before, and then you were off again, but I appreciate you including me." He paused, his lips firming for a second. "And I'm happy that was keeping you busy rather than seeking trouble."

Trina kept silent about how she'd come to the knowledge she'd used to help them all. She'd have to tell him someday because how else would she have learned about who performed the trick on him and why, but for now, she was happy to let him think kindly of her, especially when he'd been the one to suffer for her distraction.

"I'm not seeking trouble now, nor am I running off. I seem to remember we have some exercises to work through."

Azizi gave her a pointed look. "You mean I have some exercises. You've been racing so far ahead of me in these last few lessons I doubt you're lagging even with the day you spent planning how you'd approach Fred."

Trina shrugged. "Okay, you need to do them, but I'm here to help. I meant what I told them. I understand all of this only because you sat with me when I couldn't wrap my head around the workings of a ship and made sure the exercises would make sense. I never meant to abandon you. I just got distracted for a while."

"Since you treated the instructors no better, I can't really argue. And I do need the help."

They bent over his desk, going through each of the exercises as many times as it took to get a green flash. Though Trina had succeeded in her early morning session on most of these, reviewing them with Azizi gave her deeper insight that would be sure to serve her well in the future.

One problem in particular proved too hard for both of them, something about his configuration undermining it while hers had sailed right through.

"I don't see the difference," she muttered, remembering again how she couldn't replicate the juice exactly and feeling the same frustration now.

Then she burst out laughing, earning a scowl from Azizi.

"We have the answer, or at least the way to get it," she said. "I'm just not used to having a program stick well enough to remember."

Trina returned to her desk and activated her program stick. She'd had to transfer all of her work to the stick to bring it to class so it could be counted. She didn't have to work from memory. She could call up the exact exercise and they could work through the differences.

His glare softened as Azizi must have figured out what she was doing. "You have something to compare to, don't you?"

She nodded, her attention on the screen. "I completed the exercise in my room. I didn't run into the same problem, so we can look at mine and yours together to find the place where it breaks down."

"And all because you found out about these program sticks." He laughed this time as well. "As much as I appreciate the juice you made, this serves a much better purpose as far as I'm concerned. Otherwise my mind would have melted from the heat of frustration leaking out both ears."

She scowled at him, but he just laughed again, knowing she didn't mean it.

"Let's get this exercise done and make good use of our time between classes," Trina said. "I suspect we'll have to make up whatever they'd planned before learning the need for an orientation, which means more work and twice the exercises tomorrow."

He groaned, but soon his smile returned. "At least I don't have extra exercises pressing me down. Once we figure out this one, I'm as caught up as you are."

"Then get to work. It shouldn't take much longer now."

CHAPTER 25

Trina and Azizi made it almost to the classroom entrance when they saw Fred returning with the other candidates.

The sight of them set Trina's heart pounding.

They weren't supposed to return. Class had finished for the day. This meant something had gone wrong, and most likely she stood at the center of whatever had.

The thought that they'd discovered how she bypassed the locking mechanism on Sharna's door started an ache in her gut, but she dismissed it. The other candidates wouldn't have been brought here to witness her humiliation.

Each candidate filed in as if they'd just come from a lesson in a different classroom. No one looked distressed.

Fred had been counting the candidates, but when she glanced up, she gave a quick nod. "Good. You two are still here. It means I don't have to hunt you down. Take your seat please."

Only then did Trina realize they'd both frozen, not just her, and stood watching the events as if terrified.

Whatever brought the others back clearly involved everyone in the class.

Her mind spun with possibilities, settling on nothing, not even whether this would be a punishment or praise. She dropped into her chair and stared at the front, determined to take whatever came next calmly.

Fred scanned her candidates from the front of the room and relaxed enough to smile. "Good. We're all here. This is news I didn't want any to receive second hand."

She stopped for a dramatic pause, and Trina could have sworn every candidate leaned in closer, drawn by the smile to hope.

"I've just been informed that total integration with the other teams will now begin. Those responsible for judging your readiness without the bias of working with you each day have been informed of your progress. This sudden desire for extra tools"—she nodded to Trina—"made them aware of a need for a closer examination, and they liked what they saw."

Fred laughed at the frowns on some candidates' faces, but Trina felt her own expression stiffen.

"Don't worry. I'm not giving you up just yet. You've achieved base competency, but there are other aspects we still need to cover. What this does mean is you will spend half of each day in the usual training, and you'll be allowed to participate in the ship drills with the teams. I'm sure you're eager for that, having heard your teammates talk."

An excited babble filled the room and many candidates called out questions, but Trina just sank into her chair.

She'd be joining her team, the Pilots. She'd be working side by side not just with Sharna and Deluth whom she'd come to like, but with Redel. Though he had not done anything she could point to since the incident with the air stream more than three weeks before, she'd felt his animosity the few times they'd crossed paths, sometimes just in a glare across the room.

She looked to Azizi for support, but he seemed no happier.

"We know what we're doing now," Trina said with a confidence she didn't feel. "It's not like we're going in there for everyone to hold our hands. We just need to show them what we can contribute."

He twisted to stare at her. "Do you really think it will be so easy? They chose not to accept us as part of the team the moment we didn't show up for normal classes. And we won't know what we're doing. Have you ever done a ship drill? I know I have not. You think talking about it and doing exercises is the same as standing at a console while the ship is crashing into a sun, simulated or not? If the screen flashes red, you can't just reset and try again. Your whole team is affected."

"True." Fred nodded a greeting, having come up on them unnoticed. "But how is that any different than the first time you stand on a real ship with only the drills behind you? You need to learn how to adapt, but so does every member of your team. They may be the new person for their first assignment, but soon after they'll be faced with training someone even newer."

Azizi's mouth twisted in a mockery of a smile. "And are they being told this is a wonderful event? A further bit of training to make the simulation that much more real?"

Trina reached across to put a hand on his arm, reassuring him despite feeling just as unsettled.

Fred crouched down between them, leaning her arms on their desks for support. "Just what do you think they've been learning in their classes? Many of the same things, yes, but you have been excluded from the one class you're less likely to need. Every other candidate has been busy studying colonies, how they work and the different cultures found there. If they can't find a way to integrate you into the team, how will they be able to handle interactions with those founding colonies, or arrange to trade critical goods for resources the Guild needs?"

The image Fred presented offered little comfort, but Trina understood the greater purpose here. If they had not had so many needing extra training, they would have found some other way to shake up the teams. She'd wanted to be a spacer because her own life had seemed full of limitations. Now she got to see that aspect in person, with her becoming part of the difference others had to face."

As if she could read their minds, Fred rose to place a hand on one shoulder each. "Do what you've done here with each other. Find the ways your knowledge can bolster theirs as much as their experience can help you. I'm not saying it will be easy. Transitions rarely are. But this is only one of the changes you will face in becoming a spacer. Embrace it." Her sharp gaze fell on Azizi and then came to rest on Trina. "If you do not, if you cannot, you have no business becoming a spacer. The same is true of every candidate that has ever joined this program. Not all leave to start their careers."

The words sent shards of ice down Trina's spine, her instructor's warning clear.

She would do whatever she could to win Redel's respect if not his friendship. She would not be the one sent home because she could not work well with the team she'd been assigned. It seemed too much to hope the other Pilots would feel the same.

DELUTH SPRAWLED ON ONE OF the lounges, mindlessly watching a program about early colony ships, the ones that left from Earth long before the Guild even came into being. He'd hoped it would pull his thoughts away from their disastrous drill, but nothing seemed to have that power, especially with the way the few members willing to stay out here where Redel could find them spoke in hushed whispers.

He swung his legs down to the floor, wondering if he should give up and head out for his own training instead. But he didn't want to leave the others vulnerable.

Sharna had followed his lead when she'd leapt to Jessine's defense instead of listening to her own advice not to stand out. She'd taken the brunt of Redel's anger then, but from how his shipmate paced between rooms, Deluth suspected another outburst was coming. Better it fall on his shoulders.

A flicker of movement from the main entrance caught his attention. Perhaps one of the others decided to leave before the meteor shower hit.

Trina stood highlighted in the doorway for a second before she stepped inside, her gaze searching the room. From her smile, she had good news to share, something in short supply.

He thought she'd give up when Sharna couldn't be found, but her gaze brushed him and stuck.

She didn't hesitate as she strode across the room, heading right for him.

"You're a welcome sight," he said before he could school his tongue.

She stopped and tipped her head to one side, trying to puzzle out his meaning.

Deluth shrugged. "It was a long, hard day of lessons." He waved to the nearest huddle. "None of us has much to smile about."

"Is Sharna around?" Trina said, accepting his explanation without comment.

A little of the happiness she'd brought dimmed, but he forced his smile to stay steady. "No. She's resting in her room."

He'd expected her to leave, but Trina dropped onto the other lounger, tucking her feet under her as if she meant to stay.

"I wanted to tell both of you at once, but I won't disturb her, especially if the day went as poorly as you said." This time she did glance at the others, probably seeing the same despair he found in their curved shoulders and low voices.

"Tell me. I could do with some good news."

Her smile grew into a grin before she got it under control. "I'm joining the team. Only for half of the time, but still, I'll start with you tomorrow."

She bounced a little as though unable to contain her excitement, and he felt a touch of the same, the joy contagious. "You'll be taking classes with us?"

Trina shrugged. "I know I'll be working through the drills. Fred told us that much. But we won't be in every class."

Deluth felt his lips stretch with a grin of his own. "We need some new blood for the drills, especially after today. It'll mix things up a little."

"Oh? What happened anyway?"

Over her shoulder, he saw the one person he'd hoped wouldn't notice her arrival.

Redel bore down on them clearly having overheard. Trina had made no attempt to lower her voice, and why should she have?

His share of the excitement died a quick death, and he tensed, unsure what he could do to improve the situation.

Trina picked up on the change and pivoted to see what he'd been looking at in time to come almost nose to nose with Redel.

She jerked away as he slammed both hands down on the back of the lounger.

"Just what we need. Our trained team can't seem to hold things together and now we have to support a crippled team member as well?"

Trina stood, the attempt doing little to bring her to Redel's height. "I may be inexperienced, but we've been studying the ship systems extensively. I know the proper response to a hundred scenarios or more."

As much as Deluth wished she hadn't spoken, he respected her choice to stand her ground and not be bullied. Of course, that had ended poorly for Sharna already today.

Redel glared at her for what felt a long while before saying, "You think just because you added some juice to the replicator you're as good as even the worst of us? I saw Sharna over there helping you out. It might be your label, but the work is clearly hers. She must have offloaded it onto your stick as a pity gift. I'll tell you what you need to do tomorrow. You stay quiet, stay out of my way, and do exactly what I say. Nothing more, nothing less. Got that?"

He didn't wait for her response before stomping off to the meal area, though maybe he went to his room instead because they heard the sound of a door opening not much later.

Deluth turned to Trina after following Redel's progress until he'd gone out of sight.

Where he'd expected to encourage and comfort her, Trina had resumed her previous position and was watching him instead.

"It was that bad today?"

"Yes." At first, he wanted to say nothing more, but then he found the words pouring out of him. "Redel gave an incorrect command, or rather not the one I think is optimum. Peter followed it, but Jessine queried. It all went into the gravity well after that. Redel was more focused on what he saw as insubordination than a solution. Peter didn't understand the original path well enough to do the next steps on his own, and he wasn't going to switch procedures with Redel yelling at Jessine. The whole scenario collapsed with our worst score ever."

"Ouch. What about Sharna?"

"She stepped in to stand up for Jessine. That's never the best plan. When Redel's like this, keeping out of his way is the only way to survive."

Trina pursed her lips and stared after Redel though he'd long vanished. "I thought he only went after me. He should not be leading."

That surprised a laugh out of Deluth when he'd have thought it impossible in the circumstances. "He didn't give anyone much of a choice."

"He's a big man, or wants to be," she said with a nod. "I thought as much from the start, but he seemed to get along with the rest of you."

Deluth pushed to his feet and waved for her to do the same. "He does, at least until something goes wrong. I doubt this is the contest he believes it to be, but try convincing him of that. He wants our scores to be perfect every time."

"Perfect means you're not challenged."

"Exactly."

She seemed to understand his meaning about Redel and everything.

He gestured toward the meal area in a silent suggestion. Deluth felt hungry for the first time since the drill, and she'd come from class early which meant no meal with Azizi. Eating together offered an excuse to talk with her longer.

CHAPTER 26

Fred had explained they were to meet in their classroom as usual, so the next morning after telling Sharna the happy news, Trina headed off to her classroom. She set the location in the air stream and stepped on, aware that soon she would be going somewhere else in the mornings, or perhaps sometimes in the afternoons. Deluth said they switched when the drills were run to catch them at a variety of energy levels.

With the split between the two, she'd still see Azizi more than just on break days.

The classroom was almost full when she arrived, surprising as she'd come a little early. Unlike any previous day, the noise reached into the hallway. So many candidates and class not started meant a lot of talking, much in high, excited voices as the others considered what their day would hold.

Trina slipped into her seat and glanced at Azizi. "Are you looking forward to this?"

He shrugged. "It's the next step in the training. I'll do all right. My team has to accept the instructors' judgment as to my readiness."

Trina thought about Redel's reaction and said nothing.

At least she had Sharna and Deluth to balance out Redel while Azizi had no friends on his team.

Silence rolled through the classroom, the difference stark enough to catch her attention in time to see not one but nine instructors make their way to the front where they stood in a line. Trina searched their faces, but Fred was not one of them.

A man stepped out of the row and lifted a screen like those used when they'd first arrived on the station.

Tension took hold of Trina at the recognition. Why would they need a list when everyone already knew their teams? The only possible answer meant what little comfort she had in Sharna and Deluth would be stripped away.

"I'll call out your name and team assignment in order of the instructor who will take you to where they are right now. As soon as your name is called, make your way to the instructor who has a hand raised."

The announcement failed to confirm her supposition, but the surprise and complaints from the first three candidates called gave warning enough.

She remembered Fred's comment about how this would be a learning experience for the teams where they were assigned as well. The Guild wasn't taking any chances about existing friendships easing the way beyond possible connections made during the break-day gatherings.

Trina sent a nervous glance toward Azizi, only to find him more relaxed than he had been coming in despite his dismissive statement.

It shocked her to realize she should feel the same but didn't. Despite Redel, she was one of those with existing friendships, new ones, maybe, but ones she could have counted on in the confusion of entering the drills when everyone else had been involved in them from the start.

"Trina of Menthak. You are in Medical."

It took her a moment to recognize her full name, having reverted to thinking like a shafter where she laid claim only to her first, then she laughed.

After all this, they'd mixed the sisters. Katie had the head for medicine.

The lead instructor gave her an irritated look when she didn't leap up and join her guide. They wouldn't understand the humor. Not only were they unaware of Katie, but to them, the team names could not be more than convenient labels. Sharna and Deluth hadn't mentioned any special pilot training, and she knew she had received the same lessons as all in her section.

Still, if nothing else, she could consider it an omen, a connection to her far distant sister. When she had nothing else to hold onto, she'd always had Katie.

DELUTH KEPT HIS ATTENTION SPLIT between the instructor giving their morning scenario briefing and the door.

Trina said specifically that she'd be joining them for the scenarios, but it seemed cruel to bring her in after the team had already received its information. She had to show up any minute now.

He met Sharna's gaze as he turned to face the instructor, hers pointing in the direction of the door. At least one other person shared his tension.

The count raised to three when he happened to see Redel's scowl also directed at the door, though not for the same reason.

If they failed this time, it wouldn't be because of Trina as much as Redel would be sure to make it seem that way. At least the rest seemed to be listening, but that offered no guarantees when Redel ran their team like a commander rather than one member in a cooperative effort.

"Ah," their instructor said. "Just what I've been waiting for, and I suspect some of you are equally distracted."

He knew he should stay focused on the man, but Deluth turned to the door just as another purple walked in followed by Trina's friend. Deluth craned his neck, expecting to see Trina right behind them, but no other candidates stepped through.

Now he watched the instructor, or rather watched Azizi make his way to the front.

Their instructor gave the newcomers a smile as he gestured for them to turn and face the Pilots.

Deluth could hardly hear what the man said as the overwhelming question of Trina's absence screamed for an answer.

"Pilots, this is your new team member, Azizi Demai. Each team will receive a new member today as part of your training. Those of you who become spacers will both be and have new team members frequently. This is just a taste of how to integrate a new person into your team successfully."

The woman who'd delivered Azizi waved a general farewell and left Trina's friend to stand next to the instructor looking uncomfortable.

The instructor leaned over to say something quietly, and Azizi circled the edge of the assembled members to find a spot in the rear. He'd chosen to stand near Deluth, a fact Azizi didn't notice until he gave Deluth a nervous glance.

Redel let out a deep sigh, his annoyance plain. The reaction provoked a glare from Sharna, but otherwise the team ignored the change as the briefing started up again.

Deluth suspected Redel's mild response had more to do with Trina's absence than any acceptance of their new team member. He gave her friend a quick smile, though he really wanted to demand an answer to the pressing question of why Trina didn't stand in his place.

On the way to the scenario simulator, Redel passed close to where Deluth and Azizi stood. He paused long enough to say, "At least we didn't get saddled with your colony girlfriend. She'd only be dead weight. This one might know something."

Deluth bit his tongue to hold back the retort that at least Trina had been able to code a new option on the replicator while he happened to know Redel had been trying with no success. He'd been restraining the urge since Redel charged Trina of faking her drink. If Sharna had helped her, the drink would have been signed by Sharna because Trina had not received her program stick yet. She wouldn't have designed the drink at the replicator to leave it unsigned if she'd worked with someone else.

"Come on," he said to Azizi, waving the candidate to go in front of him.

Azizi hesitated.

Deluth realized he'd been less than welcoming the few times they'd crossed paths. He smiled a second time. "Look, I know things were weird when we met, if you could call it that, but you're part of the team now." His smile faded as he had another thought. "This doesn't mean Trina will be moved to another quarters, does it?"

Finally, Azizi's lips twitched up to smile though Deluth didn't think his question had any happiness in it.

"No. They would have told us, and it would defeat their purpose. They've mixed everyone up to make sure we have no friends where we land. Moving into the same quarters would reduce the effect."

Deluth limited his reaction to a nod and pointed to the entrance. "Better get going. We don't want to delay the scenario. No reason to draw more attention than you already have."

Azizi tensed at that, making Deluth wonder at the candidate's expectations. Trina probably shared her worries with Azizi when she thought she'd be here, though he hoped he hadn't been part of the list as he would have been once.

If only this scenario ran smoothly.

He refused to punish Azizi for being Trina's friend, and as much as they disagreed about almost anything at this point, he didn't want to see Redel thrown out of the program for doing something stupid either.

CHAPTER 27

The introduction to Trina's new team a week earlier had gone as well as could be expected. Groans met the original announcement, but once the Medicals learned every team would get a new member, they had collectively decided to suffer her presence without tormenting her.

Trina knew it could have been worse, but she still felt isolated with not a single friendly face.

She'd survived on classroom time with Azizi and evenings spent with him, or with Deluth and Sharna. She couldn't even tell them what bothered her as the candidates had been asked not to discuss team dynamics. The assignments had been difficult enough keeping candidates separate from those who'd tested with them.

Not that this posed a problem for Trina. She'd hardly known the ones from the colony ship. Her friends and family had been among the colonists or already in the spacer ranks.

Still, she could have used a friend this morning.

Trina waited for the others to file out of the scenario room before she left her console. She'd avoided drawing attention so far by focusing on staying out of everyone's way and learning more by observing everyone than by asking questions. A couple of the drills even fell within her strengths and she'd added something to the solution, a change recorded in their score but not one she felt comfortable pointing out for the others to see.

This morning, after seven hard days of drills, they'd pulled a situation well into Azizi's strengths, and her weaknesses. In the classroom, they would have studied the situation together with Azizi pointing things out until she could put the pieces in the right order to succeed.

Here, she'd been on her own, not wanting to interfere with whatever anyone else was doing by asking for help and yet unable to see any way her station could contribute to the overall.

"You should have backwashed the air stream system. It would have flushed the contaminant in half the time."

Trina jumped, unaware Jade, who had been acting the leader for this one, was still in the room.

Normally, the candidate avoided Trina as if she carried a contagious disease, which she supposed she did. The few comments she'd overheard referred to her as the colony girl. From other mentions, she knew Jade had come from a planet as well, but a very different one with short-hop indie trading vessels that gave Jade the chance to pilot even before she'd taken the spacer test.

"I didn't think of that," Trina said, kicking herself mentally for not connecting the air stream with a possible vent path.

"Next time, ask."

Jade didn't hang around to answer any more questions her statement might have provoked, as much, Trina knew, for fear of being branded another colonist as from a lack of interest.

She stared at the console long enough to map out the steps in her mind, the actual controls having faded along with the alarms as the contaminant spread throughout the ship until it reached every corner. This scenario hit too close to her own history for comfort.

With nothing left to learn here, Trina headed for the main room where she knew they would be discussing every step that should have been taken. Azizi would have been able to come up with five or six approaches, and perhaps the others had, but none were successful. She didn't know if hers would have been either, but everyone was too busy trying attempts from their own consoles to suggest it for her until too late.

"I'll run this through a couple times on my own after classes," Jade was saying as Trina stepped into the room. "I'd suggest you do the same. We've never had that particular drill, but we've had enough like it. We should have been able to isolate part of the ship for survivors at least."

As though coming aware of Trina's presence just then, Jade sent Trina a sharp look before pointedly turning away.

Trina slid down the far wall into a crouch and listened to each of them describe what they'd done and what the results had been. She wanted to move closer, to join them at the table, but today it did not feel wise. Whether the others felt she'd been the final flaw to secure their failure or not, Jade certainly did.

As she mulled over how she could get better when every one of them had more experience at this, Trina remembered Jade's comment. She hadn't known they were allowed to run the scenarios after class, nor had she any idea how to make that happen. But she knew whom she would have to ask.

The thought gave her a trickle of amusement despite the disappointing morning. After all, Jade had told her to do so.

They rode the air stream together to the central hub when the Medicals broke for lunch, but usually her teammates went one direction and Trina the other. Today, she caught Jade's arm to stop the other candidate from following the Medicals.

After lunch, she'd be returning to Fred's class so had no better chance.

"What is it?" Jade's irritated voice offered warning enough without how the candidate plucked Trina's hand free and dropped it as if getting rid of something particularly disgusting.

Trina straightened, her full height bringing her eyes in line with Jade's sharp, light-brown chin. She took a backward step so she could see the other candidate's face, the full expression no more welcoming than her pointy chin.

"I'd like to join you after classes. For the extra drills. To review the scenario and try out your suggestion."

"Well you can't. I'm not wasting my free time coddling you."

Jade went to join the others, but Trina slipped around her to block the way.

"It wouldn't be coddling. I don't want any favors. I need the extra training if I'm to catch up with all of you. If you help me, I'll improve that much faster. Maybe next time I'll be able to contribute and the scenario won't be a complete failure." She spoke quickly, unsure how to hold the other candidate without physically restraining her, a fight Trina could possibly win but one that would get both of them into a lot of trouble.

Jade glared down at Trina, her face a mask bordered with a severe frown. "I don't want to be seen with you."

About to protest, Trina stopped when Jade held up one finger.

"You'll meet me here, at the air stream, as soon as class ends. I won't wait long, and if anyone from my team comes before you do, I'll leave without you. The only reason I'm doing this is because as leader, I reviewed the records from previous runs. I know you've done some good, and you didn't parade it in front of us, either. You have it in you to become a decent member of the team, and you're willing to work."

Trina smiled at the other candidate's softening.

"Don't think this means anything. I've worked too hard to get the others to forget I stood on the dirt before coming here. I'm not losing all that because I spend too much time with you. It won't take much for them to remember my home planet and forget that I flew ships before they were allowed out of the family areas. You are not going to cost me what I've earned. I'll help you now, but you will stay out of my way afterward. Understood?"

The sentiment came as no surprise to Trina. She'd heard variations of it since setting foot on the station. Whatever the instructors might hope for, even they valued colony candidates less, especially those kept from technology. They'd never admit it to themselves, much less to others, but events made it obvious.

Trina wondered if other colonies held back those who might be interested in the Guild for so few to come from colony worlds rather than ships. After all, she'd spent her childhood dreaming about ships and the stars every spare moment. She couldn't imagine other colonies didn't have their share of ones like her.

"I'll stay away as long as you teach me how to do the drills on my own after this. I plan to become not just a good member, but a valuable one, and that will take more than a single extra scenario."

"Deal." She made the hand gesture Trina had only seen in her classroom, a way to signal an agreement among traders who often swapped cargo in mid space without ever having direct contact.

Rather than give a poor imitation of Jade's culture, Trina stuck with a simple nod. "Until after class."

Jade spun and headed off before Trina finished speaking, leaving her to make her way to the Pilot quarters and some form of food before the second half of the day began.

THE SIMULATOR SHUT DOWN, AND the room went dark one console at a time.

Deluth exchanged a grin with Sharna and then Azizi, but Redel spoke first with a loud, "Yes!"

This had been one of the toughest survivals they'd managed so far, and one the team had failed on four previous occasions before Azizi's quick thinking rerouted the water for the hydroponics to the tail. They'd lost two crewmembers in the flood, but the change in weight had thrown them away from the gravity well just before it gained an unbreakable hold.

The newcomer, though not so new any longer, hadn't been the first to balance crew losses with survival. His effort, however, had worked.

Deluth crossed to Azizi as they started to file out into the discussion area. "That was brilliant. You've got a knack for the environmental system and how to use it."

"Misuse it, you mean." Azizi laughed, as caught up in the elation as the rest of them. "But I can't take credit for this one. I wouldn't have thought of it except Trina did something similar by accident when struggling with her exercises."

He looked at Deluth intently, and Deluth realized he'd smiled just to hear her name.

"How is she doing with her drills?" She'd returned after he'd gone off to his room the past few days, much like how she'd behaved in the beginning.

He missed her.

Deluth swallowed the question he really wanted to ask. If she preferred Azizi's company, neither he nor Sharna had any claim.

"She's working hard," Azizi said after a pause, clearly deciding it would do no harm.

Laughing, Deluth stepped through into the discussion room with Azizi at his side. "When has she ever not? I wondered if she was avoiding us at first, but I suspect from how quickly she gained proficiency every free hour was spent much like the ones in class."

"As her study partner, I can speak to her dedication, and once she does have a firm grasp, she's happy to share that knowledge."

Redel's struggles with the replicator sprung into Deluth's mind, and he winced at the irony of what his friend needed. He should have cultivated Trina's regard instead of trying to bully her.

Their teammates headed over with broad smiles, clearly aware of just how they'd succeeded this time instead of all the previous ones.

"I see you've finally bothered to come to the discussion." Redel shoved through the others, who returned to their seats without giving the congratulations Azizi deserved.

"Is it because you'd rather hang out with the simple folks than face a challenge you can't meet? I could report you for discussing her when we've been told not to."

There was no question about whom Redel referred to, and on the heels of Deluth's thought about the replicator, he lost what little patience he'd been clinging to with his friend.

"She is more of a challenge than most candidates, a fact you'd recognize if you weren't so scared a simple colony girl would show you up," Deluth snapped, putting the same emphasis on "simple" as Redel had. "Ask her to train you on the replicator some time so you can stop wasting your energy in failure."

Red crept up Redel's pale skin until it suffused his whole face.

Deluth took a step back, realizing he'd pushed Redel too far, and he wouldn't be the one to bear the consequences.

"Now you think they're better than me? Our friendship not good enough with a whole station to choose from?" He slammed both hands onto Deluth's chest, forcing him into Azizi.

Deluth raised his arms wide. "I don't want to fight."

"You started this. You should finish it," Redel snarled. "You've never been happy with me leading the team. You think you're better at everything, and now you're collecting your own little group to break the team up. You think I didn't notice how Sharna follows your lead?"

Bracing for another attack, Deluth spoke plainly. "You pushed me and Sharna together. You thought we'd suit, and you were right. We're friends, something you used to understand."

"Used to? I used to?"

The sound of chairs moving against the floor cut into the tense pause, but Deluth didn't know whether the others would interfere or only came to watch. They didn't have much time before the instructors got involved.

Redel stared at him as if he could bore through Deluth with his gaze alone, white lines standing out stark around his eyes and mouth.

"Look, I don't want—"

Deluth's words choked off as Redel sprang across the small space separating them with no sign of reason in his expression.

Then he tripped.

Whatever Deluth had expected, for Redel to fall flat on his face had not been among the possibilities.

A giggle came from the gathered candidates, quickly smothered.

Redel shoved off the floor, swinging his gaze to take in his teammates and then Deluth, but when Deluth thought he'd return to their argument, instead he glared at Azizi.

The newcomer shrugged. "I apologize. I was trying to get to the discussion tables and didn't see you until too late."

This time the color drained from Redel, leaving him ghostly pale and shaking with anger.

Deluth caught his arm and leaned in. "Any further and the instructors will come over. You don't want that. None of us want that. We won this scenario. It's cause for celebration. You led us to victory."

He added the last, knowing the best way to break through to Redel was to pander to his ego, no matter how much the idea made his teeth grind together.

Redel took a deep breath and shook Deluth off.

Deluth stayed tense and ready, but his friend only spun in a tight circle and marched to the table. "So," he demanded. "What other ways might we have used to survive?"

Sending a grateful glance to Azizi for the save, Deluth worried Trina's friend would come to regret his assistance. Not that Redel needed another excuse to despise Azizi beyond his colony background and the fact that he'd needed assistance in tech.

Deluth rubbed a hand down his face, suddenly exhausted.

They had the potential to be a strong team. Even their weakest members had something to contribute, and despite his angry words, he didn't think Redel numbered among those. How charisma could be paired with such insecurity amazed Deluth.

He hadn't understood Redel's aggression before, but he did now. Twice, without any reason to think so, his friend had accused him of wanting to take over the team. A person secure in his own position didn't do that.

CHAPTER 28

Jade kept both her promise and then her distance, but Trina had what she needed. Every waking hour that wasn't filled with classes or official drills, she spent on the simulators. Her work had begun to pay off. Even scenarios that would have stumped her in class now triggered not just one solution but several.

Trina looked forward to her sessions with the Medicals, though she'd begun to miss the time with her own team, and Azizi was no help. He liked Deluth, hardly knew Sharna, and spoke only of their drills when he said anything at all.

It had taken a good three weeks to begin to gain the Medicals' trust, at least that she wouldn't be the one to ensure a failure every time. She couldn't give up now. She couldn't slow down no matter how much she wanted to. A break day was coming, and she planned to return from it the equal of any of the others.

Her lips curved as she considered the last drill she'd run on her own. She hadn't let her programming studies lapse just because of the drills. Instead, she'd requested scenarios designed to have solutions she could put together with her growing skills. When she could not figure out a solution, the system offered a complete assessment of where she'd gone wrong and what she should have done, teaching her by example to a level well beyond her classes. It made designing the juice seem simple.

"What are you so happy about?" Azizi said, coming up on her side as she strode to their classroom for the afternoon session.

She grinned at him, delighted he'd come early when most days he lunched with her team while she grabbed a quick meal and a quicker scenario. "My extra work is paying off. I can handle things I used to need you for."

One corner of his mouth twisted up. "Then you have no use for your old friend?"

"My use for you is as a friend now. You're no longer a crutch I have to lean on. Instead, I can enjoy your company."

He glanced at her hands, which were pantomiming a crutch to illustrate the concept. "Not many colonists on your team are there? I'll bet the ship-bred have some fancy contraption to help those injured."

"An anti-grav platter, of course." She started to ask him why when she realized what she'd done. "It's hard to remember not to explain so much. You're right about the colonists. There's one, but she'd prefer everyone, especially me, forget that fact. She knows how to give a blank look to match any of the ship-bred when she must know what I mean."

"Or maybe not. There are some colonies that might as well be ships from what I've heard. The Supply team has one, but that candidate didn't come through the extra training program. He could train the spacers if half the rumors are true."

Trina sank onto her chair and stared down at her desk. "I'd love the chance to hear some rumors," she muttered.

Fred passed them just then, and when she stopped to put a hand on Trina's shoulder, Trina knew the instructor had heard.

"Logs show just how hard you've been working. I admire your dedication, but you must take care of your other needs as well. Set time aside to spend with your friends and make new ones. They'll be who you can count on when things break down as they always do. Don't isolate yourself in the name of perfection."

Trina stared after the woman, seeing Azizi do the same out of the corner of her eye.

She turned to face him. "How come it sometimes feels as though we're being trained to adapt to the other candidates as much as practical skills?"

He shrugged. "Because maybe we are? Ships range from huge to tiny, and stations are the same. You can be the best at what you do, but if everyone despises you, they won't listen when the time comes, and that could be critical."

Trina heard the sense in his statement, but she had no experience with that in her past. She'd always been the one to work from the shadows, always alone. Katie had gone forth and made connections, friends, and a greater purpose. Trina never had.

"Sometimes I wonder if I have what the spacers need after all."

Azizi laughed so hard at that he drew the attention of every student present. "You might believe yourself a loner, and from your talk you do, but look around you. Every candidate in this room benefited from your efforts. You could have kept the knowledge of the program sticks to yourself, or only brought it to my attention. Instead, you stood up to the instructors and chastised them for forgetting all of us. That's not a loner's behavior any more than that you have people on your team asking about you, worried because they never get the chance to see you anymore."

He brushed her hand with the back of his to take the sting out of his argument. "Listen to your instincts. If you're feeling isolated, do something to change that. Spend less time studying and more with your team or me. I miss our sessions after class. You're always in such a hurry to leave. We hardly have the chance to talk anymore."

A flush heated Trina's cheeks as he mirrored her own thoughts about him. She could have followed him to the Pilot quarters any time. She could have seen Deluth and Sharna for herself instead of pushing him for whatever fragments he had to tell her. Was her growing competence worth so much more than the connections she'd made?

Tomorrow, she promised herself. Tomorrow she would skip a lunch session and spend it with her friends even if it meant getting up early enough to run a quick scenario before class.

CHAPTER 29

Deluth had looked for Trina each night, but still she stayed out until after all the other Pilots went to sleep. She should have come for Sharna if not him, though he'd thought they had started to become friends.

The mornings proved no more promising, today's no different than the rest.

Whether she left early or stayed in her room until everyone else had gone to their session, he couldn't tell. He had not earned the right to bang on her door and wouldn't give Redel another reason to complain.

Since their confrontation after the successful session, they'd been stepping carefully around each other. Deluth saw more of his friend in the behavior now that he understood the lack of confidence he'd missed behind the aggression, but that didn't excuse what Redel had done.

How they could find a way past this, he did not know.

He had no interest in driving the team, even if a chance to experience the role would be good for all of them. But Redel would never understand that, never believe it. He saw every action as an attempt to usurp what he'd claimed and never considered the possibility no one else wanted the role.

The air stream ejected Azizi, making their team count complete.

Redel said nothing.

Much to Deluth's relief, it seemed Trina's friend had been included in the uneasy truce, yet another reason why Redel and Trina were inexorably tied in his mind. Thoughts of Trina led to worries of Redel's reaction while pondering Redel's state only led to considering what it had cost Deluth, both in preventing an early friendship and possibly with why Trina kept away even now.

Azizi said little about it, keeping his comments to the classroom whether for his own comfort or to shelter Trina, Deluth couldn't tell.

He wished he had one single fact in all of this, one answer so he could move on or know the effort worth his focus. Instead, he hung in limbo at the edge of a black hole, and he didn't know whether Trina or Redel were standing in safety or deep in the center where only x-rays could escape.

A sharp pain in his side broke through his thought, and Deluth twisted to glare, expecting Redel but finding Azizi instead.

The candidate waved toward the instructor, making Deluth aware the murmur floating at the edge of his consciousness was the instructor giving their briefing.

He grimaced and listened carefully in the hopes of catching up with what he'd missed.

"On a real ship," the man was saying, "you won't always know those you are working with. Your primary team stays largely stable, but you could be asked to take a different shift, a job may require more than one group, or in an emergency, you will work with whomever is closest. There's not time to find your friends."

Deluth nodded, understanding that as obvious, but then every muscle tensed. Were they going to strip them apart just as he'd started seeing the way to help Redel? And if they did, he'd lose even the stray comments from Azizi to give him some idea of what might be passing through Trina's mind.

"Because of this," the instructor continued, "all teams will now be grouped in two. The completion of the scenario will require the combined efforts of both teams."

Tension swept Deluth as he heard the announcement.

Redel had been tracking their team statistics since the very start, and every single loss increased his aggression. Now they'd have an even greater chance of failure.

Deluth forced himself to take a deep breath. It couldn't be as bad as all that. They also had double the chance of success. More people meant more ideas and possible solutions. Just look at how Azizi had pulled off a unique solution to something they'd been struggling with.

He glanced over to Redel and could tell his friend had only the first possibility in mind. He'd see the other team as competition, and whether intended or not, unless they changed the way the results were tallied, he could make a case for it. The tallies did more than show success or failure. They also pointed to weaknesses and strengths, with those weighted against the overall. The two teams could succeed jointly, but have different scores based on the performance of each member.

Deluth rubbed the side of his head, anticipation bringing on a headache rather than any excitement, at least until he turned to see the other team step through the door.

Though half obscured by her teammates because of her slight stature, he didn't think the station could hold two short candidates with hair a blend of blond and other colors.

His first reaction was to grin, one he quickly smothered in case Redel was checking for just such a response. Thought of Redel wiped out the rest of his joy.

He'd been looking forward to working with Trina, to getting her unique perspective on what they faced. Now, they'd be on opposite sides, and if she performed as he expected her to, she'd only attract more of Redel's animosity for upsetting the balance in her team's favor.

Suddenly, the idea of avoiding their quarters in any hour where he might encounter Redel as Trina had been doing appealed to him as well. At least he'd have the chance to talk to her during the discussions after each drill. The two teams couldn't very well evaluate what they needed to change without working together no matter what Redel might prefer.

He lifted a hand on the side opposite Redel and waved a greeting.

Just as unobtrusively, Trina gave him a nod, though she could have been directing the gesture to Azizi for all he knew.

This did not look to be an easy session, and he suspected it would get worse before it got better.

TRINA HAD NO IDEA WHAT team they'd be paired with until she'd stepped through the door and found Deluth looking right at her. Stunned, she managed no more than a nod before following the others to where her drill team gathered. The instructor had carefully explained this was a joint, not competitive, exercise. Something of a relief now that she realized which team would be their partners.

She had no divided loyalties to content with, though this made discussion complicated as she now had two teams in the same place. Instinct told her the assignment had been deliberate. As much as they were trying to introduce new players, it made sense to tease the candidates with new teams that contained some who were already known. Assignments most likely crossed over more than once in a career.

Sharna offered a smile when Trina caught her gaze, but from how quickly her friend smothered the expression, Trina doubted Redel's opinion of her had changed. Azizi spoke in such general terms she didn't know whether everything had gone well or he chose not to complicate things by telling her about it.

She didn't see him until they started toward the simulation room, shocked to realize he'd been standing right next to Deluth the whole time.

He only raised his eyebrows at her, an unspoken question she answered with a shake of her head.

Luck favored Trina in keeping someone between her and Redel through the rest of the briefing, but now he managed a scowl in her direction before turning to follow the rest of his team into the other room.

The Pilots had been closer to that door, each group staying with its members, which meant they'd have first choice of the systems available. Trina hoped that would satisfy Redel, and he wouldn't cause trouble. She'd tried too hard to let animosity hinder her choices.

Besides, pushing Jade to work with her even just that once had brought nothing but rewards. Perhaps working together could do the same with Redel.

She could only hope.

Still, tension swept over her, especially when she saw they'd be paired at many stations. Trina increased her pace, even ducking around Jade to ensure she didn't end up with Redel as her partner. Despite her optimistic thoughts, she didn't think too close a contact would serve any of them well.

Finally the drill began, and everything else melted away.

Trina missed the chance to pair with Deluth, Sharna, or even Azizi, but Jessine seemed nice enough. At least he'd never attacked her.

A laugh threatened to break out when she had that thought, remembering she could not say the same of Deluth, nor could he of her.

She sobered as another warning light blinked at their console. A sudden pressure drop indicated a hull breach. Jessine stepped in to trigger the release of micro particles that were lighter than air so would be drawn to the leak quickly. As soon as any brushed metal, they linked into an unbreakable chain, filling the gap.

"Good work," she murmured, unsure why she'd said a word, but working closely together as they were, it seemed more awkward not to respond.

The meteor shower they'd been unable to avoid continued to pepper the hull with tiny fragments, but Trina saw no more warnings.

She took a quick look around the room, keeping the console in her peripheral vision.

Azizi glanced up at the same time, and she smiled, waiting for him to return the acknowledgement.

A scatter of lights in the corner of her eye distracted Trina, showing the board lit up all over the place.

Jessine reached for the same switch, but she'd covered this contingency in one of her extra trainings. With that many holes sending metal fragments into the air, the particles would bond across the chambers, failing to seal the holes and blocking all efforts to get to the remaining breaches.

Cursing under her breath, she reached for the switch with barely enough time to prevent bonding and the hull collapse that would result.

Someone slammed into her elbow, jolting her arm just enough that instead of stopping Jessine, she triggered the particles herself.

The lights flashed red and the visual display showed the hull collapsing in on itself fast enough to cascade the effect through the whole.

She had her fingers on the switch.

"This failure is all on your head."

Trina glanced up to see who had spoken, unsurprised to find Redel the one accusing her of causing the failure though she hadn't thought he'd been anywhere nearby. The command console he'd chosen stood some distance from her spot.

"I didn't—" Her explanation died as she took the almost manic glee in his expression. No matter what she said, he'd reject it, and the others would follow his lead, thinking she tried to throw the blame on someone else, especially the Pilots who had never seen her work.

"Your hand was on the switch. Don't think I didn't see that before you pulled away. If you'd left it alone, some other team member might have had the chance to enact the correct solution."

She glanced at Jessine. His expression held tension at the conflict but no sign of guilt.

Suppressing a sigh, Trina realized he hadn't even seen her go to correct the error, most likely didn't even know there was an error, and the system would show only that this console triggered the wrong solution, or rather the wrong one for that specific event. It was Redel's word against hers, and he had a following while she had just begun to prove herself.

"Didn't the instructor say we fail or succeed as a team?"

Trina stared at Jade. Of all of them, she was the last one Trina thought would speak out, and she'd assumed none would.

Then Jade continued, "There are many variables to any situation. Her action may have been the last one, but we should evaluate every single step to track how we ended up so deep in the emergency that even normal measures couldn't get us out. We'd be foolish to ignore the rest. Correcting that one misstep wouldn't have saved us."

Though not given the lead on this one because of the mixed team, Jade had done it often enough to understand the need to study all factors so they could improve. Her coming to Trina's defense had been a side effect, not the true purpose, a fact obvious to everyone.

They trooped out to the discussion area, and both Jade and Redel took seats near the screen so they could point out the problems. Trina expected a continuation of the conflict, but Redel shared the lead with Jade, pointing out one thing while she took the next.

Trina figured he was taken in by Jade's sharply defined features and tilted eyes. If he'd known Jade was colony-bred like Trina, he most likely wouldn't have let her say a word.

It only proved Jade's wish to stay separate. Too many saw the colonies as backwaters with no value beyond basic trade goods. While Ceric had denied tech a place, most others had not, and tech did not determine the usefulness of candidates anyway. She'd shown as much, even if ones like Redel would refuse to admit it.

They'd stuck with the console groupings in part because of how they'd left the room, so she could feel when Jessine tensed beside her.

Trina glanced up at the screen to see they'd reached the last part of the drill while her mind wandered.

He flushed and gave her a quick look, clearly recognizing the fault was his not hers, but when he opened his mouth to say something, she shook her head.

Someone had bumped her arm at the critical moment. The consoles were placed with enough space between them to avoid such accidental interference, and Jessine had been on her other side. Only Redel had been out of place. He'd been much too near.

If he wanted to make her fail that desperately, no effort to reveal the truth would change his loudly voiced opinion. His displeasure would just land on Jessine as well, benefiting no one.

Trina accepted the looks sent her direction as the discussion covered the error without comment or protest. Mistakes happened, whether it had been by her hand or another's. The important thing to get out of it was how to prevent the problem from reoccurring, and with Jade focusing the discussion, she knew they would cover that—in detail.

CHAPTER 30

Deluth had been watching Trina closely throughout the exercise, curious about how she worked. He might not have seen exactly what happened, but Redel should not have been over there to discover her error, if it had been hers in the first place.

From Jessine's tension whenever the team discussed it later that day after Trina left for her other classes, he suspected more to the story. But he didn't know anything. Trina had spoken little though she'd joined them for lunch for the first time.

Beyond the start of a protest right after Redel had accused her, she'd accepted the blame and said nothing more.

"So are you ready to give up on your colony girl yet? She blew the whole scenario her first time out."

Redel's question came as Deluth had been reviewing the events in his head for the hundredth time that evening when he should have been studying instead of staring into space on one of the lounges.

"Are you sure of what you saw?" he asked without thinking. As soon as the words crossed his lips, he wished them unspoken, but the reaction came too late.

"Are you accusing me of lying?" Redel's joking tone had hardened in an instant. "Her hand was on the switch. Jessine, back me up here."

The other candidate tensed again and gave a half-hearted wave. "I didn't see what she was touching." He sat down at an open terminal though he'd been on his way to the meal room from his previous trajectory.

Redel frowned, but Jessine couldn't see him so he turned to Deluth. "If I'm wrong, how come your precious colony get didn't protest?"

Deluth shoved a hand through his hair, fingers tangling as he realized it had grown even longer while he'd been at the station. "She didn't really admit to it either. And even if everything happened as you said, you saw the review just as I did. That girl from the other team, Jade, showed how each of us made a mistake or two, herself included." He added the last in the hopes Redel would recognize mistakes weren't as important as figuring out how to prevent them the next time.

"I didn't," Redel snapped, clearly missing the message.

Deluth forgot all his good intentions at Redel's flat refusal to see. "Then why were you so far out of position? If you were needed at your console, there's no way you could have gotten there in time."

"In case you didn't notice over in the corner you'd staked out, there were two people at every console. If something needed doing, that other guy could have done it."

Deluth sighed. "And what if that other guy didn't know how? This was a tough scenario, and not one we've run across. That's the real reason everything fell apart, something you'd recognize if you ever stopped trying to catch Trina in an error. We didn't know what to do. We hadn't faced something like this before, and we're not experienced enough to extrapolate the right answer."

Redel gave a sour laugh as he turned to go. "You keep telling yourself that. You'll do anything to defend her, even go against me after all we've been through. But I want you to think about one tiny flaw in your theory. With her on our joint team, we'll never have the chance to gain the experience. All it takes is one person screwing up and the cascade begins. She's going to drag down her team and us along with it. We'll see what you think of her when we all wash out of the training."

Before Deluth could come up with a coherent response, Redel had vanished into the meal area. He had no wish to continue the argument. Redel had to know his statements were false even if Trina had been responsible for the final flaw in their approach. He had to understand they were all at fault or he'd never learn. The experience they all sought would be denied him.

Deluth rubbed his temples again, hoping the return of his headache didn't signal something greater than simple frustration. How could he help Redel if his bunkmate refused to be helped? How could he prevent Redel from interfering again and making sure his prediction came true?

He reminded himself tomorrow would be another day and another scenario, this time perhaps one they knew well. Everything hung on the balance of existing knowledge paired with the ability to extrapolate to new situations. And everyone, on both teams, needed to be a part of that.

If he could manage it, Deluth decided he would pair up with Trina himself. Surely Redel wouldn't try something with him right there. At least if the failure came at Trina's hand, Deluth would be sure she'd made the mistake Redel would blame her for.

Redel needed to take care.

If he kept going as he had been, he'd tear the team apart. He'd clearly trapped Jessine in an uncomfortable situation that might just include forcing him to perpetuate a lie not of his making. All this because he couldn't handle the thought that someone born with both feet in the dirt could be a capable spacer, maybe even more capable than Redel was, or would ever be. Especially if he chose to waste his time trapping those from the colonies instead of learning how to improve.

CHAPTER 31

After talking to Redel, or rather listening to Redel spout nonsense, Deluth couldn't settle. He didn't want to eat, and even if he did, Redel most likely sat just around the corner, which meant he had no interest in going to that room.

He shoved to his feet then paused, unsure what he wanted to do.

"You all right?"

Sharna had been focused on a terminal, but perhaps it had been a defensive move like Jessine's since she seemed fully aware of what else had happened.

Deluth shrugged, unable to put his state into words. He was annoyed, angry even, at Redel, but he didn't want to confront that head on.

If Trina had stepped through the entrance just then, he'd have asked her for the truth. That would be the worst possible thing to do. She'd see it as another time when he stood up for Redel when it didn't matter if she'd made a mistake.

He knew she found his old friendship unnerving, and why shouldn't she considering how Redel tried to undercut her at every step?

Suddenly he knew with exact clarity what he wanted, and it wasn't another frustrating discussion that had him pulled in too many directions and strained his loyalties to the breaking point.

"I'm going to go do an extra training session," he said, pretending the silence after her question hadn't stretched too long.

She rose as well. "You want company?"

"No." That answer didn't take any thought at all. He planned to key up a meteor storm and sit out on the hull deflecting the rocks with his fists as long as the program would keep running. Then maybe he'd set it to run twice.

He knew he should be nervous about this increasingly violent streak he'd discovered, but at least he'd found a safe outlet. Deluth refused to think on it any further even as he stepped into the air stream and triggered his destination without hesitation.

His determination not to think, not to keep pondering the same questions until they tore him apart, held firm only until he arrived to find the first room occupied. He hadn't signed it out, but there had never been an issue before now.

Deluth turned to get a gravity suit from the supply closet near the second room when the chime sounded, indicating a scenario had completed.

With reviewing the results, the room wouldn't be ready just yet, but something made him hesitate, wondering who else pushed to practice when most were taking a well-earned rest.

The door swung open, and Trina stepped free.

He stared at her, meeting her equally shocked gaze for a long while before either of them moved.

"You look tired," he said, the first words out of his mouth and ones he would have given anything to recall.

Her eyes narrowed. "Who are you to judge?"

"It's just maybe you should take some time to absorb what you're learning," Deluth tried to explain. "I do the extra because I've been drilling since I was old enough to key in the simulators. All this is new to you. You wouldn't want to wear yourself down until you make foolish mistakes."

Again, he heard his words too late to change them. He'd meant what he said, but he didn't think she'd hear it the way he'd intended.

Her chin jutted out and the space between her legs widened as though getting a broader base for balance. "You believe anything that comes out of that guy, don't you? Have you ever thought to think for yourself? Maybe take a look around and see what is really happening?"

He ran a hand over his face, suddenly as tired as he'd thought she'd looked. She didn't seem the least bit weary now. "I wasn't talking about today's exercise. I'm still not sure what happened there. From what little Azizi said, and the fact that you're here, not with him, I can see you've been pushing yourself too hard. You don't have to be better than everyone else. You just have to be capable. And that's not something you achieve by wearing yourself to the bone."

Whether she'd believe him or not, he was worried about her.

Trina stared at the person she'd thought had become a friend. Clearly she'd been mistaken.

"You are not my parent to tell me to go to my room." Not that her mother had ever done so, and she'd never known her father. "It's good enough for you to be here, but not me? If downtime is so important, why aren't you taking it? Or are you running Redel's errands now and trying to undermine me."

He let out a sour laugh. "I don't think anything could do that. You're so busy trying to be perfect, to outperform everyone, that you have no room left for doubts, or the wisdom that comes from listening to them. This is about learning what you need to know, not fighting with the rest of us. Every single candidate has the chance of becoming a spacer. They have room for all of us and more with how quickly we're expanding through the stars."

If he knew how often she wondered why they'd chosen her over those who'd been left behind, he wouldn't be so quick to believe in her confidence. And she did have to be better, or at least so good that the doubts he found she lacked wouldn't show on the face of every other candidate assigned to work with her. But he wouldn't know anything about that. She saw little need to open her vulnerability to his scrutiny.

"You think this is some grand competition between the candidates, don't you?" he continued, apparently taking her silence as proof. "I thought you were different, but you're just like Redel. No wonder he's had it in for you from the start. He recognizes you're built in the same factory. Here I'd been trying to help you, and you're probably provoking him while I do so."

Blood leached the brown from his skin, turning the dominant color to red.

She should have taken the warning in his complexion, but Trina had faced more dangerous people than he could ever be. If she didn't stand fast, no one would be waiting to give her a boost.

"It's all very well to quote the canon with your focus on learning, but we'll see if you prove any readier to hold to it the next time your friend does something to cut the scores of a colony-bred. You think I didn't see how cautious Azizi was when with your team? You'd like to think it's me, that I'm the one at fault, but you need to look more closely at your own before you run around pointing fingers."

She hadn't meant to say anything. She'd planned just to do a better job of avoiding Redel, but she'd counted Deluth as one of her friends. The warning sounded on her session review, alerting her to the need to trigger the evaluation or save her results, but she didn't want to spend another second where Deluth might be.

Using skills learned in much rougher situations, she charged right at him, not giving him any warning. At the last second, she jerked to one side and past him, almost to the air stream before he got over his surprise enough to call her name.

She ignored him and let the rush of air sweep her as far from him as possible.

Somehow, despite everything, she'd thought he would stand strong against those who worked to make sure others failed rather than being willing to bring all of them to success.

Her chest burned as if she'd been running the streets of First City with an enforcer on her heels. She'd barely been able to concentrate on the simulation before he accused her of…

Her thoughts stalled at that.

Just what had he accused her of?

The air stream slowed and let her out, disorienting Trina before she realized she'd triggered the observation dome instead of the candidate quarters.

She crossed to under the viewport and slid against the wall, imagining she could feel the chill of space and that it, not her confused anger, had caused the cold filling her bones and making them ache.

He thought she was struggling. He never once considered she'd be able to do a spacer's duties. Even if he did question Redel's account of the session, he considered himself capable of tolerating the strain of extra training but not her, not some colony brat who hadn't even known about a program stick until he'd mentioned it.

She sat there for the longest while, staring blindly into the room. Every victory she'd had since coming weighed against each struggle until nothing she did held any value. Or maybe it was just that nothing she did would ever have value in his eyes.

Trina didn't know why that bothered her so much, but she couldn't deny it did, and her spinning thoughts offered neither a distraction nor any answer she was willing to accept.

CHAPTER 32

The next day's drill had gone better in part because Trina ended up paired with Sharna and Azizi shared a console with Jade. There wasn't much room for Redel to do anything underhanded. Especially since the Medicals declared full rotation of stations each day, something the instructor approved of.

Redel could not take command, and give himself more leeway to wander, without blatantly ignoring the instructor.

Still, she'd spent the session with her skin itching as though Deluth stared at her the whole time, waiting for her to mess up. She'd just started to gain the confidence Deluth had mocked her for, not just her own but that of her team, when the rules had changed.

The instructors had to have increased the complexity to maintain a challenge with so many candidates dissecting it. Even knowing that, when red lights flooded the simulation chamber, the failure weighed heavily on Trina.

Azizi nudged her with his elbow, bringing her attention back to the instructor and their current lesson.

Her focus kept wandering to the morning, or worse, to the moment Deluth decided she wasn't strong enough to handle the work.

She forced herself to concentrate, all too aware her drifting attention could be taken as proof she'd become too tired to care.

The instructor droned on about shipping lanes and trade routes. None of this would show up in a scenario, but it was important to know once they had their assignments. She only wished he'd chosen a more interesting way to present the material.

When he mentioned the independent traders, she listened intently for any hint that would help her understand Jade, but most of the time, she struggled to pay attention. Her one personal connection with the concepts, trading stolen goods with Fence, came from a life she'd hoped to leave behind her.

"There will be no assignments for today, but you're encouraged to review the recorded programs on the subject accessible through the screen in the gathering area of your quarters or your room terminals." The instructor laughed. "I know it was fascinating, but remember, the majority of positions have some element of trading involved, whether negotiating your ship's resupply, or figuring out how best to use any extra hull space when on an assignment. It will do you well to know not just the values each area sets, but what each is most likely to need when you are scheduled to cross through that area of space."

After a lackluster chorus of agreement, he waved them off, releasing them to their free time.

Trina headed for the air stream, thinking she should take in some of those programs before what she'd heard today faded.

Azizi caught her arm.

"You're not going for more training, are you? It's too much. Use your breaks to relax. Come have dinner with me?"

She jerked away, remembering how Deluth had mentioned Azizi spoke against her training. "I don't need a nurse to watch over me," she said, ignoring his request. "I can handle my training levels just fine."

Azizi put his hands up in surrender. "I didn't mean it that way. I just want to spend some time with you. Like we used to."

Trina scowled at him, his revision too late. She knew exactly what he'd meant, and she didn't want either of them thinking they had to treat her as if she were fragile. They had no idea what she'd lived through before coming here if they thought a few extra hours of training would tire her out.

"I didn't cause our failure this time, or the last time either."

His forehead wrinkled in confusion. "I didn't say you did. And I'm not surprised about the other day. I'd had my suspicions. Why didn't you speak out?"

Trina shook her head. "It wouldn't have done any more good than your attempt to slow me down. I will not take the chance of him catching me in an actual failure."

Though she'd intended to go to her quarters, and even if Azizi would have no way of knowing what she'd done unless Deluth or one of the others mentioned it, when Trina strode out to the air stream, she sent the simulators as her destination. She wouldn't be able to concentrate on a passive visual display right now anyway. All the frustration she'd felt when Deluth confronted her the previous night had returned intensified.

The simulators offered a way to get rid of this antsy energy without risking anything that would get her into trouble with her teams or the instructors as long as she didn't store her results. If they were setting harder, more complicated tasks, then Trina would just have to figure out how to trigger those same scenarios and work her way through each one.

CHAPTER 33

Deluth had been so sure she'd come to train despite his attempt to persuade her otherwise that he'd gone ahead to wait for her, but no one had been this way in quite some time, and he started to wonder if, perhaps, she had listened.

Redel did nothing to affect the outcome of today's simulation, though they'd failed to figure out the best approach without any assistance on his part.

Deluth had kept his attention split between Redel and Trina the whole time, meaning he'd contributed nothing to their efforts either. Only the assignment of two candidates to every station hid his distraction, but he'd wanted to make sure, whatever happened, Redel had no hand in Trina's performance, or Azizi's for that matter.

It burned that he'd consider his friend capable of harming Azizi just to pursue his unjustified anger against Trina, but he'd seen too much evidence to persuade himself that he misjudged Redel. His friend had lost true purpose in his attempts to ensure no one of colony breeding could succeed.

A groan found its way out of him as he looked at what his life had become. This was supposed to be their victory. The ultimate challenge for them to overcome on the way to becoming what they'd longed to be since as far back as he could remember.

Instead, he stood alone in a darkened corridor waiting for a person he didn't know would even come. If she wouldn't listen to his suggestion of a break, he would help her grow strong enough to defeat any attempts to make her fail. That the main offender was none other than his friend, his bunkmate, and the one he'd thought to be at his side for all time didn't matter. This was the right action to take.

"Who's there?"

The question came from the direction of the air stream, his thoughts all-consuming so he'd failed to notice her arrival. He should have been upset that she'd come after all, but instead, the very light seemed brighter.

He stepped forward, pushing off the wall he'd used as a brace while he waited. "It's just me."

She stopped walking to stare at him, first in shock but soon her expression turned to a scowl. "What are you doing here? Practicing? I thought you said to take what time they gave us for rest." She paused, but before he could reply, Trina added, "Oh, right. That wasn't for you. It's only me who needs the rest in case I find the spacer training too much."

Deluth raised a hand, not to protest but to stop her flood of bitter words.

"I'm sorry. I didn't mean— What I said didn't come out the way I'd intended, and then I got angry. Said some stupid things I wish I had not. I don't think you're weak. I swear."

She leaned all her weight on one hip, her hand braced against the opposite side. "You have a strange way of showing that."

A flush heated his neck and cheeks, but Deluth refuse to let her make him angry a second time. He'd just say something worse.

"I didn't come here to fight. I thought we could train together."

She laughed once. "Why? So you can make sure I'm not figuring anything out? So you can play tricks like your best friend in all the world and make me think I'm worthless?"

Deluth took a deep breath, held it, then let it go slowly. "No. I'm here to help you train so Redel can't do anything to trip you up. I was watching you both today—"

"I knew it," she said under her breath, interrupting him.

"—and I could tell Redel was itching to do something, only he could not. He's not a bad person. I swear he isn't. Or at least he wasn't. He's got some mixed up idea about the colony folks, and he's not ready to admit he was wrong."

"I'd say he's not. He's so determined he's willing to do what it takes to make sure he's right. That's got a name, and it's not a nice one. Pirates use it from what I've been learning in my classes. Sabotage. Or don't they think you ship breeds need any training in how the pirates disable and take ships? Maybe you know all those techniques already."

Deluth found his fists clenched at both sides and his jaw aching with how hard he closed his teeth, but he still fought the anger that seemed all too close to the surface of late. Only when he thought he could control himself did he chance speaking, and only then by ignoring her accusation. She could not know what the accusation meant to anyone who lived on a ship. He couldn't believe she would have made the charge if she had.

"Redel was my bunkmate." He kept his voice soft. "We grew up together, partnered from the moment we were released from our parents' care. He's always been competitive, and on our ship, things were a little different. Rules controlled the extent, but tricks and traps are part of that culture. It's how the ship learns who is clever enough to advance and who never will. It was normal for us then."

He thought her expression softened when he spoke of his childhood, but when he tried to explain their life before spacer training, any ease vanished.

"So he's just following the rules he was raised on? And I should excuse his attempts to make me into the fool? I was raised with my sister. Just as close as you say you were to Redel. If she tried to harm others, or caught me doing something like that, the problem would end because one or the other of us would end it. And you were raised to those rules as well. Does that mean I should expect the same from you?"

Deluth sighed. "I don't have to like everything he's done to feel the pull of loyalty, and you should have seen enough by now to know Redel doesn't respond to a direct approach. I've tried, and he's cut me down."

This time even her voice came softer as she said, "Then cut him loose. Go your own way."

"Could you do that with your sister? Could you abandon her like that?"

Trina gave a sour laugh. "I did abandon her. I came here when she did not share this dream."

He shook his head. "You didn't do it because she'd behaved against your rules. You didn't cast her off when she needed you."

She brushed by him, her words floating over her shoulder. "How would you know?"

Deluth sprinted to catch up and take hold of her arm to stop her. "Because you wouldn't do a thing like that. Would you? Tell me. Would you have left if your sister would suffer for it no matter how much she might have hurt you?"

Trina jerked free, stepping so her face fell in shadow, a move he knew had to be a deliberate attempt to hide her expression. "No," she said after a long pause. "No, I wouldn't leave her like that, not if I thought I could get through to her."

He wished he could summon up a smile at her confirmation, but instead it just made him feel as worn out as she'd looked the other night. His fingers twisted in the black strands of hair coming over his shoulder, and he stared at the shadow above her head.

"I can't abandon Redel either. There's something going on in his mind that's broken, and no one else will stand by him to figure it out.

The others are either taken in by his apparent authority or too wary of becoming his next target to say anything. We fight almost every time we speak, but at least we're still able to talk, and one of these times, I'll get through to him."

She moved then, and he thought she'd brush him off a second time, but instead she put a hand on his arm. "I can understand being trapped by loyalty better than you can imagine. Ultimately, I had to choose which side I wanted to stand on, but I didn't give up trying for a long time before it came to that."

His shoulders rose in a shrug, uncomfortable with the conversation. "Which is why I'm here, and why I'm suggesting we train together. No matter what you might think, I'm pretty sure you're as good if not better than most of the other candidates. I think I can learn something from you, and hope you'd find the same. Together, the training will have twice the value while increasing the chance that if Redel tries something—"

"When he does."

"We'll be able to counter whatever it might be long enough for him to realize how lost he's become."

That brought a smile to her lips. "You want me to train with you so I can help Redel heal his state? You must think me a generous person."

This time his lips curled to match hers. "I seem to remember someone learning how to port a replicator program just so she could gift her whole class."

She didn't respond to his comment except to wave him to follow. "If we're to do this training, we best get started."

Trina glanced over her shoulder at him, and he could have sworn he saw her wink.

"After all, I've heard it's important to get enough rest so we're not tired come the morning session. We wouldn't want to make careless errors, now would we?"

CHAPTER 34

Sympathy for how Deluth suffered between doing what was right and loyalty led her to agree at first, but Trina soon found herself looking forward to their joint training sessions at the end of every day. She'd even teased him about driving her harder than she had herself when the first week passed with no breaks. Their growing comfort showed in how he responded with a laugh instead of the anger she'd seen boiling just under his surface at the start.

"What area do you want to work on today?" Deluth asked then, hand already on the control panel.

Trina nudged him aside, eager to try something she'd figured out in theory but had not had the chance to test just yet. "I'll choose."

He raised both arms in surrender as he moved away, mocking her eagerness.

She hid a grin by keeping her gaze on the panel.

The system worked by allowing the user to set the area, but a randomizer chose what the scenario to test that function would be. They'd been switching between who chose the last few sessions, sometimes selecting it together, and sometimes choosing one that the other had to figure out during the scenario.

Deluth had been right in his thought of how well they would complement each other. Their strengths and weaknesses fell in different sections, much like how she and Azizi had been able to help each other in the class lessons. The only trouble was they were running out of ways to make the scenarios themselves challenging. They were too quick to identify the focus, and too quick to find a solution.

Trina tugged a strand of her hair, a bad habit she'd picked up from Deluth, as she stared at the screen.

Their speed had allowed them to turn around a few of the team scenarios where Trina suspected Redel of trying to set her up, but she'd been careful not to mention her suspicions or push Deluth about his friend. Either Redel would start to see the truth, or Deluth would be forced to choose, but she refused to be the one to bring things to that point.

Her job was different. She had to find a way to keep challenging them in the extra sessions. She enjoyed their training too much to call for an end, but if she and Deluth grew too quick, they'd become complacent, making exactly the type of mistake Deluth had accused her of courting through exhaustion.

She had made mistakes, as had he. They were not perfect. But a mistake because of a misunderstanding or a hole in their training was much different than one made because they didn't bother to pay attention.

"Are you done staring at that screen? I'm starting to suspect you to be the mind reader Sharna thought you were."

She laughed at the reminder. Deluth and Sharna each had told her their speculations about what would get someone with no tech knowledge into the Spacer Guild. They'd recognized her tech skills often enough now to know the thought had little grounding. Still, they liked to tease her, in part because she often noticed what another might have missed. Like with Azizi, she chose not to reveal why she'd become so observant. Her new friends were happy to enjoy her talent without questioning the source.

"Any progress?"

Trina gave up staring and started pushing commands out so they slid between the normal selections. This system had no place to insert a program stick, most likely a sign she should have taken not to mess with the settings, but no one had said it was impossible or against any rules. The better trained they were, the more the Guild would benefit once they were approved as full spacers.

"There."

She stepped away, half expecting the panel to erupt into alarm bells and burning circuits, but instead the door unlocked and slid open, welcoming them into a situation they had never experienced before, though only she knew the difference.

They each took a station, the controls compressed by the setting for only two participants. Trina had asked Jade if it resembled the smaller ships she'd flown that one time they'd trained together, but Jade only shrugged in answer. Trina had decided it both matched and did not because the smaller ships might not have had as many elements while these controls held everything that would be spread out among ten different stations in a full scenario.

A distinct hiss sounded through the room just as three warning lights came up, one on her station and two on his.

"A hull issue? And not even an outside simulation. I would have thought you'd grown tired of plugging these little holes."

Trina shrugged, letting him believe she'd chosen something simple because she wanted the rest. All the better for him to achieve the complacence she'd been worried about.

Sure enough, the next set of warnings showed a failure in the hydroponics section, this one a containment issue sending a flood of water through the two nearest parts of the ship.

Deluth cursed even as he triggered the containment barriers and sent a probe into the section.

She grinned but didn't risk a glance in his direction as she synced the probe sensors to her console and ran through the possible scans to find the source.

He leaned over her shoulder, his part complete, and together they saw the connection.

Deluth reached over to flip the same switch Redel had used to condemn her the first time they'd drilled together. He directed the component into the flooded section to bind the interior break caused by the same microscopic meteor that had damaged the hull. They'd repaired the exterior breach without considering where the projectile had landed. Every other time, it lost momentum before piercing a second wall.

The alarm bells cut off, making Trina feel deafened before the green glow announced the end to the scenario and a successful conclusion.

Trina headed for the door, eager to see the evaluation, with Deluth on her heels.

"I'll have to make it harder next time," she said as they sank down on either side of the screen controls.

"I want to know how you did that at all. I've been working with a system like this for years and never once has it crossed areas like that."

She shook her head. "It wasn't truly a cross. Both were holes."

The display lit up, and he tapped the scenario description. "Hull and food. The system agrees with me. Yes, the problems had the same root, but the results were so different they'd be handled at separate terminals and possibly no connection recognized until too late. This is way better than any scenario I've ever done. How'd you do it?"

She shrugged. "I was worried they were becoming too familiar. If we know the answer already, it's easy to forget to evaluate the whole situation."

"I've been thinking the same. The difference is I didn't know we could do anything about it."

Her cheeks heated with a blush she couldn't suppress and hoped he thought it caused by the compliment rather than the confirmation that she'd almost lost this time with him. It was different than when she worked with Azizi. She felt different. And she hadn't wanted to lose it.

"So, are you going to tell me, or will you leave me hanging."

"You won't like the answer." Considering he didn't know Sharna had played the trick on Azizi on their first break day, this strayed a little closer to condemning Redel than she'd have preferred.

"You didn't break any rules, did you? That could get both of us thrown out of the program."

She scowled at him. That's what she got for trying to protect his feelings. "No. There's no rule against it, at least not that I could find. I got the idea from that trick played on Azizi the first time we got water showers. His preferences were scrambled. I thought the only way I'd catch the person was by getting good enough to do it myself. Now that was sure to be against the rules, but I didn't interfere with the system. I just scrambled the variables a little."

"Just scrambled the variables? That's brilliant."

This time her blush did come from his words. "I wasn't sure it would work. And I half thought the system would collapse under the logic requirements or set off an alarm."

"But it did work. And with that twist, we'll never know, never be able to anticipate, because the initial setting won't be the full of the problem." He laughed. "I didn't know what I was setting myself up for when I asked to partner with you."

Though he'd been laughing, Trina tensed at the last. "I don't have to do it again."

His quiet chuckle vanished, and he stared at her with narrowed eyes. "As much I enjoy our time together, I won't work with you any longer if you stop. You were right. We've become so familiar with the scenarios we were risking becoming a danger. They don't need spacers who slap a quick answer down when a more complicated one is necessary."

Trina smiled, relieved at his answer, but his tension hadn't eased. She waited for whatever he'd say next.

"I know who did that to Azizi. It's not my secret to tell, but she had a very good reason, and she's sorry about it now. I'm sorry too. One more ship culture creating conflict."

Whatever she'd expected, for him to confess Sharna's crime, even without naming her, had not been on the list.

"It's complicated coming here, isn't it? Not just for those from colonies, but the ships each have their own rules that might or might not match what is expected here. I think that's why so much time is spent emphasizing how we need to learn to work with new people."

His mouth twisted into a broken smile. "Here I thought I'd have to convince you not to drag me before the instructors and force me to reveal the person. Somehow, I get the feeling you already knew, though you've never been vindictive."

She laughed at that. "I do know. That's how Sharna and I became friends, at least part of it, but if you remember how I accused you of the same crime, you'd know I'm not all that forgiving."

"Not when a friend is harmed. I remember."

"Our instructor, Fred, took care of the injury. Azizi was ready to let it go right then and accept it was a system error. It took me a little longer."

He tapped her hand. "I'm glad to know you're not perfect. You'd never put up with my flaws if you were."

The evaluation beeped a warning to store or start the analysis, breaking what had become intense before it could get awkward.

She triggered the analysis, allowing herself one quick glance at him, an effort met by a smile, before she turned her full attention to what they'd done right and what they could have done better.

Just because they'd been successful didn't mean there was nothing to learn.

CHAPTER 35

At the end of their third month with shared drills and separate classes, Fred informed them full integration with their drill teams would begin. Trina missed the chance to spend time with Azizi outside of the drills, but she kept herself too busy over the next two months to dwell on it. She spent every moment studying or drilling with Deluth, barely stopping to eat and sleep.

The instructors had informed them the final test was coming soon, and that it would be practical. Nothing more.

Every candidate was on edge. Even though Redel had given up on trapping Trina, Azizi became the next target.

She did her best to shield him from the brunt of it, but somehow each evaluation resulted in Redel lingering on some flaw in Azizi's performance, real or imagined. She only escaped being his target because she still counted as one of the Medicals.

"And so we missed a perfect score because one of us, Candidate Demai, failed to synchronize the trigger."

Trina gritted her teeth at the patronizing tone. If she hadn't seen Redel tap Azizi on the shoulder just as the countdown ended, she'd be with the rest in thinking Azizi had not been paying attention. But if she called him out, Redel would be sure to have a good reason for his actions, one that only made Azizi look worse. She'd learned that lesson the hard way, with Azizi suffering the consequences.

Finally, the briefing ended and the teams split to continue their lessons. Trina had been added to the Medicals' schedule just as Azizi joined the Pilots.

She paused outside the drill room, pretending to have twisted her ankle as the Pilots filed by. When Deluth would have stopped to help, she shook her head. She'd have to explain in the evening if he didn't figure it out on his own.

"Azizi." She caught his arm when he moved past her, oblivious to anything in that way he'd adopted to keep from letting Redel bother him. "Are you all right?"

He shrugged her off. "I need to stay with my team, as do you."

"Why don't you come with us for training tonight? It'll give you some time away from both of your teams and might help with Redel."

"We both know it won't. The only reason you get away with it is Redel doesn't have access to you. You're barely in your quarters at all from what Sharna tells me. Deluth, of course, is just as bad. If I start working with the two of you, word will get back to Him, and Deluth's untouchable."

She heard the capital H and knew exactly whom Azizi meant. Deluth's efforts to help had only made Redel more aggressive toward whomever Deluth wasn't shielding. The required drills had become an awkward dance between the two of them with Azizi thrust in the middle.

"I miss our time together."

He gave her a twisted smile. "You could always follow me home for dinner."

"We need to be training. With the final test coming up, and no details, the only way to survive is to prepare for anything." They'd worked almost six months preparing for this moment. She would not make Nishan and the rest regret their support.

Azizi nodded at her answer, no surprise in his expression. "I'd study with you if I could, but there's too much at risk for me to give another opening to Redel. If he had half the programming skills you've developed, he would have found a way to destroy all my exercises in every class."

She tapped his arm. "I'm sorry he hates you."

That provoked a laugh. "He doesn't hate me, Trina. He barely acknowledges me. I'm just a tool to get at you, and you're the way to Deluth. That guy has problems deeper than the air stream transport is long, but until he steps over whatever invisible line the instructors have set, I have to deal with him."

Trina frowned, wishing she could do something that wouldn't end up making a bad situation worse.

"Oh, don't look that way. It's not so bad." Azizi shrugged. "It's not like he can do any real harm. Think of it as training in how to work with unpleasant spacers. There's sure to be a few who are clever enough to get through training and skilled enough to get decent assignments. He's doing me a favor. After him, I'll be able to manage anyone who crosses my path."

She shook her head, but this time with a smile. "Don't let him crack your stoic mask then. If it's any consolation, I'd guess your lack of a reaction is driving him mad."

"Mad is what he'll be if I show up late enough to delay our next classroom session, and I don't imagine your group will be all that pleased either." He caught her arm as she turned toward the air stream. "I appreciate the effort, and the knowledge you think of me as busy as you are. I'm still your friend. I just can't afford to rile him further. The easiest way to do that is to remind him where my loyalties lie. They're certainly not with him and his claim of leadership. I'm counting the days until the final exam. One way or another, I'll be quit of him."

They walked to the transport together, but Trina let Azizi jump in first and waited the delay designed to prevent collisions. He'd been right about her team's annoyance, but they wouldn't try to make her fail because of it. She'd been working hard enough at everything to have earned their grudging respect, and in some cases perhaps, not even grudging.

CHAPTER 36

Deluth came to the next day's drill a little ahead of everyone. He'd hoped to catch a moment with Trina, who was usually among the first to arrive.

Despite sharing quarters, she needed to check in with her assigned team before starting her day, and this morning they'd had class first. She'd come to the drill area as soon as she finished her work, but he didn't see her anywhere yet.

He scowled at the empty room, wanting to talk to her if only for a few minutes. She had a way about her that grounded him, and he needed that after the disaster of class. Besides, she would not question what happened as almost any other would.

She didn't fawn over Redel.

Redel chose a different target this morning, one of the quiet members of the team who never did anything to stand out. If Deluth hadn't seen Redel reach over, he'd have been quick to deny his friend would ever change another candidate's answers, but that's exactly what Redel had done.

Deluth let out a slow breath, counting through the exhale to reduce his tension.

The breakfast Trina luckily missed had been a masterful act by Redel. He spoke in confidence to first one person then another, his voice projected to fill every corner of the room. Deluth couldn't challenge a single thing he said, either. It was all in tone and attitude. The words themselves could even be seen as kind or supportive without the full context that made them cutting.

He'd been on edge already, and seeing Redel mar someone else's score so his would look better just pushed Deluth off course. The terminal said only that the option had been selected, not who had done the selecting.

The poor, flustered candidate couldn't remember what he'd done, and under Redel's glare, would have agreed to anything. Deluth couldn't stand by and let the boy suffer.

That choice only made his day worse.

When he went to talk to the instructor, Redel made changes to his terminal as well. By the time Deluth discovered the meddling, it was too late. It appeared as if he'd set up the previous situation to cover his own errors. After all, everyone looked up to Redel.

The instructor had been kind but firm.

Deluth wanted to put his fist through the wall. He hadn't needed a solo hull scenario in weeks, but tonight, he might just have to skip out on his joint session and take a turn at punching meteors again.

The sound of approaching voices offered hope, though not of a private word with his very own touchstone. He'd have to make do with the calming influence of her presence. Maybe they'd share a terminal.

He could feel the tension ebbing. With her there, he would survive this drill without coming to blows with Redel and getting himself tossed out of the program.

The rest of the Pilots arrived at the same time as the other team, offering a jumble of faces Deluth couldn't sort out at first, but a sick feeling started in his stomach as he realized the instructors had shifted things once again.

Trina wasn't coming here. She'd been sent to a different session along with the other Medicals.

No one bothered to introduce him. They'd clearly done so generally at the transport and grouped him with the Pilots.

Sharna stepped to his side even as they all filed into the simulation room. "You look like you're about to explode. Are you all right?"

It was warning enough to get his act together. He'd thought to use Trina for control, but there would be times like now when she couldn't come, and who knew if they'd get a shared assignment. He needed to behave as if nothing had happened that morning and do his best for the team no matter how he might feel about their self-appointed leader.

He took a station off in the far corner and stared down at the console, only shifting to one side when a member of the Political team joined him. No matter what, he'd stay here and focus.

Even if Redel took to leaping from console to console as if they were floating steps in an anti-grav exercise, he wouldn't look.

The scenario reached a crisis point, and nothing Deluth or his station partner could do had any hope of affecting it.

Despite his best intentions, he glanced around the room.

"You pushed the wrong button!"

Redel's cry rang out a heartbeat before the abandon ship alarms sounded and the scenario dissolved into a flash of red light.

"I did exactly what you told me to," Azizi said, his voice low and intense.

Deluth found himself halfway over there before consciously deciding to move.

Redel stepped away and said in his deepest, projecting voice, "Isn't that like a colony-bred not to take responsibility. I didn't tell him anything. That isn't my station."

Azizi met Deluth's gaze from the three stations still separating them, but despite the plea in the other candidate's eyes, Deluth could do nothing. He had no proof that Redel did this. He'd kept his head down and focused. For all he knew, Redel had stayed at his station until the very end.

"Did none of you see him? Hear him?" Azizi demanded, but he'd been off to the side opposite Deluth, and the one station without a partner since the Political team had one fewer member.

No one spoke up as witness.

"Falsely accusing another is a serious charge," Redel said. "You'd better back down."

"To falsely accuse, the accusation has to be false."

Suspect all he could, and with the evidence of Redel's gloating expression, he did suspect Azizi of having the true account, Deluth could not speak out twice in a day without proof.

Redel had chosen his timing well. Not only had Deluth been too angry to watch for further issues, but with the Political team joining them, the other candidates had no experience with Redel's games. Why wouldn't they believe him when Azizi seemed to accuse him only because he'd called out the error?

Deluth gritted his teeth to keep his tongue behind them. He'd already been made to appear a liability to the program with this morning's mess. If he stood up for Azizi, it would only look like another effort throw blame, and his poor standing would spread to Azizi. He tried to tell Azizi to give up with his intent gaze, but the other candidate either didn't see or chose to ignore.

"You did, and you know it," the colony-bred stated with a rare stubbornness.

If only Trina had been there.

He followed the others from the room without going all the way to Azizi's side. For once, his presence would offer no benefit and could cause harm, though he did ask who hasn't made an error at this point as they went through the analysis. The new team's members were quick to agree, brushing off the issue in favor of figuring out why they hadn't been able to prevent the situation from growing into a crisis before it came to that point.

Deluth listened to them and glanced around at the other Pilots, wishing their team would be as focused on improving instead of this strange dance between Redel and whomever Redel decided was his enemy.

Sharna shifted through the others until she could put a hand on Azizi's shoulder. The colony-bred shot her a grateful glance, and Deluth sighed inwardly. He only hoped Azizi and Sharna both would understand why he'd held back. Especially with Trina missing, he suspected there would be more trouble coming.

One thing this day had showed him was the fact he'd been trying to ignore.

Redel wouldn't come to his senses. Redel wouldn't give up this competitive play and allow them all to work together.

He planned to speak with his friend after classes, and that might just be the last time he called Redel anything more than someone who hailed from the same ship.

Three spacers strode through the door, one in the instructor's purple and two in security green.

Redel pointed to Azizi. "He accused me falsely. Ask anyone. He tried to throw the blame for his error. The analysis shows clearly he was the last to touch the button."

"Only because you told me to. He did. Why should I stay quiet while he lies?"

The green suits nudged everyone else out of the way and took Azizi by the arms. "You can explain it all to the council."

Azizi stared around for Deluth again, but this had gone past where he could stop it.

Deluth stood helpless as the security officers marched Azizi away. This could not be a simple decision to remove him from the program. The instructors would have handled it. Somehow, Redel had turned the moment into a criminal act.

Once they'd vanished from sight, no one, not even Redel, seemed willing to continue the analysis.

For the first time since Redel had accused Deluth of trying to usurp his position as leader, the others on their team looked to Deluth for direction. The confusion on their faces showed they didn't understand what had happened any better than he did.

"Why don't we go to our next classes?" Deluth said, the question more of a statement or command. "There's nothing more to be learned here."

Redel shot him an approving glance, but Deluth didn't think he'd keep that opinion for long.

He waited for the two teams to file out to the transport area, then caught Redel's arm, holding on when he would have joined the others.

"Why did you do that? Whether you told him to or he misunderstood, you pushed him to argue. Azizi is not the type to throw the blame onto others. We all know that, even you."

Redel tugged free and gave a long, clearly artificial, sigh. "If you all knew it, how come no one, not even you, spoke in his defense?"

"You know exactly why I didn't," Deluth charged, scowling at his former friend. "If I had, I'd be the one carted off by Security after what you pulled this morning. You're lucky I didn't strangle you then or now."

"You never would." Redel shook his head slowly. "I don't know why I ever thought you a threat. You're loyal to a fault, to me, to Trina, and now to Azizi. Can't you see the team is stronger without them here?"

"What I see is you've fallen off course and you're threatening to take the rest of us with you. I'll speak at his council. You know I will."

Redel smiled then. "Of course you will. And when you do, your own behavior will be called up for consideration. With the unfortunate incident this morning, they'll discount your words, or you better hope they will. Otherwise, you'll be brought right up next to him."

Deluth clenched both fists at his sides, fighting for a calm that had deserted him. "Why Azizi? If this is all an effort to discredit me, to eliminate a threat that never existed beyond your twisted mind, why not call them on me this morning?"

"You know the answer to that."

Redel reached out as though to pat him on the head, but Deluth ducked to one side, barely stopping himself from slapping the hand away.

His former friend only smiled broader. "Exactly. You backed down. You avoided the confrontation growing to the point that I could not stand off without losing face. Azizi wasn't smart enough."

Deluth watched the candidate stride to the air stream without another word, seeing the boy he'd grown up with stripped away like cracked heat shields until he had no connection with what remained.

If only he knew where Trina had gone. He needed to get word to her somehow. Redel had been right about his word being tainted, but hers wouldn't be. Azizi had friends outside of this team who could speak to his character.

"YOU'RE FRIENDS WITH THAT Shekel candidate, aren't you? The pretty boy?"

Trina glanced up at Jade, surprised the other girl initiated contact, especially with their next class about to begin. "You mean Azizi."

"Yes, him. He's been taken to the council. A formal hearing. Charges laid against him and everything."

Trina surged to her feet, grabbing Jade's arm. "What are you talking about? He wouldn't have done anything to warrant that. You worked with him long enough to know he wouldn't."

The other candidate tugged free. "That's why I'm telling you. I had to run an errand before this class and bumped into a shipmate on the Political team. Like us, your Pilots were paired with another team today, the Politicals. Some guy on your team had it in for Azizi, questioning everything he did after the system recorded an error on his part. But Azizi didn't take it. He started claiming the guy had told him what to do, told him the wrong thing on purpose."

"If Azizi said it, that's the truth."

Jade shrugged. "No one saw, and the recording only holds who did what action. Whatever the guy told Security, they sure took it seriously."

"Candidates, please take your seats."

From the irritation in the instructor's tone, Trina suspected this had not been the first time they'd been told, but for once she couldn't listen. "I have to go," she told the woman. "It's important."

Her statement triggered a scowl from the instructor. "It better be. If you miss something here, you might not be able to do your exercises. Too much work left undone, and your position will be at risk."

"I understand."

Her quiet answer must have satisfied something because the woman gave a stiff nod. "Then go. You're wasting valuable class time."

She didn't wait for a second request. Her risk of facing something she couldn't understand was higher than it had ever been before if Jade had understood correctly. She'd counted on Azizi to help her whenever she faced something incomprehensible. But he deserved to be in the program and she wouldn't stand by while they threw him out.

All the way to Security, she mulled over the little information she had. The guy, though unnamed, had to be Redel. But why go after Azizi, and why so publicly. He'd chanced being caught by one of the others. If any had seen him speaking to Azizi before the event, whether they could have heard the words or not, it would call his whole accusation into question. He risked his own career for what? An unreasoned objection to anyone who'd grown up with a living planet beneath their feet?

Thought of their homes reminded her of what Azizi had told her of his colony. They provided everything anyone would need to succeed at whatever they might aspire to, but should they fail, the costs for that indulgence fell on their shoulders alone.

While it meant people wouldn't waste resources on something they'd never be able to achieve, the expense to send Azizi to spacer training had to outweigh anything he could have earned at home by a strong margin. He had not been among the wealthy to start out with or he'd have had access to every bit of tech any ship-bred candidate had.

This charge risked much more than Azizi's spacer career. She doubted Redel knew enough to realize that, but wondered if it would have changed his actions one bit.

The Security Office stood down near the entry ports, a path she hadn't traveled since she, herself, arrived. Her teeth ached from clenching them as she approached the innocuous door labeled only with a green stripe. No need to waste words when the uniform color held enough meaning to send tension down her spine.

She tried to focus on Patty, the security officer who had become a friend on the colony ship but instead her mind drew up images of every time the Ceric enforcers had come close to snatching her.

The hand she raised to trigger the door shook, but Trina could not let her fears stop her, not with Azizi's future at risk. Not with the likelihood his friendship with her rather than anything of his own nature had triggered Redel's attack.

As if to laugh at her, the door slid open to reveal a pretty woman frowning at the terminal on her desk. Her green uniform revealed her section but any resemblance to the enforcers was lost.

She looked up and blinked as she took in Trina's lack of uniform. "Can I help you?"

No one would end up coming to this office by accident, but Trina wished she could say she'd triggered the wrong door anyway. What could she do to help Azizi? She hadn't been there. If the charges were simply for claiming Redel had been responsible, wouldn't her accusations only put her in the same position? She wished she'd had time to talk to Deluth, but he'd defended his friend before this, and she didn't see him here arguing on Azizi's behalf.

"Candidate?"

She'd stood silent too long.

The woman's frown deepened, and Trina struggled for how to phrase her need.

All of a sudden, the security officer laughed, shaking her head. "I'm not some monster to gobble up children no matter what you might have been told. Us Greenies are a likable bunch on most days." She pinched the bridge of her nose. "At least when we're not weighted down with recordkeeping."

Trina shifted from foot to foot, uncomfortably aware the forms could be related to her request, but she'd come too far to give up now. "I need to speak to Azizi Demai, the candidate sent down here before lunch."

Though the woman smiled, Trina detected a flash of pity, something she'd become sensitive to in her time with Samuel's household. Only that kept her from arguing when the woman said the expected refusal.

"He's been isolated. No one can see him before the hearing. It's policy in these cases."

Trina stepped closer, trying to get a glimpse of the screen. "I'm a friend. I need to know what happened," she said to distract the officer.

With narrowed eyes, the woman swiped her screen so it went dark before Trina could make out any of the words. "You can speak for him at the hearing, not before that. It will take a lot to convince the board he's not a liability. The evidence is damning."

All her energy went into holding her tongue when Trina wanted to demand to know what evidence they could possibly have. From what Jade told her, the case was a simple matter of one account conflicting with another. Why would they have given Redel's word so much more weight?

The officer put a hand out to brush Trina's arm. "It's okay to have doubts. Sometimes we don't know people as well as we thought we did. It can happen to any of us. But go ahead and speak. If you can give the board a different picture of this candidate, perhaps they'll be willing to give him another chance. Maybe he is the person you think you know." She paused, her gaze turned inward. "You'll always have the questions if you don't go whether you speak or not. At least this way you can learn exactly what he's charged with."

"Can't you tell me?" Trina hadn't meant to play on the woman's sympathies, but clearly she knew something more. None of this made sense otherwise.

Again the officer shook her head. "I cannot speak outside of the hearing. Rumors are too quick to spread, and even if the hearing goes for the candidate, the wrong words could undermine trust. Only those committed to the case and bound by it are aware of the fullness. If you request the chance to speak, you will be held accountable should rumors begin. Know this is not a simple thing you do, but if you believe in this candidate, you may be all that stands between him and punishment."

Shaken, Trina could only nod as she headed to class. She couldn't disagree about the rumors. After all, she wouldn't have known Azizi needed her except for one of the Politicals telling Jade.

Something didn't seem right, but she couldn't know what unless she went to the hearing. It was too late to do any research on her own to offer as counter evidence. The scenario analysis must have showed nothing to help him, but how could it have condemned?

CHAPTER 37

Deluth paced the corridor between the transport and their quarters, feeling as if he spent all his time looking for Trina. He needed to tell her what had happened before Redel caught sight of her.

She would react. Who wouldn't? And he didn't want to see her in the same trouble as Azizi, especially not when Azizi needed her help.

The change in air pressure gave warning before the transport ejected its passenger.

He leaned against a wall, standing out of sight in case some other candidate stepped free as one had every other time since classes ended.

His stomach growled, a sign of just how long he'd been waiting, but she had to come to their quarters at some point. The only other person she'd eaten with had been Azizi.

Remembering how late she'd stayed with her friend offered little reassurance.

The candidate entered the corridor, and Deluth's breath rustled out on a relieved sigh as he recognized her short stature and striped blond hair.

"Trina."

The look she sent him seemed almost wary, though why she'd be uncomfortable around him, he couldn't imagine. She'd been fine when they'd finished last night's training session.

After a hesitation so slight he wasn't sure he'd seen it, she continued forward to meet him. "What are you doing here?"

"Waiting for you. I wanted to catch you before Redel does."

"Why? So you can protect him like you always do?" Her words came out hard and fast.

The vehemence stunned him for a heartbeat. "So I guess you've heard about Azizi? That's why I'm waiting for you."

"Yes, I've heard. And I can't believe none of you stood up for him. You know Azizi wouldn't lie about something like this. Since when does letting Azizi be taken by Security count as friendship. Redel has a lot to answer for."

She glared at him, and a flush heated his cheeks at the unspoken accusation. She hadn't been there, hadn't seen how quickly it all happened. He would have spoken if it would have done any good.

Then her last statement caught up with him.

Deluth grabbed her arm. "You can't do that. Don't bring your own charges against Redel."

If anything, her stare hardened as she jerked away. "Why not? He's responsible for all of this. You might consider him a friend, but he's never been one of mine. If you won't hold him accountable, be sure I will."

He moved to block her, frustration tangling his reasoned arguments. "If you do that, you'll be the one who suffers." The instructors seemed blind to Redel's faults, and Deluth felt sure at least some of the other candidate's followers would support him no matter what proof she offered.

Trina shifted her weight into a solid stance. "Are you threatening me?"

Unlike the heat of before, these words came out quiet, but he wasn't fooled. "Of course not. I'm trying to protect you."

As he watched her eyes narrow and her hands twitch, he knew he'd chosen the wrong answer.

"I don't need your protection, something you should know by now. You're just trying to protect Redel like you always do. All this time, have you been figuring out my weaknesses like you did Azizi's so when the time comes you can have Security cart me away as well?"

He rocked on his heels, stunned by the charge. "Is that what you think?"

"Why didn't you stand up for him?"

He slapped both palms against his thighs, having asked himself the same question ever since they'd been sent to quarters rather than finishing out their scheduled classes. It had seemed the best action at the time. He'd thought his intervention would only make the situation worse, but that was before Security arrived. When the guards came, he'd stood silent with the rest, stunned, confused, but silent.

"Exactly."

She shoved past him, but he couldn't let her throw her career away like Azizi had. Redel's explanation rang in his ears. Trina wouldn't back down either.

He caught her arm. "Don't go after him, Trina. Don't do it."

She tugged against the hold, but he tightened his grip, staring down at her, begging her with his gaze to save herself.

At first he thought the effort a failure, but then her eyes glazed over as though she remembered something. Her scowl didn't vanish, but she gave him a tight nod.

It wasn't much reassurance, but he had to accept it as this time she broke his hold and charged off down the corridor, clearly still angry, and clearly angry at him.

Deluth groaned, thrusting a hand through his hair as he stared after her.

He hadn't asked for much. Just to become a spacer. How could such a simple desire have come to this? Training was supposed to prepare them for the future, not destroy that chance.

DELUTH SEEMED TO STAND BY Redel no matter what his shipmate did. Her grandfather had expected the same loyalty, but in the end, she could not give it.

The Greenies might not be monsters, but in some respects they were no different than the enforcers on Ceric. Once brought to their attention, she doubted any candidate could return to the teams as if it hadn't happened.

Trina knew forcing a confrontation with Redel would do nothing to help Azizi. That, not any threats from Deluth, kept her going through the gathering and meal areas of her quarters without stopping even when Sharna called out to her. If Deluth had proven where his loyalties truly held, how could she trust Sharna? Their only connection was one of shared secrets.

She slapped the palm lock for her room, twisted through the half-open door, and triggered it to seal again.

Trina had stayed after her last class to talk to Fred. The instructor told Trina exactly what to do so she could speak for Azizi, her expression tense. It had taken all Trina's energy not to demand Fred follow the same procedures.

She had to gather calm about her before the morning. Azizi would be counting on her help, and anger only led to foolish words and greater dangers. She should have remembered that when Deluth stopped her.

The scowl returned at that thought.

She'd believed him a friend, maybe more than a friend.

They'd worked together to keep Redel in check. He'd protected Azizi before.

The bed groaned as she tossed herself onto it, staring at the blank screen of her terminal.

Every time she'd been protecting Azizi, Deluth had been ensuring his friend didn't go past the point that would threaten his standing in the program. She'd thought they were working together, but though their actions aligned, the purpose could not have been more different.

And now, someone well suited for the cooperative nature of the Spacer Guild would suffer while the one who twisted everything to his benefit would continue making trouble.

"Not if I can help it," she ground out into the silent room.

Finding her focus, Trina triggered the terminal and requested the forms to officially declare herself an advocate. She'd miss more than the half of class she'd lost today, but the form, according to Fred, would excuse her and give her time to make up the work. But more than that, the form stated unequivocally that not all of the candidates believed the charge to be true, no matter what the evidence might indicate.

The terminal hummed for a few seconds once she clicked submit.

Trina stared at the screen, wondering if it could be that simple, only to have her question answered.

The display lit with a new message, stating time and place for the hearing.

Tension coiled within her.

The very next morning would determine if Azizi would stay in the program or return to a colony that wanted him like this no more than Ceric would have welcomed her with open arms.

CHAPTER 38

Trina stayed in her room until the last second, hoping all the others would have gone before she came out. Luck was with her though she could only grab a quick serving of something called protein paste before she raced to the air stream and entered the hearing room as a destination.

Everything she knew came from one of her classes.

Her mother never spoke of what happened after she was captured beyond telling Trina never to get caught. When Patty arrested her grandfather, she had not followed him to his office, and the office down by the docking bays revealed little of how it held prisoners. Her chest burned at the thought of Azizi as a prisoner.

She stumbled when the air stream pressure died and thrust her into an unfamiliar section, one ending in a series of doors rather than corridors. She didn't know where to go.

A security officer she hadn't noticed glanced at his screen. "Trina of Menthak."

She waited for him to say something more, but he did not. After an awkward pause, she nodded. He had wanted her to confirm her identity. His flat tone sounded more like a statement than a question.

"Your papers are in order," he said without commenting on the delay. "Go through the third door on your right. Do not talk to the others waiting in the testimony box about anything pertaining to this case. You will be monitored."

Again she stood there, unsure whether she'd been released or not until he gave an impatient wave. But in the time she'd waited, she understood his words. Others had come forward to speak for Azizi after all.

Trina tugged the door open and stepped into a small, dimly lit room. The far wall revealed the reason as it looked out into a much bigger space, one she recognized from her class to be the true hearing room.

The sight distracted her enough she didn't see the others until Sharna stepped forward. Only then did she turn to see Deluth as well.

She froze, confusion fighting with hope. After their confrontation, she'd been so sure he would side with Redel, but Redel wasn't going before the council and the testimony spoke only for the accused.

"What are you doing here?" The question sprang from her before she could consider if it violated the rules set down.

Sharna shrugged, unaware the question had been intended for Deluth. "I owe him, and I owe you. That could have been me."

Trina said nothing in response.

Sharna could have been talking about a conflict with Redel, and the owing from help with their studies. Only she and the other candidate knew exactly what they held between them, and both would have to take care to keep their own failures from coming to the attention of Security here in the heart of that domain. Especially with the warning their conversation was being observed by more than Deluth, who already knew.

"They're calling us in one at a time, and each interview seems to take forever," Deluth said, still ducking her question.

"Who else?"

Sharna twisted her hands together, staring at a door Trina had missed in the dimness. "At least one instructor and a candidate I don't know."

"And one from the Politicals, the group we'd been training with," Deluth added. "He went in first."

Trina wanted to hope, but how could a person who had known Azizi such a short time be an advocate? Azizi told her he'd been the only candidate from his planet. It had been a long journey to the station, but he'd spent most of it studying.

She shifted to the far corner, keeping Deluth's position visible at the edge of her vision. If they'd called a stranger, Deluth's presence could have a very different meaning.

The inner door swung open just then, and a spacer in green stepped through. "Trina of Menthak."

Though startled when she'd been the last to arrive, this time she understood the flat tone to mean a request. She moved forward, the burning in her chest spreading to a numb tingling in her limbs.

Her words could be all to stand between Azizi and whatever punishment they chose. Understanding that more clearly than before, she pushed away any thought of bringing their attention to the troubles Redel had caused. It would not help Azizi and could bring her to face the same charge.

She regretted the decision not to bring her suspicions about Redel to the instructors earlier, but remembering how they'd responded when she'd gone with Azizi to report the harassment with the shower, she didn't think they would have listened about any other, either.

Her silent guide led her down a short corridor into an even smaller room that held a single chair.

"Trina of Menthak, you have agreed to stand advocate for Azizi Demai. Answer our questions truthfully and to the full of your knowledge."

The words issued from the wall, and Trina shifted in her seat, wishing she could see their faces and know who stood in judgment over Azizi. Not that she would know them anyway unless some were pulled from the instructors, and since she and Azizi shared most classes, she doubted they'd have done so based on her readings about impartiality.

Her thoughts spun as the judges probed her relationship with Azizi. She told them everything she could think of from the very first moment when he called her out for poor behavior on arrival day. It might not show her in the best of lights, but it proved Azizi looked to helping others more than trying to get them into trouble.

"And what of the incident on the first break period?"

Trina stared at the wall where the voices came from, wondering if they could see her confusion. "Nothing happened on the first break day," she said, thinking they were testing her.

"So unlike Azizi, you were convinced the shower malfunctioned?"

She might not have been able to see them, but she heard the contempt in that statement easily enough and pushed off her chair. "That was on the second day." She emphasized the time. "And no, I thought the event too precise to have been an accident."

As soon as the words left her mouth, Trina remembered why she shouldn't have said a thing. "Not that it mattered," she added, sinking onto the seat. "The instructor we reported it to wouldn't believe us, as I'm sure you know already." And Fred had warned against pushing.

Trina's head began to ache. She didn't understand what Sharna's prank had to do with Redel, but the parallels felt a little too close. They'd been warned to let it go or trouble would fall on their heads just as this would never have happened if Azizi accepted blame for something he did not do.

Spacers were supposed to be better than such games.

Then, as the questions probed further into his—and her—reaction to that event, she wondered if it wasn't a game after all. Had she done exactly what her mother warned against? Had she put herself in the hands of Security because they suspected her activities rather than Azizi's?

Despite the spike of fear the thought brought with it, she knew Azizi wouldn't have given her up even to save himself.

The realization gave her the strength to ignore their implications and answer the questions with Azizi firmly fixed in her mind. She offered nothing beyond what Azizi knew or had done, nothing to implicate herself, and he had never stepped outside the boundaries.

The next event they probed made her shake her head. "Azizi would have no way to affect the air stream." Though she knew someone she suspected had.

"So you are unaware of his activities in this regard? Does this not suggest you know him less than you think you do?"

A laugh burst free at the question, cutting through her tension. "You have only to look at our terminals to see just how well I know Azizi. Most nights we spent in the classroom trying to understand everything you seem to think should be basic knowledge. And if you think he became some master programmer in the time since we joined normal classes, talk to his teachers. Azizi does not have the head for it. Certainly not to program a way around the air streams."

She clamped her lips shut just in time before she gave them a hint of who had been the master programmer between the two of them. Not that she knew how to override the transport controls, but from what she had done, they might not accept her word should they start probing.

"We have talked to his teachers."

For once, the voice held something other than contempt.

"Just what do you think he's done? I thought this was about him seeming to blame another candidate, but I wasn't even there for that."

The door opened behind her, and the same spacer waved her to leave.

Trina stared at the wall. "Check his program stick, now that he finally has one. If it shows any use outside of class, I'll be surprised. Even if he wanted to do what you're saying, he just can't."

"Your advocacy has been recorded. Please leave the booth."

She glared for another few seconds before her fingers closed into fists, and she pivoted sharply to join her guide at the door. Whatever good she'd done Azizi in her advocacy, they'd decided she'd said enough.

Trina didn't think about how no one had returned when she was called until the door that opened led not to the room where the others waited but into a larger one with a desk much like the Security Office, though a man sat behind this one. Not that she could have warned Sharna, but she worried what the other candidate would do when faced with the same questions, if they even asked her the same ones.

"What happens now?" She turned to her guide, her only remaining connection to the hearing.

"Your part is done. Go confirm your status and return to your usual assignments."

"What about Azizi?"

"He will be judged."

The man offered no chance for more as he turned and left with much the same speed as she'd come from the booth.

A simple palm lock decorated the door he used.

Frustration tempted her to override it and demand a better answer, but even had the officer at the desk not been watching, the very questions showed a need to be careful. Her talents could help, but her grandfather showed how her skills could be used to harm.

Wiping her face clear of any emotions, she marched up to the desk.

"You need to indicate you did speak and confirm you will not mention any of the questions you were asked or observations you made during your advocacy. Whatever the outcome, you are bound by this agreement."

A contrary thought had her wonder what he'd do if she refused only to realize she'd end up next to Azizi.

"When will we know? Will I be able to see him if…?" She choked on the end of that question.

Something resembling pity showed in the man's eyes. "He will be released immediately, but under observation, if the judgment goes in his favor."

He didn't seem inclined to address the other outcome either, or perhaps he hesitated for her sake.

She had no other choice but to mark her agreement and go to her next class, hoping her mind would focus long enough to understand whatever they discussed.

CHAPTER 39

Deluth came out of his questioning feeling as if he, not Azizi had been on trial. They'd probed every second he'd ever spent with Azizi then questioned whether he could serve as an advocate having only seen him during sessions with a few rare exceptions, and never alone.

He'd just barely managed to keep the full answer from bursting out, but he thought they'd find his testimony worthless if they learned his trust was grounded in Trina's faith as much as his own observations of Azizi's hard work. He could appreciate the irony in considering just who had thrown his loyalty in his face. She didn't seem inclined to forgive him for the imagined betrayal either if her behavior this morning was any indication.

The worst of it was how they did not seem to question the charge at all. From their tone, they'd made up their minds and nothing would sway them. Despite depending on Trina's judgment at first, he could see no way the candidate he'd worked alongside and helped against Redel before would have done what they suspected of him, and not just because he was a good person.

Deluth tipped his body forward so the air stream pulled him ever faster to his quarters. He'd lost the whole morning, his testimony the last to be heard.

The experience had been exhausting, draining on so many levels. His body needed sustenance to replenish the energy, but his mind needed something more pressing.

He needed answers, and only one person held those.

His speed slowed only marginally as he left the air stream and marched his way down the corridor to their quarters. He stomped through the gathering area, ignoring the curious looks sent his way beyond skimming faces for the one he sought and did not find.

Sharna gave him a sympathetic nod and the realization she'd have had to lie outright to avoid joining Azizi distracted him, but only for a heartbeat. Redel had caused all of this. Azizi's troubles, the fight with Trina, and even Sharna's strain, though Redel had no way of knowing either her vulnerability or that she'd choose to stand up for one she'd scorned before.

Deluth found his target in the meal area, halfway through the same selection he would have chosen if he'd come from class with the rest.

He marched over and grabbed Redel by the arm, jerking him to his feet.

"What?"

He ignored Redel's protest as he marched them to the relative privacy of his room. He slapped a palm against the lock with a little more force than necessary and shoved Redel inside, pausing only to lock the door before turning on his shipmate.

The lack of arrogance in Redel's expression almost made him pause, but he'd built up too much anger to question it.

"What did you tell them? What did you say Azizi did? They're all set to toss him out an airlock based on your lies."

All color drained from Redel's features and when he rubbed a hand across his face, his fingers trembled. "They wouldn't do that, would they?"

"Would you care if they did?"

Redel slumped. "I didn't mean for it to go this far. I just wanted to scare him. To punish him for standing against me. I didn't think they'd find anything they could prove."

"What did you tell them?" Deluth said again, each word ground out in a fierce tone.

Staring at his hands, Redel shrugged, but there was nothing dismissing in the movement. "I suggested he'd tried to change the log. That I'd seen him hack the board and when he failed, he'd tried to blame me."

He glanced up then, but Deluth only narrowed his eyes and glared.

"I figured they'd check for tampering, find nothing, and let him go with a warning."

Deluth pushed past Redel to sink down on his bed. "This isn't the ship, Redel. It never has been. I told you from the start. Things are different here. Tampering is serious. You never think about anyone but yourself, do you? You just act and expect everyone to fall in line. Do you realize if they decide against him we'll never see him again? We won't know if they sent him home, to a prison colony, or just jetted him out into space, all based on your false testimony."

Redel straightened at that. "If they are taking this so seriously, then they found something. That means my testimony wasn't false. Maybe I didn't know about it, but he'd been doing something. Maybe I helped, did you ever think of that?"

Deluth leapt to his feet faster than Redel could step out of the way and slammed both palms onto his shipmate's chest, throwing Redel hard against the wall. "I should have told them you'd lied. The minute I figured out this wasn't about calling you out on tricking Azizi, as we both know you did, I should have thrown you out of the airlock you'd prepped for a candidate who did nothing but help people. Azizi knows what helping is."

"But you didn't."

If Redel's tone had held any fraction of challenge, Deluth would have pounded him into the floor. Instead, his shipmate's voice came out soft and with a vulnerability Deluth hadn't heard in years.

"No, I didn't."

Redel put a hand on his shoulder. "Because you understand it means Azizi did something to deserve it. They wouldn't have brought this to council if they didn't find evidence that was pretty damning. He had to have done something to be seen as guilty."

Deluth brushed Redel's hold off, but sank onto the bunk, holding his head in his hands. "Don't you understand? We're all guilty of something. Right now, you're guilty of false charges, and I had to break my word to talk about this at all." He glanced up to frown at his shipmate. "They like to turn a blind eye so they don't have to admit to knowing about things like your crusade against the colony-bred candidates. If they don't see it, it can't be happening. But you made them see. You made them look. Now they have pinned every single system change, from the simplest overrides to tools no candidate should have, on Azizi's shoulders. Any unlabeled access."

"What do you mean?"

"How many of our shipmates have the program to override air streams? On our ship, it's easy enough to win though no one official will admit to the existence any more than the instructors want to know here. What do you think the chances are a colony-bred kid who needs extra training has access to one?"

Deluth didn't need to see Redel's expression to know the question found its mark.

Tension held Redel's body taut. If he didn't have the key, he knew at least one person—Deluth—who had one. His face showed he finally understood what he'd done, understood how vulnerable he was with the tricks he played and how any of his shipmates would be.

"The rules are different here. What you do won't be brushed off or dismissed. You can cause irreparable harm, not just to careers but lives."

This time Redel met his stare, not in an aggressive way, but almost a despairing one.

"Can I go now?"

The question could have been arrogant—one day ago, it would have been—but now the words sounded defeated.

Deluth moved past him, feeling no satisfaction as Redel flinched. He opened the lock so Redel could escape to his room without touching his former friend.

He had nothing left to say. Either the message had finally reached Redel, or nothing ever would. From the change in his shipmate's attitude, Deluth suspected understanding had finally been achieved. He only hoped Azizi wouldn't have to pay the price for this critical lesson.

"I should go tell them."

Deluth stared at Redel, stunned for a heartbeat, then shook his head. "They weren't charging him for arguing with you. It would do no good, and would only increase the scrutiny on all of us.

CHAPTER 40

The afternoon's classes seemed to drag on forever, but when it came time to return to her quarters, Trina didn't want to go. She'd heard nothing about Azizi, not through official channels or even rumors from Jade.

If she went back to quarters, she'd have to face Sharna's worry and her own mixed reactions to Deluth. She wanted to believe he'd stood in advocacy. She wanted to believe he'd done what he could to help Azizi, but why hadn't he stopped Redel before it came to this? Had all the times he'd helped her stave off trouble been a ruse?

Her head ached with the complexities before her. In some ways, she felt locked in the same twist of loyalty and truth she'd felt with her grandfather. She'd tried to see the best in Samuel, blinded herself to the contradictions between what he said and what he had her do, until the consequences outweighed any delusions on her part.

Had she done the same with Deluth? Had he played on her emotions, her loyalty, to keep her from discovering his real intentions?

The questions made returning impossible, and sleep even less likely.

She spent most of the night in the observation dome, thankfully without interruption, but the lack of sleep and lack of answers made her irritable and distracted the next morning.

When she joined the Medicals in time for their first session, not even curiosity over who they'd be paired with in the training scenario could grab her interest.

She'd have to brave the Pilot quarters at lunch if only to discover whether Azizi had returned. Not knowing his fate felt worse than learning her statements had not been enough.

Trina wanted to believe he wouldn't be condemned for something he had not done, but the judges sounded so sure. She would be responsible at least in part if they punished him. She'd had too many hard lessons to trust the power of truth. Facts worked against as much as for, and the council had decided the facts weighed against Azizi before she even entered the testimony booth.

"Aren't you going to say hello?"

The soft question jerked her head up so quickly, her neck bones crackled.

"Azizi! They let you out." Her gaze swept the rest of the room, expecting to find both her teams, but the other faces were barely more than strangers—the same team they'd faced the morning everything went wrong.

He nodded. "They put me with another team—yours."

Trina stared at him, stunned for a moment before she grinned. "It'll be like it was before in the other training."

Azizi's smile barely twitched his lips as he gazed at her. "They thought it would be easier after all that had happened."

He looked away then, tension holding his shoulders rigid.

Trina put a hand on his arm, urging him to face her. "It's all over now, right? They realized they'd taken the wrong candidate? That it was a mistake?"

"It was not a mistake," Azizi said in a harsher tone than she'd ever heard him use. "I'm free because they couldn't prove anything, and because my advocates convinced them I lacked the skills for what they suspected of me."

A hint of the old Azizi showed through as his lips twisted into a sideways grin. "I'm guessing you told them about how you had to guide me through every programming step. Who knew my difficulties would turn out to save me?"

The grin fell away as he added, "I'm free, yes, but they're keeping me under observation in case I somehow managed to trick everyone."

She met his intent stare and understood all too well. Azizi knew at least some of what he'd been accused of had been her doing.

Trina half-turned away, guilt biting deep. If she had only listened to both Fred and Azizi, there would have been nothing to find.

Then she remembered the other questions. There would have been something, and worse, she couldn't have spoken so strongly without knowing at least some of his charges were false.

"You don't believe that, do you?" Azizi gripped her arm hard enough to pinch the skin. The stoic expression had vanished. "You don't think I'm sneaking around tampering."

Trina covered his fingers with her own, choosing her words carefully. His observation could all too easily turn into an investigation of her activities.

"No. I don't believe that." She shoved aside the worries and forced herself to relax. "No one could pretend to be as lost as you are when programming topics begin." Trina gave a soft laugh, grateful when he followed her.

His fingers tightened once in a squeeze then let her go.

"That's why they assigned me here. They thought it might be too difficult to be with the teams who watched Security take me off, whatever the council decided. And though they never said who advocated for me, they chose to pair me with you. There's only one reason they'd know you would stand by me."

Trina opened her mouth to tell him how many had stood up for him, but she closed it words unspoken. Not only had she signed the document promising to speak to no one about what occurred, but she still didn't know for sure whether that room had held only those speaking for him or any speaking in the case. For all she knew, Redel himself had been called before she or Sharna arrived.

"Why did you do what he told you to?" She hadn't meant to ask the question, but knew it had been chewing at her for too long to stay unspoken.

He shrugged. "I guess some small part of me thought he might be trying to help, that he might have moved beyond his hatred."

Trina couldn't stop a laugh. "All the time Deluth and Sharna worked to keep him from targeting you, and you thought he'd decided not to bother?"

Azizi shrugged a second time. "I won't be that foolish again, not about Redel or Deluth. I thought he would stand up for me as he did another that very morning, but he said nothing."

Hearing the bitterness in Azizi's tone brought back her argument with Deluth and how everything the candidate said seemed to protect Redel. But when faced with the interview, Trina saw how his advice could have been meant to protect her as he'd claimed instead. She wished she could reassure Azizi or herself, but Deluth's loyalties remained unknown.

The chime sounded, warning them to gather in the scenario room.

She laced an arm around Azizi and tugged him forward. "It was all a mistake, something they know now. Put it behind you and let's show everyone what you can do."

Even as she exchanged a nod with Jade on their way in, Trina realized another reason for them to have paired Azizi with her team. The Medicals had seen him work. They already knew Azizi gave his best effort and was happy to help others. This way, even with switching teams, he didn't have to start from scratch.

He'd built up enough trust with the Medicals for Jade to have given Trina warning. Otherwise, she'd never have known about the council. If she hadn't been there to reveal his inept programming, she shuddered to think what the judges would have decided.

JADE GAVE AZIZI AN APPROVING nod when they exited the scenario room, and the others followed suit, welcoming him as their new member. Trina didn't know what she'd expected, but such easy acceptance surprised her even though they'd been as willing to let her prove her worth when she'd come straight from the separate training.

Before she and Azizi could dwell on the fact, Fred stepped into sight.

All members of both teams came to attention in a ripple as each noticed and reacted. It had been many weeks since they had to be escorted from place to place.

Fred gave a lopsided smile in recognition of their alert nervousness. "We've decided your group is ready for the final testing of this stage. The test is a scenario, one that requires you to know not just the simulation steps but everything you've been taught at an instinctive level. You have three days to prepare, starting now. All classes are canceled."

Jade stepped forward to ask a question, but Fred shook her head once, turned around, and left.

Behind them, the warning chime sounded a reminder that they needed to trigger the analysis or it would be discarded.

One of the other team strode to the table first, but he paused with a hand over the button. "Should we review?"

"Yes."

The response came from many throats on both teams. They had to be perfect. Only those who passed the testing would be pushed into the next section. If they'd made any errors in this scenario, they needed to know what they were.

The teams completed the evaluation, and discussed a few small improvements, but both had performed quite well.

"Don't rest easy," the leader of the other team said. "We need to know everything."

There were a few chuckles in response, but his words were heard.

"We'll have to sign out the scenario rooms," Trina said. "Everyone will want extra time."

Jade nodded and crossed to the other team to arrange times for a full scenario.

Trina caught Azizi's arm. "We can probably get some extra times in the evenings if you want the practice."

"I'd be game for more," another Medical said.

Trina glanced around to see most of the others nodding as well as Azizi. She laughed. "Sure. We can all use the extra training."

It would be much different than the sessions with Deluth, but it would mean finding a room would be easier without so many competing for the extra space. She probably shouldn't have risked modifying the profiles anyway what with greater attention being paid to unusual system behavior.

Jade returned from arranging the scenario room times to find the Medicals committed to rigorous scenario training matched with review sessions held in the Medical team's quarters. Every waking moment, they planned to work, pushing themselves harder even than the instructors would have done.

Trina didn't know whether to be grateful for the excuse to avoid Deluth or frustrated. With this schedule, she would not have the chance to talk to him and discover where his loyalties rested.

She had enough to do making sure the training replaced her shafter instincts. Without succeeding there, she'd have no chance of becoming a spacer in truth.

CHAPTER 41

The three days passed in a whirlwind of training and review, but when the word came down for them to collect in the section used for break day gathers, Trina could tell the others felt no more prepared than she did.

Azizi integrated well with the Medicals, one small gift from his near removal, but he felt the strain along with the rest of them. Trina reaffirmed her decision not to tell him about Sharna. He'd accepted it as an accident, and he didn't need something else to worry about.

They had enough cause in the question of what the test would involve. So much rested on their ability to perform flawlessly, and they didn't even know what area of study would be tested.

The Medicals headed to their assignment with none of the eagerness Trina had come to expect of them. Feet dragged, and if anything, they bunched up in the air stream to provide more resistance so the current pushed them sluggishly.

Trina shared a concerned glance with Jade, and they moved to the edge until they were positioned to leave the transport first.

Together they formed a wall so their teammates had to collect there or shove by.

No one even tried.

"They wouldn't have tagged us for the test if they didn't think we were ready," Jade said as the last of the team stepped free.

"If they wanted us out of the program," Trina added, "they'd have cut us. This is a reward. Proof we're skilled."

She needed to hear the words as much as any of them.

Her stomach settled while the reduced tension in the others mirrored her own. Some even straightened and offered up cocky grins.

Jade shook her head. "Just because they think we're ready doesn't mean they'll make it easy on us. This is the first major step to becoming a spacer. People's lives, spacer lives but also those who have no training at all, will be dependent on us. They need to make sure we're capable, not just think it."

Something in her tone made Trina wonder what had happened in Jade's past that made her so aware of the need for perfection, but the other candidate said nothing further as she turned to lead them the rest of the way.

The Medicals fell into step behind her. The defeated expressions might be gone, but serious ones had replaced a temporary confidence.

Trina wondered just what they'd be walking into.

The noise reached them first, but when they turned into the gather area, every space held candidates, most familiar if only from previous gathers.

The young man next to her let out a surprised breath, and Trina felt the same. When Fred told them their group had been deemed ready, she'd assumed the Medicals, or at best, those present. Instead, it seemed as if almost as many as had gathered in the docking bay at the very beginning now crowded into a space that should have felt large.

"Candidates, your attention please."

The statement carried through the room louder than any of the discussions.

The candidates fell silent, and Trina craned her neck to see where the speaker stood. She found the man only because his platform hovered above them in the center of the room, ensuring all could see.

"Those here have been judged ready for testing. The test will be a failure of the gravity system. You will complete the test as teams, and multiple teams will be involved in each test. Return here instead of your morning sessions tomorrow."

The platform floated up to a door in the wall, giving them no opportunity to ask questions.

"A gravity failure? That's the first scenario we had," a nearby young woman said. "It's like they don't want to challenge us at all."

Others echoed her sentiment, but added how gravity was a critical system so the drill made sense.

Trina stayed silent, uneasy though she couldn't say why.

"Not that we need it," one of the Medicals said, "but we've got until morning. We should run through the drill one last time."

About to turn and join the rest, Trina's gaze fell on Deluth where he stood to one side of the Pilots.

He gave her a silent nod, recognizing her discomfort and sharing it. All the questions about his loyalty stripped away, leaving Trina longing for the time they used to spend together, challenging each other to ever more complicated drills.

Then she recalled exactly how she'd made them more complicated.

She'd been able to adjust the drills without reprogramming the whole scenario builder, almost as if it had that capability built into it.

The instructors might be planning something very different than the standard gravity failure drill they'd all become accustomed to, perhaps even to carelessness.

"Come on, Trina. One more run won't harm anything." Azizi caught her arm and tugged her after the rest, breaking the connection with Deluth.

She followed the Medicals, her mind churning through the possibilities. After Azizi's near dismissal, she had not given the scenarios even the simplest of variations, and the Medicals knew only the standard programming.

"I could run this in my sleep."

The comment drifted back to her, the source unclear. She tried to figure out how to warn them, how to prepare them, without revealing what she'd done. Azizi's monitors were still listening as far as they knew. She didn't want them to learn who had been responsible for at least some of what they'd laid at his feet even now.

CHAPTER 42

What do you think they're trying to gauge?" Redel asked as Deluth rose from the table he'd shared with his old friend and new.

Redel seemed to have undergone a real change of heart, but since none of the colony-bred candidates had been assigned to their team, Deluth remained only cautiously optimistic. At least they'd learned Azizi's fate. He would be happier with Trina than he'd ever been with the Pilots.

"Well, I think it's too simple." Sharna shook out her hair, clearly unnerved.

Deluth shrugged. "I guess it's time we find out, but I'm with Sharna. I suspect the instructors have some trick they plan to play, but I have no idea what that is." He kept quiet about how Trina tweaked their scenarios. This new peace was too fragile, and he didn't want to chance getting Trina in trouble. Unlike Azizi, no claims of ignorance would work for her, especially not after her decision to reward those in the special classes with her treat.

Anyone else would have used it as a boast but not Trina.

He remembered the joy that shot through him when their gazes tangled yesterday. They hadn't seen each other since the judgment, and he had no way of knowing what she might have thought about what happened. She'd turned away too quickly though, for him to gauge how she felt now, especially with both of them clearly thinking the same thing about this test.

The other candidates would take it at face value no matter how he tried to warn them. He'd heard of no one else who figured out a way to combine the crises. He wouldn't have thought to look.

"Are you that worried?" Redel called over a gap Deluth hadn't noticed his stride had opened between him and the other two. "Late or early, I don't think there's any way out of this but up to the next level or gone."

His pitch rose on the last word, but Deluth pretended not to notice as he sprinted the last few steps to the transport.

Every one of them had good reason to be nervous. If they failed this test, he didn't think the spacers would let them try again. Just as retests for initial qualification were almost unheard of, if these months of training weren't enough, nothing else would be.

When they reached the room, Redel and Sharna worked their way through the crowd to get to the lists announcing which testing section they'd be in.

They'd tell him soon enough where the team was assigned. He'd prefer the chance to talk to Trina and clear up any misunderstandings. The way their relationship had gone so far, Deluth had good reason to suppose she thought him firmly in the enemy camp, especially when he'd been standing with Redel when she'd seen him the previous day.

Despite his best efforts, he couldn't catch sight of her in the crowded room.

It felt as if even more candidates filled the room than yesterday. Most likely the impression came from how candidates were pushing their way forward and the loud exclamations that filled the room with enough of a roar to make any one statement unintelligible.

His failure left only one thing to do.

Deluth began to work his way toward the side where the lists were posted, as much hindered by those returning as barred by those before him. He felt no urgency so made little effort to press forward any faster than the shuffle used by the others.

"Why did they bother putting us in teams?"

"Is it always going to be like this?"

"I don't know any of them."

The comments seemed to follow the same pattern whether angry shouts or mumbles as more candidates shoved their way back. Where at first he'd been far enough for them to calm down, now he could hear their complaints, and after a bit, he started to grasp their meaning.

No longer satisfied with the slow pace, Deluth twisted his way through the crowd, a difficult endeavor when he lacked Trina's small, wiry frame.

He accepted the growls and curses as he passed, the need to see his assignment undercutting any desire to be polite.

The wall when he reached it stood as a blank frame, but he could see candidates to either side thrusting their palms forward and getting information.

Deluth copied them, impatient with the fraction of a second it took to verify his identity and his list.

First his name appeared with the number sixteen glowing above it and then those assigned as his teammates, one after the other.

He recognized most of the names from the gathers, then gave a half grin when Azizi appeared. He'd be happy to work with Trina's friend, but hoped it meant she would be assigned with him as well.

The last name appeared and clung there for some time before Deluth realized no more would be coming.

He pulled his hand away, the eagerness that drove him forward fading to a dull numbness.

She had not been on his list.

CHAPTER 43

Knowing the other candidates would be in a rush to find their assigned chambers, the Medicals didn't hurry to the gathering area. Instead, they went over their strategies one more time.

"Just remember you can't expect it to be like any of the scenarios we've done not even if we did every single one in the system," Trina said.

Jade shook her head. "Why would they go to all this trouble to train us then withhold a vital drill for testing? Isn't that counter to their own purpose?"

Trina clenched her jaw against the urge to reveal her discovery. "I don't think they would hold something back," she said after a pause, "but they could present it differently." She shrugged. "We can't be too confident is all."

The other Medical gave her a dark look. "If I didn't know better, I'd think you were trying to undercut whatever confidence we have."

The noise from the gather room reached them as they entered the corridor, removing the chance to explain even if she could have found the right words.

"Don't look so worried," Jade shouted over the swell of sound. "I know you're trying to help. We're a strong team. Whatever it is, we'll figure it out together."

Trina had to be satisfied with that, but every instinct told her the instructors took this test seriously. They'd do whatever they could to challenge the candidates, many of whom were smart enough never to have faced real adversity before in their lives. Schooling at home followed by more schooling here didn't necessarily mean they'd been challenged.

"You all wait here," Jade called. "I'll get our assignment."

Before any of the others could react, she'd squirmed away through what seemed like nothing less than an angry mob.

Trina worked her way to a wall, the others taking her lead without comment. She'd happened on a laborer protest one day on Ceric and had almost been trampled. She wasn't willing to take the chance.

Once the Medicals found a safe spot, they had nothing to do but keep an eye out for Jade.

Trina braced herself in a comfortable position and settled in to wait, trying to ignore her uneasy feeling.

"This is a mess."

"How is it even real? Spacers wouldn't throw together a whole team."

"I don't know anything about those people."

Trina shoved off the wall, the urge to see the assignments herself overwhelming even her instinct to obtain a secure spot.

She hadn't taken more than three steps before Jade stumbled across her.

"You were wrong…and you were right," the other candidate said. "The scenario might be the same, but the teams aren't."

"What do you mean? They're shuffling some members again?" Her thoughts sprang to Azizi, the newest Medical and the one with the most to lose.

Jade caught her hand before Trina could seek him out. "Not some. All of us. The lists are palm locked and not a single one of you was on mine. I'd think they were moving the leaders, but from the reactions of everyone checking when I did, they found the same."

Trina almost laughed at Jade's easy classification of herself when the Medicals rotated that assignment, but at the same time, she had become a spokesperson of sorts for the team.

Then the rest of her words sunk in.

"Everyone?"

Jade shrugged but with none of the easy confidence she'd shown before. "The only way to be sure is to go up there. I'll tell the others."

Trina watched Jade move toward where she'd just left, the other candidate's dragging steps captivating her with a morbid intensity until she forced herself to look away. She wouldn't know until she mustered up the courage to go find out.

Narrowing her eyes, Trina imagined this crowd as a festival day in a square on Ceric. She had no intention of stealing from them, but how to move through the packed bodies, ducking angry gestures, and reaching her objective without being blocked or caught remained the same.

She swerved, twisted, and wove her way past the other candidates, their half-heard complaints driving her forward until she stood in front of the wall where she'd find her answer.

Her courage failed.

Who would she be paired with? Would this new group hold the same bias against her as she'd experienced among the Pilots? She had no time to prove herself.

Someone slammed into her from behind, and Trina thrust a hand forward to catch herself even as the young woman grabbed for her with an apologetic cry.

The world narrowed to the space in front of Trina as a blank wall took on life to form first her name and then another, unfamiliar one.

She drew in a breath and held it as a complex thought occurred to her. She could as easily be paired with Deluth as any other. Her gaze sharpened, eager to read the next name.

More scrolled by, some half familiar but none known to her until the very last.

Trina stared numbly at the wall as her hand fell away and the letters faded.

She didn't resist when a candidate grabbed her shoulder and spun her around. Her dull eyes glanced up to see a face to match the last name.

"Redel."

"Don't worry, Trina. It's a good team. I know all of them. We know our way around a ship well enough to solve whatever the instructors throw at us. We can pass this with high marks."

His lips moved to form a grin, but she'd heard his message all too well.

Trina straightened and stared him right in the eye. "The scenario will be designed so we all need to solve it together whatever you might think, and I have no intention of letting you mess it up for everyone."

She pivoted on her heel and dove into the crowd before he could respond, her heart pounding too fast and her hands shaking.

Everything rested on this test, and they'd paired her with the one person who would do anything he could to stand in her way. Her only chance lay with his self-preservation driving him instead of the unreasonable hatred for her and all of those from the tech-limited colonies.

CHAPTER 44

Once everyone had received their assignments, an announcement came sending them off to meet their new teams. Deluth had no chance to find any of his friends in the crowd before they were split up.

He returned to the Pilot quarters late that evening exhausted but satisfied. His new team would work together well enough to have a chance at passing. Even Azizi seemed willing to ignore what had happened between them in favor of working together, though he'd ducked any attempt to speak privately.

A sliver of curiosity broke through his review of the day. One of the Pilots could have been assigned to Trina's group. She could have left him a message.

Even the rumble of his stomach couldn't distract him as he entered the gather area.

The few candidates present glanced up and waved, but he could see neither Redel nor Sharna. None of those present showed any interest in speaking to him.

Deluth entered the meal room, still searching, but a loud noise from the rooms beyond had him running past the space. He saw Sharna doing the same out of the corner of his eye.

"I just want to talk to you."

The strain in Redel's voice as Deluth swung to where he could see into the corridor made him tense, a state that worsened as he saw whose door his shipmate assaulted.

Deluth planted his feet and grabbed Redel's arm, the other candidate seemingly oblivious to his presence. "I thought we'd finally moved past this. I thought you had grown up."

Redel jerked free with an exasperated sigh. "Whatever you think I'm up to, you're wrong. She's wrong. I need to talk to her."

Deluth grabbed his friend's arm again and pulled Redel out into the meal area, thrusting him into a chair. Sharna took the extra one at that table without a word, leaving him to loom over the two of them, both hands braced on the back of the final chair.

"You better explain just what you were doing then," he ground out, all his frustration at missing the chance to talk to Trina himself lending force to his words.

Redel sank down in the chair and rested his head on folded arms. "She's on my team."

The words came out muffled, but clear enough to jolt Deluth. Suddenly, he wanted to make a much different command, only holding down the impulse with effort.

His shipmate looked up and gave a twisted grin at the sight of Deluth's expression. "I meant what I said the other night. I've finally figured it out. I'm slow, maybe, but I'm not stupid. When I saw her name on my list, I was happy. I thought it would be a chance to show I'd matured, to recognize the abilities I'd worked so hard to ignore."

"How did you get from there to pounding on her door?" Sharna asked before Deluth could.

Redel shrugged. "She didn't come. She never made the meeting. I had to defend her to the others, and I'm still not sure they believe me. It's my job to tell her our approach and make sure she doesn't mess it up for everyone else. All of us are hanging on this test. It's not about just me and her, if it ever was."

Deluth frowned, his mind processing the words and finding them incomplete. "She wouldn't have run away. If she was the type, the two of you would have had less to fight about."

"She didn't say she'd planned on it before the meeting locations were called, that's for sure."

"Wait. You talked to her before then?"

Redel flinched from his harsh tone, but then straightened. "Yes, I did. I told her how I thought we had a good team and a real chance."

Deluth shook his head. "How could that send her off? She'd be curious if nothing else."

"What exactly did you say?" Sharna cut in, startling Deluth who had forgotten her presence in the staring contest he'd begun with Redel.

Redel waved a hand. "I don't remember exactly. Something about how we knew our way well enough to succeed."

Deluth put himself in Trina's place, hearing the words as he'd imagine she would. He dropped into the remaining chair and groaned.

"What?" Redel demanded. "I was trying to show her."

He held up a hand to silence his friend. "And that's exactly what you did. She has no reason to trust you. No reason not to read your words differently than you intended."

"What do you mean?"

Where Deluth had expected a challenge, Redel just sounded tired.

"Oh." Sharna's breath came out in a gasp as she caught up to his meaning.

"Yes, like that. Think about it, Redel. Why would she believe your 'we' included her. She'd have no reason not to expect you to dismiss her value altogether. She'd hear what she expected, not that you thought she was an important part of the team but that the rest of you had it all covered and she was unnecessary."

This time Redel groaned loud and long enough to show he'd been telling the truth. "And she's vanished so I can't explain. We're going to be one person short, in strategy if not in reality, assuming she even shows for the test. I've looked everywhere. I even went through the training areas in case she was doing one last run."

Deluth pinched the bridge of his nose, wondering what insanity led to Trina and Redel being thrust together on the same team. He half suspected a deliberate ploy on the part of the teachers, though they'd have had to be more aware than he believed they were to pull it off.

"You won't find her unless and until she wants to be found if I know anything about Trina," Deluth said. "She comes from a hard world. This can't be the first time some arrogant, ignorant person sought to take it out on her."

Redel grimaced. "I deserve that, but it doesn't help us now. It's not just me at stake but the whole team, Trina included if she doesn't show."

"Oh, she'll be there."

Sharna nodded her agreement, adding a quiet, "No way she'd miss the test no matter what she thinks you're up to."

"You'll have to prove you've changed during the test. One more challenge to overcome, but one you're due. I just hope you don't take the rest of your team with you."

The old Redel would have blustered and argued. Deluth half expected him to object at least to the idea of being responsible for their possible failure.

Instead, he only looked embarrassed and stared down at his hands, saying nothing.

Deluth's stomach let out a harsh grumble, offering just the distraction they needed as all three gave weak laughs.

"I guess I better find something to eat, then. Tomorrow's a big day for all of us. Just remember: She wants to win as much as any of you. She won't work against your success."

"No," Redel said, pushing to his feet. "That's always been my place. I'll see you two in the morning. I don't feel much like company right now."

They watched Redel retreat, Deluth regretting the collapse of his friend's confidence, though not the arrogance that seemed to be tied directly to it.

CHAPTER 45

Trina spent the day and night before the test moving among the observation domes. She left them only for quick forays into the classrooms to access replicators.

The radiant light growing across the planet below her now sent Trina to her feet. She had to make her way to the examination chamber. The test would soon begin.

If Redel had already poisoned the team against her, she didn't want to chance them doing something to prevent her arrival. She'd heard his meaning. He planned for the ship-bred to solve everything and might be willing to take steps to prevent her from interfering. He had before.

Trina glanced out at the stars as she turned to leave and froze. Her gaze locked on one of the local constellations she'd discovered after Fred had told her about the stories and paths.

At the first sign of trouble, what had she done?

She'd gone to the closest thing this station had to tunnels, at least that she'd discovered. Few came up here, and those who did made enough noise to offer warning. She couldn't be a spacer and run. She had to stand her ground as Azizi had, even though he'd almost been thrown from the program because of it.

The scenario was sure to be harder than it appeared. She'd missed the chance to prove her experience and warn her new team because of fear. Maybe they wouldn't have been as quick to turn against her on just Redel's word, but now they had cause.

Guilt rippled through Trina, but she crushed it down. She had no time to wallow in either emotion. She needed to concentrate on doing whatever necessary for them to succeed even if it meant suffering Redel smirking at her from across the room.

Trina stopped at the supply cabinet outside the scenario rooms to get a gravity suit, but followed an impulse to carry it instead of putting it on. The others, ten in all, glanced her way when she turned the corner. Their expressions became a mix of annoyance and relief. She avoided Redel's gaze and marched over to them just as the warning bell sounded.

"There's time to get your suit on," Redel said, her attempt to avoid him failing.

The others had already started securing their helmets.

"I know."

He smiled faintly and shifted to give her room, but still she didn't move.

"You'll fall behind the rest of us," he added when it became clear she didn't intend to listen.

Trina shrugged. "Then you can leave me behind."

His interest came only out of fear that she'd slow the rest of them down, but if she was right that the answer seemed too easy, the bulky suit could hamper her.

The door opened and any response he might have made was lost as they all moved into the room beyond, their suits making the others have to file in one at a time.

Trina hung back, seeing no need to push her way forward. She knew the chamber better than most, and at least this way, she had the chance to see how they moved.

Redel had been right about one thing. Each of the members of this tossed-together team seemed comfortable and confident even in the suits, a trick when they weren't designed for maneuvering in full gravity.

Her assessment ended when she stepped through the door to join the others.

Though the helmets obscured their features, from the tilt of their heads, she guessed they were just as stunned as she was to see the familiar room transformed.

At three other points in the now cavernous space, another team gathered, making up the four groups along with Trina's, to undertake this challenge. She tried to find familiar faces, but they'd made the same choice as Redel and her teammates. Even if the distance were less, she'd have a hard time making out faces through the helmets.

The walls had been removed, transforming separate chambers into a vast cargo hold.

From their studies of different ship builds, Trina recognized this to be a freight ship hold, almost as broad as it was long unlike the cargo sections placed around the belly of the colony ship she'd been on to form a protective layer for the colonists should something strike the hull.

Independent freighter families like Jade's ran most of the cargo, but the Guild kept some freight ships for the long-haul colonies. These ships were built with minimal comforts and tiny living sections to maximize storage space.

She scanned the walls, identifying the configuration more closely so she knew where the safety overrides were placed.

Trina could see her teammates doing the same, even Redel, once again proving they had the experience to be useful if only they thought more about their need to succeed than wanting her to fail.

The space was wide open and empty.

If they lost gravity as expected, she'd be floating away with little to push off of for navigation. Cargo could be an impediment, but it could also assist. There were some grips on the wall, but no movement rungs, and without her suit on, she had no grapple to snag one of the grips.

Her stomach twinged with the fear she'd miscalculated.

The others would be able to walk around. The suits were equipped with strong electromagnets that triggered to counter gravity failures, but only when worn. Her suit would be nothing less than another piece trying to float away.

WHEN DELUTH ENTERED THE CHAMBER, he stood stunned with the rest as they discovered it was modular.

He should have considered the possibility. The scenario chamber on his home ship had been co-opted often enough for other purposes, the walls retracting smoothly.

He could see the three other doors, each with their collection of candidates. The last group made him grin.

Trina.

Even at this distance, he knew it was her, though had she put on the suit like the rest of them, she'd have been indistinguishable.

No sooner did he have that realization than he began to strip his off as well.

She was right. What would be the point in telling them enough to have them all suited up and prepared for what was supposed to be an emergency? That would never happen in a true setting, and this test was to ensure their readiness for a real spacer assignment.

Azizi leaned toward him, using gestures to question him as the helmet with its communicator had been the first to go.

Deluth pointed toward Trina. "The suits are a trick. This is a test. Why tell us in advance what crisis we'd face if not to let us make false assumptions?"

Azizi's expression clouded for a moment though he couldn't have heard the words. Then he started slowly removing the suit, too, as if questioning his sanity and Deluth's.

Whatever else might happen, Deluth could see all too easily how the suits were a quick lesson in assumptions. Assuming you're prepared for every eventuality would only get you killed. A spacer who failed to assess the true situation endangered everyone.

The scenario began without the chime used to get them into position. Instead a warning alarm sounded.

He slid down a wall that had been floor only a heartbeat earlier, one foot still trapped in the heavy fabric of his suit. The cloth weighed him down, but he'd had enough removed to prevent the magnets engaging at the gravity shift, a lucky chance when his foot could have been torn in half.

Azizi had not been so lucky. Nor had the others.

Deluth hit the floor hard but shook off the dizziness as he stared up at his teammates. Their boots stayed firmly planted on what had been the floor, but strong gravity pulled the rest of their bodies toward him.

Azizi came free first, having already been in the process of removing his suit when the gravity failed though not in the way they'd been expecting.

The internal gravity had doubled, and not evenly considering how the orientation had shifted.

It felt like being in one of the lifts common on spaceships but one designed for heavy worlders.

Deluth moved to catch Azizi, cushioning the fall with his body for lack of anything else.

The impact knocked the breath out of him and Azizi both, leaving them lying on the now floor staring up at the others who fumbled with clasps, the magnets embedded into the suit gloves to help with tool manipulation now hampering their efforts to get free.

"Boost me up."

Deluth stared at Azizi in confusion.

"I'm lighter than you are, though not by much in this situation. It's something planet-bound folks do when they can't shift the gravity. Put me on your shoulders against the wall. I might be able to reach the others and help."

The unexpected request had thrown Deluth, but soon he could see how it would work. Lifting the other candidate, no matter how light in comparison to him, would be the challenge.

CHAPTER 46

The fall, no more than half her height, had dazed Trina with its suddenness. If she'd been in her suit, she might not have fallen at all, but they'd been lucky to be in the corner of the room, so the distance between the surfaces wasn't far.

She glanced at her team members and realized the suit would have been worse. Their boots locked on, but there hadn't been enough space between wall and floor so they'd hit hard, unable to roll to absorb any of the impact.

A flush of triumph rushed through her at how she'd figured out something the ship-bred could not, but the sensation didn't last.

The test would be set to require all of them working together. She couldn't succeed without them any more than they could without her, and dividing them, or holding her forethought over them, would only cause problems.

The warning bell sounded again, and the gravity increased even more.

She pushed up to her knees and crawled over to the nearest team member, still not adjusted to the pressure.

The young woman inside the helmet looked out at her with dazed, fearful eyes.

Trina gave as reassuring a smile as she could, still not sure how they would solve this test.

Her smile faltered as she considered the possibility this hadn't been part of the test. They'd never run a scenario like this one in the drills. What if the station was at risk?

Even as the thought occurred, she dismissed it. Constant alarms would be blaring and the scenario room would have dissolved into blank walls, all resources devoted to resolving the station's condition.

"You okay?" she asked as she pulled the other candidate down out of the suit.

The young woman put a hand to her head and grimaced. "Nothing an analgesic infusion and quiet won't solve."

That startled a laugh from Trina, her reaction as unexpected as the sour comment. "I think you'll have to wait on both of those. We have a scenario to solve."

The candidate's features hardened, and she nodded, her lips pressed together against the pain. "I'm well enough to help you get the others out. We're lucky you didn't suit up. Smart decision."

Before Trina could react to the unexpected compliment, the candidate moved toward another suit to continue freeing their team.

As the helmet came off, Trina realized the young woman had chosen Redel, saving Trina from having to fight her lingering resentment. She focused instead on checking each team member and getting them all safe.

Once the whole team stood, sat, or lay on the newly made floor, Trina scanned for the nearest safety override.

Floating, she could have reached it easily, but suit or not, she was firmly anchored to the ground with the rest of them.

The nearest grip offered nothing useful. If they'd been maneuvering rungs, they'd be spaced close enough to act like a ladder. As it was, she knew exactly how to use them in Zero G as launching points, or to flip from one orientation to another. Now they mocked her, just out of reach.

"What are we supposed to do now?"

Trina turned to stare at Redel, him the least of any of them to ask such a question. She'd expected him to bluster or state some solution no matter how wild to gain authority over the others. Even less expected, he looked to her as much as any of the team.

If only she had an answer.

The safety switches hung many body lengths above them, well out of reach even of most ladders found on Ceric, farther than the tallest of the polit buildings.

Trina scanned the room, expecting nothing because she'd already assessed it, but she had to do something.

Her gaze tripped over the group half way across the new floor. Her pulse leapt when she recognized Deluth and then Azizi, friendly faces where she'd expected none.

A heartbeat later, she realized what they were doing.

Her team had been close enough to the wall that became a floor to have been touching the new ground. Deluth and Azizi worked to free teammates hanging suspended from their ankles a good bit up the new wall. They formed a human ladder to reach far enough.

"We were lucky," the first candidate Trina had freed said. "I'll take a headache over the muscle pulls they'll suffer. I just hope no one broke anything."

About to object at the risk, Trina realized this test had none of the precautions programmed into the other scenarios. They could get hurt, and hurt badly, before the time ran out.

As though to emphasize the realization, the warning bell sounded a third time just as the pressure on her intensified, driving her back to hands and knees.

She stared at her hands as she waited to adjust to the new weight of gravity. They wouldn't be able to take many more increases before the pressure knocked them out. If they were to succeed, they had to act quickly.

Her position, hands splayed and knees tucked in under her with toes curled against the surface triggered a memory not from her spacer training but from long ago when she taught herself how to scale walls so she could reach the bigger wins hiding in polit houses.

She glanced again at the safety switch and then over to the human ladder which had grown by one person to reach the last two of their team.

None of the ship-bred had a solution for this scenario, but she wasn't ship-bred. She wasn't what most expected of colony-bred either.

They hadn't chosen her for what she could learn, and certainly not for any prior knowledge or skill.

Nishan had been right when she'd convinced Trina to take the spacer test. They were interested in her because her skills might prove useful, because she had abilities from her shafter life no one else would.

The distance might be taller than any polit building, but she was older and stronger too.

"I can get up high enough," Trina said, startling all of them into staring at her. "I can use the corner."

"How?" Redel's forehead pinched together.

Trina's mind shut down, unable to come up with anything she'd seen in ship life that would explain how to work by counter pressure. "I just push off of one side for the grip to hold me on the other side. I used to climb walls on Ceric like this all the time."

She did not say why she'd been climbing them in the first place, and luckily no one asked.

"You can't. Your colony tricks won't work here. The gravity is too strong."

Trina braced both hands on her hips and glared at Redel. "Do you have a better idea?" She waited several seconds for a response she knew wouldn't come. "Well then we don't have anything to lose."

He scowled, reminding Trina of Deluth all of a sudden. "You could get hurt." Redel waved at the abandoned suits. "The safety limits are clearly off."

Whatever argument she'd expected him to use, this hadn't even been in the running.

She dropped her aggressive stance. "We don't have a choice. I need to pass this test as much as any of you."

"What do you need?" A young woman stepped between them.

Trina glanced at the corner then at the distant safety unit. She'd have to figure out how to get to the switch once she was high enough. "A brace to get me started will have to do." They didn't really have anything else.

"Wait." Redel blocked her path again.

"There isn't time. It gets more dangerous with each increase." She glared at him, wondering what was behind his sudden interest in her wellbeing. He must have been trying to keep her from saving them all.

"Make time. If we cannibalize the suits for their grappling ropes, you can secure them to the rungs. At least then if the gravity gets too strong, you'll only fall the length of the rope."

Her eyes widened as she stared at the one she'd been sure would work against her at every turn. "That's a good idea."

Almost before she finished, he moved to the nearest suit, pulled free a utility knife, and started cutting the mechanism loose. "I'm leaving the trigger attached. You'll have to use it to move the tether to a higher rung."

Trina knelt next to him, taking up the slack as he released it so she could make a coil. She paused just as he tucked the knife away, resting one hand on his forearm. "Thank you."

She'd expected a curt nod or some dismissive comment, but instead he smiled.

Something had changed. They didn't have time for her to discover what, so she rose and crossed to the corner, the rope in one hand.

"Couldn't you use the boots too?" one of the others asked. "If Redel can disable the trigger for the grappler."

She looked to Redel for the answer, but he shook his head.

"That trigger is tied to biometrics. You have to be in the suit, and once you are, you wouldn't be able to shut it on and off at will." A more familiar grin crossed his face. "If I could work that out, I'd just walk up the wall itself to the safety."

Trina liked that solution better than scaling a smooth surface taller than any she'd tried with the possibly of gravity shifts at any moment. But again, it would have been too easy.

"Right. Then at least we have this way."

Half the group stepped forward to boost her into a starting position. She scrambled up a ladder built of hands, but paused at the top. "Work out a way to get from the corner over to the safety, would you?"

The chorus of "we will" that came in response freed Trina to focus on keeping her grip and working her way up the wall. At least she could count on Redel's safety line if she fell.

With that thought, she paused to toss out the line and secure it, now high enough to need the measure. Her first toss fell too quickly and missed the grip, but she compensated and the next held firm.

Trina sent a smile down to Redel, something she'd never thought would happen.

They'd piled the discarded suits beneath her as an extra cushion should she fall straight down, but she did not intend to take that route.

AZIZI'S PEOPLE LADDER STRETCHED to an awkward height but the two grips they'd reached helped secure it long enough to bring down the last team member safely.

"That was a good idea, Azizi."

A handful of the others added their approval to Deluth's.

"I don't know if I could have hung on up there much longer." The youngest of the candidates had also been the last to come down, and he huddled on the floor in shock from the look of his shivers.

"You wouldn't have had a choice," one of the others said, shaking her head.

None of them looked ready to continue the test as they sank to the ground in a ragged circle, but Deluth doubted they wanted to fail any more than he did.

"We have to figure out the best steps to solve this problem. The overrides are all out of reach even if every one of us joined the ladder." He glanced at the shivering boy, unsure if that would be possible. "Any other ideas?"

As they tossed around answers, none any more viable than the human ladder, Deluth scanned the room for inspiration. Some tools had come loose in the reorientation he'd failed to notice before, falling not far from where he stood.

A bracing rod, a length of rope, and a couple of hand tools from what he could see. Nothing useful even if the rod could stretch high enough to reach the panel. The overrides would be bio-matched to the crew to avoid accidents with shifting cargo. If not, hitting the panel randomly with the rod would be just as likely to make things worse as better, maybe more so.

Deluth half smiled as he overheard one of his team run through the same jolt of hope turned to regret. At least they weren't grabbing onto a path without thinking it through, but he'd yet to figure out something that could work.

His gaze drifted to where Trina's, and therefore Redel's, team ended up. Those team members stood aimlessly staring at the overrides as well. They had no better luck in figuring it out as far as he could tell.

Then he saw one of them cup a hand to her mouth and call something up.

He followed the direction of their gaze, and his eyes narrowed.

He'd recognize that wiry form even at this distance. She performed some strangely splayed walk that allowed her to progress up the wall despite the gravity.

At first he watched in admiration, but then his mind caught up to the facts, and he considered how she did this. She used the corner, the angle allowing her to create pressure by shifting her weight. It was ingenious, but no more effective than anything they'd come up with he realized.

She'd have no way to traverse the wall between the corner and overrides even should she come close enough. The overrides weren't designed for easy access, after all. They held critical functions, but mostly the position had to do with increasing the wall space for securing cargo. A simple anti-grav would lift any spacer up if they needed it.

Deluth searched again, this time for an anti-grav plate, but none of those lay around conveniently waiting for him to notice.

He went back to watching Trina for lack of anything else to do, hoping she had some grand idea in mind he couldn't see. He'd prefer any team succeeded than for them all to fail. He didn't know how it would reflect on his own standing, but he suspected this test, and their spacer future, rested on something more than a green or red light. They didn't know how long the test would run, or how many more gravity increases they'd experience. Someone could get seriously hurt.

A glance at the boy, Kai, who was still in shock made him revise the thought. Someone already had on his team. There could be more on the others.

Trina swung a tether out, the first time he'd recognized the meaning of the rope strand between her and the nearest grip. The tether must have come from the suits considering how it appeared to have a triggered mechanism, but that still wouldn't be enough to get her to the overrides, not without an anchor right next to them.

She'd reached the height of the overrides.

He stared, waiting for her next move to learn the answer, but she only clung there.

She called down to the group below. From their shaking heads, it seemed they didn't know what to do next either.

His gaze fell on the rod again. It could act as the anchor point she needed, but only if he could find an anti-grav plate, and then he wouldn't need her at all.

"No more ideas?" he asked his team.

Deluth kept Trina in the corner of his eye as if his attention alone could keep her safe.

The glum expressions that met his question offered his team's answer.

"Azizi? You knew to make a human ladder. Any other planet things that might work with the tech failing?"

Azizi shrugged. "If gravity shifted on the planet like this, everyone would be dead already."

Deluth wasn't listening.

"We couldn't reach the override with your ladder, but we could get high enough to set the anchor if everyone goes."

"An anchor for what?"

He waved toward Trina in answer to the question from one of his teammates. "They've got someone high enough." He noticed Azizi's eyes widening when the young man realized who it was. "She can't get across. If we use that bracing rod and set it high enough above the overrides, she might be able to swing over."

"Wouldn't they win then? And all of us fail?"

"I've been thinking about that," Deluth told the young woman who'd asked. "This is a simulation of real spacers. What if part of the test is to see if we work together? In a true crisis, everyone would be asked to pitch in or stay out of the way. Spacer, colonist, ship-bred, it wouldn't matter if you had something to contribute. Training only takes us so far."

Azizi rose. "I'll do it. Whether you're wrong or right, I'd prefer to help another team win than sit here and let everyone fail."

One after another, the others rose as well, their gloom easing with the chance to do something.

Deluth turned to look at the one team member remaining. "How about it, Kai? You're the lightest of us. You could be raised the highest to set the rod. Are you up for it?"

The boy stared at his hands for what felt like an age, then sprang upright as though the shock had never happened. "I can do it."

Returning Kai's grin, Deluth pointed to the rod. "Then we'd best be at it. I don't know how long Trina can stay balanced up there."

They all turned to stare at the distant figure, but the paralysis broke when one young woman sprinted over to the rod, or rather she started to sprint but her energy flagged with the battle against gravity despite no more increases.

They'd have to be quick and careful, but it was their only chance.

CHAPTER 47

Trina could hardly miss the effort attempted by Deluth's team when she paused to take a rest. After all, that safety override had been her target as well.

One after another, the team members clambered up the human ladder, Deluth at the bottom.

There weren't enough of them. There was no way they could reach the override.

The last of their team was the smallest.

She understood why. Deluth must be suffering under all that weight even with the wall to brace them. They didn't have the grips this time because it would have put them on a different line. Then they'd be stuck just like she was, only she'd attained the necessary height.

Trina tried to refocus on the problem, glancing down at her own team in the hopes they had a suggestion, but something about the last candidate's climb drew her attention.

He struggled not just with the pressure of extra gravity but because he carried a bulky rod under one arm.

It made no sense.

The keypad had a bio lock. The rod might make the group tall enough, but it wouldn't do anything useful.

The candidate extended the rod to its full telescoping height as she watched. It stretched a length above the switch, next to, but not touching the controls.

As it suctioned to the wall, Trina realized their purpose. Next they'd attach a rope and someone would attempt to climb the last measure, though how they'd manage with nothing but a slick rod to grab hold of, she couldn't imagine.

The human ladder disassembled the same way it had grown into being, if a lot faster.

No rope hung down.

Deluth seemed to stare right at her.

Trina raised one hand in a wave, her feet braced to support her.

It had been a good effort despite failing. At least they'd tried.

He started waving back, but his gestures seemed too forced, too sharp.

It wasn't until he picked up a rope and swung it much like how she'd swung her safety line that she understood.

He'd given her something to latch onto. No team could do this on their own, and he decided cooperation would lead to success.

She grinned wide enough her cheeks ached as she disconnected and reeled in her lower safety line. The magnet on the end provided enough of a weight to combat the pull of gravity, but the line fell short.

She tried again only to realize the problem wasn't her throw.

Shouts came from her team below as they recognized the same thing she had. Two choices remained: to climb down and get another length or to use her upper safety line as well.

The second line came free with a quiet click. She didn't know if she had the strength to go that distance a second time, and if this worked, she'd be on the ground soon enough. She knotted the two together, all too aware of her precarious position. If she swung too hard, nothing remained to catch her.

Fear made the first try with the new line drop short of the rod as well, but she gathered up the length and put more force into the toss. Her feet slipped ever so slightly before she planted them again.

The cry came from many voices below as her line hit and latched onto the rod.

She glanced down to find the other two teams gathering as well, and from how they brought everything they'd found, it seemed everyone had decided to cooperate. A quick scan showed a couple of candidates she'd met, and a few she'd seen at the special classes, but Sharna, Jade, and any others she'd worked with closely were missing. She had no way to judge the abilities of strangers so turned back to what she could affect.

Trina secured the line to her waist. She took a deep breath and shoved off the wall, determined to make this joint effort work.

She fell toward the floor at a speed much higher than she'd expected. Terror flashed through her mind. She'd made the rope too long. The magnet would break its bond. Her knots wouldn't hold.

Just as she knew with certainty the floor would come up to meet her, the line tautened and she began to curve.

Relief held her for a heartbeat before she realized she'd have to use the pendulum momentum and cut it short at just the right time. Otherwise, she'd swing back and forth until she hung too far beneath to climb up and too high to reach the floor.

She brushed the wall at the same time as she jerked the rope. Its length stretched far and above the override.

Again she fell, but this time she knew the rope would catch her if she failed. Success meant grabbing the rod when it came into reach.

A clear memory of leaping through the air between roofs of Ceric houses overtook her, complete with the sharp scent of desert and sun.

It gave her the confidence she needed to time her grab.

Hard metal slapped her palm with enough force to make her cry out, but she clenched her fingers and ignored the burn as she slid partway down its length before she brought her feet to the wall to stop herself.

Every muscle in her body screamed. She pulled herself up the wall using the rope, the rod, and her braced feet until she hung next to the panel.

The effort to reset the system to normal gravity felt anti-climactic after everything it had taken to get there, but at least the commands worked.

She waved the others to stand along the real floor and waited for them before completing the last step of changing the orientation.

The simulated ship moved slowly to correct, but not slowly enough for her to secure herself when she realized she'd be left hanging halfway up the wall.

Trina had no choice but to let go.

Deluth was watching Trina and saw the second she let go. He pushed to his feet and staggered, the simulated ship still re-establishing its orientation. Even without that, she fell too quickly for him to make it over there.

He tried anyway, getting his balance more with each step, but the better the orientation became, the worse it was for Trina. As long as some slant existed, she could roll down the wall, using it to slow her momentum.

She hit the floor with a solid thud when Deluth was still several strides away.

He pushed harder and skidded to his knees next to her, barely aware of the thunder of running steps behind him as the others came as well. She hadn't moved since falling.

Disheveled hair obscured her face, and he brushed it aside too better assess her state.

Bright, aware eyes stared up at him.

"You're okay." He made it sound like a statement but it felt more like a question to him.

Trina tried to nod and groaned, the movement revealing bruises she clearly hadn't noticed yet.

"Don't move. We just have to wait for the announcement, and you'll be taken to the infirmary."

The other candidates gathered, sitting or crouched, around the two of them.

Trina rolled to one side and pushed to a sitting position. "It's over?"

"It has to be." Deluth swallowed his protest at her movement.

"It wouldn't have been without you," Redel said, coming down on Trina's other side. "That was dangerous, but it worked."

"It would have been more so without your tether."

Deluth looked between the two and saw a reluctant acceptance in Trina's eyes, as if she didn't want to believe but had seen Redel's transformation herself.

When she turned to him, her expression brightened. "And would have been worthless without your team's anchor point." She put out a hand to brush his knee. "Whatever the instructors might think, working together makes sense for a crisis."

He shrugged, unsurprised she saw the reasoning so well. "Maybe that's what they were trying to show us."

"Then why haven't they come?" another candidate asked, tension in her voice.

"What if it was real?"

Though only two had spoken, he could see the panic spreading.

Trina raised both hands to get their attention. "It couldn't have been. Remember, we're on a station. The simulation was something that could happen to a ship, and this simulated cargo bay wouldn't be here in an emergency."

"Then why isn't it over?"

Deluth glanced at Trina, and together they said, "It couldn't have been that simple."

"You call that simple?" Redel shook his head. "I'd hate to see what constitutes a hard test in your mind."

Trina put out a hand, and Deluth helped her to her feet. "This was supposed to be a crisis. No one is dead or even severely injured."

"But the real answer," Deluth chimed in, "is we don't know the cause. We've solved the effect, but this isn't a simple system malfunction. What made the gravity heavier, and at a different orientation?"

He met several dubious looks when he glanced at the others, but then someone from the third team waved a hand.

"This isn't a class. Just tell us." Trina said, then shrugged as if apologizing for her sharp tone.

"What if the ship is being pulled in by something bigger?"

"Would we have been able to correct it?"

"What if…?"

He'd expected chaos. Instead, all four teams jumped in, asking questions, exploring options, and considering what each of them were saying.

"It can't be a sun. The ship is sophisticated enough to avoid something like that. There are protocols to prevent such things."

"My father was most likely lost with his ship, so things can happen, or at least could less than twenty years ago."

Trina's blunt statement caused a momentary lull.

Deluth struggled to come up with a response, but before he could, she continued.

"It's the best answer we have. It's not perfect, but we have to start somewhere. Who are the strongest coders here?"

A couple of hands rose tentatively, and Deluth nudged Trina to raise her own.

She gave him an odd look, then did so.

"Okay, that's four of us. We need to get to the console and break in to see what the state of the ship is."

"Isn't that against the rules?"

The question came from a young man who had not claimed programming skills.

Deluth remembered Azizi's trial and glanced toward Trina's friend just as Azizi stepped forward.

"The rules are meant for normal, everyday life. Why do they teach us enough to get us into trouble if we didn't have need of it? There is a difference between using the knowledge to harm and using it in a crisis." He turned away from Deluth to face Trina. "You'll need to check the ship's position relative to the orientation it had been on before we fixed that."

Deluth half expected Trina to shake off the warning, but instead she smiled. "I will. For now, we need to make another ladder. A strong one because you'll have to hold us at the console."

He glanced at the distance, grateful only that the reorientation brought the console a lot closer. "I'll be part of the base."

As he stepped into position, Redel joined him and locked arms. The next group did the same, one layer up and so on until they'd made a structure that should hold. With all four teams working together, they would reach just high enough.

Trina smiled at him before launching herself up the human ladder as if born for climbing.

WITH FOUR OF THEM WORKING together, it proved easy to overcome the console protocols and gain access to the whole environment. None of them had all the answers, but with a little from how Trina overcame simple palm locks combined with similar specific knowledge from the others, they worked around the blocks to get through from the cargo hold to the engine room's information.

The hardest part had been retaining their position so they could all see the console.

One of the programmers gave a low whistle. "We're caught all right."

Trina twisted to see what he indicated and almost slipped off the human ladder.

"Got you," another of the four said as she grabbed Trina's shoulder. "See what you can, Fireen, and let's get down so we can figure out what to do about it."

If only they had a way to project the results below.

A tap on her ankle startled Trina. She glanced down to see something being passed up that resembled a very thick version of her program stick.

"Beautiful," Fireen said as he snatched it from her hand. "I didn't know any of us had a screened one. You all start climbing down. I'll follow as soon as I get the data transferred."

There was nothing to be gained in crowding around the console now, though Trina itched for a closer look at the tool he'd been given.

By the time they all reached the bottom and the ladder dissolved, no sense of individual teams remained. The murmurs she'd ignored while working had established the various strengths. They had at least two candidates capable of representing each of the spacer divisions. She only hoped it would be enough.

The female candidate who had first given the tentative suggestion of a sun leaned over to see the data. "It's not a sun, but it's something huge."

Trina got her chance to see the tool for a moment as she scanned the data and passed it along. Not the most efficient way, but better than shuttling each of them up a human ladder.

"We were supposed to fail."

The deep-voiced comment cut through all the chatter as everyone turned to the young man who'd made it. He waved at the program stick he'd handed to the next person. "We're going nose down toward it. Think of a skipping stone on a lake. You want an angle almost flat to the surface so you skim along it. Too high, and you lose your forward momentum and sink. Too low, you hit head on and sink. The weird angle was so we'd skim off the top of the object's atmosphere and bounce to safety."

Trina shared the bewilderment in the faces around her despite the idea coming from someone clearly colony-bred. She'd never had access to water wide enough to balance a stone though she'd seen such expanses in pictures since coming here.

Closing her eyes, she ran through the description again, trying to find a parallel. "It's like the air stream transport."

Her words came out louder than she'd intended, with everyone now staring at her. "You lean into the current and you go faster. Lean too far away, and the same effect."

"Exactly," the first candidate said, his teeth showing bright against his dark skin. "Only you've breached the surface already so you can't bounce off."

"But when you step into it, you have to push," Redel chimed in.

Sharna laughed. "Equal and opposite reaction. If we don't push through, but let ourselves be pushed away, we're safe. Brilliant."

"Only we 'fixed' that," one of the other candidates said, making quotation marks with her fingers. "So now we're going to crash right into whatever is pulling on us."

Trina leapt up. "Oh no we're not. We need to fashion a swing for the person up at the console, one that will keep them steady in both rotations. And use the suits for padding and protection for the rest of us."

Azizi gave her a puzzled look even though he'd already regained his feet, clearly ready to follow her lead.

"You're going to unfix it, aren't you?" Deluth asked, his words spreading comprehension among the other candidates.

"And quickly." Trina turned to search out another of the rods. "If we had two rods, we could stretch a rope swing between them."

A candidate stepped forward with another rod, this one compressed to its smallest height.

"The rope swing has to have enough give to move between the orientations," Redel said.

Trina nodded, still surprised to find him helping but unwilling to waste time figuring out what happened. "You're the best with knots. Can you do this?"

He gave her a wide grin for an answer and dove toward the pile of discarded suits, presumably to strip off more rope.

"There's a real rope here," someone called, tossing him a wound cable.

"Thanks."

Even as he accepted the rod and rope, others were already rebuilding the ladder for him to climb.

"You know it'll be you up there," Deluth said. "You undid the change. You have the best chance of restoring it."

Trina nodded her acceptance of Deluth's statement. She'd also have the best chance of clinging to a rod should the swing fail. She doubted any of this group had hung in the open from the edge of a rooftop as she had many times while learning how best to navigate the buildings.

"You'll have to do a steeper curve this time." Fireen pushed the program stick at her, the screen allowing for some calculations on the device itself. "We've changed the variables."

She accepted the device with a grateful smile. "Of course. It wouldn't have worked if I'd moved back to the old orientation because we're closer now. Good thinking."

A glance to the console showed Redel climbing down, the swing complete. Trina didn't waste another second, knowing Fireen's calculations would become less and less true the longer it took.

"I'm secure," she said as she reached the console. The swing held her weight.

The human ladder dissolved, and everyone ran to the join between the floor and what would be the floor when she'd finished. They braced each other in standing positions that would become prone soon enough.

Trina set up the commands she'd need using Fireen's numbers and watched until everyone looked secure. The change would happen rapidly. It had to if they were to have any hope of success.

She gripped the rope and triggered the final sequence, swallowing a gasp as the orientation shifted and she swung from where she'd been to almost upside down before finding her new position.

Even if she could see the console from here, she wouldn't be able to reach the keys in time should anything go wrong. Like everyone else, she just had to wait it out.

CHAPTER 49

The sound of clapping startled Deluth and caused those around him to jerk.

They'd stayed in position long after the return to the false orientation, hoping against hope they'd somehow restored the fix in time.

An anti-grav platform floated into sight, moving toward the console with five instructors on its surface, two of them unknown to him and the rest from his classes.

"Trina, could you reset to normal orientation?" one of the unknown instructors asked with clear familiarity.

Even as the request came, Deluth saw Trina claw her way up the rope to the console and enter the same commands she had thought were the solution the first time. The test must have used a true gravity shift outside of the simulator's control system.

His head spun with the room, but not enough to keep him from realizing the instructors had arrived on the anti-grav because they'd expected to correct the orientation once the timer had run out. They hadn't expected the teams to solve this problem.

Kenner held out a hand to Trina once the room stabilized, and she leapt from the swing with a surprising grace.

Down they came, delivering her to where the rest of the candidates now stood, each with an expression ranging from hope to despair.

Deluth wondered what his own face revealed, his thoughts too muddled to figure out where he stood. Somehow, he felt, like the test, their assessment would not follow expectations built from the previous examinations. He didn't know whether the difference would work for or against them.

"The final test is tailored to each session based on the strengths and weaknesses of each included candidate as observed during your studies."

Deluth jerked to attention as Kenner began speaking before the platform touched the ground and Trina rejoined the other candidates.

Another instructor he knew caught Trina's shoulder and passed her to the fifth. Deluth's gut tensed, suddenly sure the difference would work against them.

The other unknown instructor, and the oldest, stepped to the front, his frown cutting deep lines in an already wrinkled face. "We've rarely seen a group as competitive as your session. Despite shifting members, different classes, and joint endeavors, the majority of you candidates identified with one team, working with others grudgingly when required."

The fourth, Lalia, tucked her hair out of the way, but her bangs swung forward to half-obscure her expression when she shook her head. "I don't think we've seen as many tricks or attempts to undermine before."

The oldest laughed, muttering, "Wait until you're my age," under his breath.

Deluth only heard him because he stood at the front, a position he regretted as he waited for the last instructor, the one holding Trina, to speak.

"Where divisions didn't exist, you created them," she said after a pause. "And never more strongly than with those starting at a disadvantage."

He fought the need to glance at Redel with as much energy as he struggled to contain his protests.

Hadn't they shown in the test they'd grown beyond those differences?

The oldest instructor gave Deluth a nod as though he could read minds. "We'd all but given up on everyone included in this test session and one other. This isn't some insulated ship family. This is the Spacer Guild. We are the thread that is woven throughout all known space. In the Guild, you will find members from every group, and with every background. Some might not share your experiences, but they'll have strengths of their own. We can't have spacers who fail to understand that, who look for difference instead of commonality."

Redel stepped forward. "Not everyone worked on division."

Before he could say anything else, Kenner put up his hand. "Have you not seen from this enough to realize how little that mattered? Whether you actively worked to divide, whether you only set your sights on winning at any cost, whether you stood aside and let it happen, or whether you chose to fight against it, every single one of you was complicit. We were ready to throw out each candidate in this room. You had already failed your test. The actual scenario seemed a formality at the most."

Deluth focused on the one word in that whole statement which offered any hope: "seemed."

The woman holding Trina laughed then, and Deluth glanced around to see the same desperate hope on all their faces.

"Yes," she said. "You are to be congratulated. We were sure you would fail, but something changed between the planning and this test. You're about to be someone else's problem. Deluth of The Headway, step forward."

Only her congratulations gave him the strength to move, but he sought Trina's gaze as he did so.

She gave a little shrug, clearly as innocent of the reason for their separation.

"Every one of you have made mistakes in your training." The second instructor swept the room with a gesture. "Here's the secret: so did each of us up here. The difference is whether you let those mistakes define you. These two worked the hardest against the raw tendencies of your session, making connections across the lines of prejudice and even working together when most saw every other person as a rival. They were not alone in these behaviors, but they showed the most initiative, the ability to command, and the strength to bring together those who stood the farthest apart."

The fifth instructor dropped her hold on Trina and added, "Even if those methods sometimes went directly against what you were instructed to do. There will be times when the ability to see beyond orders will save lives and every person in your charge will be grateful for what you have demonstrated here."

Deluth exchanged another look with Trina, this one stunned.

Kenner stepped behind them to place a hand on their nearest shoulders. "These two stand before you because they will be leading you forward to the next stage of your training. You've passed beyond classes. Beyond drills. Beyond pretending. You will be assigned a mission just as though you were full spacers, only you will have experienced instructors available to ensure your mission succeeds whether or not you do. That is your true final assessment, and it won't be an easy one."

"So," the oldest instructor broke in, "take your rest now, because you won't have much time for it soon enough. Through the door to your left you will find a party set up to celebrate all successful sessions. Go enjoy this night. Tomorrow you will be shifted to your ship."

TRINA STOOD THERE, THE SHOUTS and laughter of the other candidates reaching her through a fog that began when Fred asked her to reset the gravity a third time.

They'd done it. They'd passed, and she had done well enough to be paired with Deluth to lead.

As much as the thoughts echoed in her head, they didn't sink in as well as the other statements from the instructors had.

She'd been a part of the problem. Fred warned her when she said to leave the prank against Azizi alone, but Trina hadn't listened. She had neither reported nor dismissed the game Redel played with the air stream either. She'd held it against him, worked against him, instead of making any attempt to resolve their conflict.

A hand caught her arm, and she raised her eyes to see Deluth. She'd been just as wary of him, and for all the wrong reasons.

"We should go. This might be our last break day in a long while."

Trina glanced around to see the scenario room almost empty. Still unsure whether the instructors saw something in her that didn't exist, her gaze crossed that of Redel.

He smiled and waved her on.

"Yes, we should," Trina said with the first bit of confidence filling her. "I want to see who else passed their sessions."

She might not have trusted Redel before today, but they'd worked together to solve a difficult problem. And one from the underlying tone of the instructors, they'd been expected to fail. Even worse, the instructors thought they'd fall to infighting.

Perhaps what the testers saw in her, in all of them, had been there after all.

The room holding their celebration seemed tiny in comparison to the simulated cargo space. Noise assaulted her as she stepped through the doors, Deluth at her side.

Trina scanned the room, catching sight of Jade by a replicator and Jessine talking to an instructor, before candidates from their session came up to the two of them and offered congratulations.

She didn't sense any resentment. Mostly they seemed relieved, though whether because they'd passed or the responsibility of leadership passed over them, she couldn't tell.

"Why do I get the feeling most don't think we're lucky to have been chosen?" Deluth whispered into her ear.

Trina twisted to grin up at him. "Of all the candidates I've met, you're the last to shy away from hard work."

He quirked an eyebrow at her. "This from the candidate who worked so hard not even her home team had the chance to meet her?"

"Neither of you showed much sign of slacking off," Sharna said, appearing out of the crowd.

A tension she hadn't acknowledged drained out of Trina at the sight of her friend. She'd known not everyone would pass this test, but hadn't wanted to believe Sharna one of those that hadn't.

Sharna gave a twisted smile as she took in Trina's expression. "Sorry I was late to the party." She waved a hand at her left arm, making Trina aware of how it floated on a platform against Sharna's chest.

"What happened?" Deluth asked the question Trina had been about to.

"These sessions are designed to test us to our limits. We passed." Sharna shrugged. "The rest will heal."

With a sharp nod, Trina accepted the answer. "We were lucky not to have any serious injuries in our session."

Then she laughed. "Azizi and I were wondering how you ship-bred dealt with broken bones. We'd guessed on the anti-grav."

Sharna ducked her head. "On my ship, I wouldn't leave my quarters like this."

Deluth chuckled. "I doubt spacers would accept the excuse. They'd expect you to keep working with your good arm."

"Well perhaps I should make the most of this break while we have it." Sharna seemed to have recovered from her embarrassment as she headed for the replicator.

Trina glanced down at her empty hand, tempted to follow her friend, but at the same time, she wanted to hear Deluth's thoughts on the coming mission. "Maybe that's at the root of why we were chosen," Trina said with a laugh as she realized what she'd been doing.

Deluth smiled down at her. "What's that?"

"We work too hard."

They both laughed then, but their humor cut short when they heard, "An aspect, perhaps, but not the only one."

They turned together to meet the newcomer.

"Fred. I didn't expect you to be here." Trina waved at the party, but meant the assessment as well.

Her instructor shrugged. "I knew all of those who required extra classes and your session had more than most. That familiarity is how your examination team is put together. Each test is tailored to push the specific candidates within it."

Deluth stepped forward. "So we have you to thank for the difficulty."

Fred accepted the charge with a sharp nod, lifting her glass in salute.

Trina eyed the purplish liquid.

"Yes," Fred answered her unasked question. "Your juice has been added to the replicator here, and everywhere I'd guess. When you offered it to the class that day, you won many supporters, and not just for your generosity. There's a complexity to this flavor profile rarely achieved by the molecular experts. You surprised everyone."

Seeing Deluth's grin in the corner of her eye, Trina remembered him describing the drink to her in glowing terms before he knew she'd been the one to assemble it. "I only tried to match something I'd had on Ceric."

"And that's exactly why spacers need colony blood." Fred paused for another sip. "It's easy to become isolated when you only see the sun through a viewport. There's more to this galaxy than held inside metal walls."

Trina smiled at that. "I spent all my time on Ceric wishing for nothing else but to get inside these walls. Colonies can be insulated as well."

"Which is why a mix is great. People come at problems from different directions, and combining can have surprising results."

Deluth shifted from foot to foot, clearly aware of the same hint of something more in Fred's tone.

"We weren't supposed to solve the scenario, were we?" The question had been hovering in the back of Trina's mind ever since they'd had to reset the ship's orientation, and she wasn't the only one to notice.

Fred gave a startled laugh. "You're not supposed to know that. Considering how things went, we felt you would think it rigged to ensure your failure." Her voice had lowered so they had to lean in. "Your scenario, unlike the others, was supposed to teach you there are times when you can't win, that sometimes the best action is not to act. How you responded to the fact would show whether you were ready to be a part of the Guild or more interested in making sure the fault fell on other heads."

Trina nodded slowly. She understood the lesson better than most. Her choice to act at times had horrible consequences counter to her intentions. Had she refused her grandfather…but then he would have been waiting for a better opportunity.

"No one, not even I, thought it was solvable." Fred grinned at them. "The console was out of reach, and you had just enough equipment to frustrate. Then, instead of attacking each other, you stunned us all by working together. You solved the unsolvable not once but twice, using amazing climbing skills, cannibalizing the suits for equipment you shouldn't have had, and the human ladder. None of us anticipated your thinking patterns. That's exactly what we look for in new spacers, and what we'd despaired of finding in you."

"It wasn't just us," Trina said. "The idea to strip the suits came from Redel, and many others helped figure out what happened."

"Azizi set up the ladder." Deluth's firm tone made it clear he would not accept credit for something he had not done.

Fred waved her glass at the others in the space. "That's what I meant. All of you. Each brought something, and those who didn't were quick enough to help with the ideas of others. Spacers work together. That's the hardest lesson to teach to candidates, but it's one we must before giving you any chance at a real assignment."

"Can you tell us anything about the mission?" Deluth broke in.

She shook her head. "You'll find out soon enough. Know only you'll be responsible for coordinating the teams and pushing everyone to succeed. That's enough for now."

Fred raised her empty glass. "I'm going for some more juice. You should enjoy yourself. It'll be a long while before you get a break again."

She wandered off before they could say anything more.

Trina brushed Deluth's arm. "What do you think?"

His stomach rumbled beneath the noise of the party, and he laughed. "I guess that's answer enough. Shall we find the replicator?"

Their first act of command, and they had only themselves to direct. Still, the results proved satisfying, as did the company.

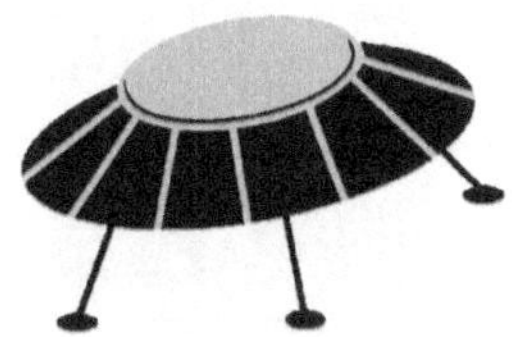

Thank You for Reading

I hope you enjoyed going through training in the Spacer Guild with Trina and her new friends.

I love to hear about your experiences with my characters, so drop me a line in email to:

* author@margaretmcgaffeyfisk.com

or use the contact form on:

* margaretmcgaffeyfisk.com

And while you're there, if you sign up for my monthly newsletter, I'll share a bit of my writing and publishing journey, fun events, and even snippets or pre-publication stories as a thank you for letting me into your inbox. You can also choose to receive release announcements, which are split into genre and go out only when a new title is available in that genre. Feel free to select as many options as you'd like.

Finally, can I ask a favor? If you're willing, I'd appreciate an honest review of *Trainee*. Your feedback will help Seeds Among the Stars find the right audience. If you choose to review on your website as well as retail and/or reader sites, you can also send me the link with permission to include it on that book's information page, if you're so inclined.

If you'd like to read an excerpt from the next Seeds Among the Stars title, *Apprentice*, please turn the page.

APPRENTICE
SEEDS AMONG THE STARS, BOOK III

Assigned to a simple trading mission, Trina and Deluth find proving they are Spacer Guild material is much more difficult than they'd expected.

Trina woke, her eyes opening to a dark room. It didn't feel early. She didn't feel tired. Her alarm should have woken her long ago.

She sat up with a jerk, throwing the covers off in a desperate scramble to get to class on time.

The lights came up slowly, and the events of the previous day spilled into her mind.

There were no more classes, no more simulations, no more tests. She'd passed despite everything. She'd be getting her first assignment today.

That sent her scrambling out of bed just as quickly, but instead of panic, her cheeks ached from the force of her grin.

"I did it, Katie. I really did."

As though her sister stood here with Trina instead of on a colony many light years away, warmth filled Trina. She savored the feeling before dragging on clothes and triggering the door. Her sister might not be here, but Trina had a good number of friends who would be waiting for her, ready and impatient to begin their last stage before becoming full spacers.

The corridor, revealed as the door slid open, held only a few bodies instead of the usual crowd on class days.

"Hey, sleepyhead." Sharna teased as she passed on her way to breakfast.

"I'm not that far behind you," Trina called after, hoping there wouldn't be a line at the cleanser.

The four others in the hall were all ready to go, leaving the sonic washroom free, a rare occurrence when normally the morning alarms triggered at the same time.

Trina smiled at Peter and gave the other two a quick wave as she ducked around them. Their expressions reflected the joy in her own.

Her hand lifted toward the palm reader before she realized another explanation existed for the light traffic.

Not every member of the Pilot team had been present at the previous night's celebration. Their session might have been expected to fail, but not all members of the other sessions had made it through, whether they demonstrated behaviors incompatible with a spacer life or collapsed under the pressure of the test.

Trina remembered what the officer who had tested her on the colony ship said about regrets. She understood the demand for eager trainees better now.

It wasn't a simple matter of dismissing strangers. The further each candidate got in the training, the more they became companions, friends even. And some of those would be sent back to whatever ship or planet they'd come from. She might never see them again.

The cleanser door came open suddenly.

Trina, in her distraction, hadn't noticed the delayed response to her touch until Redel stepped out almost on top of her.

"Sorry."

Not so many days ago, that single word would have been delivered with a shove or a mocking tone. So much had changed.

Trina grinned and shook her head at the same time.

"I should have noticed it was occupied."

He shrugged, returning her grin. "I think we're all a little distracted right now. See you out there."

She turned to watch him go, stunned to realize she was grateful he'd passed the test. She would have missed Redel.

After all the time he'd spent trying to make her fail, when it counted, he'd found his own confidence and so no longer needed to shove Trina and the rest down. More than that, he'd helped everyone succeed. If he hadn't, she did not know whether the spacers would have let a single member of their session, or at least of the team she'd been part of, continue on.

Deluth had told her a little of what happened to bring about Redel's change at yesterday's gathering. She didn't think she'd have been able to forgive Redel if Azizi had been thrown from the program, but then, it didn't sound like he'd have been any more forgiving of himself.

Still, hadn't she needed to see the lengths her grandfather would go to before she would accept he wasn't who she'd thought him to be? She should have been able to detect his true nature, but she'd let her dreams blind her. Who's to say Redel hadn't done the same, blind to his own nature?

The last edge of melancholy left her as she finished preparing for the day as fast as she could. Her friends waited just outside the corridor, people she'd spend time with on her next assignment, or maybe a later one depending on where they were placed. Fred had been unwilling to tell them anything at first, but when she and Deluth caught the instructor later in the night, Fred told them enough to know the presentation of the two of them as leaders in the session meant little. Each person would be assigned based on the best place for them to serve out their apprenticeship. They had no guarantee of sharing a leadership role, or even being on the same ship.

Trina planned to enjoy the company of her friends for as long as she could, whether today or the whole of their apprenticeship. Who knew when their paths would cross again if they were placed on different ships? Even if they weren't, she remembered how huge The Starshiner had been. Though spacers had come to the colonists' gatherings, and she'd made a point of meeting every one of them when she'd finally given up her self-imposed isolation, often she'd seen new faces. With so many needed to run the ship, they might not spend any time with each other, especially if posted to different sections.

Trina burst into the meal area, her gaze already scanning the tables to choose where she wanted to sit. Any of her friends could vanish in the next few days not to be seen for months or even years.

Her hand came up in a wave as she saw Deluth, Sharna, and Redel at the same table. Not so long ago, she'd have avoided her two friends rather than join where Redel held a seat. Now, she appreciated having those of the Pilot team she knew the best all gathered together.

She pointed to the replicator, the room filled with noisy chatter. Even the three missing from their number could not dampen their excitement. A smile twitched her lips at how the volume might have sent her scurrying in the other direction when she'd haunted the walls of The Starshiner. So much had changed in the six months of her training. It made her question what would change in the length of her apprenticeship. The thought only made the need to know where the Spacer Guild planned to send her bite harder.

Patience had been a struggle to master when she'd been nothing more than a thief on the colony of Ceric. She'd had little need to maintain the skill during training here on the station where her teachers encouraged action over waiting. If only she could act in a way that would bring their assignments faster.

Trina laughed as she selected her juice paired with a breakfast of grain, meat, and sharp spices Azizi had introduced her to. She'd grown used to much more than strange flavors since coming here.

She turned around to scan the room again, this time not looking for anything specific but more trying to imprint the room, their quarters, and the whole station into her memory much like she used to do with the places she planned to rob. Only this time, rather than looking for vulnerabilities, Trina saw only strengths.

It hadn't been easy, but she'd learned so much here. She would leave this station with regret and missing many of those she left behind. Only Piper, the true friend of her childhood, had inspired that emotion when leaving Ceric.

Her pensive mood vanished as movement drew her gaze to the visible portion of the gathering area.

Three instructors stepped through the entrance and sank into seats at the nearest table, which stood open both because of the missing members and because it sat the farthest from the replicator.

Whether her tension translated to the others, or they noticed the entrance at the same time she had, the conversations fell silent one after another, leaving an expectant tension in their wake. Every conversation that was except for the one the three instructors were having.

They chatted with each other seemingly oblivious to the impact of their arrival, as though random, purple-clad strangers wandered in at meal times every day.

Trina stared at them for what felt like forever but must have been mere seconds. They showed no awareness of her attention.

She swallowed a frustrated sigh and turned to join her friends at their table, fighting to keep her shoulders straight when every instinct told her she mattered not at all.

The table came into view, her downcast gaze giving little warning before she reached the empty place she'd planned to claim.

Suddenly, the idea of slipping into a chair and huddling in silence with the others while the instructors finished their conversation and deigned to reveal the reason they'd come lost its appeal. She let her tray fall to the table with a loud clatter, Deluth thrusting a hand out just in time to catch her juice before the glass tipped and spilled it all over the table. Trina gave him a quick nod in thanks before she spun to face the room once again.

"If we're still here," she stated to the whole room, ignoring the conspicuous absences, "then we have passed. They have no more power over us. We are done with classes and instructors."

That brought the attention she'd wanted so desperately a heartbeat earlier and now Trina wished she'd kept her mouth shut.

The spacers turned to face the room, revealing one of three to be an instructor she'd met in her separate classes. Reviewing trade agreements, however, had little insight to offer in this moment, making him no more readable than the strangers.

She straightened her back and stilled her features so they couldn't see how much she regretted the outburst. Trina wished more than anything to sit down in the chair that faced nothing more pressing than the wall if she avoided Sharna's gaze.

Then the instructors raised their hands and started to clap, one after another.

The man she knew slightly rose to his feet and nodded at her. "I can see why they chose you as captain of your trial," he said. "I wouldn't have expected it from your presence in my lessons, Trina of Menthak, but I can see you have other virtues." His expression lightened into a smile.

Trina wanted to correct the assumption as she had not captained anything in the trial, but the group gave her no chance to explain as the second man continued.

"We were going to wait for you all to eat your fill, but I see that was a bad decision as we've put you off your food." He gave a short laugh.

The woman of the group picked up the explanation with, "There are three ships currently available that are appropriate for apprentices. Your assignments have been chosen—well, for most of you—and we've come to collect you for the briefings.

Portable screens Trina hadn't seen in use since rejoining the full training had been lying unnoticed on the instructors' table. She bit back a groan at the sight.

Each time instructors had used the devices, it meant taking her away from what comfort she'd secured and any friends she'd made. Her thoughts about the different assignments seemed all too true now, and the announcement of a joint command with Deluth more of an encouragement than any hope. These instructors believed her role part of the training she'd be leaving behind. Even if they planned to give her some responsibility, surely an experienced spacer would be in charge of the ship itself.

The idea of making her captain seemed laughable. Simulated training had little weight compared to real experience.

Trina glanced around at the others and saw the same edge of fear in their eyes now that the time had come.

She curled her lips into a smile, hoping to encourage her friends, but she didn't keep her attention on them long enough to see whether she'd succeeded. The instructors, and the screens before them, drew Trina stronger than the starships had through the fence separating them from the rest of Ceric.

The instructor she knew gave a shrug and sat back down, the others following his example. "We'd tell you the split now, but no doubt you'll be too full of questions to finish your meal. Eat. It may be some time before you have another opportunity. If the Spacer Guild has taught us anything, it's to take your chances when they come."

Learn more about *Apprentice* on MargaretMcGaffeyFisk.com.

About the Author

Margaret McGaffey Fisk is a storyteller who explores tales across genres and worlds. Raised in the Foreign Service where she developed a love for anthropology, she has been a data entry clerk, veterinary tech, editor, support engineer, and programmer, among other roles. She pulls on her studies and experiences to give depth to the cultures and people that form the heart of her stories. As her website is titled, she offers tales to tide you over.

She'd love to hear from you through any of the contact points or social media accounts listed on her website, or you can subscribe to one of her newsletters for release announcements, snippets, and other news:

margaretmcgaffeyfisk.com/subscribe-to-my-newsletter/

Website
MargaretMcGaffeyFisk.com

Acknowledgments

The very first thank you must go to my loyal readers without whom *Trainee* would never have been written. I originally believed *Shafter* to be a standalone title and had made no plans to continue the series. Then I received notes from my readers wondering when the next book would be available. No need to worry. Once that door has been opened, it refuses to shut. There will be more Seeds Among the Stars to follow.

My supportive, patient, and willing husband, Colin Fisk, deserves a mention as always along with my sister Jennifer McGaffey; my mother, Elizabeth McGaffey; and my son Jacob Fisk. Other members of my family have also encouraged my writing in more ways than will fit on this page, including critiquing stories, covers, and whatever else I needed feedback on. Some families offer either blind support or none at all. My husband and I met in creative writing classes, my parents both did stints as English teachers, and my sisters and sons are all avid readers. They'll tell me when something works, but they'll also point out where and why it doesn't, a trust and honesty I depend on.

The members of my writing groups are much the same, offering support, edits, and a place to explore ideas or work through blocks. Dawn Hebein and Erin Hartshorn were especially helpful with this book.

I am lucky to be surrounded with friends, family, and fellow writers who believe blunt truth the best help a person can give, and readers who are willing to reach out so I know what you all enjoy.

www.ingramcontent.com/pod-product-compliance
Lightning Source LLC
Chambersburg PA
CBHW030611120726
47904CB00006B/1859